PENGUIN BOOKS

The Thief

Clive Cussler is the author or co-author of a great number of international bestsellers, including the famous Dirk Pitt adventures, such as *Crescent Dawn*; the NUMA Files adventures, most recently *Devil's Gate*; the *Oregon* Files, such as *The Silent Sea*; the Isaac Bell Adventures, which began with *The Chase*, and the recent Fargo adventures. His non-fiction works include *The Sea Hunters* and *The Sea Hunters II*; these describe the true adventures of the real NUMA, which, led by Cussler, searches for lost ships of historic significance. With his crew of volunteers, Cussler has discovered more than sixty ships, including the long-lost Confederate submarine *Hunley*. He lives in Arizona.

Justin Scott's twenty-four novels include *The Shipkiller* and *Normandie Triangle*; the Ben Abbot detective series; and five modern sea thrillers published under his pen name Paul Garrison. He lives in Connecticut with his wife, the filmmaker Amber Edwards.

DIRK PITT® ADVENTURES
BY CLIVE CUSSLER

CRESCENT DAWN *(with Dirk Cussler)*
ARCTIC DRIFT *(with Dirk Cussler)*
TREASURE OF KHAN *(with Dirk Cussler)*
BLACK WIND *(with Dirk Cussler)*
TROJAN ODYSSEY
VALHALLA RISING
ATLANTIS FOUND
FLOOD TIDE
SHOCK WAVE
INCA GOLD
SAHARA
DRAGON
TREASURE
CYCLOPS
DEEP SIX
PACIFIC VORTEX!
NIGHT PROBE!
VIXEN 03
RAISE THE TITANIC!
ICEBERG
THE MEDITERRANEAN CAPER

FARGO ADVENTURES
BY CLIVE CUSSLER
With Grant Blackwood

THE KINGDOM
LOST EMPIRE
SPARTAN GOLD

ISAAC BELL NOVELS
BY CLIVE CUSSLER

THE RACE *(with Justin Scott)*
THE SPY *(with Justin Scott)*
THE WRECKER *(with Justin Scott)*
THE CHASE

KURT AUSTIN ADVENTURES
BY CLIVE CUSSLER
With Graham Brown

DEVIL'S GATE

With Paul Kemprecos

MEDUSA
WHITE DEATH
THE NAVIGATOR
FIRE ICE
POLAR SHIFT
BLUE GOLD
LOST CITY
SERPENT

OREGON FILES ADVENTURES
BY CLIVE CUSSLER
With Jack Du Brul

THE JUNGLE
THE SILENT SEA
CORSAIR
PLAGUE SHIP
SKELETON COAST
DARK WATCH

With Craig Dirgo

GOLDEN BUDDHA
SACRED STONE

NON-FICTION BY CLIVE CUSSLER
AND CRAIG DIRGO

THE SEA HUNTERS
THE SEA HUNTERS II
CLIVE CUSSLER AND DIRK PITT
REVEALED

BUILT FOR ADVENTURE: THE
CLASSIC AUTOMOBILES OF CLIVE
CUSSLER AND DIRK PITT®

The Thief

CLIVE CUSSLER
and JUSTIN SCOTT

PENGUIN BOOKS

PENGUIN BOOKS

Published by the Penguin Group
Penguin Books Ltd, 80 Strand, London WC2R ORL, England
Penguin Group (USA) Inc., 375 Hudson Street, New York, New York 10014, USA
Penguin Group (Canada), 90 Eglinton Avenue East, Suite 700, Toronto, Ontario, Canada M4P 2Y3
(a division of Pearson Penguin Canada Inc.)
Penguin Ireland, 25 St Stephen's Green, Dublin 2, Ireland (a division of Penguin Books Ltd)
Penguin Group (Australia), 707 Collins Street, Melbourne, Victoria 3008, Australia
(a division of Pearson Australia Group Pty Ltd)
Penguin Books India Pvt Ltd, 11 Community Centre, Panchsheel Park, New Delhi – 110 017, India
Penguin Group (NZ), 67 Apollo Drive, Rosedale, Auckland 0632, New Zealand
(a division of Pearson New Zealand Ltd)
Penguin Books (South Africa) (Pty) Ltd, Block D, Rosebank Office Park, 181 Jan Smuts Avenue,
Parktown North, Gauteng 2193, South Africa

Penguin Books Ltd, Registered Offices: 80 Strand, London WC2R ORL, England

www.penguin.com

First published in the United States of America by G. P. Putnam's Sons 2012
First published in Great Britain by Michael Joseph 2012
Published in Penguin Books 2013

001

Copyright © Sandecker, RLLLP, 2012
All rights reserved

The moral right of the authors has been asserted

Typeset by Palimpsest Book Production Ltd, Falkirk, Stirlingshire
Printed in Great Britain by Clays Ltd, St Ives plc

Except in the United States of America, this book is sold subject to the condition that it shall not, by
way of trade or otherwise, be lent, re-sold, hired out, or otherwise circulated without the publisher's
prior consent in any form of binding or cover other than that in which it is published and without a
similar condition including this condition being imposed on the subsequent purchaser

B-format ISBN: 978-0-241-95801-8
A-format ISBN: 978-1-405-92957-8

www.greenpenguin.co.uk

Penguin Books is committed to a sustainable
future for our business, our readers and our planet.
This book is made from Forest Stewardship
Council™ certified paper.

BOOK ONE
Talking Pictures

I

The Cunard Flyer Mauretania
Crossing the Bar

'Hear that?'

'Hear what?' asked Archie.

'Fast motorboat.'

'You have ears like a bat, Isaac. All I hear is the ship.'

Isaac Bell, a tall, lean man of thirty with a golden head of hair and a thick, impeccably groomed mustache, strode to the boat deck railing and stared intently into the dark. He wore the costume of a sober Hartford, Connecticut, insurance executive: a sailing day suit of Harris tweed, a low-crowned hat with a broad brim, made-to-order boots, and a gold watch chain draped across his narrow waist.

'It's not the ship.'

They were sailing home to America on the Cunard flyer *Mauretania*, the fastest liner in the world, bound for New York with twenty-two hundred passengers, eight hundred crew, and six thousand sacks of mail. Down in the fiery darkness of her stokehold, hundreds of men labored, stripped to the waist, shoveling coal to raise steam for a four-and-a-half-day dash across the Atlantic Ocean. But she was still creeping quietly in the channel, crossing the Mersey Bar with mere inches of tide beneath her keel and a black night ahead. Six decks above her furnaces and five

3

hundred feet ahead of the nearest propeller, Isaac Bell heard only the motorboat.

The sound was out of place. It was the crisp rumble of a thirty-knot racer powered by V-8 gasoline engines – an English-built Wolseley-Siddeley, Bell guessed. But such exuberant noise spoke of a Côte d'Azur regatta on a sunny day, not a pitch-dark night in the steamer lanes.

He looked back. No boat showed a light. All he saw was the dying glow of Liverpool, the last of England, eleven miles astern.

Next to the ship, nothing moved in the invisible intersection of inky water and clouded sky.

Ahead, the sea buoy flashed intermittently.

The sound faded. A trick of the wind gusting in from the Irish Sea perhaps, rattling the canvas that covered the lifeboats suspended outside the teak rail.

Archie opened a gold cigar case with a ceremonial flourish. He extracted two La Aroma de Cubas. 'How about a victory smoke?' He patted his vest pockets. 'Forgot my cutter. Got your knife?'

Bell drew a throwing knife from his boot in a flicker of motion quicker than the eye and cut the Havanas' heads as cleanly as a guillotine.

Archie – redheaded Archibald Angell Abbott IV, a socially prominent New Yorker – looked like a well-off man-about-town, a gilt-edged disguise he adopted when he traveled with his young wife, Lillian, the daughter of America's boldest railroad tycoon. Only the ship's captain and chief purser knew that Archie was a private detective with the Van Dorn Agency and that Isaac Bell was Van Dorn's chief investigator.

They lighted up, sheltering from the wind in the lee of a web support, to celebrate capturing a Wall Street stock swindler whose depredations had shut mills and thrown thousands out of work. The swindler had fled to a luxurious European exile on the mistaken assumption that the Van Dorn detectives' motto – 'We Never Give Up! Never!' – lost its teeth at the water's edge. Bell and Abbott had run him to ground in a Nice casino. Locked in the *Mauretania*'s forward baggage room in a lion cage rented from a circus – the liner's brig already occupied – he was headed for trial in Manhattan, guarded by a Van Dorn Protective Services operative.

Bell and Abbott, who had been best friends since fighting a legendary intercollegiate boxing match – Bell for Yale, Archie for Princeton – circled the boat deck alone. The hour was late, and the cold wind and fog had driven the *Mauretania*'s First, Second, and Third Class passengers to their respective staterooms, cabins, and galvanized-iron berths.

'We were discussing,' Archie said, only half in jest, 'your not-so-impending marriage to Miss Marion Morgan.'

'We are married in our hearts.'

Isaac Bell's fiancée was in the moving picture line. She had caught the last boat train from London after photographing King Edward VII's funeral procession for Picture World News Reels. Cine-negatives from the taking machines she had stationed along the route had been immediately developed, washed, dried, and printed. Tonight – only nine hours after old 'King Teddy' had been buried – five hundred and twenty feet of 'topical film' was showing in the Piccadilly theaters, and the hardworking director was enjoying a hot bath in her First Class room along the *Mauretania*'s promenade deck.

'No one doubts the ardor of your courtship,' Archie said with a wink so suggestive it would have earned any other man a fist in the eye. 'And who but the blind could fail to notice the colossal emerald on her finger that signifies your engagement? Yet friends observe that it's been a while since you announced . . . cold feet?'

'Not mine,' said Bell. 'Nor Marion's,' he added hastily. 'We're both so busy we haven't time to nail down a date.'

'Now's your chance. Four and a half days on the high seas. She can't escape.' Archie gestured with his cigar up at the *Mauretania*'s darkened bridge and asked casually, as if he and his wife had not conjured up this conversation the day they booked passage, 'What do you say we ask the captain to marry you?'

'Miles ahead of you, Archie.'

'What do you mean?'

A big grin lighted Bell's face with a row of strong, even teeth that practically flashed in the dark. 'I've already spoken with Captain Turner.'

'*We're on!*' Archie grabbed Bell's hand and shook it vigorously. 'I'm best man. Lillian's matron of honor. And we've got a boatload of wedding guests. I snuck a look at the manifest. *Mauretania* is carrying half the "Four Hundred" and a fair slice of *Burke's Peerage*.'

Bell's grin set in a determined smile. 'Now all I have to do is corral Marion.'

Archie, who was recuperating from a gunshot wound, announced abruptly that he was going to bed. Bell could feel him trembling as he helped him through a heavy door that led into a companionway.

'I'll walk down with you.'

'Waste of good tobacco,' said Archie, holding tight to the banister. 'Finish your cigar. I'll make it under my own steam.'

Bell listened until Archie had safely descended. Then he stepped back out on deck, where he lingered, his ears cocked to the dark sea.

He leaned over the rail. Sixty feet below, the water swirled in the lights of the pilot boat lumbering close, belching smoke and steam. The helmsman pressed his bow skillfully to the moving black cliff of the *Mauretania*'s riveted hull. The pilot who had guided the mammoth steamer out of the river and over the sandbar descended a rope-and-wood Jacob's ladder. It was neatly done, and in another minute the two vessels disengaged, the smaller extinguishing her deck lights and disappearing astern, the larger gaining speed.

Bell was still peering speculatively into the night when he heard the crisp V-8 rumble again. This time it sounded nearer. A quarter mile or less, he estimated, and approaching rapidly. The motorboat closed within a hundred yards. Bell still could not see it, but he could hear it running alongside, pacing the steamship, no small job in the steepening seas. He thought it odd, if not plain dangerous, that the vessel showed no lights. Suddenly it did – not running lights but a shielded Aldis signal lamp flashing code.

Isaac Bell looked up at the open overhang that extended from the bridge, expecting the *Mauretania*'s answering flash. But the bridge wing was deserted of officers and seamen, and no one signaled back. He saw no response either from the foremast that towered invisibly two hundred feet into the dark sky. The lookout perched in his crow's nest watched ahead of the ship, not to the side where the Aldis lamp had aimed its narrow beam.

Suddenly Bell saw the splash of a bow wave. It gleamed white, in sharp contrast to the black water. Then he saw the boat itself veering close. It *was* a Wolseley-Siddeley, burying its nose in the steep seas, hurling spray, and tearing ahead in the hands of a helmsman who knew his business. It drew alongside directly under him, forty feet long, sharp as a knife, spewing a bright feather of propeller wash.

Bell heard a shout behind him, a frightened cry stifled abruptly. He whirled around and scanned the dark boat deck. Then he heard a grunt of pain and a sudden rush of feet.

From the companionway where he had said good night to Archie burst a tight knot of men in fierce struggle. Their silhouettes lurched past the light spilling from the First Class library windows. Three big men were forcing two smaller fellows to the rail. Bell heard another shout, a cry for help, a hard blow, a muffled groan. A victim doubled over, clutching his stomach, the wind knocked out of him.

Isaac Bell sprinted the distance that separated them.

He moved in utter silence.

So intent were the three that the first they knew of the tall detective's approach was the crack of a powerful right fist knocking the nearest man to the deck. Bell wheeled on the balls of his feet and launched a left-hand haymaker with all his weight and strength behind it. Had it landed, he would have evened the odds at one to one.

Bell's target moved with superhuman speed. He slipped the punch so it missed his head and smashed his shoulder. It still connected with sufficient power to drive the man to the deck. But he was carrying a heavy rope looped over his shoulder, and the springy Manila coils absorbed the shock.

A counterpunch exploded from the dark with the concentrated violence of a pile driver. Isaac Bell rolled with it, sloughing off some of the impact, but the momentum pinwheeled him into the railing and so far over it that he found himself gazing down at the motorboat pressed against the hull directly under him. The man who had unleashed the blow that sent Isaac Bell flying dragged his two victims to the rail. At a grunted command, his accomplice jumped over the body of their fallen comrade and charged Bell to finish him off.

Bell saw a knife flash in the light from the library.

He twisted off the rail, regained his feet, and tried to sidestep a vicious thrust. The blade passed an inch from his face. Bell kicked hard. His boot landed solidly. The man hit the railing and tumbled over it. A shriek of pain and fear ended abruptly with the sickening thud of his body smashing on the motorboat sixty feet below.

The boat sped away with a roar of throttles opened wide.

Isaac Bell whipped a Browning automatic from his coat.

'Elevate!' he commanded the astonishingly quick and powerful man with the rope, whom he could see only as a shadow. 'Hands in the air.'

But again the leader of the attack moved like lightning. He threw the coiled rope. Loops of it entangled Bell's gun hand. In the instant it took to untangle himself, Bell was astonished to see the attacker scoop his unconscious accomplice off the deck and throw him over the railing into the sea. Then he ran.

Bell threw off the rope and leveled his pistol: 'Halt!'

The attacker kept running.

Isaac Bell waited coolly for him to reach the light spill from the library in order to get a clear shot to shoot the man's legs out from under him. His highly accurate Browning No. 2 semi-automatic firing .380 caliber cartridges could not miss. Just before reaching the lights, the running man clapped both hands on the rail, flipped high in the air like a circus acrobat, and tumbled into the dark.

Bell ran to the spot the man had jumped from and looked over the side of the ship.

The water was black, bearded white where the *Mauretania*'s hull raced through. Bell could not see whether the man was swimming or had sunk beneath the waves. In either event, unless the motorboat returned and its crew was extraordinarily lucky in their search, it was highly unlikely they would pull him out before the bitter-cold Irish Sea sucked the life from his body.

Bell holstered his pistol and buttoned his coat over it. What he had just seen was singular in his experience. What would possess the man to throw his unconscious accomplice overboard to certain death, then hurl himself to the same fate?

'Thank you, sir, thank you so very much,' spoke a voice in the accent and baroque cadence of a cultured Viennese. 'Surely we owe our lives to your swift and courageous action.'

Bell peered down at a compact shadow. Another voice, a voice that sounded American, groaned, 'Wish you'd saved us before he socked me in the breadbasket. Feels like I got run over by a streetcar.'

'Are you all right, Clyde?' asked the Viennese.

'Nothing a month of nursing by a qualified blonde won't cure.' Clyde climbed unsteadily to his feet. 'Thanks, mister. You saved our bacon.'

Isaac Bell asked, 'Were they trying to kill you or kidnap you?'

'Kidnap.'

'Why?'

'That's a long story.'

'I've got all night,' said Isaac Bell in a tone that demanded answers. 'Did you know those men?'

'By their actions and their reputation,' said the Viennese. 'But thanks to you, sir, we were never formally introduced.'

Gripping each man firmly by the arm, Bell walked them

inside the ship and back to the smoking room, sat them in adjoining armchairs, and took a good look at their faces. The American was young, a tousle-headed, mustachioed dandy in his early twenties who was going to wake up with a black eye as well as a sore belly.

The Viennese was middle-aged, a kindly-looking, dignified gentleman with pink-tinted pince-nez eyeglasses that had stayed miraculously clipped to his nose, a high forehead and intelligent eyes. His suit of clothes was of good quality. He wore a dark necktie and a round-collar shirt. In contrast to his sober outfit, he had an elaborate mustache that curled up at the tips. Bell pegged him for an academic, which proved to be not far off. He, too, was going to have a shiner. And blood was oozing from a split lip.

'We should not be here,' the Viennese said, gazing in wonder at the richly carved wood paneling and elaborate plaster ceiling of the enormous lounge, which was decorated in the manner of the Italian Renaissance. 'This is the First Class smoking room. We voyage in Second Class.'

'You're my guests,' Bell said tersely. 'What was all that about?'

The smoking room steward appeared, cast a chilly eye on the Second Class passengers, and told Bell as solicitously as such an announcement could be uttered that the bar was closed.

'I want towels and ice for these gentlemen's bruises,' Isaac Bell said, 'an immediate visit from the ship's surgeon, and stiff scotch whiskeys all around. We'll start with the whiskeys, please. Bring the bottle.'

'No need, no need.'

The American concurred hastily. 'We're fine, mister. You've gone to plenty trouble already. We oughta just go to bed.'

'My name is Bell. Isaac Bell. What are yours?'

'Forgive my ill manners,' said the Viennese, bowing and pawing at his vest with shaking fingers, muttering distractedly, 'I appear to have lost my cards in the struggle.' He stopped searching and said, 'I am Beiderbecke, Professor Franz Bismarck Beiderbecke.'

Beiderbecke offered his hand, and Bell took it.

'May I present my young associate, Clyde Lynds?'

Clyde Lynds threw Bell a mock salute. Bell reached for his hand and looked him in the face, gauging his worth. Lynds stopped clowning and met his gaze, and Bell saw a steadiness not immediately apparent.

'Why did they try to kidnap you?'

The two exchanged wary looks. Beiderbecke spoke first. 'We can only presume they were agents of a munitions trust.'

'What munitions trust?'

'A German outfit,' said Lynds. 'Krieg Rüstungswerk GmbH.'

Bell took note of Lynds's fluent pronunciation. 'Where did you learn to speak German, Mr Lynds?'

'My mother was German, but she married a lot. I spent some of my childhood on my Swedish-immigrant father's North Dakota wheat farm, some in Chicago, and a bunch of time backstage in New York City theaters. "Mutter" finally hooked a Viennese, which she wanted all along only didn't know it, and I landed in Vienna, where the good Professor here took me in.'

'Fortunate Professor, is the truth of the matter, Mr Bell. Clyde is a brilliant scientist. My colleagues are still gnashing their teeth that he chose to work in my laboratory.'

'That's because I came cheap,' Clyde Lynds grinned.

Bell asked, 'Why would agents of a munitions company kidnap you?'

'To steal our invention,' said Beiderbecke.

'What sort of invention?' asked Bell.

'Our *secret* invention,' Lynds answered before the Professor could speak. He turned to the older man and said, 'Sir, we did agree that secrecy was all.'

'Yes, of course, of course, but Mr Bell has so kindly treated us. He saved our lives, at no small risk to his own.'

'Mr Bell is a handy fellow with his fists. What else do we know about him? I recommend we stick to our deal to keep quiet about it, like we agreed.'

'Of course, of course. You're right, of course.' Professor Beiderbecke turned embarrassedly to Bell. 'Forgive me, sir. Despite my age, I am not a man of the world. My brilliant young protégé has persuaded me that I am too trusting. Obviously, you're a gentleman. Obviously, you sprang to our defense while never pausing to consider your own safety. On the other hand, it behooves me to remember that we have been sorely used by others who appeared to be gentlemen.'

'And who tried to yank the fillings from our teeth,' grinned Lynds. 'Sorry, Mr Bell. You understand what I'm saying, don't you? Not that we're not grateful for you charging to the rescue.'

Isaac Bell returned what could be judged a friendly smile.

'Your gratitude does not have to take the form of giving away an important secret.' His mild answer disguised curiosity that would be best satisfied by biding his time. As Archie had noted, for the next four and half days on the high seas no one was going anywhere. 'But I am concerned for your safety,' he added. 'These munitions people mounted an audacious campaign with military precision to kidnap you from a British liner putting to sea. What makes you think they won't try again?'

'Not on a British liner,' Lynds fired back. 'On a German ship we'd worry about the crew. That's why we took a British ship.'

'You mean they tried before?'

'In Bremen.'

'How did you happen to give them the slip?'

'Got lucky,' said Lynds. 'We saw them coming, so we made a big show of booking passage on the *Prinz Wilhelm*. Then we ran like heck the other way, to Rotterdam, and caught a steamer to Hull. By the time they figured out we hadn't sailed on the *Wilhelm*, we were on the train to London.'

Bell had many more questions, but they were forestalled by the arrival of the ship's doctor. When the chief officer bustled in right behind the doctor, Bell emptied his whiskey glass into a spittoon before the officer could see and conspicuously poured another from the bottle.

The chief officer listened with an increasingly skeptical expression as the Professor and Lynds described an attack by three men who subsequently fell overboard. Then, while the doctor examined Beiderbecke's cut lip and Lynds's swelling eye, the officer said quietly to Bell, with a significant glance at the whiskey in his hand, 'One cannot help but wonder whether those two gentlemen had a falling out and covered it up with a tall tale of, shall we say, "piracy in Liverpool Bay"?'

Isaac Bell sipped his whiskey. He intended to get to the bottom of the bizarre attack, as well as the nature of Beiderbecke and Lynds's self-described secret invention, which had provoked it. But the kidnappers had drowned in the night, miles behind the ship. The Austrian and the American-raised German-Swede were the only sources of information available. And the *Mauretania*'s officers were even less qualified than a small town police force to investigate the motive for the attack. They would only get in his way.

'I say . . .' the chief officer went on. He had begun politely, almost diffidently, the model of the smooth company man unfazed by the peccadillos of wealthy passengers. Now he fixed Bell with a flinty eye practiced at terrorizing junior officers: 'As no one jumped, fell, or was thrown overboard, I am curious how they induced you, Mr Bell, to embroider their story.'

'Sympathy,' Isaac Bell smiled. He touched the whiskey to his lips. 'Poor chaps were so embarrassed by their behavior . . . and I had had a drink or two.' He peered into his glass. 'Seemed like a good idea at the time . . .' He looked the officer full in the face and grinned sheepishly. 'It felt jolly good to be a hero, even for a moment . . .'

'I appreciate your candor, Mr Bell. I am sure that you will agree that as soon as the surgeon has done his work it will be best if we all turn in for the night and let sleeping dogs lie.'

*

'Krieg Rüstungswerk GmbH?' echoed Archie Abbott, who had traveled regularly back and forth to Europe his whole life. Most recently, in the course of an extended honeymoon, he had laid the groundwork for overseas Van Dorn field offices. 'They're a private munitions outfit with strong Army connections. As you'd expect of a cannon manufacturer gearing up for a European war.'

Isaac Bell had joined him in the dining saloon moments after the breakfast bugle had blown. The *Mauretania* was steaming past Malin Head on the northern tip of Ireland, and as she left the Irish Sea in her wake, the liner had begun lifting her bow into unusually tall Atlantic swells, churning rumors in the elevators and vestibules of rough weather ahead.

'Why do you ask?'

'Do you recall the motorboat you could not hear last night?'

'If I couldn't hear it, how could I recall it?'

Bell told him what had happened. Archie was crestfallen. 'Of all the darned times to go to bed early. *All* three overboard?'

'The one who tried to stab me, the one who got tossed by his boss. And the boss under his own steam.'

'You have all the fun, Isaac.'

'What sort of lunatic drowns himself?'

Archie smiled. 'Is it possible he was afraid of a fellow who had already floored two of his gang and was suddenly waving a gun?'

Bell shook his head. 'A man afraid would not have taken the time to throw his accomplice overboard. No, he made sure there was no one left to confess. Not even himself. Lunacy.'

'Are you sure he didn't jump into a lifeboat?'

'Positive. I went back and looked later. He was along that open stretch in the middle where there aren't any boats. Ten yards at least from the nearest one.'

Archie forked down several bites of kippered herring. 'I'd say less *lunatic* than *fanatic*. Krieg Rüstungswerk operates hand in glove with the Imperial German Army. So if Krieg Rüstungswerk wants the Professor's "secret invention" it must be some sort of war machine, right?'

'Undoubtedly a war machine.'

'Then Krieg might well recruit German Army officers to snatch it. They're fanatical on the subject of *"Der Tag"* – "the Day" – to kick off Kaiser Wilhelm's "Will to deeds". And we all know what "Will to deeds" means.'

'Shorthand for "Start a war,"' said Bell. 'Though I keep hoping that the European war talk is just talk.'

'So do I,' said Archie. 'But Great Britain is paranoid about German dreadnoughts, and Imperial Germany is ambitious. The kaiser loves his Army, and the Army rules society – just like in old Prussia. Everyone's drafted for three years, and the bourgeoisie are so nuts for uniforms they take reserve commissions just so they can dress up like soldiers.'

'Soldiers didn't build German industry. Civilians did.'

'No doubt millions of hardworking Germans would rather get rich and send their kids to school than fight a war. The question is, can the kaiser stampede them into battle – But enough small talk about war and secret weapons! Dare I ask – has Marion said yes again?'

'Haven't braced her yet.'

'Too busy tossing miscreants overboard? Hey, where are you going? You haven't finished your breakfast.'

'I am marconigraphing the Berlin office before we steam out of range. Get Art Curtis cracking on Lynds, Beiderbecke, and Krieg Rüstungswerk.'

'Good luck. Art's only a one-man office, and he just got there.'

'Art Curtis is quicker than a mongoose and smart as a whip – plus he speaks fluent German. Why do you think Mr Van Dorn gave him Berlin?'

'I'll meet you in the smoking room. We have to talk about you taking your beautiful bull by her horns – Say, Isaac? What happened to the rope he threw at you?'

'The rope was gone when I went back to look.'

'A crewman must have scooped it up.'

'Or an accomplice.'

Bell picked up a blank from the purser's desk and filled out his message. Rather than pass it before inquiring eyes, he carried the form directly to the Marconi house on the top deck of the ship between Funnels 2 and 3.

A window curtain, gray with coal smoke, flapped in the wind as Bell walked into the radio room extending a British pound sterling note – five dollars, two days' pay – to derail ahead of time any suggestion that he send his message through the purser. Nor did the operator, who was not a member of the *Mauretania*'s crew but employed by the Marconi Wireless Telegraph Company, remark that Bell's message looked like gibberish, as it was written out in cipher.

Bell stood by as the operator dispatched his message by Morse code to a shore station at Malin Head. From there it would be relayed overland by telegraph and under the Irish Sea and English Channel by cable and back onto telegraph wires across the continent to the Van Dorn field office in Berlin. Depending how far at sea the *Mauretania* had preceded, Arthur Curtis's reply would be transmitted from Ireland or relayed by other ships.

'Just in time for the bloviating,' Archie greeted Isaac Bell when the tall detective joined him in the smoking saloon. Midmorning, the male haven was crowded with gents smoking cigars, pipes, and cigarettes, playing chess and solitaire, and reading the ship's newspaper. Thin northern daylight, filtered through stained glass and tobacco smoke, shone upon settees, tables, and armchairs grouped on a pale green carpet. Two ruddy-faced middle-aged men were arguing in raised voices. Bell cocked an ear. In smokers and club cars, even the judicious sank to braggadocio, spilling priceless information by the boatload.

'Who's the large gent in tents of tweed?' he asked Archie.

'Earl of Strone, retired British Army.'

'Who's that Strone's squaring off against?'

'Karl Schultz, a Pan-Germanist coal-mining magnate known not so affectionately by the Ruhr Valley laboring classes as the "Chimney Baron". Before they get any louder, let me imbue you with courage. I implore you, my friend, moor the fair Marion before she drifts off.'

'Midnight tonight,' said Isaac Bell. 'Every detail lined up. Champagne and music for the kickoff.'

'You can't go wrong with champagne. But where will

you get an orchestra at midnight? Even the steward who bugles goes to bed after he blows "Sunset".'

'I'm going to surprise her with a gramophone.'

'Won't a gramophone horn flaring from your dinner jacket spoil the surprise?'

'The horn is made of cardboard. The whole thing folds flat in a little box no bigger than a camera case.'

Archie looked at him with genuine admiration. 'You are relentlessly strategic, Isaac.'

'Lillian's pacing outside the door. You can give her the thumbs-up. It's in the bag.'

'Is it too early in the morning to drink to your success?'

Bell had already caught the steward's eye. 'Two McEwan's Exports, please.'

'I'll be darned,' said Archie, rising to his feet and waving. 'That's Hermann Wagner, the banker. He hosted a dinner for us on our honeymoon in Berlin. Herr Wagner!'

Wagner came over, smiling. Bell noticed the air of the sophisticated Berliner about him, the elegant inverse of his coarse-grained countryman Chimney Baron Karl Schultz. While exchanging passenger chitchat about the rumored rough weather and agreeing that the *Mauretania* was already pitching heavily for such a long vessel, they were suddenly interrupted by the Earl of Strone heard across the saloon.

'What possible need has Germany for more dreadnoughts?'

'Because now strikes the hour of Germany's rising power,' replied Schultz, as loudly.

Conversation ceased. Every man in the smoker waited for Lord Strone's response.

21

The Briton tugged a watch from his vest. He thumbed it open, peered at the face, and announced to laughter, 'The hour, by my timepiece, appears to be half-eleven.'

'I refer to Germany's achievements,' Karl Schultz replied proudly. 'We have surpassed England in the production of coal and steel, and our scientists are dominant in chemicals and electricity. We produce half the world's electrical equipment. And we have a superior culture of music, poetry, and philosophy.'

Archie's friend Hermann Wagner interrupted in a gentle voice. '"Superior" is perhaps a strong word among shipmates. From strength comes humility.'

'Humility is for fools,' Schultz growled. 'We are neither despots like the Russians nor weakling democrats like the French. Our achievements give Germany the right, the duty, the *lofty* duty, to seek more colonies.'

'Good God, man, you've got German East Africa and German South-West Africa. You've even got a sliver of Togoland, as I recall. What more do you need?'

'Leopold, king of minuscule Belgium, has the *entire Congo*. Germany demands her rightful share of Africa. *And* South America, *and* the Pacific, *and* China. England has had too much for too long.'

The earl's lips tightened, and he started to rise to his feet.

Hermann Wagner intervened, placating him with smiles and pleasantries. Strone settled back down in his chair, harrumphing like an indignant mastiff, 'The colonies are already spoken for.'

'Strone's a darned good actor,' Isaac Bell told Archie.

'Actor? What do you mean?'

'Ten-to-one he's British Military Intelligence.'

Archie Abbott looked more closely.

'And twenty-to-one,' Bell added, 'he's *not* retired.'

Archie, who himself would have become an actor if his mother had not forbidden such a leap from society's bosom, nodded agreement. 'No bet.'

The Briton said to the German, 'You want war in hopes of grasping the spoils of war.'

'Those powers that try to impede German ascendancy will eventually recover from the weakening we mete out and accept their place in the new order.'

Lord Strone rounded suddenly on Isaac Bell. 'You, sir, you look like an American.'

'I have that honor.'

'Will the United States accept the "new order"?'

Bell answered diplomatically. 'Britain's navy rules the seas, and the German Army is the largest in the world. We have every hope that you will work out your differences. In fact,' he added sternly, 'we *expect* you to work out your differences.'

'Not likely so long as Germany keeps building dreadnoughts,' said the earl.

Schultz's cheeks flushed crimson. 'I quote Kaiser Wilhelm: "Our armor must be without flaw."'

Hermann Wagner intervened again, smiling polite apologies for his countryman's florid aggressiveness. 'But if – God forbid – Great Britain and the German Empire are on a collision course, on which side will America stand?'

'On the far side of the Atlantic Ocean,' drawled Archie Abbott, sparking laughter around the room.

The Berliner laughed with them and even the Chimney Baron smiled. But Lord Strone replied gravely, 'We are sailing in a four-day ship, sir. *Mauretania* steams to New York at twenty-six knots. The world is closer than Americans think.'

'Not so close we won't see it coming,' said Isaac Bell.

The men laughed again, sipped their drinks, and drew on cigarettes and cigars.

Hermann Wagner broke the silence, and Isaac Bell wondered why he persisted so. 'But if America had to choose, was *forced* to choose, to whom would you gravitate?'

'Germany,' Schultz answered. 'More Germans have emigrated to the United States than from any other nation.'

'Americans and Englishmen share blood and centuries of tradition,' countered the Earl of Strone. 'We are brothers.'

'But Americans fought their brothers in the Civil War.'

A grim glance flickered between Isaac Bell and Archie Abbott. It sounded as if the German Empire and the British Empire would fight sooner than later. God knows if France, Russia, Italy, and Austria would pile on. But the two detectives had no doubt that the United States of America should steer clear of Europe's chaotic politics.

Isaac Bell stood to his full height and looked the certainly not retired military intelligence officer in the eye. The Briton, at least, ought to know that the days of romantic cavalry charges were long dead. Then he widened his commanding gaze to encompass the Germans and said to all, 'Before you resort to war, I recommend you observe closely the effects of up-to-date machine guns. If you gents can't sort out your differences, you'll turn Europe into a slaughterhouse.'

'Are you in the arms trade, Mr Bell?' asked Wagner.

'Insurance.'

'Oh, really? May I ask what firm?'

'Dagget, Staples and Hitchcock.'

'Venerable firm,' Lord Strone rumbled. 'My solicitors engage them for my American holdings. But tell me, old chap, is it common for insurance men to observe the effects of modern machine guns?'

'We number among our clients Connecticut and Massachusetts arms factories,' Bell answered smoothly. 'And by extension, factories with whom they conduct business abroad. Vickers, of course, in England,' he said to Strone, and to Schultz, 'Krieg Rüstungswerk in Germany. Are you familiar with Krieg?'

'Only by reputation,' Hermann Wagner answered, as the Chimney Baron glanced aside.

'What is Krieg's reputation?'

'Innovative,' Hermann Wagner interrupted, again. 'Full of get-up-and-go, as Americans would say.'

3

Arthur Curtis, who manned the Van Dorn Detective Agency's one-room Berlin field office, was a short, rotund Coloradan. With a quick, sunny smile, a friendly glint in his blue eyes, and a potbelly straining his vest, Art Curtis looked less like a first-class private investigator than a prosperous liquor salesman.

He got busy on Beiderbecke and Lynds the instant he received Bell's marconigram. It was in his nature to get right to it, but in the case of Isaac Bell, he would never forget that when his old partner Glenn Irvine was killed by the Butcher Bandit, it had been Bell, shot twice in that gun battle, who paid from his own pocket to look after the dead detective's aged mother.

Curtis had operated in Berlin less than a year and was still developing the network of contacts – in government, business, the military, police, and criminals – that he would need to raise the field office to Van Dorn standards. He made swift progress nonetheless, establishing that Professor Franz Bismark Biederbecke held a prestigious chair at Vienna's Imperial-Royal Polytechnic Institute and that Clyde Lynds's multiple degrees confirmed that he was the genius his mentor had proclaimed him to be.

But he ran smack into a stone wall when he popped his first question about the munitions trust. A policeman he had cultivated, a middle-ranked detective, fell silent on the telephone. Curtis listened to the wires hiss, wondering why the sudden reticence. Finally, the policeman said, 'It could be dangerous.'

'What could be dangerous?'

'When Krieg Rüstungswerk GmbH hears that you are asking questions, it will be very dangerous.'

Threatening Arthur Curtis was a surefire way to get his dander up. 'Is that so?'

'That is so, Herr Private Detective,' said the German. 'I have kept you far too long on the telephone. Good day, sir.'

Arthur Curtis returned the earpiece to his telephone, took out his favorite pistol, a finely crafted lightweight Browning 1899 that fit his small hand, and broke it down and cleaned it to clear his mind. A sharp knock at the door alerted him to trouble.

'I told you,' he said, without looking up as the door opened, 'go away.'

'I am here for your own good,' Pauline Grandzau replied, stepping in uninvited and draping the coat and hat she had already taken off on the clothes tree. 'You need me.'

Art Curtis ground his teeth. He had come to think of her as Pauline the Plague.

'For the last time: I do not need a girl in this office. Even if I did, which I don't, I would not need a girl who is only seventeen years old and is probably lying about her actual age which is plausibly sixteen or less.'

'Every great detective needs an apprentice.'

Curtis looked up, wearily. This had been going on for weeks. She was standing there with that same hopeful smile on her freckled face, a skinny little German student with yellow braids, bright blue eyes, and the moxie of a Berlin street fighter.

'I'm not a great detective,' said Curtis, who could play disguises with the best of them. He wheeled out a favorite: roughhewn Westerner. 'I'm not that fancy Sherlock Holmes you're always reading about. I'm just a working stiff. That lets me off the hook.'

'It is your duty to society to take an apprentice. How else will the young learn?'

'I don't believe in girl detectives. And I'm not running a charity for society. Go away.'

She had already moved closer, edging up behind him, peering over his shoulder at the papers on his desk. Lots of luck reading Van Dorn cipher, he thought.

'You know you'll hire me in the end,' she said blithely. 'You need me. I speak perfect English. I am studying library and can look up anything. I am even a powerful skier, taught by my grandfather in the Alps.' Curtis put his head in his hands. He knew what was coming next. Sure enough, she quoted the infernal Holmes. '"When the other fellow has all the trumps, it saves time to throw down your hand."'

'Out!'

Pauline Grandzau grabbed her coat and hat and waved as she left the office. Art Curtis locked the door. Her English was actually pretty good – not as good as she thought, and not that he needed a German-English translator.

He trolled through his growing list of acquaintances, telephoned a talkative bank manager he had befriended and invited him to a beer garden, where they sat in companionable conversation on bentwood chairs under the shade trees, occasionally clinking their pewter steins and puffing their own contributions to the blue haze of cigar smoke.

The bank manager knew a bit about Krieg Rüstungswerk. The munitions manufacturer was controlled by the ancient Prussian Roth family, known to be secretive, which was hardly surprising in the arms trade. Krieg, as it was known colloquially, was especially well connected with the Army because it was 'smiled upon' by the kaiser. Krieg also had a penchant for buying up firms in unrelated businesses. Unlike the policeman on the telephone, the bank manager made no mention of any danger from asking questions. Curtis was just shaking hands good-bye, intending to move on to a working class beer garden where a retired German Army sergeant drank, when the bank manager said casually, 'I know a chap who works in their Berlin office.'

'Really? On what level?'

'Rather high up, actually. An executive.'

'I would like to meet him. Would that be possible?'

'It will cost you an expensive meal. He is greedy.'

'Why don't we all three dine together?' asked Arthur, which was exactly what the bank manager wanted to hear.

Arthur went on to his next beer garden. The retired sergeant was there. Plied with a fresh stein, he spoke admiringly of a highly accurate Krieg Rüstungswerk rifled cannon and repeated what Curtis had heard about the kaiser's warm feelings for the firm. With another stein down the hatch, the sergeant recalled fondly the time his regiment was reviewed by the kaiser himself dressed in the black uniform of the Death's Head Hussars.

Arthur Curtis went back to the office to draft a reply to Isaac Bell.

He unlocked his door and stepped inside. Hairs prickled the back of his neck. He slewed sideways, pressed his back to the wall, and slid his pistol from his shoulder holster.

'It is only me,' said the shadow sitting at his desk.

'Pauline, how did you get in here?'

'But if I had been Colonel Moran I could have shot you with my silent air gun. No one in the building would hear.'

'Who the devil is Colonel Moran?'

'He tried to kill Sherlock Holmes. Holmes arrested him.'

'I said, how did you get in here?'

She pointed at the window, accessed by an alley fire ladder, which Curtis occasionally used to leave the office undetected. 'As Sherlock told Watson in "The Adventure of the Crooked Man": "Elementary."'

'Elementary? Here's elementary.' Curtis picked up his telephone. 'I'm going to call the cops and have you arrested for breaking and entering if you don't get lost once and for all.'

'Guess what I found in the library about Clyde Lynds.'

Art Curtis felt his jaw drop. 'How do you know that name?'

'It's in the marconigram you received from the *Mauretania*. The one about Professor Beiderbecke and Krieg Rüstungswerk.'

'That marconigram was in code.'

Pauline shrugged. 'It's not a hard code.'

4

'You are up to something.'

Marion braced herself against the movement of the ship and regarded Isaac Bell with a dreadnought admiral's collected gaze. Her coral-sea green eyes, her loveliest feature, Bell thought, if forced to choose only one, shimmered with equal parts warm love and healthy skepticism.

'A picnic,' he answered.

'It's midnight. We're the only two passengers not seasick in their cabins. I see no wicker hamper. Though for some reason you're carrying a camera.'

'It only appears to be a camera. Take my arm so we don't fall down the stairs.'

The seas were heavy. The broad grand staircase swayed as the ship rose and fell with stately precision, but after twenty-four hours in a North Atlantic gale, they were getting the hang of it. Bell gripped the banister and they climbed together, gauging the pitch, compensating for the roll. At the top of the stairs, Bell led Marion through the vestibule into the First Class music room, a domed lounge with a thick floral carpet and brocaded furniture in hues of pink, blue, red, and yellow. The lights were low and it was empty of people but for a sleepy saloon steward standing by with a bucket of champagne anchored between a couch and a pillar. Bell tipped him, lavishly. 'I'll open it, thank you. Good night.'

The man left, smiling.

Marion said, 'Now you'll try to make me tipsy.'

'Would you dance with me?'

'Delighted. As soon as the orchestra arrives.'

Bell opened his camera case and wedged it in a corner of the couch. Marion leaned in close. Wisps of her golden champagne hair brushed his cheek. 'What is that? Oh my gosh, a little gramophone. Where's the horn?'

Bell unfolded a flat piece of cardboard and formed it into a horn, which he attached to the cylinder player. He turned a tiny crank, winding the mechanism, put on a two-minute cylinder, and started it.

'Remember this? We saw the show on Broadway.'

'"Heaven Will Protect the Working Girl,"' Marion answered when the first notes emerged thinly from the horn. The latest musical comedy sensation was a satire of the old 1890s romantic ballads.

Isaac Bell sang along in a credible baritone.

He treated her respectful as those villains always do,
And she supposed he was a perfect gent.
But she found diff'rent when one night she went with him to dine
Into a table d'hôte so blithe and gay.
And he says to her: After this we'll have a demitasse!

Marion sang,

Then to him these brave words the girl did say:

and took up the chorus:

Stand back, villain, go your way!
You may tempt the upper classes
With your villainous demitasses,
But Heaven will protect the working girl.

Bell opened the bottle of Mumm and poured two glasses. 'To what?' asked Marion.

'Love?'

'Love it is.'

They locked eyes, kissed, and drank. Bell changed cylinders, and strains of another new song, the romantic hit 'Let Me Call You Sweetheart', played through the cardboard horn.

'May I have this dance?'

He took Marion in his arms and wove a waltz through the furniture as if the rolling, carpeted deck were a crowded dance floor. 'Do you recall the first time I asked you to marry me?'

She pressed her cheek to his. 'Yes. It was during an earthquake.'

'And the second?'

'In the lobby of the St Francis Hotel. I said I was too old for you. You claimed that I was not.'

'And the third?'

'In New York. When you gave me this lovely emerald, which I thought too bright at first but have grown to love as our lucky charm.'

'And the fourth?'

'Above the Golden Gate. In your flying machine.'

'Will you marry me?'

'Of course.'

'Tomorrow,' said Isaac Bell.

'Tomorrow?'

Marion gave him a curious smile. The music stopped. She stepped back out of his arms, looked searchingly into his eyes, then down at her emerald ring. 'Funny you should ask.'

'What is funny about a man asking his fiancée five times to marry him?'

She did not seem to hear him, but marveled, instead, 'At the very last minute as I was racing to Euston Station to catch the boat train I made the driver stop at Hanover Square so I could run into Lucile's to buy a dress. Obviously, there wasn't time to make one, but a Russian woman I met in London told me that there was such a run on black dresses for mourning King Edward – it turned out he had *many* more mistresses than rumored – that Lucile's had scads of *not* black dresses just hanging about, deeply discounted. I wanted to ask your opinion of it, before I wore it. Now I can't.'

'Of course you can't. It's bad luck to see the bride before the wedding.'

She looked him in the face, and her beautiful eyes filled with tears.

'You're crying. What's wrong?'

'I am so happy.'

'But –'

'I love you so much.'

'But –'

'May I have your handkerchief?'

Bell handed Marion a square of snowy linen.

'I'm surprised by how totally happy you've made me. I

think I got used to the idea of us always being engaged. That was fine, but I love you with all my heart. I know you love me. But I guess I was holding back a little, because I really, really want to marry you – Isaac, are you sure Captain Turner will marry us? I've heard he's very gruff.'

'It was touch and go,' Bell admitted. 'He has a low opinion of First Class passengers and asked straight off why would we want a "bunch of bloomin' monkeys" at our wedding. I assured him that some of our best friends were monkeys. He didn't crack a smile. Just said that having been divorced, he was not, as he put it, "much of a hand in the wedding line."'

'How did you change his mind? Show him your gun?'

'I was about to. But he caught sight of you running aboard from the boat train and was suddenly all smiles. Practically fell in the drink leaning over the rail to watch your progress. I said, "That is my fiancée." Captain Turner said, "By Jove, I'll wear my full dress uniform. The whole bloomin' rig!"'

'I would not call my dress "full dress". It's not quite white. It is rather creamy, though more an evening dress than a traditional wedding dress.' She gave her eyes one last dab of his handkerchief and handed it back. 'Speaking of tradition, Isaac, isn't it traditional for a man to kiss the woman he's asked to marry when she says yes?'

Isaac Bell swept Marion back into his arms. 'I couldn't recall whether it's bad luck or good luck to kiss the bride before the wedding.'

'It is required,' said Marion.

'The very night before?'

'All night.'

5

'Third Class passengers are never admitted to First Class sections of the ship,' Isaac Bell was informed by *Mauretania*'s chief purser when they met to arrange the wedding. 'Not even briefly to celebrate your marriage, I'm sorry to say. Not even "moving picture people" known to your fiancée. You may invite a few from Second Class, provided they come properly attired, but we draw the line at Third mingling with the superior classes for one simple reason.'

'And what is that?' Bell inquired with a dangerous glint in his eye. He could not abide bigotry. That Marion's acquaintances were traveling on the cheap was no reason to exclude them.

'A reason that even the most ardent "democrat" will sympathize with. Were Third Class to mingle with the superior classes and one of their lot were to arrive in New York exhibiting symptoms of measles or mumps or some other of the infectious diseases spread by immigrants, the entire vessel and all who sail in her would be held at Quarantine. No one – not even you and your fellow First Class passengers – would be permitted ashore until the doctors could guarantee no outbreak of infectious disease, which would take weeks. Weeks! Imagine, Mr Bell, confined to the ship anchored offshore, staring helplessly at New York City, so near but so far.'

'My fiancée's acquaintances are not immigrants. They're artists saving on expenses, trying to make ends meet.'

'Infectious diseases do not distinguish between motives. I am sorry, but surely you understand.'

'What's tomorrow's dinner menu in steerage?' asked Bell, using the popular term for Third Class.

'A nourishing soup with bits of beef in it.'

'May I see tomorrow's First Class dinner menu?'

The purser produced a tall menu card beautifully illustrated with a color print of the immensely tall and narrow four-stack *Mauretania* framed by pink roses. Bell read it from top to bottom.

'I see nothing here that displeases. For our wedding feast, my bride and I will have prime sirloin and ribs o' beef, roast turkey poulet, quarters of lamb, smoked ox tongue, and Rouen ducklings sent down to steerage.'

'Excellent! Give me your acquaintances' names, and I will see –'

'To *everyone* in steerage.'

'Everyone?'

'Everyone will enjoy our wedding feast.'

'Most generous, sir,' the chief purser said drily. 'May I remind you that we have one thousand one hundred and thirty-five passengers in steer – Third Class.'

'What's for dessert in steerage?'

'On Sunday they'll get some marmalade.'

Bell referred back to the First Class menu. 'We'll send down apple tart, petits fours, French ice cream, and rum cake.'

The chief purser looked around his office, confirming they were alone and the door was closed. 'I don't presume to ask what a private detective earns, sir, but the cost of feeding First Class fare to over a thousand souls will be considerable.'

'Fortunately,' Isaac Bell smiled, 'I had a kindly grandfather. He blessed me with a legacy. Which reminds me, how many children are in steerage?'

'Many.'

'Better lay on extra ice cream.'

'Marconigram for Mr Bell,' piped a twelve-year-old call boy in a blue uniform.

'Don't move, nervous groom,' said Archie. 'I'll get it.'

The normally nimble-fingered Isaac Bell was having trouble knotting his tie, so best man Archibald Angell Abbott IV was attempting to tie it for him. Archie tossed the boy a coin that made his eyes widen and handed Bell the orange Marconi Wireless envelope.

Bell tore it open, unfolded the buff-colored marconigram, noted the date and the notation 'Handed in at SS Adriatic,' indicating the White Star liner had relayed the radio signal from a shore station, and then began to decipher its handwritten contents while Archie started over again on his tie.

'This is odd.'

'Hold still! What's odd?'

'Art Curtis says that Professor Beiderbecke is not a munitions inventor.'

'What does he invent?'

'Hang on, I'm still trying to figure ...' Ordinarily as quick with figures as he was nimble-fingered, he was having trouble reading the familiar Van Dorn code.

'I have never seen a more jittery groom,' said Archie.

'*You* were walking into walls at your wedding. Here we go! Professor Beiderbecke is an electro-acoustic scientist at Vienna's Imperial-Royal Polytechnic Institute.'

'What the heck is an electro-acoustic scientist?'

'Art says he holds patents for recording and amplifying speech and music.'

'Gramophones?'

The two detectives looked at each other. 'What does a munitions outfit care about gramophones?'

Archie laughed. 'If Krieg Rüstungswerk challenges Mr Thomas Edison's phonograph patents they'll see what war really is.' He saw expressions of puzzlement and intense curiosity cross Isaac Bell's face. 'What else?'

'Clyde Lynds is an honors graduate of the Polytechnic Institute.'

'Like they told you.'

'But they didn't tell me he's taken it on the lam.'

'Who's chasing him?'

'The Imperial German Army issued an arrest warrant for desertion – that makes no sense at all. The kid's no soldier.'

'Maybe that's why he deserted.'

Bell nodded. 'But he grew up in the United States, and he's been studying in Austria. You'd think he wasn't subject to the German draft.'

'Maybe they drafted him anyway and he didn't show up.'

'Art speaks fluent German, and he always chooses his words precisely. He writes "desertion". Meaning Clyde Lynds was already in the Army – come on, let's go.'

39

'Where?'

'I'm going to ask Beiderbecke why a munitions outfit is trying to steal his gramophone.'

As Bell yanked open the door, a page boy came along banging a Chinese gong.

'There goes the dressing gong. You don't have time. The captain's tying your knot in half an hour.'

'And I'm going to keep asking until he gives me an answer.'

'But your wedding –'

Bell was already out the door. 'When we get up there, peel Lynds away from Beiderbecke so I can talk to the Professor alone.'

Dozens of guests had arrived early in the First Class saloon lounge, the men in white tie, the ladies in gowns, and all wearing the tentatively relieved expressions of people whose seasickness was fading into memory. As Clyde Lynds put it when Bell and Archie approached him and Beiderbecke, 'Getting over seasickness is like being let out of jail.'

Archie took Lynds's elbow. 'You must tell me about your jail experiences.'

Bell steered Beiderbecke into the small bar at the front end of the lounge. 'I've got a case of groom's jumps. I hope you'll join me in a drink?'

'I am not quite over my seasickness.'

'A "stabilizer" for the gentleman,' Bell told the barman. 'A dash and a splash for me, please.' 'The stabilizer is half brandy, half port,' he explained to Beiderbecke.

Beiderbecke shuddered.

'Trust me, it works.'

'It is gracious of you to invite us to your wedding.' The Viennese professor flourished his invitation, a thick sheet of parchment paper that had been embossed in *Mauretania*'s print shop, and marveled, 'With this document in hand, barriers between Second and First Class tumbled like the walls of Jericho. Young Clyde slept with his under his pillow, lest villains steal it.'

Bell raised his whiskey and soda to the Viennese. 'Continued smoother sailing.'

'And to your bride's happiness.'

Beiderbecke sipped doubtfully and looked surprised. 'The effect is immediate.'

'I told you you can trust me,' said Bell. 'Now, can you tell *me* what exactly does an electro-acoustic scientist do?'

Franz Beiderbecke looked guilelessly at the tall detective. 'I experiment how sounds might be recorded faithfully by employing electricity instead of mechanical means.'

'Can that be done?'

'That is my hope. In theory, it is a simple matter of amplifying and regenerating weak electrical signals. Though the actual doing of it is not so simple. But wait –' He blinked, perplexedly. 'Wait! How do you know that? I did not discuss my field with you.'

'I was curious,' said Bell. 'I marconigraphed a colleague in Berlin, who informed me that you are a famous scientist in the field of electro-acoustics.'

'Marconigrams are dear. You went to considerable expense to inquire about me.'

'I don't often meet inventors of so-called secret inventions.'

'Can you blame my protégé for being cautious?'

'I blame Clyde for risking your lives,' Bell said bluntly. 'He may be smart, but he's not smart enough to distinguish friend from foe. *You* know that I won't betray you to the people I stopped from kidnapping you.'

Beiderbecke touched the stabilizer to his lips. 'Don't you find protégés are more interesting that one's own children?'

'Don't talk circles around a deadly subject, Professor. You and Clyde are in danger. What if they have accomplices on the ship? If you do make it to New York intact, what makes you think that a powerful trust like Krieg Rüstungswerk can't grab you in America?'

'I think of Prussians as pathologically insular.'

'You have invented something that those Prussians regard as unique. What sort of a weapon is it?'

'Weapon? *Sprechendlichtspieltheater* is not a weapon.'

'*Sprechend*-what?'

Beiderbecke put his glass down and repeated staunchly, 'It is not a weapon. And I will say no more of it. I gave Clyde my word.'

'If it's not a weapon why does a munitions trust want it?'

'I do not know. It is not for war. It is for education. It is for science. For communication. Industrial improvement. Even public amusement. It is –'

Clyde Lynds was approaching, trailed closely by Archie, who gave Bell a look that said he had diverted him as long as he could. Beiderbecke appeared deeply relieved by the interruption. 'Ah, Clyde. I was just giving Mr Bell an older man's advice on how to survive marriage.'

'Wha'd he tell you, Mr Bell?'

Bell said, 'Say it again, Professor. I could never put it so eloquently.'

'I shall attempt to repeat it,' said Beiderbecke, shooting Bell a grateful look for going along with his dodge. 'Since men and women are such different types of creatures, their only hope of getting along with each other is to love each other.'

'In other words,' said Isaac Bell, 'The love they have in common is all they need in common.'

Archie Abbott opened his watch. 'Assuming Miss Marion Morgan has not jumped ship, it's time to test that theory.'

6

'Shipmates!' roared Captain William Turner, a short, square-jawed, squint-eyed man in his fifties with a great ship's prow of a nose and enormous ears. His hearty seaman's voice carried to every corner of the *Mauretania*'s Saloon Lounge, where hundreds of First Class passengers had come dressed in their best to celebrate the novelty of a wedding at sea.

None were disappointed.

The bride was bewitchingly beautiful in a daring, close-fitting cream-colored dress with a high waistline that suited her erect carriage and a sash of diaphanous silk that promised, discreetly, an enchanting décolletage. Her blond hair was swept up high on her head, circled by an abbreviated veil that graced her high brow, and capped with a tiara made of rosebuds instead of diamonds. Diamonds, all agreed, would have paled beside her dazzling eyes.

Her golden-haired groom stood proudly at her side in a tailcoat. He was tall and straight-backed as a cavalry officer. Beneath his gold mustache, his lips parted in a smile that twitched repeatedly into a broad grin.

The beautiful matron of honor and handsome best man wore expressions of sheer delight for their friends. The *Mauretania*'s famously standoffish captain was a vision of cordiality, aglitter in the dress uniform of the Royal

Naval Reserve, with buttons, belt, braid, and epaulets of gold, a sword at his side, and a hat cocked fore and aft on his head.

'We are gathered together in the sight of God and in the face of *Mauretania*'s passengers and ship's company to join this man and this woman in matrimony, which is an honorable estate . . .'

With the attention of the entire ship riveted by the wedding, Professor Beiderbecke calculated it would be safe to visit the baggage hold, deep below and far to the back, to check on the well-being of his machines and instruments. He retreated before the ceremony began, pleading that his seasickness was worse, even though the sea had calmed and most passengers were moving about with color restored to their faces.

Clyde had barely noticed. The young man was in a high state of excitement, put there initially by gaining entrance to the sumptuous First Class lounge, then by being seated next to an exotic Russian woman of Marion's acquaintance. Dark-eyed Mademoiselle Viorets was no exception to Beiderbecke's experience that Russian women were intoxicating. Poor Clyde was panting like a Austrian Brandlbracke puppy.

Fearing that the way into the bowels of the gigantic ship would be a confusing labyrinth of stairs and passageways, the Professor had studied builders' drawings in the library and committed them to memory just as he would schematics for arcane electrical circuits or the latest triode vacuum tubes.

Rich carpets and runners in the corridors of passenger

quarters gave way to plebeian rubber tiling. Wide stair-cases narrowed into steel-shrouded companionways. He dodged crew when he saw them in time, and directed at those he could not avoid a haughty stare: Make way for Professor Franz Bismark Beiderbecke in his old-fashioned frock coat and silver-headed walking stick.

Suddenly he had a strange feeling that someone was watching him. His first terrible thought was that the *Akrobat* – as he had dubbed the long-armed, agile thief who had tried twice to steal his *Sprechendlichtspieltheater* machine – was stalking him again.

Impossible. Beiderbecke had seen with his own eyes the mysterious *Akrobat* jump off the *Mauretania* into the sea. Nonetheless, he stopped in his tracks and cast a fearful glance up the stairs. No one. He craned his neck to peer down another flight. No one. He poked his head into a corridor, saw no one, and continued down into a crew section, past rudimentary sleeping quarters and lavatories, storage rooms, and pantries. The air grew oppressive.

The engines made their presence felt, resonating in the steel around him, ever more strongly the deeper he descended, a muted roar that grew louder and louder. Beiderbecke stopped again and looked back, cocking his ears for footfalls. Silliness! What could he hear over the thunder of the furnaces and the whine of the turbines? Besides, despite Isaac Bell's efforts to frighten him into revealing his secret, the *Akrobat* no longer existed.

Real as it was, the sense of being watched was an irrational feeling, he told himself. A shadow flew near. Beiderbecke shrank into a shallow alcove formed by massive steel ribs. He pressed against the steel, which vibrated and felt hot, as if the fires that powered the behemoth ship were burning right behind him. The shadow, cast by electric bulbs caged in the low ceiling, crept along the corridor toward where he cowered. A crewman hurried by, cap and face and clothing black with coal dust.

Beiderbecke waited until he had gone, then darted along the corridor and down a flight of steps to the orlop deck, where he found himself yards from the stern of the ship in an area shared with sleeping barracks for three dozen cooks and stewards. The noise was deafening. Picturing the builders' drawings, he realized that he was standing below the waterline. Just outside the hull's shell plating, the propellers pounded a relentless din as they churned the sea at one hundred and eighty revolutions per minute.

He saw another shadow coming toward him and ducked through a door and down a companionway. At last he reached a door that should open – if he had not blundered himself utterly lost – into the corridor to the baggage room where the wooden crate that held his machine was concealed in a shipment of a dozen similar crates. All were addressed to a warehouse on New York City's 14th Street – a short walk, Clyde had assured him, from the Cunard Line pier where the *Mauretania* would land.

He opened the door and bumped into a broad-shouldered seaman who was just leaving the baggage room. 'Begging your pardon, sir?'

Beiderbecke said, 'I wonder if you could help me? I'm looking for my shipment of crates.'

'Crates, sir?'

'Wooden crates. There is something I must get from one.'

'There's no crates in here, sir. Just luggage.'

'No crates?' he echoed, aghast. Had Krieg Rüstungswerk stolen them? 'But they were loaded down here.'

'No, no, no, bless you, sir. In the *forward* baggage room is where you'll find crates. That's where they stow crates, whip them down the cargo hatch into the forward baggage room, they do. In the bows, sir. The front.'

'On which deck will I find this room?'

'Lower deck, sir. Directly under the main deck.'

'This plethora of decks – upper, lower, orlop, shelter – appear designed to breed confusion,' said Beiderbecke, taking out his wallet. 'Could I possibly prevail upon you to show me the way?'

'Bless you, sir, I wish I could. But passengers really oughtn't to be down here.'

'I'm afraid I'm lost,' Beiderbecke said, extracting a pound note.

The seaman stared at the money, wet his lips, then sadly shook his head. 'I'm afraid that the best I can do for you, sir, is lead you up to the shelter deck. There I'll point you forward on the Third Class promenade. When you have walked all the way to the bow, go down three decks to the lower deck and perhaps someone can show you the baggage room.'

Franz Bismark Beiderbecke trudged up narrow stairs after the seaman. Then he walked forward over six hundred feet along the Third Class promenade, which was crowded with immigrants – Croats, Bohemians, Romanians, Italians, Hungarians, and Czechs, as if half the

48

Austro-Hungary Empire had decided to regroup in America. The promenade ended at the Third Class smoking room near the front of the ship. He found the way down blocked by a scissors gate and climbed upstairs to go around. His pound sterling note persuaded a rough-looking steward to let him around a barrier.

Beyond that barrier, he looked out of a porthole down onto the open foredeck and saw, between the mast and an enormous anchor, a cargo hatch. There! That must cover the hole through which the cranes had lowered his crates. He headed downstairs for several decks. Racking his memory of the builders' plans, he finally opened a door on what could be, hopefully, the forward baggage room.

His heart froze.

The *Akrobat*, whom Beiderbecke had seen leap into the sea, was loping sure-footedly along the passageway, peering into every nook and cranny. Slung over his back was an enormous silver-colored steamer trunk. Judging by how effortlessly the *Akrobat* carried it, the trunk was empty.

7

Isaac Bell promised Marion '. . . to have and to hold from this day forward, for better, for worse, for richer, for poorer, in sickness and in health, to love and to cherish, till death us do part.'

When Marion promised to love and cherish him, she added in a strong voice, 'with all my heart, forever and ever and ever,' and Bell's blue-violet eyes swam with emotion as he placed beside their lucky emerald a plain gold wedding ring he had purchased long ago in San Francisco. Then Captain Turner repeated their vows in seamen's terms, commanding them to 'sail in company, in fair winds or foul, on calm seas or rough, in vessels great and small,' and concluded in a mighty voice, 'By the powers I hold as master of *Mauretania* I pronounce you man and wife.'

Hastily, he added, 'You may kiss the bride.'

Isaac Bell was already doing that.

Flanked by Archie and Lillian and Captain Turner, the newly wed Mr and Mrs Isaac Bell greeted their guests on a receiving line.

Mademoiselle Viorets and Clyde Lynds brought up the rear.

'In Russia we do everything backwards,' she proclaimed dramatically. 'Instead of gentlemen kissing bride, in Russia is the custom for ladies to kiss the groom. Firmly on the lips.'

'Irina,' Marion Bell warned with a steely gaze, 'we are not in Russia. If you must kiss someone firmly on the lips, start with that handsome boy trailing you with adoring eyes. Isaac, I want you to meet my very good friend Irina Viorets. It was Irina who told me about this dress.'

'A pleasure.' Bell shook the dark-eyed beauty's hand. 'From what Marion's told me you two had more fun in London than is usual at royal funerals.'

'We are kindred spirits. Marion, I have arranged for you and your handsome husband a special wedding gift to wish you happiness in your marriage.'

'What is it?'

'An entertainment.' She snapped her fingers and took command of a phalanx of saloon stewards, who marched into the crowded lounge carrying an Edison film projector and a screen improvised from a square of sailcloth.

'That is one energetic woman,' Bell whispered to Marion.

'A bit too energetic. She escaped Russia one step ahead of the secret police.'

'How did she annoy the Okhrana?'

'By making a film that the czarina deemed "risqué". I didn't get the whole story, and it changed a little with each glass of wine, but she's hoping to start over again in the movie business in New York.'

'Taking pictures?'

'Manufacturing. She told me, "Dis time I vill be boss."'

'Have I told you that you look absolutely gorgeous in that dress?'

'Only twice since we were married.' She stepped closer to press her lips to his. 'Isn't it wonderful? Now people expect us to kiss in public — Oh my, Irina is giving us a Talking Pictures play.'

The stewards suspended the sailcloth beside the piano. Actors, two men and a woman, positioned themselves behind the cloth with an array of gongs, triangles, drumsticks, whistles, and washboards.

'Where did she find a Humanova Troupe in the middle of the ocean?' marveled Marion.

'I say, what is a Humanova Troupe?' asked Lord Strone. The British colonel had been hovering near Mademoiselle Viorets.

'Humanovas make sound for the movies,' Marion told Strone.

'Sound? In the cinema? Do you mean like the orchestra?'

'Much more than an orchestra. The actors speak lines of dialogue. And make effects.'

'Effects?'

'Gunshots, whistles, bells. Surely you've heard Humanovas in London. Or Actologues?'

'Rarely get to town anymore, m'dear. Retired, don't you know?'

Bell concealed a smile at the sight of Archie's red eyebrow cocked toward the skylight. Strone was laying it on with a trowel, but a flurry of marconigrams from Van Dorn informants in England had repeated, in guarded language, rumors that His Lordship was, as Bell suspected, attached to Great Britain's newly formed Secret Service Bureau with offices at Whitehall in the center of London.

He left London only to undermine England's enemies abroad.

Urged on by Irina Viorets, the stewards arranged chairs facing the improvised screen, and within minutes the lounge had been transformed into a moving picture theater. Members of the ship's orchestra gathered around the piano with violins and a trumpet. They struck a clarion chord.

The wedding guests took their seats. The lamps were lowered. The projector clattered and light flickered on the screen. From behind the screen, an actor read aloud the movie's title card.

'Is This Seat Taken?'

'It's a Biograph comic,' Marion whispered to Bell. 'Florence Lawrence is in it.'

The scene was laid in a ten-cent moving picture theater just as the movie ended. A well-dressed audience applauded when a woman with a pistol arrested a villain, who was marched off by a policeman. The actors behind the sailcloth clapped their hands as the movie audience applauded. The next film on the ten-cent theater screen showed a conductor and piano player auditioning singers and dancers.

The actors behind the sailcloth sang and shuffled their feet on the washboards, and the ship's piano played ragtime.

A lady looking very much like the woman with the pistol walked into the ten-cent theater wearing an enormous hat and looked for a seat. An actress called, repeatedly, 'Is this seat taken?' Theater patrons refused to move, protesting that her hat would block their view of the screen.

The lady in the big hat was followed by a man in a top hat, who looked very much like the villain just arrested. An actor called in a strong voice, 'Is this seat taken?'

Theater patrons yelled that his hat was too big. Shouting matches ensued – angry words and a general banging came from behind the sailcloth.

Lord Strone laughed, 'If my wife could see the thoroughly unpleasant sort who attend the cinema, she'd stop badgering me to take her there.'

The ship's orchestra took up an aria from *La Bohème*.

On the theater screen, the director threw auditioning singers out the door.

Behind the sailcloth, the door banged and actors laughed.

In the ten-cent theater, ladies in increasingly large hats took their seats, provoking a riot.

A whistle blew behind the sailcloth. In the ten-cent theater, the clamshell jaws of a steam shovel descended from the ceiling and plucked off a lady's hat. Ladies removed their hats. The lady in the biggest hat refused. The jaws descended again and lifted her, hat and all, out of the ten-cent theater. The actors behind the sailcloth cheered.

Lord Strone led the laughter. 'I say! That'll teach her. Whisked off like rubbish.'

'Irina!' cried Marion as the lights came back on, 'That was splendid. Thank you.'

Irina stood and bowed. 'Could we have a hand for the players?'

The Humanova troupe stepped out from behind the sailcloth. The wedding guests clapped.

Isaac Bell shook the actors' hands, pressing into each a ten-dollar gold piece. 'Thank you for a memorable performance.'

'Would that we could have rehearsed longer,' one sighed, 'but Mademoiselle Viorets kept changing the dialogue.'

The wedding party trooped down *Mauretania*'s grand staircase to the dining saloon. Bell and Marion made the rounds of the tables, thanking guests for coming and fielding questions.

'To the beautiful bride!' shouted a red-faced Chimney Baron, draining his glass and waving for a refill. '*Und* to you, Mr Bell, as ve say in Germany, *Da hast du Glück gehabt!*'

'Which means,' Herr Wagner translated, 'Did you get lucky!'

'*Danke schön!*' Bell grinned back.

They were making their way back to their own table when Clyde Lynds hurried up, his face pale, his expression grave. 'Mr Bell!'

'Are you all right, Clyde?'

'I can't find the Professor anywhere. He's not in his cabin, he's not on deck, he's not here, and he's not in the Second Class dining room.'

'When did he leave the party?'

'Before the ceremony. He said he felt seasick again.' Lynds lowered his voice and whispered, 'I had a feeling he was heading down to the baggage rooms. I went down there. I didn't see him. I checked both of them, back in the stern and up in the bow. He wasn't in, either.'

'Why would he go there?'

Clyde Lynds shrugged. 'To check on our things, I guess.'

'What things?' Bell asked. 'Luggage?' The Professor and his protégé had danced repeatedly around the subject of the actual 'secret invention'. Was it aboard the ship? Was it in their heads? Was it on another ship? Did it consist only of drawings? Bell had no idea, but now it sounded as if the invention was physically on the *Mauretania*. It was be ironical if whatever the machine was, it was riding in the same luggage room as a Van Dorn Detective Agency prisoner.

'What's in his luggage, Clyde?'

Lynds hesitated. Then he ducked his head and said, 'The Professor had some crates.'

'Go sit with Mademoiselle Viorets. I'll have a look.'

'Don't you want me to come with you?'

'No.'

8

'Marion, I'm afraid I'm going to have to excuse myself. Beiderbecke has disappeared. Clyde is worried, and so am I.'

'I'll hold the fort.'

Bell walked Marion to her chair and nodded to Archie. The two men left the party separately and joined up in Bell's stateroom, where Bell slipped a pocket pistol into his trousers and tossed Archie another. 'Beiderbecke's gone missing. Clyde thought he went down to the baggage rooms, but he couldn't find him there.'

'We've got our Protective Services boy in the forward one.'

'Let's see what he has to tell us.'

They bounded down the grand staircase faster than the elevator would take them, past promenade deck, shelter deck, upper, main, and lower, and hurried forward to the front of the ship, following a route they knew well from visits to their prisoner, the swindler, and his bored and lonely guard. Archie was soon breathing hard, but insisted on matching Bell's pace. Bell grabbed him suddenly and stopped him in his tracks. 'Watch it.'

He scooped Professor Beiderbecke's pince-nez spectacles off the deck. They examined them in the light of a ceiling bulb. One of the lenses had cracked. 'His all right, pink tint to the glass, like he wore.'

The forward baggage room was cavernous – over sixty feet long and nearly forty feet wide, although so close to the *Mauretania*'s bow that its width tapered to sixteen feet as it traced the sharpening line of the hull. It held far more bales and wooden crates than luggage, rows and rows of shipping barrels marked 'Fragile' and 'China', oak casks of wine and brandy, a pair of Daimler limousines, and a handsome yellow Wolseley-Siddeley touring car. Bell smelled something in the fetid air, not the autos' gasoline odor, which he had noted on earlier visits, but a more acrid stink, like coal tar, or, he thought, simply the ubiquitous odor of paint from the constant maintenance performed by the ship's crew.

The lion cage sat near the front. As Bell and Archie pushed through the door, they saw that their Van Dorn Protective Services operative had fallen asleep beside the cage and that their swindler, a lanky, middle-aged sharper with a matinee idol's leonine mane of hair and a choirboy's trustworthy smile, was straining to reach through the bars for the keys.

'Lawrence Block?' asked Archie, using the alias under which he had conducted his stock manipulations. 'Even if you got the door open, where do you think you would go on a steamer in the middle of the Atlantic Ocean?'

'For a walk,' said the swindler. 'Maybe even find someone to talk to. This fellow and I have run out of subjects of interest to either of us. Failing that, maybe I'd bust into one of those brandy casks and get drunk.'

The guard woke with a start and jumped to his feet. 'Sorry, Mr Bell. The boat keeps moving up and down, and there's a smell in the air that makes me tired.'

Archie said, 'Next time hide your keys.'

Bell said, 'We're looking for a middle-aged Viennese gentleman with a fancy mustache and pince-nez glasses. He was wearing a frock coat and carrying a walking stick with a silver head. Has anyone of that description come in here?'

'No, sir.'

'Has anyone at all come in here while you were awake?'

'Just a young feller looking for the same guy you're looking for. Ran in, ran out.'

That would be Clyde. 'No one else?'

'Nope.'

Swindler Block called, 'What about the guy who took a trunk?'

'What guy?' asked Bell.

'Just a crewman,' said the PS guard.

'What did he want?'

'Took a trunk. They're in and out all the time. They get sent down for trunks when folks in First Class want something they forgot.'

'He wasn't crew,' said the swindler.

'What?' Bell looked at him gripping the bars of the lion cage, glad as any prisoner of a break in his empty routine. 'What are you talking about, Mr Block?'

'He wasn't crew.'

'He was so crew,' protested the Protective Services man. 'I saw him with my own eyes.'

Bell ignored him and asked Block, 'Why do you say the fellow you saw was not a member of the ship's company?'

Block said, 'The food down here is lousy. I want a good meal.'

'You'll get one if you tell me what you mean.'

'He was pretending he was crew.'

'The hell he was,' said the Protective Services man.

'The hell he wasn't,' said the swindler.

'Archie!'

Archie marched the Protective Services man out the door. Bell asked Block, 'How do you know that the man who took the trunk was not a member of the ship's company?'

'Do I get a meal?'

'Prime sirloin and ribs o' beef, roast turkey poulet, quarters of lamb, smoked ox tongue, and Rouen ducklings. *If* you help me. How do you know?'

'I just know.'

'You better know more than "just know" or you'll be dining on bread and water.'

'I'm not dodging you, Mr Bell. I'm telling you that it takes one to know one. I smoked right off that the fellow was an imposter. For one thing, he was covered in coal dust. Like a stoker. Well, do they send a stoker to retrieve a rich man's shiny clean steamer trunk? Of course they don't. They send a shiny clean bedroom steward. You get my meaning?'

'And for another thing?'

'The stewards usually come in pairs, help each other carry. He was alone.'

'What did he look like?'

'Like I just told you. Like a stoker. Hard as nails tough from the black gang.'

'Big man?'

'Not so big. Powerful build, though. Long arms. Like an ape. Like I said, what you'd expect shoveling coal.'

'Long arms? Did you see his face?'

'Black with soot.'

'Would you recognize him if you saw him again?'

'I doubt it.'

'Why not?' Bell demanded.

The swindler answered, 'Cap pulled down over his eyes, collar up round his ears. All that soot on his face, for all I saw he could have been dancing in a minstrel show.'

Bell looked at him with a wintry eye. Block was a very intelligent crook.

'What color was the trunk?'

'Silver.'

'How long ago was this?'

'Hour? Little more.'

'Enjoy your dinner.' Bell started out the door, then stopped with a new thought. 'Was there a sticker on the trunk indicating the passenger's class?'

'First.'

'Lawrence Block, you've earned your first honest meal since you graduated reform school.'

Bell sent the PS man back in with a stern warning to stay on his toes. Then he told Archie, 'A coal stoker, or someone who looked like a coal stoker, lifted a silver-colored steamer trunk with a First Class sticker. Question is, why?'

'Assuming the Professor's been kidnapped, I'd say they stashed him inside it so they could smuggle him into a cabin they booked somewhere in First Class.'

'So would I.'

'But,' Archie said, 'we found his glasses down here.

How would they know he was coming down here? Maybe they have someone in the crew watching him.'

'Or a passenger,' said Isaac Bell. 'We better get Captain Turner to rustle up a search party.'

9

'Isaac! They found the trunk on the promenade deck!'

Bell passed Archie at a dead run, climbing the grand staircase. There was a mob at the top of the stairs. The corridors converging outside a service pantry were jammed with the junior officers: saloon, deck, and bedroom stewards and seamen who had been pressed into the search. Bell saw a saloon steward sprawled on his back, his normally immaculate tunic filthy, and beside him the silver trunk. A husky seaman stood over it, aiming a fire ax at the lock.

'I'll open it,' said Bell, shouldering him aside. He knelt by the trunk and felt with his hands that it was heavy. 'Would there be a wine screw handy?'

The sommelier's assistant produced a corkscrew. Bell twisted it into the lock, manipulated for a moment while gazing into the middle distance, and the lock clicked open. To the murmur of acclaim, and before anyone asked how an insurance executive happened to know the fine art of lock picking, he said, 'Parlor trick my great-aunt Isabel taught me. She was a regular whiz.'

Stewards and seamen laughed.

'Never would say where she learned it,' Bell added, and the officers laughed, too.

He hinged the hasp up and lifted the lid. The laughter died.

Professor Beiderbecke had been squeezed into the trunk. His legs were bent sharply to his chest, his arms pressed about his head. His eyes were wide open. His face was rigid with pain and fear. His skin was blue.

Without a word, an elderly dining saloon steward passed Isaac Bell a gleaming fish knife. Bell held it to Beiderbecke's nostrils. He did not expect that the poor man's breath would cloud the silver, but it did.

'He's alive!' A dozen hands helped Bell pull Beiderbecke out of the trunk. They laid him on the rubber-tile floor and gently straightened his limbs. Beiderbecke groaned, gasped, and inhaled fitfully.

'Doctor!'

'Get the surgeon.'

Bell leaned closer, searching for a spark in his wide-open eyes. They seemed to focus on him. 'You'll be fine,' said Bell. 'The doctor's coming.'

Beiderbecke's body convulsed. 'My heart,' he whispered. Racked with pain, he clutched his chest. 'Bell!' he gasped.

'I'm right here, Professor.'

'Bell. My . . . protégé . . .'

'Don't worry, I'll look out for Clyde.'

'Protect him, please.'

'I will.'

'Protect him from the akkk . . .'

'From what?' Bell put his ear to Beiderbecke's lips, for the man was surely dying. 'From what?'

'Akrobat.'

The ship's surgeon arrived, shooing people from his path. Bell stood up to make room for him, then watched as the surgeon parted vest and shirt with sure hands and pressed a stethoscope to Beiderbecke's chest. He listened for a long time, shaking his head, and finally removed the instrument.

'What did Beiderbecke say? Archie asked Bell.

'Made me promise to protect Clyde.'

'From Krieg?'

'I suppose,' Bell answered. 'But that wasn't all he said.'

'What else did he say?'

'A name or a word that sounded like "acrobat." How do you say it in German?'

'The same, except spelled with a "k",' said Archie. 'But what did Beiderbecke mean by "acrobat"?'

'A man,' Isaac Bell mused thoughtfully, 'who can fly.'

'Like the one who jumped overboard.'

'And somehow flew back.'

Archie said, 'But acrobats can't really fly.'

'Maybe not. But the best of them can do a darned good imitation . . .' Isaac Bell thought hard. '*Mauretania*'s carrying three thousand people, passengers and crew. Whoever killed Beiderbecke is hiding among them.'

'That's like hiding in a city.'

'We need a witness. Let's ask this steward if he got a look at who knocked him down.'

The steward, who was sitting up blearily, shook his head. 'Sorry, guv. Jumped me from behind, he did, when I walked in the pantry.'

Bell helped him to his feet. 'Not even a glimpse as you fell? Did you see how big he was or what he was wearing?'

'Not a peep, guv.' He looked at his tunic sleeve, then down at the trousers. 'Blimey, am I a sight. Better get out of these before the boss sees me.'

Bell noticed brown grease stains on his trousers from the pantry floor. But the smudges on his sleeve looked like soot. He ran his finger on one.

'Coal dust,' he told Archie. 'Let's go visit the black gang.'

Block, the swindler, swore up and down, again, that he had not seen the face of the black gang crewman who had taken the silver trunk from the baggage room, but Isaac Bell brought him along anyway, intending to watch *his* face for signs of lying as they scrutinized the men who stoked the furnaces. He brought the saloon steward, too, on the theory that the man who knocked him down could not know beyond a doubt that the steward hadn't seen his face. The sight of two witnesses might set off a case of nerves. Or so he thought until he clapped eyes on the stokers and the hellish place where they worked.

'Three hundred and twenty passers, trimmers and firemen, mostly Irish from Liverpool,' said the *Mauretania*'s chief engineer, a compact, no-nonsense Scot with a walrus mustache and four gold stripes on his sleeve. 'Plus your odd foreigner.' Captain Turner had ordered him to escort Bell and Archie and their witnesses down to the stokehold.

He pressed an electric switch, and a massive watertight steel door ground open on a sulfurous scene of heat and thunder. Men stripped to the waist and hunched double were shoveling coal and wheeling barrows in near darkness.

The chief engineer had to shout for Bell to hear him

warn, 'Doubt you'll get much out of 'em. The black gang are a hard lot.'

'I'd be amazed if they weren't.'

'You should see 'em brawl. We dog the hatches till the fightin's over. Mind, it's no picnic. Our *Maury* wants a thousand tons a day to make her knots.'

The devil, thought Isaac Bell, would feel right at home deep in the ship. It was one thing to envision the principle that fire heated water into steam that spun the blades of *Mauretania*'s turbines that turned the propellers that drove her through the sea. It was another to peer through air thick with eye-stinging coal dust at scores of men sweating to feed her.

Timing gongs clanged. Furnace doors flew open. In the leaping light of flames, firemen with wet rags tied over their faces for protection from the heat thrust ten-foot steel-slicing bars into seething beds of yellow embers. They stabbed white-hot clinkers of fused impurities loose from the fire grates, smashed the clinkers, and raked away the pieces. They dug their shovels into coal heaped on the deck. They straightened up and scattered a scoopful into the furnaces, bent over and dug up another. Scoop after scoop after scoop after scoop they scattered onto the fires. They worked fast, endeavoring to open the furnace doors for the shortest possible time to keep the heat up. For seven minutes the firemen sliced and raked and shoveled, skillfully spreading even layers of fresh fuel on the incandescent coals. The searing heat dried their face rags stiff.

Furnace doors banged shut. Darkness fell. The firemen lunged for water buckets. Sweating trimmers manhandled wheelbarrows into the fire aisle and tipped them on the deck, heaping new coal beside the furnace doors. The trimmers raced back to the bunkers for more. Inside the bunkers themselves, Bell could see passers shifting coal from the back to the front. The gongs rang again, and the stoking indicator showed the number of the next furnace to be fed.

'How are long are their shifts?' Bell asked the chief engineer.

'Four hours on, eight off.'

Bell led the steward and the swindler along the fire aisles of all four boiler rooms, past one hundred and ninety-two furnaces under twenty-four boilers, in and out of bunkers, then by trimmers greasing machinery and shoveling white-hot cinders from ash pits into ejectors. Finally, he walked them through the fetid passers' and trimmers' barracks on the lower deck and the firemen's on the main deck, where exhausted men sprawled on tightly stacked berths. Not a single glowering face of those awake or those unmasked in dreamless sleep sparked a memory that swindler Block or the steward would admit to.

Returning from the wedding feast, Hermann Wagner opened the door to his Regal Suite. Truly fit for a king, he smiled, with two bedrooms, a parlor, his own dining room, and a second entrance through a pantry for the servants. Oddly, the lights were out. On previous nights a well-lit cabin had welcomed him after dinner with his bed turned down, a pot of his favorite hot chocolate on the night-stand, and a brandy beside the chocolate. Well, if the newly minted Mr and Mrs Bell's wedding had thrown the entire ship into a tizzy, it was worth the trouble. It had been a wonderful party with a dazzling bride and groom, excellent food and wine, great dollops of love in the air, even a whiff of mystery. It was rumored that half the ship's company was knocking on doors searching for a passenger who had gone missing from Second Class.

Strange, too, was a scent hanging in the air, a heavy, acrid odor, as if the smoke billowing from the *Mauretania*'s stacks had drifted down the vents into his quarters. He had never smelled coal smoke in his stateroom while crossing the Atlantic in First Class. With British and German and French ships competing for the wealthiest passengers, every detail was *de luxe*.

He felt cautiously for the light switch. The champagne had made him clumsy. He bumped into a lamp and lunged to rescue it before he realized that it was anchored securely against the motion of the ship. Behind him, he heard a metallic click. What had he knocked over, he wondered? Then he realized the sound had been the door being locked. Something brushed close to him. A steely hand closed around his arm. He felt himself dragged backwards against a rock-hard body.

Another hand clamped his mouth shut before he could even yelp in surprise, much less shout for help. Hermann Wagner was young and athletic. He fought hard to break free. But his captor held him with astonishing strength. It was the man crushing the life out of him who reeked of coal.

Suddenly salvation! A knock at the door. 'Steward, sir. May I enter?'

Wagner kicked out, hoping to knock something to the

floor that would make a noise. The knock was repeated with a firm rap of impatient knuckles, not the usual deferential forgive-the-interruption-sir, but a demanding open-the-door-and-let-me-in. The missing passenger! The crew was searching the ship. He struggled harder. The hand over his mouth slid down his chin and closed around his throat. Neither blood nor air could rise to his brain. He felt his legs give out from under him and he realized with a loss of all hope that he was being strangled to death.

'Sir? Are you there, sir?'

The man who stunk of coal muttered in Wagner's ear. *'Ich bin Donar.'*

It was the most beautiful sound that Wagner had ever heard in his life. *Donar*. German for Thor, god of thunder. It meant that he would not die. *Donar* named the leader of a secret Imperial German Army plan, blessed, Wagner had been assured beyond any doubt, by the kaiser himself.

The grip on his throat eased fractionally.

Wagner nodded, confirming what he had sworn in blood: obey without question.

The hand eased a little more, just enough for Wagner to whisper, 'Forgive me, please. I didn't know.'

'Tell the steward that you are sleeping. Tell him to go away.'

'What if he won't go? They're searching the ship.'

'If he insists, let him in, but not into your bedroom. Tell him there is a lady there who wishes to remain anonymous. Do you understand?'

'Yes, sir.' said Wagner. He had an impulse to salute. The

last man to speak to him with such compelling authority had been his colonel in the Army.

'Do it!'

'Do you suppose they're looking for the German?'

Two young trimmers in the No. 1 boiler room – Bill Chambers from County Mayo and Parnell Hall from Munster – passed in opposite directions, heaving wheelbarrows between the forward cross-bunker and the firing aisle. They had no fear of being heard over the thundering furnaces. Besides, the chief engineer, the American swell, the saloon steward, and the prisoner who'd been locked in the baggage room had finally left the stokehold.

'Who else?'

Chambers and Hall were leaders of a new breed of the Irish Republican Brotherhood. To hell with compromising old men. They were true rebels, and they had vowed to drive British rulers out of Ireland or die trying. Neither would deny they were hotheads. In fact, they would accept that charge as a compliment. Nor would anyone who had seen them harry English Army patrols with rocks and slingshots deny their bravery. As for being seduced by promises of rifles and explosives in exchange for helping the German, that depended on your definition of seduction.

'Think they'll find him?'

'If they do they'll wish they hadn't.'

Though both were young and brave and had fought the patrols, Bill Chambers and Parnell Hall let go of their wheelbarrows and made the sign of the cross. The man they knew as the German was in a fighting class by himself.

As the poet said, plague and famine ran together.

Through his Regal Suite bathroom door, Hermann Wagner listened to the leader of the Donar Plan wash off the coal dust in the needle-spray shower affixed to his porcelain tub.

'Turn around,' Donar called through the door. Earlier, he had warned in a cold voice that left no doubt of the consequence, 'Never look upon my face.'

Wagner stepped into the parlor and turned his back. His throat hurt since the man had nearly squeezed the life out of him.

'Order your dinner in your suite tonight so you may stand guard while I sleep.'

Wagner, who sang in his church choir and had an ear for voices, heard something slightly off-key in Donar's High German accent. While smooth and guttural, with the expected educated flair, now and then the tones of the Prussian upper crust roughened like a peasant's. 'Shall I order food for you, too?'

'Don't be ridiculous. One passenger doesn't eat two meals.'

'I meant so you might have dinner, too.'

'I'll eat yours.'

'Yes, of course. I see.' He heard Donar walk from the bathroom into his bedroom.

'Wipe up that coal dust before the bath steward sees it.'

Hermann Wagner got down on his hands and knees to scrub his own bathroom, something he had not done since he was twelve years old, in the strict boarding school his father had sent him to 'make him hard'.

He did not mind. It was an honor to be among the elite diplomats, bankers, and merchants drafted into the Donar Plan. Admittedly, he was no soldier. Nor was he privy to the details of the military scheme. But he could travel freely in the United States of America while conducting legitimate business and mingle in the highest echelons.

Der Tag was coming. Victory depended not only on soldiers. There would be no victory unless a patriot like Hermann Wagner did his part to persuade Americans to join the war on Germany's side – or at least stay out of it while Germany destroyed Russia, France, and Britain.

At dawn the newly wed Isaac Bell slipped silently out of bed, kissed his sleeping bride softly on her brow, dressed quietly, and went out on the promenade deck. It was bitter cold, and the sea was making up again. Long, evenly spaced rollers marched out of the northwest. The sky was clear but for jagged clouds stacked on the horizon like ice-capped mountains. The wind was strong, and the smoke from *Mauretania*'s tall red funnels streamed flat behind her.

He went straight to the point on the starboard side that the man who jumped from the boat deck would have passed as he fell. Somehow, Bell suspected, he had managed to land safely on the promenade deck – although that did not seem possible, as the boat deck was not set back and the promenade deck did not thrust farther out. But Beiderbecke had called him an acrobat.

Bell paced the area, his eyes roaming. Assume, he thought, that the *Akrobat* was a real acrobat. Assume he was a trained circus tumbler or trapeze artist. Assume he was extraordinarily strong, astonishingly agile, with no fear of heights and nerves of steel.

Bell smiled, suddenly gripped by a fond memory. He had run away from home to join the circus when he was a boy. Before his father caught up with him in a Mississippi fairground, he had befriended animal tamers, clowns, horseback performers, and especially the acrobats, whom he revered for their bravery and their strength.

Assume this *Akrobat* possessed every power of a professional big top performer who had honed his skills since childhood, as circus stars did. Surely, from what Bell had seen the night they sailed, the man was indeed strong and agile, with no fear of heights and nerves of steel. Was it possible for such a man to jump off the boat deck, drop ten feet down the sheer side of the ship, and swing back aboard on the promenade deck?

The answer was no.

Bell leaned over the railing and looked straight down at the water. Then he looked up the side of the Marconi house. As he had told Archie, the nearest lifeboat hanging from davits beside the boat deck was thirty feet from where the Acrobat jumped the railing. A quick count of boats revealed something he had never really thought about before. They had room for only five hundred people, while *Mauretania* carried three thousand . . .

Suddenly Isaac Bell bolted to the nearest companionway and bounded up the stairs. Would he have noticed in the dark if the Acrobat had jumped *up* rather than down? *Up* to one of the many stays and cables rising to the sundeck, immediately above the boat deck, where the Marconi house sat. Would he have seen him grip a line and scramble up to the sundeck?

Bell ran along the boat deck past the library windows that had backlighted the scene that night and saw immediately that the answer was no. There were no stays remotely near enough for a man to jump to. Therefore, if the Acrobat hadn't fallen into the sea, he had to have landed on the deck below the boat deck. Also impossible. Baffled, Isaac Bell wandered slowly back down to the promenade deck.

Two seamen were smoothing the wood railing with rasps and sandpaper.

'Good morning, sir.'

'Good morning, gents. Up early?'

'Soon as we can see to work,' said one.

The other said, 'If we let wear and tear go, the ship would be a bloomin' embarrassment. Look at this gouge! Fairly tore the rail in half.' He stepped back to show Bell their repair of what was actually the minutest gouge in the teak, which only an eagle-eyed bosun would notice.

Oddly, the gouge traced the full twelve-inch curve of the wood from inboard to outboard as if something flexible had wrapped around it. 'What do you suppose caused that?' Bell asked.

'Some bloomin' swell, begging your pardon, sir, must have whacked it with his walking stick.'

'Or sword,' ventured his mate.

'Sword?' the first echoed derisively.

'The grain of the wood is cut.'

'It ain't a cut. It's a gouge.'

'You can call it a gouge if you like, mate, but I say he whacked it with a sword.'

'Where the bloomin' hell would a First Cabin nob get his paws on a sword?'

'Concealed in his walking stick. Wouldn't you agree, sir?' he added, enlisting support when he saw Isaac Bell studying the gouge intently.

'Wire,' Isaac Bell said.

'Beg your pardon, sir?'

'Wire. A thin braided-wire cable.'

'Well, yes, it could be braided cable, sir. On the other hand, you might ask where would the swell get a braided cable and why would he whack the rail with it? Unless he was an out-and-out vandal. Not that we don't get the odd one or two of them aboard – You'll recall, Jake, there was that Frenchman.'

'What do you expect?'

'An acrobat,' Bell said, half aloud. Had the Acrobat somehow grappled the railing with a flexible wire cable?

'Acrobat? No, sir, begging your pardon, that Frenchie was no acrobat.'

'A German acrobat.'

The seamen traded baffled looks.'Well, if you say so, sir.'

'An acrobat it is, sir.'

As Bell hurried away, he heard whispers behind him. 'What the blazes was he rattlin' on about?'

'Acrobats.'

'Next'll be monkeys.'

Isaac Bell walked faster. He could imagine that a superb athlete, a muscular, lithe acrobat, could stop his fall by hooking a thin cable over the railing. But he could not imagine where the man could suddenly get the cable. Nor how he had secured it in the split second that he hurtled past the railing. Nor why the wire didn't slip through his hands. Or cut him to the bone if he wrapped it around his wrist.

Bell passed a barrier into Second Class, said good morning to the seaman Captain Turner had assigned to stand guard outside Clyde Lynds's cabin door, and knocked loudly. 'It's Isaac Bell, Clyde. Open up.'

Lynds let him into the cramped, windowless space he had shared with the Professor. He appeared to have slept in his shirt and trousers.

'You look a mess,' said Bell.

'Didn't sleep a wink. The Professor was a good man. A kind man. He didn't deserve dying that way.'

'You wouldn't either,' said Bell.

'Am I next?'

'Make a clean breast of it, Clyde. Your life's in danger. Who are they? What do they want?'

'I swear I don't know them.'

'Does it have to do with you deserting the German Army?'

'I didn't desert. I was never in the Army. I've never been a soldier.'

'Then why is the German Army after you?'

'I don't know. They're lying.'

'Why would the Army lie? If they are lying, why are they hunting you?'

'I don't know.'

'Yes, you do.'

'I am not a deserter.'

'I know you're not. That's what makes it worse.'

'Worse?'

'The German Army is helping Krieg Rüstungswerk steal your invention.'

'I'll be O.K. when I get to America.'

Isaac Bell asked the question he had come to Clyde's cabin to ask. 'Did you ever hear the Professor mention a name or a word that sounded like "acrobat"?'

Lynds turned pale. 'Why do you ask?'

'When Professor Beiderbecke asked me to protect you, it was the last word he spoke. "Acrobat."'

'Oh my Lord,' Clyde Lynds breathed. 'Are you telling me the guy didn't fall overboard?'

'You know who I mean.'

'Yes,' Clyde admitted. 'He's the one. Is he really on the ship?'

'I think the Professor saw him. I think this acrobat locked him in the trunk. If that's true, then you're being stalked not by his accomplices, but by the man himself, the same man who tried get you in Bremen and again the night we sailed from Liverpool. You were lucky that night that I just happened to be there. Last night the Professor's luck ran out. Whoever killed Professor Beiderbecke is hiding among either the passengers or the crew. He will not be found before disembarking in New York, at which point he will disappear into the city – where he will find you easily, Clyde. A man who has hunted in the confines of a steamship with nearly a thousand crew to take notice is a formidable hunter. He will find you.'

Clyde Lynds puffed up. 'What does an insurance man care about this?' he demanded, truculently.

'I don't give a hang about this or you,' Isaac Bell shot back.

'You don't?'

'If I hadn't promised the Professor to look out for your prevaricating hide, I'd let you to swing it out with this murderer we're calling the Acrobat. But I did promise. So you're stuck with my help, like it or not.'

'Can you really protect me?'

'Only if you can tell me what I'm protecting you from. What is your "secret invention"? Why do they want it?'

'OK. OK. We'll do it your way.'

Lynds sat silent for a long moment. Bell prompted him, saying, 'Professor Beiderbecke started to name it when we had a drink before my wedding. He called it "*Sprechend*-something" before he clammed up.'

Clyde Lynds laughed.

'What the devil is funny?'

'*Sprechendlichtspieltheater*.'

'*Sprechendlichtspieltheater*? What is *Sprechendlichtspieltheater*?'

'A ridiculous name. I told him we needed an American name. So he came up with "Animatophone". I told him that was worse. So he said, "How about 'Photokinema'?" Which is a bad joke. I couldn't get it through his head that we needed a snappy name we could sell.'

'But what is it?' demanded Bell.

'Professor Beiderbecke and I have invented a machine that reproduces sound perfectly.'

'What kind of war machine is that?'

'It's not a weapon.'

'That's what Beiderbecke told me. I thought he was lying.' Bell recalled Beiderbecke's claims for education and science, communication, industrial improvement, even public amusement. It was quite a laundry list, but a better gramophone might fit that. 'What is it, a gramophone?'

'It is much more than a gramophone. Much, much more than a gramophone. We perfected a way to add sounds to moving pictures. A machine to make talking pictures.'

'Talking pictures?'

'That's what I named it. Talking Pictures. Snappy, eh?'

'Better than *Sprechendlichtspieltheater*,' Bell admitted with a smile.

Lynds shook his head ruefully and ran his fingers through his tousled hair.

'Word got out. We were approached immediately by the biggest film manufacturer in Germany. They wanted to make a deal. Invited us to Berlin, First Class, all expenses paid, put us up in the best hotel. But then we learned that the firm was owned by Krieg Rüstungswerk, and we knew they would steal it. The Professor knew a scientist whose invention they robbed. So we decided we would do much better taking it to America to sell it to Thomas Edison . . . Boy, were we babes in the woods. Never occurred to us they'd try to stop us from leaving Germany. Or that the munitions trust was so in cahoots with the German Army that the Army would help track us when we cut and ran. Blind luck, we got away. That phony warrant gave them the power to have me arrested for desertion and the Professor for harboring a draft dodger. We barely made it out of there with that Rotterdam hocus-pocus. But when we got aboard *Mauretania* we thought we were free to sell Talking Pictures in America. Then surprise, surprise . . .'

'What do they want it for?' asked Bell.

'It is very valuable,' Lynds answered.

'But the German Army isn't in the movie line.'

Lynds shrugged. 'Maybe they want to be.'

'Somehow,' said Marion, smiling awake at the sight of Isaac Bell perched on the edge of their bed with a cup of tea for her, 'I always assumed I would see more of you when we married. At least the morning after the wedding.'

'Forgive me. But I'm afraid we've landed in a case.'

'Of course you've landed a case. After you saved poor Professor Beiderbecke from being kidnapped, he was murdered. That makes him your personal case.' She hugged him and took her tea. 'What have you learned since we kissed good-night?'

'Clyde Lynds finally told me what the kidnappers want. But I'm having a hard time believing it.'

Bell reported word for word what Lynds had told him. He often talked through cases with Marion. She had a razor-sharp mind and an uncanny ability to approach an idea from an unexpected angle. In the case of Talking Pictures, she was uniquely qualified to help him as an expert in the moving picture line.

When he was done, Marion put down her cup and sat up straight.

'Talking Pictures? *Real* talking pictures?'

'What do you mean real?'

'Not someone behind the screen, but actors actually speaking on the screen? Pictures with sound?'

'That's what he says.'

'Isaac! Pictures with sound are the Holy Grail. I don't know how he would do it – scores have tried and failed – but if he could, it would be worth a fortune. It would change everything. Right now we're stuck in wordless drama. Pantomime.'

'The Humanova troupe got around that.'

'But what are Humanovas and Actologues but a traveling vaudeville show staging the same drama night after night in a single theater? They're *less* than movies, not more, saddled with all the expense of touring players – payroll, train tickets, room and board. With real talking pictures, hundreds of copies could be exhibited simultaneously. Film reels don't need to eat or sleep.'

'Like a frying pan factory that didn't need to pay workmen because machines make frying pans automatically.'

'Exactly. All each theater needs is a projector with a sound machine.'

'You're very excited by this. Your eyes are shining.'

'You bet I'm excited. It's like you told me I could suddenly fly to the moon – Don't you see? Ten-minute, eight-hundred-foot one-reel movies have been playing forever in nickelodeons. But there's a potential for a huge new audience. Theater- and operagoers would flock to longer two- and three-reelers. Sound would let us tell bigger stories. I would quit Picture World in a flash to make talking pictures.'

'So young Clyde has his hands on something very valuable.'

'If it works,' said Marion.

'Why wouldn't it?'

'There are three technical problems that no one has

been able to solve.' She enumerated them on the long, graceful fingers of her left hand, starting at her index finger and ending on her ring finger, where beside her emerald nestled the gold band from San Francisco.

'One: synchronizing the sound with the picture; the actor's words must match the movements of his lips, just as a theater audience hears what it sees on the stage. Two: amplifying sound; it must be loud so thousands can hear movies in big theaters. Three: fidelity; so they feel the power of human voices and the beauty of music.'

'What you'd expect in a great opera house.'

'*Hundreds* of opera houses! Simultaneously! Talking Pictures could play in every city at once. Seen and heard by millions. But so far, no one in Europe or America has come close to solving those three problems. Those who tried have given up, ruined. Beiderbecke and Lynds's Talking Pictures machine has to solve all three.'

'If it does,' said Bell, 'they own a commercial gold mine.'

'And an artistic treasure. Isaac, this is so exciting.'

'What do you think of Lynds's scheme to sell it to Thomas Edison?'

Marion thought on Bell's question.

'It is very risky to bring a new idea to Thomas Edison. He doesn't want new inventions unless they're his own. He fights tooth and nail to keep his monopoly over moving pictures by licensing his cameras and projectors and banning the competition. His Motion Picture Patents Company has US marshals and his own private detectives investigating patent infringements, and he hauls independent filmmakers into court for the smallest thing. The courts are on his side because he's made friends in the legislatures by supporting the reformers' silly "recruiting stations of vice" nonsense against nickelodeons – But worst of all, if you're not working under his Edison Company license, you can't buy perforated Eastman Kodak film stock, which means that you can't take quality pictures. And frankly, that is the reason I don't mind working with Preston Whiteway on Picture World. Edison can't touch me. Topical films occupy a separate universe, and Preston is too rich to be intimidated.'

'And too unpleasant,' said Bell. 'Who should Clyde go to instead?'

'There's the rub.' Again, she answered carefully. 'He has little choice. Edison will be the only market Lynds can sell to – unless he's willing to risk joining up with an independent who could be crushed any moment by the Trust. You know, maybe you should invest in it. Put some of your grandfather's fortune to good use.'

'Grandfather Ebenezer told me on his deathbed that a man who acts as his own banker has a fool for a client.'

'I've heard that said by lawyers.'

'I mentioned as much, and Grandfather gasped, "Lawyers stole that expression from bankers." His dying words: "Spend all you like on wine, women, and song, but swear to me you won't invest it." So I'll leave investing in Talking Pictures to the professionals. But I have an idea about getting Joe Van Dorn to waive the agency's protection fee in exchange for Clyde sharing a piece of his profits.'

'Where is Clyde now?'

'He's safe. Archie's with him.'

Marion frowned. 'Lillian told me that Archie is still not entirely well.'

'Archie promised to shoot first and avoid fisticuffs.'

'But is he well? Lillian says he still drifts off to sleep sometimes.'

Bell nodded. 'It happened last week in Nice. But he snapped out of it. The fact is it's important to Archie that he pull his own weight. I have to honor that,' he added evenly. 'Whether I like it or not.' A warm smile softened his no-nonsense expression. 'Which leaves me with time on my hands until we join Captain Turner for dinner tonight. Is there anything you would like to do on our last day at sea?'

Marion stretched across the bed and lifted the receiver from the switch hook of a white telephone affixed to the paneling. 'If you would like to shed your scratchy outdoorsy tweeds, you'll find in that closet a silk dressing gown that I bought for you at Selfridges – Oh, yes, good morning, steward. We would like our breakfast in bed, please – They're asking what we want.'

'Honeymoon specials.'

That night, their last night at sea, Isaac and Marion and Lillian Hennessy Abbott ate at the Captain's table in the First Class dining saloon. Archibald Angell Abbott IV sent his regrets. He was busy babysitting Clyde Lynds.

I 2

Clyde Lynds watched Archie Abbott drift toward sleep, start awake, then drift again.

Isaac Bell's redheaded pal would be a goner in ten more minutes, he predicted, and indeed in eight he was fast asleep, sitting up in the chair squeezed into a corner of Clyde's cabin. Having noticed Archie's condition, Clyde had prepared for this opportunity by visiting the purser's office to remove some money from the wallets he and the Professor had left in the safe.

He slipped quietly out the door and signaled a deck steward he had primed to wait, touching a finger to his lips to ensure silence. The steward hurried off and returned quickly with two mates, bigger men then he. They padded quietly along the corridor, their shoes making no sound on the rubber tiles. All three were grinning like men who were about to earn enormous tips for very little effort.

'Ready?'

'Ready, sir.'

'I don't expect trouble, but just in case.'

'Don't you worry, sir,' all three assured him.

'If trouble they want, trouble they'll have.'

'Bet yer sweet life.'

He knew this was crazy. But he had to get a look at the machine to be sure it was OK. It was a move like this that got the poor Professor the ax, which was why he was paying good money to husky stewards to make sure it didn't happen to him.

'You know the way?'

'Follow us, sir.'

'Where you headed, Clyde?'

Clyde Lynds whirled around to discover a wide-awake, hard-eyed Archie Abbott in the doorway behind him. The stewards rushed to his rescue, then thought better of it.

'Whoa, Emma!'

Archie held a pistol tucked tight to his torso. 'Take it easy, boys. Where are you headed, Clyde?'

Clyde Lynds explained that he had hired the stewards to escort him safely to the baggage hold so he could see his machine. 'I just have to make sure it's OK, Mr Abbott. Can you understand? It's really important.'

Archie took a close look at Clyde's 'protection squad'. Second Class stewards were a tougher lot than he'd seen in First. And one bruiser looked like he'd stepped into the prize ring, though not recently.

'All right.' He pocketed his pistol. 'I'm rear guard. Go ahead, gents. Lead the way.'

They went quickly along the corridor and down companionways, Clyde close behind the stewards and Archie lagging behind Clyde, breathing hard and thinking to himself, I could be dining with my wife instead of herding this motley crew into the bowels of an ocean liner.

Both the swindler and his guard were fast asleep under blankets. Neither stirred when Archie, Lynds, and the stewards crowded into the baggage room. Archie smelled something sharp and acrid that he hadn't noticed on his last visit. Clyde smelled it, too. He stopped abruptly in front of the row of wooden crates from which the smell emanated.

'I smell tar,' said Archie.

'Could be the wine went bad,' said a steward and laughed, 'Why don't we sample some, see if it's all right?'

Clyde did not laugh, Archie noticed. The young man wet his lips and looked around nervously.

'What's the matter, Clyde?'

'Uhhmm.'

'You look like you've seen a ghost.'

'Do you smell something sharp?' Clyde asked.

'Yes, I just said that. So do they. What's going on?'

'I don't know,' Clyde answered, slowly, though Archie bet that he did. He laid a tentative hand on one of the crates, bent over it, and sniffed the wood. When he straightened up, Archie thought that he looked terrified.

'Mr Abbott, we'd better open all the doors and hatches in this baggage room. Immediately – all you men! Open everything. Now!'

The stewards looked about, uncomprehending.

Archie said, 'What is going on, Clyde?'

'Unless I'm mistaken,' said Clyde, 'these crates contain raw celluloid film stock. Movie film. The tar smell indicates that it's old and decomposing.'

'So what?'

'It breaks down chemically into a volatile nitrate gas. It will explode.'

'How do you know?'

'I'm a scientist! I experiment all the time with celluloid film. It's manufactured by dissolving nitrocellulose in camphor and alcohol.'

'Guncotton,' said Archie, as the penny finally dropped. 'Highly flammable.'

'The gas generated by the breakdown will do more than burn. First it will explode. *Then* the film will burn. We have to vent the gas before something detonates it.'

'Open everything!' Archie ordered the stewards. 'Do it now. Open every door.'

They ran to obey.

Clyde Lynds looked up at a ten-by-ten square opening in the ceiling. 'The cargo hatch!'

'What are you doing?' said Archie.

Lynds scrambled onto a crate, reached up, and pulled himself onto the bottom rungs of a ladder that rose into the darkness overhead. 'The cargo hatch,' he called down. 'If I can open it, the shaft will suck the gas out like a chimney.'

Many decks higher and three hundred feet aft in the First Class dining saloon, Marion said, 'Captain, I can't help but notice that eight of the twelve seats at your table are empty. Surely it can't be for lack of guests who want to dine with you. This is a splendid dinner, and you are a charming host.'

'Thank you, Mrs Bell,' Turner replied, studiously ignoring the titans of industry, the London aristocrats, and the American millionaires at nearby tables who were attempting to catch his eye. 'I will carry your sweet compliment to my grave. But I only dine with passengers when I feel like it, which is not often. They tend to be a bunch of bloomin' monkeys, present company excepted.'

'Doesn't the line object? Isn't the captain supposed to woo wealthy passengers?'

'Cunard have taken notice of a curious fact,' the captain answered. 'The more I insult First Class passengers, the more First Class passengers wish to sail in my ship. It was the same way on the *Lusitania*, my previous command. For some reason the wealthy, particularly the newly wealthy, court abuse. As you know' – Turner lowered his voice and beckoned them closer, conspiratorially – 'the White Star Line will soon launch *Olympic* and *Titanic*. Neither will ever match *Mauretania*'s speed, of course, but they will be bigger, and there's always the appeal of novelty, so competition will be hotter than ever. With that in mind, I've suggested to the chairman that I drive up ticket sales by treating passengers in First Class to old-fashioned Royal Navy floggings.'

Isaac Bell and Marion burst out laughing.

'Haven't heard back from him yet,' Captain Turner chortled. 'Presumably he's debating it with his directors.'

Their laughter was abruptly quelled by a hard thump that rattled the silverware. Crystal rang musically. Five hundred people in the enormous dining saloon fell silent.

Bell thought it felt as if something heavy had smashed the carpeted deck under their feet. Either another vessel had struck the ship, or somewhere in the eight-hundred-and-ninety-foot hull something had exploded with terrific force. Then came the most frightening cry heard at sea.

'Fire!'

BOOK TWO
Flickers

13

'Fire! Fire in the forward baggage room!'

Isaac Bell raced down the grand staircase.

Captain Turner was running up the stairs, heading for the bridge, shouting orders to turn the *Mauretania* away from the wind to keep it from fanning the flames.

Bell ran to the fire. His prisoner was trapped in the baggage room in the bow. He had to get the man and his PS guard to safety.

The bugle shrieked the alarm. *Fight fire! Fight fire!*

Passengers milled. Stewards tried to calm them but had no answers to their frightened questions. The ship heeled, leaning away from a sharp turn that put her stern to the weather. The decks lurched. Ship's officers bellowed into megaphones: 'Passengers to the boat deck. All passengers to the boat deck.'

The stewards began pleading with people to put on their life vests.

A woman screamed.

Isaac Bell smelled smoke before he got close enough to see the fire. It was a bitter chemical blend of coal tar and gunpowder oddly layered with sweet whiffs of brandy. Suddenly he saw flames explode from the end of a corridor. It was as strikingly bright a fire as he had ever seen, with an intense white-orange color. He felt the heat fifty feet away.

He saw a band of stewards whose uniforms had been burnt to smoldering rags stagger from a cross-corridor dragging a hose. Bell ran to help them charge the flames. They were led by a tall man singed half bald. His green eyes blazed in a face black with soot.

'Archie?'

'How was dinner?' asked Archie, striding into the burning baggage room, spewing steam from the hose.

'You OK?'

'Tip-top. Most of the explosion went up the hatch, and our PS boy did himself proud getting Block out.'

'What's burning?'

'Nitrate film stock. Clyde says it feeds on its own oxygen.'

Bell asked, 'Any more hoses?'

'This is steam. There's a saltwater hose in the companionway.'

Bell unreeled it and followed Archie into the burning room. 'Where's Clyde?'

'He went up the hatchway ladder to vent the fumes.'

Bell looked at the square opening in the ceiling. The bitter, undoubtedly poisonous smoke was billowing up it. 'Is he all right?'

'I don't know. It blew soon after he left. But it looks to me like he got the hatch open. Unless it blew open.'

Three dozen seaman streamed down from their sleeping berths directly above the fire. Stewards joined them, mobbing the forward baggage room with long hoses, directing steam and salt water into the furious orange maw of poisonous smoke and intense heat that threatened the ship. The water tended to spread the burning film, scattering it. The steam was better at smothering it.

As they fought to confine the fire to the baggage room, paint on surrounding bulkheads was bubbling from the heat, all three automobiles exploded, and the brandy, a dining saloon steward shouted, threatened to 'turn the bloomin' ship into *Maury flambé*'.

With the crew fighting the fire, and his saltwater hose a less effective extinguisher than the low-pressure steam that Archie refused to relinquish, Isaac Bell ran up the companionways looking for Clyde. He could see that the steel hatchway that rose forty feet from the baggage room to the foredeck had directed the flaming force of the explosion straight up like an enormous square cannon, past the cram-packed quarters of seamen and stewards on the upper deck, and past the officers' mess hall on the shelter deck. He stepped out on the open foredeck. A pillar of flame and smoke pouring skyward from the open hatch lighted the *Mauretania*'s mast, vents, and smokestacks bright as day.

He found Clyde Lynds sprawled facedown on the spare anchor, coughing and retching the poison fumes out of his lungs and gulping water from a bucket held by a pair of black and greasy stokers, who pounded him on the back and poured more water into him, shouting, 'Good lad. Spit it up, lad. Spit it up. You'll be right as rain.'

They told Isaac Bell that they had just sneaked out for a breath of fresh air on the dark foredeck when they heard his frantic pounding on the hatch. 'Undogged the hatch, he did, but it was too heavy for him to lift. Good luck we was there to help him out. And we opened it just in the nick. The lad's a bloomin' hero, he is. Saved the ship. Spit it up, lad! Spit it up.'

*

Late that night, Isaac Bell interviewed Archie Abbott, Clyde Lynds, the *Mauretania*'s chief purser, and finally the bosun's mate, who had operated the winch that had loaded cargo and luggage down the forward hatch the day they sailed from Liverpool. He reported privately to Captain Turner on the bridge.

'As you know, the entire contents of the forward baggage room were incinerated. Nothing remains but ash, so hot was the fire. But I can tell you with some confidence that the fire was caused by the spontaneous explosion of a large shipment of deteriorating celluloid film stock. I'm sure you're aware that film-stock smugglers profit by going around the Edison Trust to sell to independent manufacturers who can't buy direct from Eastman Kodak.'

The mariner was livid. 'I will personally hang them from *Mauretania*'s foremast if I ever got my hands on them. This has happened time and again in the past year, endangering ships at sea.'

'There were as many as eight wooden crates disguised as a shipment of rare books destined to a bibliophile in Reistertown, Maryland – a gentleman whom I strongly doubt was expecting more than a single crate. The books were a clever device as they're very heavy, much like film stock.'

'Damned smugglers! Have they no regard for the lives of three thousand souls?'

Captain Turner agreed with the stokers that Clyde Lynds was a hero. In a brisk early-morning ceremony on the flying bridge – while down on the forepeak seamen in a paint party were touching up the blackened hatchway – he pinned a medal on Clyde's chest. 'For quick thinking and brave action that prevented a catastrophic explosion. I'll lend you one of mine for the moment until the line strikes a proper one for you.'

'The stokers who helped me deserve medals, too.'

'I've already presented theirs, not to worry, lad.'

Clyde looked questioningly at Bell, and the detective thought that the normally brash scientist seemed uncharacteristically reluctant to accept the honor. 'What do you think, Mr Bell?'

'I think it is the least you deserve. Hopefully it will make up a little for your losing your crate in the fire.'

Oddly, the mention of the loss caused the young man to break into a broad grin, the first Bell had seen on his face since Professor Beiderbecke had died.

'Wasn't it important?' Bell asked.

Instead of answering, Lynds said, briskly, 'Thank you, Captain Turner. And thank you for the temporary loan of your medal until they strike mine. What did you get yours for?'

'Good day, gentlemen,' Turner dismissed them brusquely. 'As I have promised the company a quick turnaround rehearsing for the Christmas voyages, I have to land my ship, disgorge passengers, and load coal and victual for the next lot at breakneck speed.'

Walking down the grand staircase as the luncheon bugle blew, Bell asked again, 'Wasn't your crate important?'

'It sure was. It held the only prototype of the Beiderbecke and Lynds Talking Pictures machine.'

'Then why were you smiling?'

'It's safe in my head. Give me some time and some dough and I can replicate it even without poor Professor Beiderbecke.'

Isaac Bell stopped in the middle of the grand staircase and took Lynds firmly by the arm. 'Clyde, you are a first-rate jackass.'

'You think I'm bragging? Listen, I'm not saying it'll be a snap, but give me several years with proper financing and a top-notch laboratory, and I can do it. And I'll build it even better than it was. After we finished, we kept thinking about ways to perfect it. It's not like I'm starting from scratch. We solved most of the big problems, and the solutions are safe in my head.' He tapped his head with one finger. 'Right here. Deep in my skull.'

Isaac Bell said, 'If your enemies suspect that, you're in more danger than ever.'

Hermann Wagner filled out a marconigram blank and gave it to an assistant purser.

The assistant purser, who had been thoroughly briefed on the identity of all important passengers before the *Mauretania* left Liverpool, was not surprised that a leading Berlin banker would send his marconigrams in cipher, particularly a message addressed to the German consulate in New York City. Bankers had secrets to guard, and you could double that for diplomats.

The assistant purser noticed that Wagner's hands were shaking, but of course he did not remark upon it. Even stolid German bankers were known to indulge in a few too many schnapps on their last night at sea. A good night's sleep ashore and the banker would be nose to the grindstone tomorrow morning.

'They'll send this immediately, Herr Wagner. May we help arrange your lodgings in New York?'

'No, thank you. Everything is planned.'

14

'"Colossal" is the only word to describe the new steam-ship terminal of the Chelsea Improvement,' said Archie Abbott, who was as tireless a promoter of his beloved New York as a Chamber of Commerce publicity man. To shelter as many as sixteen express liners as big as the *Mauretania*, he enthused, the terminal's piers extended six hundred feet into the Hudson River and burrowed two hundred feet inland for three-quarters of a mile from Little West 12th Street all the way to West 23rd.

'There's even room for *Titanic* when she goes into ser-vice. And wait till you see the portals on West Street – pink granite! An eyesore of a waterfront is transformed.'

'Not entirely transformed,' said Isaac Bell, studying the pier through field glasses. Crowds of people had stepped out of the second-story waiting room onto the pier's apron to wave handkerchiefs to friends and relatives on the approaching ship.

Earlier, steaming up the harbor, Isaac and Marion Bell and Archie and Lillian Abbott had stood arm in arm admiring the city from the promenade deck railing. It was a beautiful day. The air was crisp. A stiff northeast wind parted the coal smoke that normally blanketed the harbor. Manhattan's skyscrapers gleamed in a blue sky.

Now, as music from a ragtime band danced on the water and tugboats battled to land thirty-two thousand tons of *Mauretania* against the wind pushing her lofty superstructure, the detectives were concentrating on getting their prisoner and Clyde Lynds safely ashore, after which they would meet up with their wives at Archie and Lillian's town house on East 64th, where the newlyweds were invited to stay.

'What do you mean not entirely?' Archie protested. 'We sailed from Hoboken last month. You haven't seen the Chelsea portals or the magnificent waiting rooms. The elevators are solid bronze. There's never been a city project like it.'

Bell passed him the field glasses. 'They forgot to transform the plug-uglies.'

'You'll always find a couple of pickpockets when a ship lands,' Archie scoffed.

'I'm not talking about pickpockets. Look closer.'

A thousand people awaited the liner at Pier 54. Longshoremen were poised to work ship, heaving lines and unloading mail and baggage. Treasury Department customs agents swarmed the pier's lower deck to inspect luggage for dutiable gowns and jewels being smuggled. On coal barges in the slip, trimmers had gathered before the usual time to refill the *Mauretania's* bunkers for Captain Turner's extraordinarily speedy turnaround. And up on the second-story waiting room terrace, the regular contingents of sneak thieves sidled among the passengers' friends and relatives, crackerjack vendors, newspaper reporters, and moving picture operators. But it was six Hell's Kitchen gangsters who had caught Bell's attention.

'Gophers!' said Archie.

The Gophers, pronounced 'goofers,' were snappy

dressers, favoring tight suits, pearl gray bowler hats, fancy shoes, and colorful hose.

'Who the heck gave them pier passes?'

'It's possible they know someone in Tammany Hall,' Bell said, drily. In New York, politicians, builders, priests, cops, and gangsters shared the spoils, a system derailed only occasionally by the reformers. 'Do you see who they brought with them?'

'Molls,' said Archie, focusing on a cluster of extravagantly coiffed women in towering hats and elaborate dresses.

'Not a good sign.'

The Police Department had been cracking down on firearms lately. Faced with arrest if caught in possession, the gangsters had taken to stashing their pistols in their girlfriends' hats and bustles.

'Loaded for bear. Who do you suppose they came to meet?'

Bell took back the field glasses. The gangsters were glowering at the back of the ship, where the Second Class passengers would go ashore. In a sight that would be comic if it didn't mean someone was going to get badly hurt, a burly Gopher raked the Second Class embarkation port with dainty mother-of-pearl opera glasses he had stolen from somewhere.

'Archie, do you recognize the thug with the opera glasses?'

Archie, whose pride in New York extended even to the superior ferocity of its street gangs, took a look. 'Might be Blinky Armstrong.'

'Is he a boss?'

'Not yet, that I've heard.'

'It looks like he's running that crew. Soon as the switchboard's hooked up, telephone the office. Tell Harry Warren to bring his gang squad.'

'Why?'

'I have an unpleasant feeling.'

The *Mauretania*'s private-branch telephone system switchboard would plug into the New York City exchanges the moment the ship docked. The Van Dorn New York field office was in the Knickerbocker Hotel on 42nd Street, and while the streets would be clogged with traffic, the magic carpet of the Ninth Avenue Elevated Express could speed Detective Harry Warren and his gang specialists downtown in a flash.

'Harry'll know if it's Blinky.'

With the tugboats almost overwhelmed by her tonnage and the wind, it was fully half an hour before they had *Mauretania* enough inside the slip for her seamen to throw lightweight messenger lines. Longshoremen used them to drag her heavy hawsers ashore.

At last, the bugle blew to announce they were fast to the pier. Engines stopped.

The First Class gangway was hoisted from the cavernous waiting room. First ashore, stiffly ignoring each other, were Lord Strone and Karl Schultz. The Chimney Baron was greeted by a brace of pretty girls, granddaughters, Bell guessed, by the joyful way they took his hands and spirited him, laughing, through the crowds and out the doors to West Street. Strone stepped off alone and discreetly followed a young man, whom Bell supposed was from the British consulate, to the stairs to the lower deck, where the steam yacht *Ringer* out of Greenwich – which had trailed the ship from Quarantine – would whisk him to his American estate in Connecticut.

Explosions of photographers' flashlights at the foot of the gangway told Bell that the newspaper reporters had caught sight of Marion and Lillian disembarking, and he could imagine from experience the shouted queries. Had Miss Morgan come back to New York to take new moving pictures? Was it true Miss Morgan had been married to an insurance executive? Had the ceremony actually been performed by the captain of the *Mauretania*? What did Mrs Abbott think of the new fashions in London? Was there truth to the rumors that her father had secretly amassed a controlling interest in the Atchison, Topeka and Santa Fe?

The Second Class gangway would rise as soon as First Class had cleared the ship. Third Class, Marion had told Bell, was doomed to spend the night aboard. Two names on the passenger list couldn't be found. Miscounts were not uncommon, but everyone in Third Class – immigrants and citizens alike, including the moving picture people – would be held on the ship for officials to tally again. Isaac Bell had to wonder whether those missing had been the Acrobat's accomplices. The chief officer bamboozled that night in the smoking room was probably wondering, too.

'OK, Archie. Go telephone Harry Warren. I'll get Clyde. You grab Block and our PS boy. When things settle down, we'll go off together from Second Class.'

Bell hurried back toward Second Class. He found Clyde Lynds in the embarkation vestibule and tipped the seamen

Captain Turner had assigned to guard him. 'I'll take it from here, gents, thanks.'

Clyde, grip in hand, was anxiously studying the crowds.

'See anyone down there you know?' Bell asked, watching for his reaction.

'I doubt it,' Clyde answered, even as his eye locked on the knot of Gophers staring back in his direction. 'Been quite a while since I was in town.'

'In the theater, you said?'

'My last stepfather, minus one, was a stage manager.'

'At what theater?'

'All over. Downtown. Fourteenth Street. Then for a while on Broadway. The Hammerstein.'

'Did you live in that neighborhood?' Bell asked. Blinky Armstrong was aiming his opera glasses exactly where he and Clyde were standing.

'Around the corner on Forty-sixth Street.'

'Isn't that near Hell's Kitchen?'

Clyde laughed, nervously. 'Fortunately, not too near.'

But near enough, thought Bell, that a gang of Gophers just might have gathered to welcome you home. Had the kid somehow offended them? Or had the Krieg Trust perhaps hired Gophers to grab him as he left the boat? From the little Bell could see through the waiting room windows, it appeared that the Gophers' numbers had swelled. He counted a dozen gangsters converging on the back of the ship. They shoved through the crowd surrounding the foot of the Second Class gangway, which was ascending.

Isaac Bell was liking the situation less and less. He was fully armed, but that would do no good, as gunfire would be lethal to countless innocents. He saw a couple of cops patrolling the waiting room and a few more scattered on the lower level, but not enough to thwart a concentrated attack, if that's what the Gophers were planning.

Archie hurried into the vestibule, leading the PS man, who had handcuffed himself to a disconsolate-looking Lawrence Block. 'Harry Warren's on his way.'

'Hang on to Clyde,' Bell whispered. 'Don't let him ashore.'

'Where you going?'

'I'm going to find out why the Gophers are staring at Clyde like they want to eat him for lunch.'

Bell turned to Clyde Lynds. 'Stay here with Archie. Do not leave the ship until I come back for you.'

'What's up?'

Bell shoved past the seamen at the embarkation port and jumped for the top of the Second Class gangway, which the longshoremen were pivoting toward the ship. It was five feet short of being secured to the hull, and it swayed wildly under his weight. Bell ran down it and into the waiting room.

'Hold on there!' shouted a Cunard official.

Isaac Bell brushed past him and headed straight for Blinky Armstrong, who had pocketed his opera glasses and was glowering up at Clyde Lynds and smacking a meaty fist into a stony palm. The tall detective was twenty feet away from the gangster, his progress slowed by thickening crowds, when suddenly a woman screamed. The sound parting her lips was as much a shout as a scream, a feral noise that spoke more hate than fear.

Two gangsters were fighting, rolling around on the asphalt, kicking and gouging and smashing each other with blackjacks. Blood flew. Two more piled on, and ordinary people ran screaming from the vicious tangle. Only when a flying wedge of gangsters tore through the crowd, hurling men, women, and children from their path, and swinging fists and lengths of lead pipe, did Isaac Bell realize that the newcomers were not more Gophers but attackers from a rival gang.

The melee spread like wildfire. Fifteen men pummeled one another. A tall cop charged, swinging his nightstick. Strong and agile, he floored three gangsters like bowling pins. A fallen man's boot snagged his ankle, and the tall cop went down in the tangle and disappeared as if swallowed whole.

Knives flashed, eliciting angry shouts and screams of pain.

Then a shot rang out, stunningly loud.

Wild-eyed gangsters ran to their women cheering on the sidelines, snatched their revolvers, and raked the pier with gunfire. Bullets banged on corrugated-iron doors and shattered glass. Citizens nearby flattened themselves on the asphalt, and Bell saw the way suddenly clear as if a swaying field of wheat had been mowed by a giant McCormick reaper. He saw Blinky Armstrong and two of his Gophers sprint toward the West Street portal, trampling cowering citizens and knocking down those too terrified to move.

Isaac Bell tore after them.

Halfway to West Street, they ducked into a stairwell.

Bell followed, pounding down steel steps that led to

the baggage deck below. The Gophers were racing along-side the *Mauretania* toward the rows of doors that led off the pier onto West Street. Before they could get out the doors, squads of cops arrived on the run, reserves from nearby station houses, and the Gophers and the rivals who had attacked them were suddenly in a mad rush to avoid arrest.

Instead of trying to escape directly toward West Street, where they could melt into the neighborhoods, they turned back toward the water to get rid of their weapons. Revolvers, pocket pistols, and sleeve guns clanged against *Mauretania*'s black hull and splashed into the slip.

Isaac Bell cut the corner of the dogleg the gangsters had turned to the slip and caught up with them. He was close enough to see the seams in Armstrong's coat and was just about to launch a diving tackle at the big man's ankles when he passed the *Mauretania*'s bow and could suddenly see two hundred feet across the slip to the next pier. Lighters were moored there to shuttle sheets, towels, napkins, and tablecloths to the city's laundries. Chandlers' boats waited to deliver fresh supplies. Tugboats maneu-vered coal barges with shovel-wielding trimmers to replenish *Mauretania*'s bunkers.

Oblivious to the tumult on the pier – or capitalizing on the distraction of fleeing gangsters and pursuing cops – two bill posters steered a little steam launch under the flare of *Mauretania*'s bow, took up long-handled brushes, and began to plaster advertisements on the express liner's hull as if she were a billboard.

THE ELECTRIC THEATER
323 West 14th Street
Finest
MOVING PICTURE PALACE
in
New York City
'NEW SHOWS DAILY'

Twenty more cops stormed in the West Street doors.

The Gophers jinked abruptly to the right.

Isaac Bell veered after them.

The Gopher ahead of Armstrong leaped from the pier toward the landward edge of the slip, missed his footing, and fell into the water. Armstrong jumped next, made it, and ran past *Mauretania*'s bow. Bell leaped the same watery corner and landed running full tilt. He put on a burst of speed to dive for Armstrong. But just as he was about to launch himself in the air, he sensed as much as saw in the corner of his eye an eerie flicker of a familiar grim silhouette moving down the side of the ship with sure-footed grace.

15

Isaac Bell skidded to a stop, hardly believing his eyes. Coal chutes gaped open along the middle of the hull, fifteen feet above the barges. Beneath each hung staging, wooden platforms suspended by ropes for the trimmers to stand on. On the farthest stage, halfway back along the *Mauretania*'s hull, four hundred feet toward the river – and nearly obscured by shadows and work gangs hoisting buckets from the barges into the chutes – crouched the long-armed, almost simian silhouette of the kidnapper Bell had seen jump from the boat deck the night they sailed from Liverpool.

Bell looked for the fastest route out there. It would take too long to go back through the ship. He had to get across the water. He spotted the enterprising bill posters slathering the *Mauretania* with advertisements from the bobbing perch of their steam launch.

'Bill posters! You men, there! Bill posters!'

They heard him, he saw by the way they ducked their heads, but their only response was to glue faster. Accustomed to being chased off private property, they were trying to slap on as many ads as they could until they had to run from shipowners and pier officials. Before Isaac Bell could get their attention, the man that Professor Beiderbecke had dubbed the *Akrobat* glided down a rope holding a stage. He dropped lightly onto a barge riding high in the water that the trimmers had unloaded. A tug was already approaching, deckhands poised with lines, to back the empty barge away and make room for a fresh load.

The Acrobat, Bell realized, had timed his drop to coincide with the barge's removal. Dispensing fat bribes to the boatmen, he would ride the empty barge ashore in the guise of an American trimmer and step onto dry land in a distant coal yard, neatly dodging the customs agents and immigration officials guarding the *Mauretania*'s pier.

Bell cupped his hands. *'Fifty dollars for a boat ride.'*

The bill posters' eyes swiveled at him like searchlights.

Bell yanked his wallet from his coat and waved the money.

A poster that proclaimed

DREAMLAND THEATER
9 West 9th Street
NEW 'MOVIES' EVERY DAY

was abandoned in a flash.

One man used his brush like a barge pole to shove off the *Mauretania* as if the ship were on fire while the other seized the helm and shoved the steam quadrant full ahead. The launch shot toward the pier. Bell jumped eight feet to the deck, nearly capsizing the narrow craft, and pointed at the tug hipped alongside the empty coal barge. 'Follow that barge.'

'Gimme the dough!' cried the man with the brush.

Bell smacked it into his hand.

'On the jump!'

The steam engine chugged. The propeller spun, and

the sharp-bowed little boat turned around and gathered way alongside the *Mauretania*. They passed the last of the open coal chutes, where Bell had first spotted the Acrobat, and pulled into the wake of the tugboat propelling the empty barge.

Bell heard a sharp two-finger whistle, an urgent warning. The Acrobat was signaling someone on the ship.

Bell turned to see who his accomplice was.

He saw a blur of movement in one of the chutes and glimpsed a chunk of coal with sharp, gleaming facets fly at his head. He ducked, turning his face, but it came too fast – no man could throw so hard, it had to have been hurled from a sling. Turning saved his face, but nothing could stop the jagged shard from smashing his hat into the water and slicing his skull.

Isaac Bell heard a hollow explosion like a firecracker dropped in a barrel. A sharp pain shot down his spine. He felt his knees buckle, and he sensed that he was tumbling. He heard the bill poster who was steering the launch shout, 'Catch him!' He saw the brush extended for him to grab hold. But the hand he reached with was too heavy to lift.

Bell gathered all his strength for a massive last-ditch effort. He raised his leaden hand higher. He felt the brush in his fingers, and he grasped it as tightly as he could. The bristles slipped through his fingers, and there was nothing the tall detective could do to stop himself from falling backwards into the water.

16

Isaac Bell fell flat on his back and sank like a stone.

The slack tide on which the *Mauretania* had landed had begun to ebb, and cold river water was swirling through the slip. The deeper he sank, the harder the current pushed him. He felt it sluice him across the slip, and he slammed hard into something solid – one of the piles on which sat the pier. The current pinned him against it. Then something grabbed his foot. It was soft but insistent, and it pulled him farther down. Mud? he wondered, vaguely. He had sunk to the bottom of the slip, and the mud wanted to hold him there as if it were alive and hungry.

Something started pounding. Then his face was suddenly cold as if someone had thrown a champagne bucket of ice water in his face. Not 'someone.' Marion. It was Marion throwing ice water in his face. 'Wake up, Isaac. Wake up! Wake up! Please wake up!'

He awakened and suddenly knew a lot. The pounding was his own heart. The ice water was an invigorating tongue of cold river current. The mud indicated he was thirty-five feet beneath the surface. He had to breathe air or he would die. He kicked the mud and pulled himself up the slippery piling. The water grew warmer, the current less strong. He kicked harder and rose faster. Instinct told him to place one hand on his head to protect it, and a moment after he did he bumped up against an underwater crossbeam that braced two pilings. He was out of air. His heart thundered. Lights stormed in front of his eyes. He couldn't hold his breath any longer. He opened his mouth and inhaled, and suddenly sunlight was blazing in his face.

'Isaac!'

He spit water and gulped air, coughed, gulped more air, and swam toward the shouting. They were yelling about a ladder. He found it fixed to a pile and pulled himself onto it. He held on a while, ignoring the shouting, breathing, collecting himself.

Isaac Bell climbed out of the river in a foul mood. The Acrobat had gotten clean away. His head ached. Blood was stinging his eyes. And he'd lost his hat and his favorite derringer.

'You OK, Isaac?'

It was Harry Warren – head of the Van Dorn Detective Agency's New York gang squad – a studiedly nondescript-looking fellow who wore a loose-fitting dark suit with plenty of pockets for sidearms and a black derby with a reinforced crown. Harry's face, normally as expressionless as the lid of an ashcan, was clenched with worry, a look repeated on the scarred countenances of his hard-bitten detectives, who were watching over Harry's shoulder as Isaac Bell gathered his feet under him and rose, swaying.

Harry handed Bell a handkerchief. 'You're bleeding.'

Bell said, 'Find out who was mixing it up with the Gophers.'

'What?'

Bell mopped the blood off his face and wadded the

cloth against the source, a ragged furrow parting his hair. 'I want to know what the devil was going on. We didn't just *happen* to land in a gang war. The Gophers were waiting for someone on the ship. I want to know who and why. And I want to know why those other boys came along at that moment. On the jump!'

Warren and his boys trooped off. Bell went looking for dry clothes.

Early the next morning, in Archie Abbott's library, Marion read aloud to Isaac Bell the *New York Times* account of yesterday's shootout on Pier 54. Steered by Cunard Line publicists charged with maintaining the steamship company's reputation for safety, and threatened, Bell presumed, by red-faced police and docks commissioners, the newspaper blamed the gunfire on 'disgruntled Italian longshoremen'.

Bell laughed, which made his head hurt.

'"The Italians all escaped in the confusion,"' Marion concluded her reading. '"Arrests are imminent," vowed the commissioners.'

Archie's butler appeared and said, 'A Mr Harry Warren to see you at the kitchen door, sir.'

'Bring him in,' said Marion.

'I tried, Mrs Bell. He won't come past the kitchen.'

The cook poured Harry coffee and made herself scarce.

Harry stared in some amazement at Bell, who was attired in his customary white linen suit and had combed his thick golden hair to hide a row of surgical stitches. 'If you wasn't white as your duds, no one would know you was recently brained and partly drowned.'

'He looks better than he is,' said Marion. 'The doctor said he ought to be in bed.'

'I'm fine,' said Bell.

Harry Warren and Marion Bell traded glances of concern. 'You know, boss, Mrs Bell is right to be worried. So's the doc. Knocks on the noggin rate respect.'

'Thank you, Harry,' said Marion. 'Could you help me walk him upstairs?'

'What have you found?' Bell demanded.

'The Gophers didn't believe there was a fire on the *Mauretania*.'

'What business was it of theirs? It so happens there *was* a fire. I saw it with my own eyes. It burned up everything in the forward baggage room, including the smuggled film stock that ignited it.'

'That's what the Gophers didn't believe.'

Bell looked at Marion. The penny dropped. 'You mean the *Gophers* were smuggling the film stock?'

'They put up the dough for the shipment. When they heard about the fire, they decided that the guy they paid to smuggle it into New York was welshing on the deal, selling the stock to another buyer for more dough.'

'Where did they get that idea?'

'They're Gophers! They get ideas like that. They figure that what they would do to somebody, somebody would do to them. Like the Golden Rule. Backwards. So they met the ship to deal with the guy who they thought welshed.'

'Who is he?'

'Clyde Lynds.'

Bell exchanged a second glance with Marion and shook

his head in disgust, setting off new jolts of pain. 'I was afraid you were going to say that. Clyde smelled the film going bad and knew exactly what it was because it was his stock.'

Marion said, 'The "hero" who saved the ship is the smuggler who almost sank the ship.'

'In a nutshell,' Harry Warren agreed. He stood up and put on his derby. 'Anyway, when the Yorkville boys showed up, the Gophers jumped to the conclusion that they were taking delivery of the film stock they'd bought out from under them. Fighting ensued.'

'In a nutshell . . .'

'Thanks for the coffee.'

'Who are the Yorkville boys?'

'From the new German district up in Yorkville. Uptown, on the East Side.'

'Germans?'

'Germans are leaving downtown since the *General Slocum* fire. You know, the excursion-boat fire when all their poor children were killed. Tore the heart out of the old neighborhood, and they've just kind of been retreating north – lock, stock, and breweries.'

'What's the gang called?'

'Marzipan Boys.'

'Like the candy?'

'The old gangs mocked 'em with that name. Now they're proud of it since they've been whaling the heck out of everybody. They're a tough bunch.'

Harry Warren was halfway out the back door when Bell called, 'But why did the Marzipan Boys go to Pier 54?'

'What do you mean?'

'The film stock *did* burn in the fire,' Bell said with elaborate patience. 'Clyde Lynds didn't welsh on the deal. The Marzipan Boys didn't buy it out from underneath the Gophers, therefore they weren't there to pick up film stock they didn't even know about. *So why did the Yorkville gang meet the* Mauretania*?*'

Harry Warren's blank expression got blanker. 'Haven't found out yet.'

'Find out! Report to me at the office.'

'Isaac,' said Marion. 'The doctor said to stay home today.'

'OK,' said Bell. 'I'll stay home today. Harry, report to me at the office tonight.'

17

'Clyde,' said Isaac Bell, 'you're going to have to return Captain Turner's medal.'

'What do you mean, Mr Bell?'

Bell fixed him with an icy stare.

Clyde Lynds hung his head. 'I'm sorry, Mr Bell. I am so sorry.'

Bell asked, 'Sorry for what? Spit it out! What?'

'The film stock. It was mine.'

'Go on.'

Clyde said, 'We needed the money to escape from Germany. I mean, I wanted so much to succeed with Talking Pictures. But I was scared crazy for our lives. When the Army issued that phony warrant, I knew my goose was cooked.'

Bell bored into him with his eyes. Then he asked, softly, 'Was this smuggling scheme Professor Beiderbecke's idea?'

'No!'

'Are you sure?'

'The poor old guy didn't have a clue. It was all my idea. Remember I told you I got lucky? What happened was I bumped into a Gopher I used to know in New York when he was a sceneshifter at the Hammerstein. He had moved up in the Gophers, and they sent him to Germany looking for film stock. He had the dough. I knew an outfit I'd bought from and they steered me to a shipper to pack it and hide it. We worked a deal.' He hung his head again. 'I thought, What the heck, everyone smuggles film stock, why not me? I didn't realize the stuff was so old it was unstable.' He barked a bitter laugh. 'I got taken like a rube. Seven crates of garbage.'

'Deadly garbage.'

'I swear, I didn't know it was old. I think they switched it on me. I mean, I wouldn't risk hurting all those people.'

'And you are absolutely positive that Beiderbecke had nothing to do with it?'

'I didn't tell him until it was on the boat . . . What are you going to do?'

Isaac Bell sighed. 'I'm afraid you leave me no choice but to help keep you alive and unkidnapped while you build a new Talking Pictures machine.'

'Help me? Why? It was terrible. All those people could have died.'

'Why? You're a jackass. But you're an honest jackass. I just gave you an easy out and you didn't take it. All you had to do was blame the Professor, but you didn't. That's good enough for me.'

'Somebody put the fear of God into those Marzipan Boys,' Harry Warren told Isaac Bell that night at Van Dorn headquarters in the Knickerbocker Hotel, 'which ain't easy to do.'

'How'd they manage that?'

'The guy who led the raid on Pier 54?'

'What about him?'

As the agency's New York gang specialist, rubbing

shoulders with Gophers, Dusters, and Chinatown tongs, Detective Harry Warren had seen his share of evil in the slums. But his hands were shaking as he tugged a flask from his hip pocket, took a long pull on it, then passed it to Isaac Bell.

'They burned him alive in a brewery furnace.' Harry took the flask back, wiped it with his sleeve, and drank again. 'The guy's brother told me.'

'Why'd he tell you?'

'Good question. It was like whoever did this has different stripes than he's used to. It was like the Gophers and the Marzipans and the Van Dorns and even the cops are on one side of a big hole in the street, like from an earthquake or something, and these folks roasting his brother are on the other.'

Bell asked, 'What else did he tell you?'

'Nothing. Clammed up.'

Bell said, 'Let's go see him.'

Isaac Bell and Harry Warren made the rounds of dives in the East Eighties and finally found the dead man's brother leaning on a saloon front under the Third Avenue El. He was fumbling for money in empty pockets. His name was Frank, and he was a tall, handsome, broad-shouldered German-American with a street fighter's scarred face and fists. He assessed Isaac Bell in a glance and nodded his head as if to say he would fight the tall detective if he had to, but he didn't want to. Bell read something else in the resigned nod, a confirmation of what Harry Warren had told him. The gangster had seen evil that shook him to the core.

They took Frank into the saloon and bought a bottle.

Bell said, 'I'm sorry about your brother.'

'Yeah.'

'Were you and Bruno close?'

'Used to be. When we was kids. Not so much now.'

'Did your brother tell you what the deal was at the pier?'

Frank shrugged. 'Grab a fellow who got off the boat.'

'What did this fellow look like?'

'Twenties, five-six, mussed brown hair, blue eyes, pencil mustache.'

Clyde Lynds to a T.

'He say why?'

'No.'

'Did your brother say who you were grabbing the guy for?'

'No.'

'Did you ever see him?'

'How could I see him? Bruno kept him to himself.'

'Did your brother tell you how much the guy was paying?'

Frank shook his head. 'Bruno would never tell me. He'd take what it was and pay us what he felt like.'

'Hard man, your brother.'

'Not as a hard as them.'

'No, I suppose not . . . Mind me asking something?'

'Nothing's stopped you so far.'

'Nothing's stopped you from answering, and I do appreciate that, especially at such a hard time.'

'You gunning for those guys?'

'Yes,' said Bell.

Frank nodded. 'What was you asking?'

'Did your brother ever work for them before?'

Frank hesitated.

Bell asked, 'Was this the first time?'

'I dunno. I mean, I dunno if it was the same or who knew the same. You know what I mean?'

'No.'

'I mean, for when they have a party, sometimes, we sell 'em dust. We sell 'em goils.'

'Who?'

'They might have been who told this guy about my brother.'

'Could have been,' Bell agreed. 'Who are they?'

Frank hesitated. 'I don't want to queer things with them. Maybe it wasn't them who told the guy about us. I don't want to . . .'

'You don't want to mess up a good arrangement,' said Bell. 'I don't blame you.'

'Neither do I,' said Harry Warren.

'Yeah, I mean, steady money is steady money.'

'With your brother out of action, money's going to be tight,' said Bell. 'At least until your crew gets back on its feet. Look, Harry's standing so no one can see me handing you this. Just a couple of hundred dollars to tide you over.'

'Two hundred bucks? Crissakes, mister. What do you get outta this?'

'I get the guy who killed your brother. If you can tell me who introduced him to your brother. Was it the customers who buy your cocaine and your girls?'

'Yeah.'

'And who are they?'

'They live at the consulate.'

Bell found himself holding his breath. 'Which consulate?'

'The German consulate.'

Isaac Bell and Harry Warren walked quickly to the Third Avenue El and rode downtown to the tip of lower Manhattan. They got off at South Ferry and strolled up Broadway. Deep in conversation as they passed the handsome sixteen-story Bowling Green Office Building, they barely glanced at the Hellenic Renaissance granite, white brick, and terracotta facade.

Of the thirteen bays of windows from ground floor to roof, all but two were dark this late at night. The White Star and American Line shippers, the naval architects, bankers, and lawyers who conducted business at the prestigious address were home in their beds. Of the lights still burning, both were on the ninth floor, which housed the offices of the German consul general.

'Cover the place,' Isaac Bell ordered. 'Try to pick up something more.'

18

'I heard that the agency had a protection contract with the German consul general of New York City back in '02,' said Isaac Bell, when he strode into Joseph Van Dorn's walnut-paneled Washington, DC, headquarters office in the Willard Hotel, two blocks from the White House. The boss spent the majority of his time in Washington these days drumming up business from the Justice Department, Congress, and the Navy, and was intimate with the workings of the capital city.

Van Dorn laughed heartily. 'We did indeed, and I'll never forget it.'

Mirth reddened his face – a grand moon of an affair wreathed in robust red whiskers and splendid burnsides and topped by a shining bald crown – and his hooded eyes almost disappeared as their lids crinkled around them. He was a large, powerfully built man. His affable manner and ready laughter disguised ambition, ferocious intelligence, and an unyielding love of justice that made him the scourge of criminals.

'Prince Henry of Prussia was touring the country,' Van Dorn explained in a rich voice softened by the faintest of Irish accents. 'After all the assassinations in Europe, who knew if some anarchist or homicidal crank might take a potshot at him? The Germans had battalions of their own agents, of course, plus the Secret Service on loan from the Treasury Department, but they hired us, along with local cops, rail dicks to guard his trains, and some of the lesser private agencies. Turned into a regular Chinese fire drill: thirteen varieties of detectives were covering Henry, most blissfully unaware of one another's identity. He was lucky to get home alive before some sorry Pinkerton shot him by mistake.'

'What did you mean the Germans' "own agents"?'

'Foreign consulates import their secret police to shadow their countrymen who live or travel in America, keeping an eye on criminals and anarchists who might go back to Europe and make trouble.'

Isaac Bell said, 'I understand that German consulates also field spies disguised as legitimate military and commercial attachés.'

'As do the British, French, Austrians, Italians, Spanish, Chinese, and Japanese. Why did you ask about the contract?'

'Do they also have dealings with local criminals?'

'Ah, that's where you're headed . . . I wouldn't read a lot into "dealings with local criminals". The consuls and vice-consuls stationed in the field are not what the Germans call *hoffähig* – gents, to the manner born – compared to the aristo diplomats in the Washington embassies. Consuls and vice-consuls mix it up with businessmen and cops and all sorts of troublemakers that traveling foreigners run into.'

Bell seemed to change the subject. 'I received several cables from Art Curtis.'

Van Dorn frowned. 'At your instigation, Curtis is pestering me to authorize hefty expenditures for information about the inner workings of Krieg Rüstungswerk GmbH. Information about something that no one has seen fit to inform me of yet,' Van Dorn added tartly. 'Leaving the proprietor of this detective agency to speculate whether he will be the last to know what's going on, and whether it has anything to do with that fire on the *Mauretania*, or that shootout on Pier 54, or the rumor that two or three people fell off the ship you happened to be sailing in, Isaac.'

'Art Curtis's information is gold,' said Bell. 'Pure gold. He turned up a disgruntled Krieg employee, a company executive, who claims that in New York and Los Angeles Krieg pays commissions to German consulate staff to act as unofficial sales representatives.'

'Gold?' Van Dorn scoffed. 'Foreign consuls are *supposed* to grease the wheels of commerce. That's their main job. Trade. Introductions. Selling.'

'Except these consular staff don't sell anything. Nor do they arrange introductions. Nor do they court American customers. But they get paid commissions as if they do. In other words, Krieg is paying German consuls under the table. Don't you wonder what kind of favors consulate staff grant in return?'

Isaac Bell was gratified to see that the boss had stopped laughing. In fact, he wasn't even smiling. But his eyes were on fire, like a grizzly sniffing prey.

'That is interesting.'

'Art Curtis is the best,' said Bell. 'I don't know another man who could get so deep inside so quickly. But suborning a highly placed informant costs a lot of money. In other words, this executive Art turned up is accustomed to first-class remuneration.'

Van Dorn stood up from his desk and lumbered to the windows, where his second-floor corner office let him view people approaching the Willard's front and side entrances. Then he wandered to the interior wall and inspected the reception room through a peephole drilled through the eye of Ben Franklin, whose portrait greeted visitors to the detective agency.

Bell sat still as ice, patient and silent.

At last, the boss faced him inquiringly. 'Is this why you traveled all the way to Washington instead of telephoning me long-distance?'

'No. I came to tell you something *more* interesting.'

Hans Reuter – Arthur Curtis's painstakingly cultivated informant inside the Krieg Rüstungswerk munitions combine – refused to meet in a beer garden anymore. 'Too many people,' he kept saying. 'Too many people are seeing us together.'

Had they been speaking face-to-face instead of on the telephone, Arthur would have folded his hands calmly over his potbelly and listened with a sympathetic expression. All he had on the phone was a soothing voice and simple logic. 'They don't know what we talk about. They don't know that I pay you money.'

'I was followed last time.'

'Are you sure?' Arthur Curtis asked more casually than he felt. The fact was, after their last meeting, when Reuter dropped the bombshell that Krieg had German consuls in America on its payroll, Curtis had wondered whether he was being followed and had returned to the office by a circuitous route, after going to great lengths to shake the shadow, if indeed there had been a shadow. Now it sounded like there had been, and a very stealthy one at that. He had to hand it to Krieg. It hadn't taken long to catch on to him. He knew he had to do something to end the threat. The trouble was, his frightened informant still had a lot of good information bubbling in his embittered mind, although he was doling it out very slowly.

'I am deadly sure,' Reuter replied. 'For all we know, they are listening in on this telephone wire.'

'They would have to be soothsayers to listen in on telephone kiosks in post offices on opposite sides of Berlin.'

'I would not be surprised if they were.'

'I have an idea,' said Arthur Curtis.

'No more ideas,' said Hans Reuter, and broke the connection.

Arthur Curtis worked his way slowly back to the office. Redoubling ordinary habits of caution, watching reflections in shop windows, changing trams repeatedly, stepping in and out of bakeries and cafes, he did not enter his building until he was one hundred percent sure that he was not being observed.

Pauline was sitting behind his desk, reading his mail.

'You should be home in bed. It's late.'

'I'm not tired.'

'Don't you have school tomorrow?'

'My mother's friend is visiting. He'll be gone at midnight.'

'Have you had your supper?'

'I'm not hungry.'

'Here.' He handed Pauline a sweet bun he had picked up just in case and watched her tear into it like a timber wolf taking down a mule deer. And then the darnedest thing happened. Art Curtis was suddenly scared. Not for himself but for her, the silly kid hanging around. What if they did catch up with him and she was here? What would they do to her when they got done doing him?

'"Flickers" have been around for years,' Joseph Van Dorn protested.

Issac Bell had just concluded the story of Beiderbecke and Clyde Lynds and their Talking Pictures machine with the recommendation that the Van Dorn agency take up the job of protecting Lynds while he built a new machine in exchange for a share of the profits.

'Moving pictures won't be mere "flickers" anymore when sound makes them so visceral, they play on the emotions. The Talking Pictures machine is revolutionary.'

Van Dorn shrugged. 'I attended a talking picture once in Cincinnati. They called it a "Kinetophone" or some such, and the advertisement claimed that the songs followed in perfect unison the movements of the actors' lips. But in fact the lips and words were at sixes and sevens, making it impossible to follow the story.'

'Synchronization is the crux of the problem.'

'Besides, there was the usual unnatural and discordant mechanical grate you hear from talking machines.'

'Amplification is another problem Lynds and Beiderbecke claim to have solved.'

'I'll say it's a problem. I attempted to hear an Actologue troupe in Detroit. One poor player had a feeble voice that was unable to penetrate the picture screen. Every word he uttered disappeared straight up into the fly loft.'

'You bought tickets,' said Bell. 'You paid money to see these various attempts at talking pictures. That proves there's a demand for this kind of attraction. But the way they're going about is too expensive. Marion says a typical Actologue company consists of at least eight people, including the machine operator, piano player, singers, manager, and actors to imitate the parts behind the screen. That same film shown by Lynds's Talking Pictures machines could be distributed to a thousand theaters at once. Film reels don't eat, don't sleep, and don't demand a salary. It would be like a frying pan factory that doesn't need to pay workmen because machines make frying pans automatically.'

Van Dorn, as hard-nosed and tightfisted a businessman as Bell had ever met, smiled at the thought of not having to pay labor. 'You are very persuasive, Isaac. When you put it that way, you make me think he's got something worth protecting.'

The savvy founder of the detective agency stroked his chin, ruminated silently, and fiddled absently with his candlestick telephone and his speaking tube. 'But Professor Beiderbecke is dead. Can Clyde Lynds reproduce Talking Pictures without him?'

'Beiderbecke claimed Clyde is smart as a whip. The German Army believes he can. So do the German consuls.'

'I find it hard to believe the kaiser's army is fighting this hard just for the money.'

'I agree,' said Bell. 'They're not businessmen. They're soldiers. There's something more to this.'

Van Dorn nodded vigorously. 'Find out what,' he ordered. 'Continue to watch developments at the New York consulate. I'll nose around here in Washington.'

'Why not invite the German ambassador to lunch at the Cosmos Club?'

'I'll do it tomorrow. But don't get your hopes up. His Excellency is not likely to be informed of such a vicious operation, particularly if it's a military scheme.'

'Will you give Art a free hand in Berlin?'

'Yes, yes, yes,' Van Dorn growled, reluctantly.

'I'd rather he didn't waste time clearing each payment through you.'

Van Dorn grimaced. 'OK, dammit. You're authorized to spend what you need.'

'Don't worry. Art won't squander a penny.'

'Just remember that while you're trying to figure out what the Germans are up to, our valuable young genius is already in their crosshairs. Keep him safe – Where is he right now?'

'Lipsher's got him.'

'Who's Lipsher?'

'The PS boy who guarded Block on the ship. Turned out to be a good man in a pinch.' Bell stood up. 'If you will clear it with Dagget's managing director, I'll continue under my insurance executive guise and spread the word that Dagget, Staples and Hitchcock is investing in Lynds's invention. That such a staid old firm is interested ought to burnish its appeal.'

'Dagget, Staples and Hitchcock consorting with moving picture people?' Van Dorn laughed. 'The founders will be spinning in their graves. But you're right. Keep us out of it as long as you can. Best to not show our hand till we know who's across the table.'

'And what he wants,' said Isaac Bell, grabbing his hat and charging out the door.

'Where you headed?'

'Union Station. I'm meeting Clyde in West Orange, New Jersey.'

'Thomas Edison's laboratory? Hang on to the fillings in your teeth.'

19

Isaac Bell was surprised twice upon arriving at the red brick building that housed Thomas Edison's laboratory in West Orange, New Jersey. It had never occurred to him how young Edison's scientists would be. The laboratories were teeming with nattily dressed bright young fellows like Clyde Lynds. Nor had he expected Edison, with his reputation for hard bargaining, to have such a warm smile. It widened his full mouth engagingly and lighted his deep-set eyes.

Bell was not surprised, when a functionary led them into a soundproof phonograph-cylinder recording room, by the sight of the great man trying to hear music by biting down on the piano lid. Edison's deafness was public knowledge. He stood up from the piano, dismissed the man playing it with a pleasant nod, and said in a loud but friendly voice, 'Never go deaf. You'll hate it. You must be Mr Bell.'

Bell shook the strong hand Edison extended.

'And you, young fellow, must be Mr Lynds, about whom Mr Bell has telegraphed so glowingly. Shrewd move with the telegraph, Mr Bell. I am hopeless on the telephone. All right, come in, sit down. Tell me what you've brought me.'

Clyde had prepared a sketchbook with drawings and titles written out in block letters. Thomas nodded appreciatively. 'This even beats Mr Bell's telegram.' He flipped through the pages. "'Pictures that talk'? Everyone brings me pictures that talk. Trouble is, none of them work.'

Clyde Lynds faced the inventor and spoke loudly and slowly, moving his lips to exaggerate each word. 'This. One. Works.'

'You don't say? OK, show me. Where is it?'

Lynds tapped the sketch pad and then tapped his head. 'In here.'

'What was that?'

Bell watched with admiration as Clyde turned a page of his pad to display the words he had written out ahead of time: *The first machine was lost. I need a laboratory, machine shops, and money to build a new one.*

'What do you mean "lost"?' Edison shouted.

Clyde flipped to the next page, on which he had written *In a fire*, and Isaac Bell's admiration went up a notch. The penniless young scientist was choreographing his conversation with the richest, most famous inventor in the world.

Edison glanced at Bell. Whatever the expression in his eyes, it was lost in the shadow of his brow, but Bell sensed a shift in his attitude. 'Mr Bell,' he said briskly, suddenly all business, 'I suspect that the purely scientific conversation we are about to embark on will bore you. I've arranged a tour of my laboratories for your enjoyment while Mr Lynds and I pursue what makes his talking pictures different from all the others.'

'Thoughtful of you,' said Bell, rising to his feet. 'I'm curious to see your operation.' Clearly, Edison wanted to get rid of him. But just as clearly, Bell concluded, Clyde could take care of himself. Besides, they had made a pact that Clyde would sign no papers without Van Dorn attorneys reading them first.

The functionary sprang into the room as if he had had his ear pressed to the door, and Isaac Bell allowed him to walk him through a standard canned tour of the Edison laboratory. He saw the chemical plant, machine shops, laboratories. At the storeroom he watched a clerk dispense a length of manatee skin, which would be fashioned into belt drives, his guide told him. From a gallery Bell could look down at Mr Edison's two-story, book-lined office. The functionary pointed out Edison's marble statue of an angel shining an electric lightbulb on a heap of broken oil lamps.

'What's that?' Bell asked. They were passing a door marked 'Kinetophone Laboratory' and through the top glass he could see an older bearded man hunched over a cat's cradle of wires and pulleys that linked a moving picture projector to a phonograph. Joe Van Dorn, Bell recalled, had been disappointed by a Kinetophone. 'I said, "What's that?"'

'Just an experiment.'

'I'd like to see it.'

'It's not ready to be seen.'

'I don't mind,' said Bell, and pushed through the door, ignoring his guide's protests. The bearded old man looked up, blinking in surprise, as if unaccustomed to visitors.

'We should not be in here, Mr Bell,' said the functionary. 'This experiment is very important to Mr Edison. Much is riding on it.'

'Go ask Mr Edison's permission,' said Bell. 'I'll wait here. Go on!'

The functionary scuttled out. Bell said to the old man, 'A fellow I know saw one of these in Cincinnati. Is this one that you're repairing?'

'Repairing? Don't make me laugh. God Himself couldn't repair this piece of trash.'

'What's wrong with it? Why is it trash?'

'Listen.' He moved an electric switch, and the machine projected on the wall a moving picture of a woman singing. At the same time, the phonograph cylinder began spinning. The wires connecting the two machines whirred, their pulleys clattered, and the woman's voice emerged from the phonograph horn, thin, harsh, and grating, as Van Dorn had said. Within ten seconds her voice had fallen behind the movement of her lips.

'She doesn't sound synchronized with her picture,' said Bell.

'And never will be,' said the old man.

The song ended, but the woman appeared to keep on singing. Her mouth opened wide, holding a note, while from the horn a male voice said, 'What a fine voice you have.' Five seconds later a man appeared, mouthing the words he had spoken earlier and clapping silently as an invisible violin played. At last the violinist appeared.

'That's rather funny,' said Bell.

'It is supposed to be a drama.'

'If it can't be fixed, why are you working on it?'

'Because this is the only job Edison will give me,' the old man answered bitterly. 'He has younger men working on similar experiments, but they're all trash.'

'Why don't you work elsewhere?'

The old man looked at Isaac Bell. A strange light shone

in his eyes as if he were staring so deeply inward that he could not quite see what was in front of him. 'Edison bankrupted me. I had debts I could never repay. Edison bought them up. I owe him. I am forced to work here.'

'Why would Mr Edison want you to work on something that doesn't work?'

'Don't you understand?' the old man railed, and Bell wondered about the man's sanity. 'He keeps me from inventing things that would put him out of business. He stole my greatest invention, and now he makes sure I will never invent another.'

'What invention?' Bell asked gently, feeling sorrow for the man's distress.

'I invented an inexpensive gramophone. Edison copied it – poorly, shabbily. Mine was better, but he undercut the price and inundated the market with cheap copies. He named his "phonograph", People fell for it – people are such fools – and bought the less expensive one. He drove me out of business.'

'When was this?' asked Bell.

'Long, long ago.' His face worked, contorted, and he shouted, 'Mine was a beautiful machine. He is a monster.'

The door flew open. The functionary had returned with a heavyset bruiser whose coat bulged with saps and a pistol. 'OK, mister, out of here,' he ordered, and took Bell's arm.

The tall detective turned eyes on him as bleak as an ice field and said, very softly, 'Don't.'

The bruiser let go.

'Take me back to Mr Edison.'

*

Thomas Edison was not smiling when Isaac walked into the soundproof recording room, and Clyde Lynds's normally cheery countenance had hardened into one tight-lipped with anger.

'There you are, Mr Bell. We were just finishing up our discussion. Clyde, I look forward to hearing back from you as soon as you've had the opportunity to speak with your lawyer. Good day, gentlemen.'

The shadow of a grin crossed Clyde's face, and he scrawled on his sketch pad, *Good day*.

'Would you leave your drawings with me?' Edison asked. 'Let me peruse them at my leisure.'

To Isaac Bell's surprise, Clyde handed them over.

He was unusually quiet on the trolley to Newark. Bell waited until they boarded a train for Pennsylvania Station to ask, 'What did Mr Edison think of your machine?'

'I believe he thinks that it is very, very valuable. Of course he didn't say that.'

'What did he say?'

'In exchange for providing a laboratory, he demands complete control of the patent, not just license to manufacture it. In other words, he would own it.'

'Those are harsh terms.'

Clyde grinned. 'I'm taking them as a genuine vote of confidence. If a man as smart as Thomas Edison wants to steal it, Talking Pictures must be worth a fortune.'

Bell said, 'I had a gander at his "Kinetophone". It didn't strike me it's going anywhere.'

'All mechanical methods of synchronization are doomed to failure,' Clyde said, flatly. 'The Professor and I figured out at the start that we'd never get two separate machines to run precisely synchronized. We knew we had to invent a better way. And we did. Better and completely different.'

'Wasn't it risky giving Edison your plans?'

Clyde laughed. 'I gave him fake plans.'

'Did you really? That was slickly done,' said Bell. 'I never tumbled.'

'I gave him notes for an acoustic microphone instead of the Professor's electrical one, and I gave him drawings for a synchronization contraption similar to the Kinetophone you saw at the laboratory.'

'Similar? How do you know?'

'The Professor and I studied every cockamamie talker scheme in the world – French, Russian, German, British – plus every damned one Edison copied from someone else.'

Isaac Bell was fast coming to the conclusion that Clyde Lynds was shrewder than he had let on. 'So you weren't surprised by Edison's move this afternoon.'

Clyde Lynds sighed and looked suddenly weary. 'Not surprised, but I am disappointed. The Professor and I had hoped our superior machine would convince Edison to treat us like equals. So I'm going to have to go it alone.'

Isaac Bell smiled. 'Not quite alone.'

'What do you mean?'

'My wife pulled some wires for you in case things didn't work out with Edison. She's lined it up for you to meet an independent called the Pirate King. He's top dog among fellows who make movies outside the Edison Trust.'

'That's mighty kind of her.'

'Better than kind. Marion's rooting for you. She intends to make the first real talking picture.'

20

'Don't interrupt moving picture people when the sun is shining,' Marion warned her husband. 'They hate to waste the light.'

Isaac Bell searched the sky for a promising hint of haze as the ferry to the Fort Lee district of New Jersey crossed the Hudson River. A sultry southwest wind suggested that clouds were in the offing. With any luck, he told Clyde Lynds, the skies would darken by noon.

They rented a Ford auto at a general store with a gasoline pump in front and drove up the steep palisade. In the village of Fort Lee they passed motion picture factories sanctioned by the Edison Trust. Through the glass walls and roofs of barn-like structures, they could see arc lights hanging from the rafters and banks of Cooper-Hewitt mercury-vapor lamps to boost the sunlight. Substantial brick outbuildings housed scenery, property, and costume shops, offices, film-processing laboratories, machine shops to maintain the cameras, and dynamos to power the Cooper-Hewitts.

Bell kept driving, heading north on narrow roads along the top ridge of the Palisades. Following Marion's directions, he located a turnoff in the middle of nowhere that took them west, deeper and deeper into the countryside. Finally, he pulled into a dairy farm barnyard, hidden from the road, where the independent Pirate King Jay Tarses was shooting outside pictures of a troupe of players costumed like Crusaders, Arabs, and Vestal Virgins.

A herd of horses was skittering nervously around a corral, spooked by camels that Tarses had gathered for his Arabs. From what Marion had told him, the camera operator draped over an enormously bulky Bianchi camera was actually cranking an Edison-patented camera concealed inside it.

Isaac Bell stopped the car at a distance to stay out of the picture. An assistant, one of several petite dark-haired girls hanging around Tarses, approached with trepidation.

'Don't worry,' Bell told her. 'We're not Edison bulls. I'm Isaac Bell, and my wife, Marion, arranged for me and Mr Clyde Lynds to visit Mr Tarses.'

'Of course,' she exclaimed. 'I'll tell him you're here.'

'Don't interrupt the picture taking,' said Bell. 'We'll wait for the clouds.'

By half past one the sun had disappeared. As the players opened box lunches, the assistant led Bell and Lynds to Pirate King Jay Tarses, an unshaven fellow in a slouch hat, shirt-sleeves, and vest who was telling a bespectacled man with ink-stained fingers, 'Twenty-five dollars is the most I pay for a scenario converted into a complete photoplay.'

'I think I deserve fifty.'

Tarses lighted a five-cent cigar. 'If it makes a hit, we'll send another check for the same sum.'

'But when I write a short story, the magazines pay two hundred dollars.'

'The people who watch my pictures don't know how to read,' said Tarses, turning his back on the writer.

He cast an amiable smile at Isaac Bell. 'Any husband of Marion is a friend of mine, Mr Bell. She scored a headliner in her first picture. *Hot Time in the Old Town Tonight* was alive with human interest. What can I do for you?'

Bell began what Clyde Lynds called a 'spiel'.

'I represent Dagget, Staples and Hitchcock of Hartford, Connecticut.'

'Unfortunately,' Tarses interrupted, 'I've never had the pleasure of borrowing money from them, as they're not the sort that consorts with my sort.'

'Your luck is about to improve. Dagget, Staples and Hitchcock is considering entering the moving picture business.'

'I am all ears,' said Tarses. Money talked in a business where it had to be borrowed daily, and a prosperous-looking insurance executive dressed in a bespoke suit and made-to-order boots was listened to.

'Our first step is to invest in Mr Lynds's Talking Pictures machine. We are looking for partners among moving picture folk, experienced manufacturers who are up to taking superior pictures with the same photography and finish as the French. Mr Lynds will explain the technical details.'

Tarses's response was to change the subject. 'Is your wife still making those topical films for Whiteway?'

'You can bet she'll make talking pictures when Mr Lynds perfects his machine,' said Bell, and turned the spiel over to Lynds. It was up to Clyde to sell his scheme, and Bell had no doubt that he was a born salesman.

'Wait,' said Tarses 'What do you want from me?'

'To start, Mr Lynds needs a laboratory, chemists, machine shops, and moving picture mechanicians.'

Tarses glanced around the barnyard. A gesture with his cigar indicated horses, camels, and actors. 'I don't have any of that stuff.'

'You can get it in a flash,' Bell retorted. 'My wife chose wisely, Mr Tarses. You know all the moving picture folk in all the aspects of the business and manufacture. Plus, you're a natural-born manager. Everyone in the motion picture business says that if you didn't hate the Trust, you'd be ramrodding your own big outfit.'

'Yeah, well, I don't get along with bosses.'

'When his machine is perfected, Mr Lynds will need a movie manufacturer who knows the line from top to bottom to take charge. You'll be your own boss, making the pictures and distributing.'

'But who needs Talking Pictures?'

Clyde was dumbstruck. He looked at Bell in disbelief. Hadn't Krieg and the German Army made it painfully clear that they needed it?

'Who *needs* them?' shouted Clyde, suddenly red in the face and finding the words to denounce the absurd question. 'The world needs them. Talking pictures will enable motion picture men to take pictures that are crackerjacks, full of snap and go, and energy and push. We'll tell stories of original situations dear to the heart of the exchange men, who will know darned well that exhibitors will recognize great features for their audiences.'

Jay Tarses crossed his arms over his chest and stated flatly, 'Talking pictures will never happen.'

'Give me one reason why.'

'I'll give you four. One: Audiences are happy; they don't want smart-aleck talk, they want pictures that move. Two:

How will foreigners understand what the players are saying? Three: Who's gonna pay for installing Talking Pictures machines in every theater? Exhibitors hate spending money. Four: Who would dare distribute Talking Pictures? If they're any good, the Edison Trust will block them.'

'He's wrong,' Marion said fiercely when Bell reported back to the Abbott town house on how they were rebuffed. 'Tarses is so busy trying to stay a step ahead of the sheriff, he doesn't understand. I'm so sorry, I thought he was smarter than that. Isaac, this is so important, we must help Clyde.'

'Who else can we approach?'

'I wonder . . .'

Bell waited. They were in Archie's library. From the drawing room came the sounds of a dinner party gathering for cocktails. 'Why don't you get dressed?' said Marion. 'Let me think on this.'

When Bell returned in a midnight blue dinner jacket, Marion was fired up and supremely confident. 'There is an innovative director at the Biograph Company – bold and very clever.'

'But Biograph is part of the Trust.'

'He's chafing under company rule. He wants to make his own pictures. He's so forward-thinking – he's invented all sorts of wonderful tricks with the camera – he might realize the potential of Clyde's machine.'

'Let's go see him.'

'He just took fifty people to California. He's making a Biograph picture in some little village outside Los Angeles.'

'What's his name?'

'Griffith. You've seen his pictures. D. W. Griffth.'

'Of course! He made *Is This Seat Taken?*'

'He's your man.'

Isaac Bell said, 'I hate to leave you so soon after our wedding, but I had better take Clyde to see him.'

Marion said, 'I would love to visit my father in San Francisco and tell him all about the wedding.'

'Wonderful! 'Frisco's only five hours on the train. We'll meet in the middle.'

Marion straightened his bow tie and pressed close. 'I don't suppose there's any chance we could travel together to California?'

Bell shook his head with a rueful smile. 'I wish we could.'

'I love riding trains with you.' She laughed. 'Now that we're married, we don't have to book two staterooms for propriety's sake.'

'Unfortunately, escorting Clyde, I'm obliged to double up with him to keep a close watch.'

'Do you expect Krieg to try to kidnap him?'

'No, no, no. Just to be on the safe side. Don't worry, after we meet Mr Griffith, I'll stash Clyde with the Los Angeles office for a weekend, and you and I can rendezvous in Santa Barbara.'

'And after I've seen my father, I'll come down to Los Angeles to find some work.'

The old Grand Central Station was no more. Its classical facade and its six-hundred-and-fifty-foot glass train shed had just been razed, and now steam shovels and hard-rock miners were burrowing sixty feet into the Manhattan schist to make room for a new, two-level Grand Central Terminal.

Isaac Bell led Clyde Lynds into a temporary station that was operating out of the Grand Central Palace, a convention and trade fair building around the corner on Lexington Avenue, and headed for the makeshift gate marked '20th Century Limited'. The chaos of new construction had not persuaded the crack Chicago-bound express to lower its standards. Temporary or not, its famous red carpet had been rolled out the length of the platform.

'Hang on a minute,' said Bell. 'Loose shoelace.' He planted his foot on a fire department standpipe protruding from a wall and busied his hands around his boot.

'How can you have a loose shoelace?' asked Clyde. 'Your boots don't have laces.'

'Don't tell anyone.' Bell straightened up and headed for the telephones. 'I have to phone the office. Stick close.'

'I heard there's a phone on the train.'

'There will be a line of businessmen waiting to telephone their offices that they didn't miss the train. Stick close.'

Bell told the operator at the front desk, 'Van Dorn Agency, Knickerbocker Hotel,' and followed the attendant to a paneled booth. When the Van Dorn operator answered, he asked for the duty man.

'This is Chief Investigator Bell. Two tall yellow-haired men in dark suits and derbies followed me across Forty-second Street and into the Grand Central Palace. They're hanging around the waiting room pretending not to watch the Twentieth Century gate. One has a mustache and is wearing a green four-in-hand necktie. The other is clean-shaven, with a dark bow tie. I'll telephone again when we change locomotives at Harmon.'

Bell paid the attendant.

'Let's go buy some magazines, Clyde — No, don't look in their direction.'

21

Forty-five minutes after leaving New York, the 20th Century Limited stopped in Harmon to exchange the electric engine that had hauled it out of the Manhattan tunnels for a high-wheeled 4-4-2 Atlantic steamer that would rocket it north to Albany at seventy-five miles an hour. While train and yard crews swiftly uncoupled the old and coupled the new, Isaac Bell ran to the New York Central dispatcher's office, identified himself as a Van Dorn detective, and asked to use their telephone.

The duty man at the Knickerbocker reported that Van Dorn operatives were trailing the 'gentlemen thugs' who had followed Bell across 42nd Street.

A wire waiting for Bell at Albany, where the flyer got a fresh locomotive and a dining car, reported laconically,

NOTHING YET.

After dinner, there was nothing at Syracuse.

Bell had booked a stateroom with two narrow berths. He stretched out on the bottom berth, fully clothed.

Clyde said, 'You know I could have saved money sleeping in a Pullman berth.'

'I assure you, Clyde, you would not be my first choice of company for a night on an express train, but this way I can keep an eye on you.'

'Who were those men? Krieg?'

'I should know for sure by morning.'

'How would they know to follow us from your detective agency?'

'They followed us from the *hotel*, not the agency.' Bell had stashed Clyde for safekeeping in a room at the Knickerbocker next door to the Van Dorn bull pen. The hotel was enormous, and the Krieg agents would have no reason to connect Clyde to Van Dorn.

'How'd they know what hotel?'

'They probably followed us to the Knickerbocker from Edison's laboratory. I believe you did mention Thomas Edison while discussing your machine with Krieg?'

'Sure. I wanted Krieg to know there were others we could go to.'

'You can bet they've been watching the Edison laboratory since the *Mauretania* landed, waiting for you to show up.'

Bell locked the door and closed his eyes, recalling nights on the 20th Century when he and Marion would drink champagne in the privacy of adjoining staterooms.

At Rochester, the telegraph delivered pay dirt.

GTS TO ATTACHE AT GC.

Isaac Bell broke into a lupine smile.

Translated, the wire read that the 'gentleman thugs' who had followed him to the train had reported to a diplomatic attaché whom the Van Dorn detectives covering the Bowling Green Office Building had already identified at the German consulate. In other words, Krieg and the

German Army knew that he and Clyde were steaming to Chicago. But they did not know that Bell knew.

He wired the Chicago field office from the next engine stop.

The 'Drummers's Table' in the breakfast room at the exclusive Palmer House Hotel in Chicago was like a private club, but any traveling salesman who could afford the best hotel in town was welcome to sit in. The club brothers – valuable men who worked on commission only and paid their own expenses – had expensive suits, florid complexions, and proud bellies, and they laughed louder and told newer jokes than the founders of steel and slaughterhouse fortunes at the surrounding tables.

The top salesman for the Locomobile Company of America was telling a new story he had heard two days earlier at the Bridgeport, Connecticut, front office involving accidentally switched department store deliveries of ladies' gloves and undergarments.

The representative of the Victor Talking Machine Company interrupted. 'Hey, here's Fritz!'

'Hello, Fritz! Haven't seen you in a coon's age.'

Men shuffled around to make room for the new arrival, a broad-shouldered, light-on-his feet German in his mid-thirties who traveled America peddling church organs and parlor pianos.

'Waiter! Waiter! Breakfast for Mr Wunderlich.'

'Only time for coffee. I'm catching the train for Los Angeles.'

Fritz Wunderlich was a funny-looking fellow, with heavy brow ridges, a mighty anvil of a jaw, and long arms like a gorilla, but he had a smile that any drummer would give his eye-teeth for. It opened wide as the prairie and bright as the sun and pulled the customers in like suction from a sinking ship.

Fritz worked hard as a nailer – 'Eight days in the week, thirteen months in the year' – and it paid off, judging by the cut of his funereal black suit, his immaculate linen, his fine homburg, his weighty gold watch chain, and the ten-cent polish on his shoes.

'Coffee for Fritz!'

'*Mit schlag!*'

'Hear that, waiter? *Mit schlag.*'

'Vat is the story I interrupt?'

The Locomobile drummer started over again, repeating the beginning about the mixed-up ladies' gloves and undergarments. 'So then the lady who received the panties gets a letter from the fellow who sent her his gift of gloves. Here's what he wrote.'

Fritz broke in with the last line of the joke: 'Whoever sees you in these vill admire my good taste and your delicate looks!'

The table roared with laughter and choruses of 'That's a good one!'

'But it's a brand-new joke,' protested the drummer from Bridgeport. 'How'd you hear it? I came direct to Chicago on the Pennsylvania Limited.'

'I heard it in 'Frisco last veek,' said Fritz.

''Frisco? How? Did anyone else at the table ever hear it before?'

Salesmen shook their heads. 'New to me, Jake.'

The youngest, a Chicago hometown fellow making big

money on a line from the Gillette Safety Razor Company, had the explanation: 'Electricity is faster than steam.'

'What the heck do you mean by that?' asked the Locomobile representative.

'He means,' said Fritz Wunderlich, 'vile you ride the train, your joke flies to San Francisco on the telegraph vire.'

'Who can afford to telegraph jokes?'

'No one goes to the expense. But late at night when the wires are quiet and the operators have nothing else to do, they click jokes to one another.'

The Quaker Oats salesman nodded. 'They know their pals by their "fists". One pal clicks another, city to city, and the jokes get passed along the wire all the way across the continent.'

'Fritz? How are things in Leipzig?'

'I am happy to say that America remains a nation of God-fearing, music-loving churchgoers, so things in Leipzig are very vell indeed. At least among the organ builders, *danke. Und* you, gentlemen? All are vell?'

'Very well, Fritz. Say, weren't you trying to sell a new organ to that big church in St Louis last time? How did that go?'

'Detroit, if I recall. And thank you, it vent OK.'

'They bought the new organ?'

'Two!'

'Two organs for one church? Why did they buy two?'

Wunderlich's smile warmed the table, and his response was the drummer's anthem: 'It seemed like a good idea at the time.'

The table roared. Salesmen slapped their thighs. Those

indulging in eye-openers signaled the waiters for another round.

'Must go. Time is money. *Ja!* I almost forget. I took on a new line. Hymnals. Here, sample pages.' He opened a calfskin satchel decorated in solid brass and passed around beautifully printed single sheets.

'Onvard, Christian Soldiers,' he sang as he bundled up his things. His beautiful voice, a thrilling lyric tenor, stopped every conversation in the room. 'Marching as to Var.'

The drummers took up the hymn, beating time with coffee cups and highball glasses and waving farewell to good old Fritz, who was running to catch his train.

'That is one tip-top traveling man,' said the Locomobile representative loud enough for Fritz to hear.

'"Eight days in the veek,"' chuckled another as the German disappeared out the door. '"Thirteen months in the year."'

'"Time is money!"'

'"*Mit schlag.*"'

'Funny thing, though,' said the Gillette Razor man.

'What's that?'

'I stopped in one of his firms' piano shops in Akron. They said they couldn't take any orders, they was all backed up.'

'You heard Fritz. Business is booming.'

'Yeah, except it weren't the kind of shop you'd think. Dusty old place. Surly fella behind the desk looked more like the "floor manager" in a saloon than a piano sales-man. Hard to believe anybody ever bought anything there.'

'Maybe you just stopped by on a bad day.'

'Suppose.'

General Major Christian Semmler, Imperial German Army, Division of Military Intelligence, hurried out of the Palmer House, basking in the drummers' laughter and their warm farewells. As a child in the circus Semmler had learned from the clowns that an actor who *inhabited* an alias would never be caught out of character.

There was a 'Drummers' Table' in every fine hotel in America. In this club, 'Fritz Wunderlich,' commission salesman of organs and pianos, was a brother.

'Fritz Wunderlich' could travel where he pleased.

Christian Semmler, mastermind of the Donar Plan, never had to explain himself.

22

Isaac Bell and Clyde Lynds changed trains at Chicago to continue across the continent on the Rock Island's all-Pullman Golden State Limited to Los Angeles. Van Dorn detectives shadowed them so discreetly from the 20th Century's LaSalle Street Station to the Golden State's Dearborn Station that even Bell only spotted them twice.

Once aboard the Golden State, he asked a Van Dorn agent costumed as a conductor if they'd been followed. He was assured, categorically, no. Bell figured it was quite likely true. Joseph Van Dorn had founded the agency in Chicago. The detectives headquartered in the Palmer House were top-notch and proud of it.

The Golden State Limited was a transcontinental express that would stop only at major stations along a 2,400-mile run south and west on the low-altitude El Paso Route. A luxurious 'heavyweight', it consisted of a drawing room sleeper, a stateroom and drawing room sleeper, a stateroom car of smaller cabins – where Bell had again booked top and bottom berths – the dining car, and a buffet-library-observation car in the back of the train. Mail, baggage, and express cars rode at the front end directly behind the tender that carried coal and water for the Pacific 4-6-2 locomotive.

Five minutes before its scheduled departure from Chicago, a slab-sided Bellamore Armored Steel Bank Car bearing the name of the Continental & Commercial National Bank rumbled on solid rubber tires into the Dearborn Station's train shed. It stopped beside the Golden State. Shotgun-toting guards unloaded an oversized strongbox into the express car.

The strongbox, as long as a coffin, was addressed to the Los Angeles Trust and Savings Bank at 561 South Spring Street. The destination, and the closemouthed guards who wrestled it into the express car, guaranteed that it was packed with gold, negotiable bearer bonds, banknotes, or a strikingly valuable combination of all three. A friendly remark by the express car messenger, that when he was recently in Los Angeles the bank's building on South Spring Street was still under construction, was met with cold stares and a curt 'Sign here'.

The express messenger, Pete Stock, a cool customer with a well-oiled Smith & Wesson on his hip, was nearing retirement with every expectation of receiving a fine Waltham watch for brave service to the company. Having guarded innumerable shipments of specie, paper money, and ingots of silver and gold – and having shot it out more than once with gunmen intending to 'transact business with the express car' – he checked carefully that the paperwork the brusque Bellamore guard handed him tallied with his manifest, and then he signed.

Isaac Bell sent and received telegrams at every station stop.

At Kansas City, Kansas, a wire from Marion, who never wasted money on telegraphed words, read:

    GRIFFITH AWAITS CLYDE.
    BRIDE MISSES GROOM.

Griffith, similarly parsimonious as well as courteous, wired:

    EXPECTANT.

Pondering the Acrobat, Bell wired Harry Warren in New York:

    MISSED A BET? BRUNO DIDN'T TELL BROTHER FRANK
    WHO HIRED HIM. BUT DID BRUNO TELL HIS
    GIRLFRIEND?

Harry Warren's response caught up with Bell the next night. The train was taking on an additional 'helper' locomotive to climb the mountains, seventy miles east of the Arizona Territory border at Deming, New Mexico Territory.

    BRUNO TOLD GIRLFRIEND OF COAL STOKER LIKE
    APE.
    SOUND FAMILIAR?

Familiar. And odd. The same man seemed to be everywhere, and it occurred to Isaac Bell that the Acrobat was an unusually deadly type rarely encountered in the underworld – a criminal mastermind who did his own dirty work. Whether outlaw or foreign spy, lone operators were elusive, being immune to betrayal by inept subordinates.

Bell chewed on this while he watched a precision rail-yard ballet performed by the Deming brakemen coupling on the helper. A thought struck him like a bolt of lightning. Despite the military precision of the Acrobat's attack that had almost succeeded in kidnapping Lynds and Beiderbecke off the *Mauretania*, if he was a soldier, the Acrobat was no ordinary soldier.

Military men were not by nature lone operators. Soldiers accepted discipline from above and dispensed orders below. The Acrobat may have been a soldier once, but he wasn't one anymore. Or if he still was, then he had carved out a unique and exclusive niche above and beyond the supervision and encumbrance of an army.

Bell cabled Art Curtis in Berlin:

ACROBAT? MAYBE CIRCUS PERFORMER? MAYBE
SOLDIER? NOW? BUSINESSMAN WITH KRIEG
RUSTUNGSWERK GMBH???

Bell was painfully aware that it was expecting a lot to believe a one-man field office could unearth facts to support such vague speculation – even with as superb a detective as Art Curtis – so he wired the same message to Archie Abbott in New York. And then, just as the Golden State Limited sounded the double-whistle 'Ahead,' Bell fired off another copy to Joseph Van Dorn in Washington.

A train wrecker wielded a track wrench by starlight. He was twenty-five miles west of Deming and ten miles from the Continental Divide, where the grade climbed steeply on the Southern Pacific line over which the Rock Island trains ran between El Paso and the West Coast. He was unbolting a fishplate that held the butt ends of two rails together.

His partner was prying up spikes that fastened the steel rails to the wooden ties. With every bolt and spike removed, the strong cradle built to support hundred-ton locomotives was rendered weaker and weaker. Substantial weight on the rails would now spread them apart. The rails did not have to move far. A single inch would make all the difference between safe passage and eternity.

But to ensure success, when the wreckers were done removing bolts and spikes, they reeved a longer bolt through a hole in the side of the rail that had carried a fishtail bolt and fastened it to the last link of a logging chain. They had already laid the chain out to its full length along an arroyo, a dry creek bed deep enough to hide the Rolls-Royce touring car they had stolen from a wealthy tourist visiting Lordsburg.

They were just in time. A haze of locomotive head-lamps was brightening in the east.

A piercing two-finger whistle alerted their man, who was farther up the hill with the horses. The hostler whis-tled back. Message received – he would commence buckling cinches and loading saddlebags bulging with food and water for the long trek to Mexico.

The wreckers started the auto and eased it ahead to take the slack out of the chain. Then they waited, the soft mutter of the Rolls's finely turned motor gradually drowned out by the deepening thunder of twin Pacifics pulling in tandem. When the train was too close to stop even if the engineer happened to see his rail suddenly break loose, they throttled the Rolls-Royce ahead. The rail resisted. The tires spun in sand. But they only had to pull one inch.

Had the Golden State Limited been distinguishing herself at her usual mile-a-minute clip, the entire train would have jumped the tracks, rolled down the embankment, been set ablaze by the coals in her firebox, and burned to the wheels. But the wreckers were old hands in the sabotage line, and they had deliberately chosen the heavy grade rising up from Demings toward the Divide. Even with her helper locomotive, the train was barely doing thirty miles an hour when they ripped the rail from under her.

Locomotives, tenders, and the first express car crashed eight inches between the spreading rails and crunched along the ties, splintering wood and scattering ballast. For what on board the train seemed like an eternity, she skidded along in a cacophony of screeching steel.

The coupler between the express car and the mail car parted. Electric cables, plumbing pipes, and pneumatic hoses tore loose. With air pressure gone, the rearmost cars' air brakes clenched their shoes on the wheels. Slowed by the additional drag, the Golden State's mail car, diner, and sleeping cars finally ground to a stop, half on the tracks and half on the ballast, still upright though leaning at a frightening angle, and plunged into darkness.

23

When the lights went out, the German whom Professor Beiderbecke had dubbed the Acrobat climbed out of the Continental & Commercial National Bank of Chicago strongbox. Express messenger Pete Stock had already located a flashlight, but he hesitated a fatal, disbelieving half second before reaching for the Smith & Wesson on his gun belt.

The Acrobat spooled a thin braided cable from a leather gauntlet buckled to his powerful wrist, looped it around Stock's neck, and strangled him. Then he went hunting for Clyde Lynds, confident that his people had everything in place to execute a swift and orderly escape: across the Mexican border on horseback, a special train to Veracruz, a North German Lloyd freighter, and home to Prussia, where the inventor would be persuaded to rebuild his machine.

He jumped off the train and ran back toward the Pullmans, counting cars in the starlight as he loped past baggage, mail, diner, and two drawing-room stateroom cars and finally climbing up into the vestibule of the regular stateroom car where Clyde Lynds had just woken up to the chaos of derailment.

Isaac Bell made a practice of sleeping with his feet to the front of a train. Awakened abruptly when his feet smashed into the bulkhead, he pulled on his boots and his shoulder holster.

'What happened?' Clyde called sleepily from the upper berth.

'She's on the ground.'

'Derailed?'

Bell drew his Browning and chambered a round. 'Climbing slowly on a straight track? Two to one, she had help.'

'What are you doing?'

'Soon as I'm out the door, lock it. Let no one in, not even the conductor.'

Bell stepped into the pitch-black corridor and shut the door behind him. As far as he could see, the corridor was empty. He could hear people shouting in their staterooms. They sounded more confused than frightened. Train wreck was never far from any traveler's mind, but the Limited's stop, while sudden, had not ended in the splintered wood, twisted metal, smashed bones, and burning flesh that got their names among the dead and injured in tomorrow's newspapers.

Bell stood still with his back pressed against the door. His eyes adjusted to the dark in seconds. The corridor was still empty. He could see the shapes of the windows on the opposite side of the narrow corridor outlined by the starlight that bathed the high-desert floor. Outside in the starlit dark he saw a flicker of motion. Were his eyes playing tricks or did he see horses clumped close together, a hundred yards from the train? It was too far and too dark to see if they were saddled, but wild animals so near the thundering derailment would have stampeded to the far side of the mountains by now. These were horses with men.

Bell saw a flashlight at the head end of the car and, in its flickering back glow, the snow-white uniform of the Pullman porter, Edward, roused from a nap in his pantry. Bell closed one eye to protect his night vision. He sensed motion behind Edward. Before he could shout a warning, the porter crumpled silently to the floor. His flashlight fell beside him, arcing its beam along the corridor toward Bell.

A stateroom door flew open, and a fat man in pajamas stepped out, shouting, 'Porter!'

More doors banged open. Passengers stumbled into the dark corridor, and Bell realized that the Acrobat's plan had suddenly gone wrong. He saw the shadowy figure who had knocked down the porter move oddly, thrusting one arm out and folding the other across his face.

Bell smelled a familiar scent and covered his eyes. He heard a champagne cork *pop*. A blaze of intensely white light flooded the corridor. Blinded, the passengers fell back into their staterooms, crying out in fear and dismay.

No one stood between the Acrobat and Clyde Lynds's door except Isaac Bell.

Bell had remembered from his circus days the peculiar odor of flash cotton. The clowns loved the gag of igniting cloth impregnated with nitrocellulose to shoot fire from their fingertips, and he had recognized its smell in time to avoid being blinded.

He charged into the dark straight at the starlit simian shape of the Acrobat.

'I can't see!' cried the fat man, stumbling back into the

corridor. The tall detective slammed into the fat man. Both lost their footing, and the pair went down in a tangle. Bell somersaulted off and rolled to his feet. The fat man grabbed his ankle in a surprisingly strong grip.

Bell wrenched himself loose and ran to the head of the car and through the vestibules into the next car. At the far end, flame from the spirit stove for brewing tea in that car's porter's closet illuminated a broad-shouldered, long-armed silhouette running past. That porter, too, lay on the floor, either out cold or dead. The tall detective raised his gun and did not waste time ordering the Acrobat to stop.

Bell aimed for his legs and squeezed the trigger.

Just as the weapon's firing pin descended on the rim of the cartridge, detonating the charge within, Isaac Bell jerked the gun upward with all his might. A woman in a dressing gown that glowed white in the starlight had stepped out of her stateroom. She screamed and Bell saw her sleeping cap fly from her head.

'Are you all right?' an aghast Isaac Bell cried. This was his nightmare: an innocent had stepped into his line of fire. He ran to her, feeling his way along the row of stateroom doors. Then he felt a stinging sensation in his hand – wooden splinters his bullet had gouged from her door – and he realized with enormous relief that no woman shot in the head could keep screaming that loudly. He confirmed that she was unhurt, guided her gently back to her berth, then charged after the Acrobat.

Unlike Isaac Bell, the German was not slowed by confused and frightened passengers blundering out of their staterooms yelling for porters and demanding explanations. He smashed through them, knocking bodies to the floor and shattering glass as he pushed others through the windows. The derailment had extinguished the lights, so no one could see him – although at the moment his own wife would not recognize his face, so contorted was it by rage. Twice now Isaac Bell had upended an intricately planned and precisely executed operation.

He ran toward the head of the train, and when he reached the mail car whose couplers had parted, he jumped to the ballast and ran past the express cars and the tender. He heard Isaac Bell pound after him. Seizing a golden opportunity to put a stop to Bell's interference once and for all, the German climbed the side of the helper locomotive.

Out of nowhere, a brakeman grabbed his ankle.

The German laid him flat with a kick so powerful the man's neck broke. But the impact caused him to lose his own balance. He started to fall backwards. Reacting coolly, with a cat's economy of motion, he flipped his left hand forward. Launched from the gauntlet buckled to his wrist, the weighted end of the wire he had used to strangle the express messenger whirled around a handrail.

24

Isaac Bell saw the Acrobat jump onto the cylinder rod that connected the piston to the drive wheels of the helper engine, and he saw the shadow of a trainman who tried to stop him fall to the ground. For a second, Bell thought the Acrobat himself was falling off. Instead, his arm shot up in a peculiar overhead motion. Suddenly he appeared to fly from the connecting rod up past the wheel fender to a handrail above it. He gripped the rail and flipped backwards. The simian silhouette blurred the stars atop the big helper engine, and then he was gone, disappearing like smoke.

Bell scrambled after him. The locomotive was festooned with handholds and steps so workmen could reach every part that had to be oiled, greased, cleaned, and adjusted. The fender above the Pacific's seven-foot-high drive wheels formed a ledge alongside the boiler. He jumped onto the connecting rod, hauled himself on the ledge, stood up, and reached for the handrail. Only after he had locked both hands on it and was clenching his arms to pull himself up did he see the shadow of a boot cannonballing at his face. The Acrobat had not fled, but was waiting on top.

Bell whipped his head back and sideways, as if slipping a punch.

The boot whizzed past his ear and smashed into his shoulder. The Acrobat wore boots with india rubber soles and heels, Bell realized. A kick that hard with leather soles would have shattered bone.

The impact threw him off the locomotive. He fell backwards, tucking into a ball to protect his head. Tucking, twisting, he fought to regain his equilibrium in the air. If he could somehow land on the steeply angled side of the track bed instead of the flat top, he might survive the fall. The star-speckled sky spun circles like a black-and-white kaleidoscope. The dark ground rushed at his face. He hit the lip between flat and slope and skidded down the slope into a dry ditch.

Bell sprawled there, the stars still spinning. He heard a drumming noise, like hoofbeats. He wondered if he had cracked his skull again. But he hadn't. His head, in fact, was about the only part of him that wasn't going to hurt for a week. Scrambling to his feet, ignoring sharp pains in his shoulders and both knees, he heard the sound fade in the distance. Hoofbeats, of course. He had seen horses in starlight. And horses were the fastest way out of rough country.

He climbed up the embankment and came face-to-face with Clyde Lynds.

'Are you OK, Mr Bell?'

'I told you to stay inside and lock the door.'

'They're gone. They rode away on horses.'

'Happen to catch a look at any faces?'

'No. But . . . Uh . . .'

'But what?' Bell demanded sharply, hoping for some clue.

'One of the horses had no rider,' Lynds said, looking around fearfully at the passengers clustered beside the derailed train. 'Maybe he's still here . . .'

'No, Clyde. That empty saddle was reserved for you.'

*

'Mister, if you'll get off that locomotive,' bellowed a red-headed giant of a railroad wreck master, 'we can put this train back together.'

First light found Isaac Bell poring over the Golden State's helper locomotive with a magnifying glass. A wreck train had finally steamed up the grade from Deming, while out of the west another had just arrived from Lordsburg. Between them, the two were preparing to hoist the Limited back on the tracks, piece by piece.

'I'll just be a minute,' Bell called down.

'Get off my train!' roared the giant, clambering up the locomotive onto the drive wheel fender.

Bell turned with a smile and thrust out his hand. 'Mike Malone. I would recognize that Irish brogue in a thunderstorm.'

'Well, I'll be damned. Isaac Bell. Put 'er there.'

They shook hands – two tall men, one lean as a rail, the other with limbs thick as chestnut crossties.

'What are you doing here?'

'Escort job,' Bell answered cryptically. He had known Mike since they had come within inches of being blown to smithereens by dynamite ingeniously hidden under Osgood Hennessy's Southern Pacific Railroad tracks.

'Under guise,' he added, encouraging Mike to refrain from asking what Bell's magnifying glass had to do with an escort job – not to mention the express messenger found strangled in his car and the Rolls-Royce auto chained to a broken rail.

Malone winked. 'Mum's the word.'

Bell showed him a groove rubbed in the handrail. 'What do you think made this mark?'

The wreck master ran his calloused finger over it. 'Hacksaw?'

'How about a braided cable?'

Malone shrugged mighty shoulders. 'Could be.'

'Wouldn't happen to have a small cutting pliers on that wreck train I could borrow?'

'Linesman's pliers do you?'

'Long as they're sharp as the devil and small enough to slip up my sleeve.'

'Never seen them that small. I'll have my toolmaker run 'em up for you. Where should I send them?'

'Los Angeles.'

Isaac Bell was sure that the intention of the attack was to kidnap Clyde Lynds, not injure him. But it had come close to succeeding, and Clyde was terrified. The bravado and smart-aleck talk had been frightened out of him. His eyes were darting everywhere, seeking solace, finding fear.

Bell had no intention of walking away from the Krieg investigation. But the detective felt honor bound to ask the young scientist whether he would rather take the safe course and sell his machine to Thomas Edison so the Germans would stop plaguing him. 'You'd be free of this mess in a flash.'

Clyde asked if Bell was abandoning him.

'Absolutely not. But I am saying that the attack came close, and the next might succeed, even though the Van Dorn Agency – and I in particular – will lay our lives on the line to protect you.'

'Why? What do you care? It could be years before Van Dorn sees any money out of Talking Pictures.'

To Isaac Bell, the innocent were sacred and must always be protected. But to answer Clyde, he only laughed. 'I already told you. Marion hopes that your invention will help her make ever-better moving pictures. That's good enough for me.'

'If you say so,' Clyde said, his eyes still darting, 'I guess it's good enough for me, too.'

'Are you sure, Clyde? I can't *guarantee* your safety. I can only guarantee that I will do whatever is required to keep you alive, but I can't guarantee we will succeed. The Acrobat is no slouch.'

Clyde conjured a brave smile. 'What about Van Dorn's motto, "We never give up. Never!"'

'Oh, we'll get him in the end,' Bell smiled back.

'Lot of good that will do me if he gets me first.'

'That's why I'm asking if you're sure.'

Clyde took a deep breath. 'I'm sure.'

'Good man.'

In Berlin, Arthur Curtis wandered in and out of the Tiergarten, passing through the park's huge Egyptian gates twice in twenty minutes. The skittish Hans Reuter had failed to show up for a meeting. Curtis had hoped that his greed, if not his hatred of his employer, had made him brave again. The nattily dressed, potbellied Van Dorn started to enter the park a third time, but gave it up when he noticed a plainclothes policeman noticing him.

Seeing his jaunty stride, no one would guess that Arthur Curtis had shifted into a state of high alert and was employing every trick he knew to determine, before he returned to his office, whether he was being followed.

The contact could have turned on him. It was a remote possibility, but not impossible, that he had confessed to his employer that he was selling Krieg company secrets. He might even have gone to the police; guilty men were prone to panic, and panic made fools.

Curtis worked his way cautiously through the diplomatic quarter adjoining the park, taking his time on the handsome streets that served the mansions of the ambassadors. There were Army officers aplenty in the neighborhood. It seemed every second German was wearing a uniform. By sheer coincidence, he bumped into an acquaintance, a minor British embassy official with a taste for French brandy, who said, 'You're looking all spiffed today, Arthur, what? Did you win the lottery?'

Curtis winked, 'I was just visiting a friend,' which drew a lewd grin and the expected, 'Might she have a sister?'

'I'll inquire next time,' said Curtis, and they parted on a laugh.

When he reached a commercial district, he watched for reflections in the shop windows. All seemed well until a fellow in a fine gabardine coat appeared on the sidewalk ahead, twenty minutes after Curtis had first noticed him.

The man was richly dressed for a detective or a secret policeman. But Krieg and the German Army could afford the best, couldn't they? When he noticed a uniformed mounted police officer signal someone with a nod, Arthur Curtis hopped onto a tram, partly to think things over and partly to watch who got on next. A portly fellow in an expensive homburg boarded at the next stop, perspiring from a hard run, and Curtis knew that he was either paranoid or in trouble and had to act as if it were the latter.

On the other hand, he thought with a smile that broadcast innocence, he'd been working the private detective game for fifteen years – nearly twenty if he counted his apprenticeship with a Denver-based bullion-escort outfit ramrodded by a couple of old Indian fighters – and since arriving in Germany, he'd devoted every spare moment to learning the ins and outs of the Berlin neighborhoods. He jumped off the tram and onto another.

The street traffic changed from autos to bicyclists and horsecarts, and he hopped down in a workers' district of five-story tenements interspersed with coal yards where homburgs and gabardine coats would stand out like sore thumbs. He walked purposefully, like a man headed home – or, considering the quality of his clothing, come to collect the rent. He continued down several streets, fingering the money clip in his pocket. He rounded a corner, flashed marks at a teenager on a bicycle, and bought the bike for double its value. Then he pedaled away at three times the speed a shadow could run, hoping no cop behind him had flashed a badge at another bike rider.

It felt like a clean getaway. But getting away was not the same as getting the job done. Isaac Bell was pressing him hard, and Arthur Curtis wanted to deliver the goods. But if he couldn't corral his man inside Krieg, how could he ask whether a former Army officer now held a high position in the company?

25

Isaac Bell was first off the Limited in Los Angeles.

Boots to the platform while the train was still rolling into La Grande Station, guiding Clyde Lynds firmly by the elbow and trading discreet nods with a Van Dorn detective attired as a porter, Bell burst from the station into the fierce morning sun. He looked for an olive green Santa Monica trolley with the dash sign 'Hollywood' and they jumped off thirty minutes later at a brick depot that served the farm village.

While the electric sped out of town, Bell scrutinized the tourists who had gotten off with them and confirmed the all-clear from a Van Dorn buying picture postcards. He entered the nearest of the hotels and guesthouses clustered around the depot and asked the front-desk clerk, 'Where is Mr D. W. Griffith taking pictures?'

'Right around the corner. It's a two-reeler called *In Old California*. But you won't find work. There's fourteen players lined up ahead of you. I'm number twelve.'

'Thanks for the warning – come along,' Bell said to Clyde.

Clyde had recovered from his scare on the train. 'Who the heck cares about old California? Griffith could use a snappier title. Like *The Girls of Old California*.'

'Stick close,' said Bell.

He traced the Griffith movie by the growl of a dynamo

powering the lights. It was a big outside operation in a vacant lot with a distant view of majestic mountains. Bell counted more than fifty people engaged – horse wranglers, mechanicians, actors, and scene shifters, and a camera operator he recognized as a valuable man named Bitzer who had worked for Marion and was known as the best in the business.

Griffith, a lanky man of thirty-five or so, was directing from a chair, his face shaded by an enormous, floppy straw hat. He had a soft Kentucky accent and a revolver tucked in his waistband.

'Now, young lady,' he told an actress dressed in an old-fashioned Spanish señorita gown and shawl, 'you will try again to walk from where you are currently standing to that tree.'

'Yes, Mr Griffith.'

Griffith raised a two-foot megaphone to his lips. 'Lights!'

The Cooper-Hewitts flared, doubling the effect of the brilliant sun.

'Camera!'

Bitzer focused and started cranking.

'Speed!'

Bitzer cranked to a speed that sent the film past the camera lens at a rate of a thousand feet in twelve and a half minutes.

'*Action!*'

The señorita pointed at the tree.

'*Stop!*'

The camera operator stopped cranking. Griffith slumped a little lower under his hat and drawled, politely but firmly, 'Billy's camera will present you as a close-up figure. In return for that honor Ah would appreciate a certain restraint of expression.'

'I have to point out to the audience where I'm heading next.'

'The least patient among them will soon see where you are headed next. Don't point. And stop looking at the camera.'

'Yes, Mr Griffith.'

'Speed!'

The señorita having reached the tree at last and lunch finally announced, Griffith retreated under the shade of an umbrella and removed his floppy hat, revealing jet-black hair, an incipient widow's peak, a strong hawk nose, and the deeply set, soulful eyes of a matinee idol. A smile warmed them when Bell was introduced.

'May I congratulate you, sir, on your marriage to a wonderful lady and a fine director.'

'Thank you, Mr Griffith. We had the pleasure of seeing *Is This Seat Taken?* shown by a Humanova troupe at our wedding feast on *Mauretania*.'

Griffith rolled his eyes. 'With the director putting words in my actors' mouths?'

'I'm afraid so. That's what we've come to talk to you about. This is Mr Clyde Lynds. He has invented a wonderful machine to make and show talking pictures.'

'That's been tried before.'

'But mine works,' said Clyde.

'I've never seen voice and picture synchronized for longer than five seconds.'

'You'll see mine for five *reels*.'

Griffith glanced from the brash young scientist into the steady gaze of the tall detective.

'My firm, Dagget, Staples and Hitchcock, is betting it will work,' said Bell. 'Clyde developed a new process with Professor Franz Beiderbecke, who was an electroacoustic scientist at the Imperial-Royal Polytechnic Institute in Vienna.'

Griffith said, 'I would love to make talking pictures. The human voice is a wondrous factor at intense moments But I am not in any position to invest.'

'I don't need your money,' Clyde shot back. 'All I need is a laboratory like you've set up in that shed. And a machine shop like you have for the cameras. And –'

'Most of all,' Isaac Bell interrupted, 'Clyde needs an important director to make a picture show with his machine.'

'That would be me,' said Griffith, 'Except I'm only here until we finish *In Old California*. Then it's back to New York, and I doubt very much that Biograph will have any interest in a machine that would compete with Mr Edison. But –' Here, with a dramatic pause, he raised a finger for emphasis. 'By coincidence, I was, only yesterday, approached by the Imperial Film Manufacturing Company offering to woo me away from Biograph.'

Bell did not like coincidences. 'Who is Imperial?'

'They showed me their cinematography studio, and I'll tell you it's the finest motion picture plant in the West. Four hundred hands, a corps of stage directors, magnificent stages, complete laboratories, darkrooms, and machine shops. All installed at a cost that must have run into big money, thanks to financial backing by the Artists Syndicate.'

'What is the Artists Syndicate?' asked Bell.

'They're a combine of Wall Street bankers who don't give a hoot for the Edison Trust. Wait until you see Imperial. They have a wealth of brand-new equipment capable of turning out a quantity of film, and they've engaged stars, both legit and vaud. They're all set to make big plays – longer, multi-reel pictures.'

Clyde said to Isaac Bell, 'Imperial sounds up-to-date.'

'Could you arrange an appointment, Mr Griffith?'

'I'll do better than arrange an appointment. I'll tell them I'll make the first picture with sound as soon as you've perfected it. That ought to get their attention.'

'Don't you have a contract with Biograph?'

Griffith placed his right hand over his heart. 'I promise that I will break my contract with Biograph in a flash for a chance to direct moving pictures that can truly make the sound of human voices. But it's up to you, Mr Bell, to sell them the machine, and you, Mr Lynds, to perfect it. I'll telephone Imperial right away.'

'Before you phone,' said Bell. 'May I do you a kindness in return?'

'What did you have in mind?'

'I notice you carry a six-shooter.'

'Old habit from before Biograph joined the Trust,' Griffith grinned, joking, with a theatrical wink, 'Haven't shot an Edison thug in years.'

'May I see it?'

'Sure.' Griffith tugged the revolver from his waistband. Bell opened the cylinder, counted six cartridges, and removed one. 'Gents I know who carry a six-gun in their waistband make a habit of leaving the hammer on an empty chamber. At least so long as they intend to father children.'

Isaac Bell left Clyde Lynds in the care of the Los Angeles Van Dorn field office and went alone to his appointment at Imperial Film, intending to get a clear-eyed look at what had fallen into their laps. He found a brand-new, ten-story red sandstone building with a glass penthouse that towered over a newly surveyed block of lots for sale. The neighborhood looked destined to become the next center of the up-and-coming city, and the substantial modern headquarters seemed proof that the independent movie factory had deep enough Wall Street pockets to defy Edison's Patents Trust.

Motorcycle messengers with sidecars full were rushing reels of film in and out of Imperial's first-floor film exchange. The exchange was plastered with 'No Smoking Allowed' signs, which none of the cyclists distributing highly flammable reels to exhibitors were obeying. The building directory listed offices and lofts on the upper floors housing laboratories, machine and repair shops, properties and costume wardrobes, and a main studio containing Stage 1 and Stage 2 in the glass penthouse.

The entire second floor was devoted to the factory's own moving picture theater – the Imperial. Newspaper reviews posted in the lobby called it a 'Movie Palace', and while absorbing the details of the building and the people coming and going, Bell read of gleaming gilt cherubs in a 'finely appointed place that will draw the more wealthy classes who do not patronize moving picture shows except on "slumming" exhibitions.'

The doormen patrolling the lobby were harder-cased than he would expect to find wearing uniforms as lavishly gilded as Captain Turner's. That a bruiser corps was considered a wise precaution for an independent a full three thousand miles from New Jersey spoke volumes about the power of the Edison Trust. One of the doormen watching Bell read the reviews swaggered over to investigate.

Bell said, 'It says here that ladies who come downtown on shopping expeditions spend an hour in the Imperial.'

'And bring their friends next time. What can we do for you, mister?'

'I have an appointment with the managing director.'

'Seventh floor, sir.'

The elevator operators were unusually young and fit. On the seventh floor a male receptionist, who looked like he had learned his trade in a football flying wedge, led him through a locked door to a secretary who ushered him into a large office, curtained against the blazing sun. To Isaac Bell's surprise, the managing director who rose smiling from her desk was Marion's beautiful, dark-eyed Russian friend Irina Viorets.

She was dressed in a stylish suit, with a long skirt and jacket that hugged her closely, and she had collected her beautiful hair high in the back as the women directors did to allow them to peer through the lens of the camera.

'You look surprised, Isaac,' she greeted him with a warm laugh. 'I assure you, no one is more surprised than I.'

Bell took the hand she offered. 'May I congratulate you on what must be the quickest immigrant success story in America? You have landed on your feet and then some.'

'Sheer luck. I bumped into an old friend who knew my work in Russia. He introduced me to a banker, who introduced me to a group of Wall Street men who had already jumped on the movie bandwagon and suddenly had this factory and no one to run it. I leaped at the chance. Moving pictures will all be made in California. The sun shines here every day.'

'Quite a leap,' Bell marveled, 'from making pictures to running the entire factory.'

'Well,' she said, lowering her eyes modestly, 'I had experience of business in Petersburg. But I don't overrate my position here. The Wall Street bankers back in New York call the tune. I am merely the piper. Or, at best, the arranger. They burn the telegraph wires firing demands across the continent night and day. Where is your lovely bride? Taking pictures of Jersey scenery?'

'San Francisco, visiting her father.'

'What does she do next?'

'She's contemplating her next move.'

'Perfect. We must get Marion to join us here, where she may take pictures of things more attractive than "Jersey scenery".'

'I imagine she would like that. I certainly would.'

'In the meantime, come to lunch and tell me all about "Talking Pictures".'

They rode the elevator down to a staff commissary feeding actors costumed as plutocrats, policemen, washerwomen, countesses, cowboys, and Indians. Many were grease-painted with purple lips, green skin, and orange hair to show up in the chartreuse glow of the Cooper-Hewitts. Irina sashayed among them, exchanging friendly waves and greetings, and into an exquisite private dining room that looked like it had been removed board by board from a London club and reassembled in the new building.

Bell asked, 'Did Clyde mention anything about his Talking Pictures machine on the boat?'

'Just enough to make me think, when Mr Griffith telephoned, that it could be exactly what my investors in the Artists Syndicate are looking for.'

Isaac Bell enjoyed a flirtatious lunch with Irina Viorets while making it clear he was a one-woman man, and Marion was that one woman. But he had the strong impression that Irina's smiles, flashing eyes, and light touches on his arm were more for show than intent.

'I meant to ask on the ship, how do you happen to speak such interesting English? Sometimes you sound almost like a native-born American.'

'Almost, but not quite. Though I'm improving. It is a wondrous language.'

'How did you learn it?'

'In Petersburg my father played the piano at the American embassy. I had many friends among the children.'

For some reason, thought Isaac Bell, that was a story he wanted Van Dorn Research to verify. In fact, there was something about this whole setup that rang a little false. Perhaps it was just the incredible speed with which Irina's good fortune had unfolded, or perhaps the detective's nemesis, coincidence. Or maybe it was simply a memory of Marion saying that Irina's story about fleeing the Okhrana changed with each glass of wine, though there was no wine at this lunch, merely orange juice and water.

'When was that?'

'Let me think,' she said. 'Oh, Isaac, it's embarrassing how long ago that was. Bloody Nicholas hadn't taken the throne.'

'Before, when was that, 1894?'

'Not too far before,' Irina said, her full lips parting in a warm smile. 'Allow a woman a certain latitude with her age.'

'Forgive me,' Bell smiled back, satisfied that Grady Forrer – the brilliant head of Van Dorn Research, a large man in whose presence barroom brawls tended to peter out quickly and a hound dog of a tracker – would soon put the question to American embassy officers who had served in Russia when Czar Alexander III still reigned.

'Tell me, Irina, will you miss directing pictures now that you're running the whole show?'

'Will I miss positioning the camera and waiting for the sun for hours so I may transfer full beauty to the negative? Yes, very much. Will I miss a banker who lent me the money to position the camera for hours telling me that it would be better if I positioned it *there*, instead of *there*? No! Not one bit. Now my only "boss" is the Artists Syndicate, and they are three thousand miles away in New York.'

'Who are the investors in the Artists Syndicate?'

'The syndicate is closely held. I met none of them. I don't even know their names.'

'Why do you suppose they are so secretive?'

'For two reasons,' she answered, with a laugh that did not conceal a certain discomfort, Bell thought. 'They are probably respectable bankers who don't want their wives, club brothers, and fellow progressive reformers to know with whom they rub shoulders. Don't forget, motion picture manufacturers are thought to be either risqué or tainted by sinful nickelodeon profits or careers that started in carnival shows and low-class vaudeville. I am told that this is a uniquely American attitude, but I saw the same snobbishness in London.'

'And the second reason?'

'The second reason is what I suspect is the real reason: fear. As wealthy as they are, they are not as powerful as Thomas Edison. They're afraid that if Edison interests learn who they are, the Trust will fight back by shutting them out of their *other* businesses, not only moving pictures.'

Bell eyed her closely. There was something about the Russian woman he liked – a sense of decency, he supposed, and her liveliness. And she certainly was easy on the eyes. But he wondered, would she ever question the nature of the investors backing her dream of being a boss? Or would her ambition still her doubts?

'We have a proverb,' he said. '"She who sups with the devil should have a long spoon."'

Irina Viorets laughed it off. 'Russians have a proverb, too: "When the devil finds a lazy woman, he puts her to work." I admit to many flaws, but sloth is not among them. And I never forget that we Russians also say, "God keeps her safe who keeps herself safe."'

Isaac Bell reckoned he might have opened a chink in

her armor. Nonetheless, he would wire a second inquiry to Grady Forrer:

WHO PAYS THE BILLS FOR IMPERIAL FILM???

After lunch they got down to business, with Bell acting his part as a Dagget, Staples & Hitchcock insurance executive anxious to invest in the movies. Bearing in mind the outright rejection by Pirate King Tarses, he opened with Marion's fierce defense. 'Without pictures that talk, the screen shrinks drama, tragedy, comedy, and farce to pantomime.'

'But the screen is democracy,' said Viorets, 'if not socialism. We are reproducing the rich man's tragedies, comedies, and farces in pantomime that men on the street can afford.'

'Clyde has invented a way to do it with words and music instead of pantomime,' said Isaac Bell.

Irina nodded. 'I heard that your insurance firm was investing in Clyde's Talking Pictures machine. That's really why I was intrigued when Mr Griffith telephoned.'

'Where did you hear that?'

'From moving picture people you were shopping it to in New Jersey.'

'Then you heard that my firm seeks manufacturers who are up to taking superior pictures with the same photography and finish as the French.'

Irina Viorets reached across the table and placed a pretty hand on Bell's arm. 'I promise you, Mr Bell, Imperial will out-French the French – let me show you,' she said, and took him on a tour of the Imperial Building that left Bell with no doubt that Irina Viorets was in command of a going concern.

She showed him the laboratories and machine, repair, and carpentry shops that Griffith had raved about. He saw printing and perforating instruments in the darkrooms, properties and wardrobe rooms of costumes for hundreds of soldiers, police, and cowboys, and rows of flats in the scenic department painted black and white. On the fourth floor was a soundproof recording room, like Edison's, the walls padded, the floor corked tile, with an array of acoustic horns to capture sound.

She took him outside. In a vacant lot on the south side of the building, a mock street facing toward the sun could be made to look like New York, or London, or medieval Paris.

Next to the building was a life net. Ordinarily held by firemen to catch people jumping from a burning house, this one was permanently fixed. 'For catching actors,' Irina laughed, pointing at the building's parapet a hundred feet off the ground. 'Just outside of camera range.'

Bell quoted Clyde Lynds: 'Providing thrills dear to the heart of the exhibitor.'

They went back indoors and rode the elevator ten stories to the roof. Irina said, 'The best photoplays of the future will be those that are created inside the film studio.'

The picture-taking studio had room for several cinematograph studio stages with glass ceilings to capture natural light. At one edge of the roof stood a stone wall that could serve as a precipice or a building. Bell leaned over and looked down. The life net winked back at him, no bigger than a dime.

'I have one more thing to show you.' She took him

down to the eighth floor to a gleaming camera and projector machine shop, with a laboratory attached.

'Everything is up-to-date. Would you like to use our facility, Isaac?'

'Will your Artists Syndicate allow it?'

'I will deal with the Artists Syndicate. You and Clyde will deal with me.'

'Done,' said Isaac Bell. 'With one proviso. My firm will staff Lynds's workshop with mechanicians.'

'If you like, though we already have the best in Los Angeles.'

'And we will provide our own guards.'

'Whatever for? This building is a fortress.'

'So I noticed. Nonetheless, my directors are conservative. They will demand that we do everything possible to protect Lynds's invention.'

'Perhaps you could convince them that the building is safe.'

'My directors remember what happened on the *Mauretania*. Professor Beiderbecke was killed. And the machine was destroyed in a fire. You can imagine why they insist that we protect our investment.'

'I understand,' she said reluctantly.

'I hope this wouldn't cause trouble with the Artists Syndicate.'

'I told you. I will contend with the syndicate. Let us shake hands on our deal.'

On his way back to Van Dorn headquarters, Isaac Bell rented a house big enough for Clyde Lynds to share with Lipsher and two more bruisers from Protective Services.

*

Irina Viorets locked the door to her office in the Imperial Film Manufacturing Building and lifted a leather-bound copy of the novel *War and Peace* from her bookcase, causing the case to slide open on a private stairway. She climbed two flights to a suite hidden on the ninth floor. Its windows were heavily draped, making it cool and dark. To a northern European, it offered welcome refuge from the Los Angeles heat and sunlight.

The man waiting for her report sat behind his desk with his face in shadow.

'I'm sorry,' she said. 'Bell insists on posting his own guards.'

BOOK THREE
Hollywood

26

General Christian Semmler laughed at Irina Viorets.

'Of course he wants his own guards. He's cautious. What do you expect of an "insurance man"?'

'How would I know what to expect? I am not a soldier, only an artist.'

'You are "only an artist" like a cobra is only a snake.'

'You have no right to mock me. I have done exactly as you wanted.'

'And will continue to.' Christian Semmler watched her gather her courage, then brutally cut the legs out from under her. 'No! To answer the question forming on your lovely lips, I have no message for you from your fiancé.'

'You promised,' she said bleakly.

'I promised I would *try* to get a message.'

He watched tears fill her eyes. When he took mercy upon her, it was not really mercy, but merely another way to make her toe the line. 'I can tell you that he is still safe in Germany.'

'In prison.'

'If the czar's secret police were hunting *me*,' Christian Semmler replied with withering disdain for her foolish lover, 'I would rather be in a German prison than out in the open. The Okhrana are as determined as they are cruel. So if it puts your mind at rest, remember that your young man is safe in an Imperial German Army prison deep inside Prussia. And no one enters that particular prison without my express permission. Or leaves it, for that matter.'

'May I go now?' she said, rising with strength and dignity.

She was a strong woman, Semmler had to admit. He had chosen well. Better than she had. The fool she was engaged to marry, one of her benighted nation's thousands of impoverished princes, had bungled a quixotic attack on the czar in the name of some murky Russian amalgam of democracy and socialism. Which gave Semmler all the leverage he needed to make Irina Viorets serve the Donar Plan.

'You may go,' he said. 'Get Lynds established in his laboratory immediately and do everything necessary to make him productive.'

27

'Isaac! What are you doing in Los Angeles?'

'Hoping you'll help me, Uncle Andy.'

'Don't call me Uncle Andy. It makes me feel old, and I am not your uncle.'

Bell regarded the impish-looking Andrew Rubenoff with affection. 'You're my father's special friend. That makes you uncle enough for me.'

Rubenoff was a dark-haired man in his forties, who wore an impeccably tailored suit of worsted wool and, on his head, a disc of velvet, the yarmulke of the Hebrew faith. A banker like Bell's father, he was shifting his assets out of coal, steel, and railroads into the three newest industries in America: automobiles, flying machines, and moving pictures. Colleagues who thought him lunatic before he doubled his fortune were further appalled when he pulled up stakes and moved from New York City to Los Angeles. As Bell's father had put it, 'They act as if President Taft had moved the White House to Tokyo. The fact is, Andrew emigrated from Russia to New York to San Francisco and back to New York. There is a bit of the gypsy in the fellow.'

'I need your help,' said Bell. 'How would you like to be a detective?'

'I would rather play piano in a Barbary Coast bordello.'

'You've already done that, Uncle Andy. I am offering a new experience.'

Andrew Rubenoff gestured out the windows of his hilltop mansion, indicating his pleasure with the views of the mountains to the north and east, the flat coastal plain stretching to the blue Pacific Ocean, and the hazy outline of Catalina Island. Within his lavish office, fine furniture shared the space with oil paintings by the radical artists Marcel Duchamp and John Sloan and his beloved Mason & Hamlin grand piano, which had traveled with him from New York. 'I am enjoying this experience, thank you very much. Will you have tea, Isaac?'

A handsome male secretary brought tea in tall glasses. In New York, Bell recalled, the secetary had been matronly. Rubenoff sipped his tea through a cube of sugar. Bell followed suit, burning his tongue as usual.

'What have you heard about the Imperial Film Manufacturing Company?'

'I heard this morning that Imperial is dropping the word "Manufacturing" from its name. All the picture firms are doing it. It's dawned on them that movies are more interesting than anvil foundries. And far more complicated.'

'Before this morning, what had you heard about Imperial?'

'Big and rich.'

'But they just got started. They built an expensive building but have just begun distributing films. How did they get so big and rich?'

'Artists Syndicate.'

'Who are Artists Syndicate's investors?'

'Finally, you ask an interesting question. But a hard one.'

'You're the man to answer hard questions,' Bell said bluntly.

'Do you know anything about the movies?' Rubenoff asked. 'Other than being married to a woman who makes them.'

'She's taught me a lot,' said Bell. 'And by the way, thank you again for the silver service. Next time we have thirty-six to dinner we'll put it to good use.'

Rubenoff waved his thanks aside. 'Ah, the least – you see, Isaac, I find this disturbing. I don't *know* who invests in Artists Syndicate and Imperial Film.'

'Disturbing?'

'I should know. They're potentially my competitors – if not, one day, partners. I should know if I am up against a bunch of furriers from Manhattan, a combine of distributors from Springfield, or a furniture magnate from Ohio who knows a young lady who should be a star, clothiers from Philadelphia, or glovers from Gloversville, or Frenchmen fronting for Pathé. Or English lords snapping up yet another American enterprise. Why is Artists Syndicate so anxious to remain private?'

Bell nodded uncomfortably. The banker was confirming his own worry that he had he steered Clyde Lynds in a potentially dangerous direction. While Grady Forrer had found State Department people who confirmed Irina Viorets's story of spending her childhood with American embassy children, Van Dorn Research had made no headway on the question of who paid the bills for Imperial Film.

Nor could he forget that Arthur Curtis had cabled early on that Krieg Rüstungswerk had an 'appetite' for unrelated businesses.

'Seriously, Andrew. Can I persuade you to play detective for me?'

Rubenoff returned a puckish smile. 'Will I have to bear sidearms?'

'Not unless you're frightened by the sight of a beautiful woman.'

Arthur Curtis opened an envelope containing an enciphered cablegram from Isaac Bell. Pauline read it aloud over his shoulder, decoding it faster than he could. It was apparent by now that she had a true photographic memory for both sights and sounds.

NEED MORE ON KRIEG RÜSTUNGSWERK.
NEED KRIEG MAN IN AMERICA.
BOSS AUTHORIZES PAY ANY PRICE.
ON THE JUMP!

'What is the meaning of "On the jump"? Like it sounds?'

'Exactly like it sounds. Get moving without delay. Immediately.'

'What are you going to do on the jump, Detective Curtis?'

'Send you home and go to work.'

Curtis climbed into his coat and felt in the pockets for a couple of apples he had bought earlier.

'Should I come with you?' she asked.

'Go home. It's bedtime. Here.' He handed her the apples. 'Give one to your mother.' He ushered her out and locked the door. Then he turned off the light and watched from the window until she disappeared around the corner. No one else was out at this hour, and no one was watching the office. He went out the back window and down the fire ladder and hurried to a neighborhood *Kintopp*, hoping to get lucky.

A groschen bought him a pint *Topp* of beer and entry to the *Kino* which showed moving pictures in a long, narrow space formed by three apartment flats strung together. The films on the screen this evening would have not passed the test for a police license. Arthur Curtis had been a detective long enough to have only a passing interest in what in his boyhood would have been called 'dirty pictures'. But Hans Reuter, his man inside Krieg's Berlin office, liked them, and this working-class moving picture theater was a sufficiently long walk from Reuter's expensive neighborhood that he felt safe frequenting it without the locals telling his wife. So Arthur Curtis sipped his beer and pretended to be engrossed in the goings-on flickering on the screen while he kept an eye on the men drifting in from the beer bar.

Curtis sat for two hours in the dark. The place had emptied out a bit, and he was having trouble staying awake, when, all of a sudden, in walked his man from Krieg, hugging his beer and looking for an empty place on the bench that he favored in the back row. Curtis moved over. Herr Reuter sat, sipped, and stared.

The short, round Van Dorn detective remained as silent as the film until the waiters finally interrupted with loud offers of 'Beer?' During the storm of affirmative replies, he leaned closer to Reuter and whispered, 'Triple.'

'What?' Reuter turned. His mouth tightened when he realized that the man who had been sitting next to him all along was Arthur Curtis. 'I said, no more.'

'I can now pay triple,' whispered Curtis. 'Three times as much. If you're interested, meet me in the bar.'

Reuter kept him waiting, but not for long. Greed, in the immortal words of Chief Investigator Isaac Bell, worked wonders.

'Triple?' Reuter echoed in disbelief.

Arthur Curtis passed him the fresh *Topp* he had ordered and took a sip from his own. 'Triple. But only for something special.'

'Like what?'

'Something unique. You know the situation at your employer. You're best qualified to suggest something that I would really need. Aren't you?'

Hans Reuter looked worried. 'But how am I to guess?'

Curtis shrugged. 'Let me guess for you. How many Krieg company executives and directors are former Army officers?'

'Very few.'

'Do you know any?'

'Not personally. I mean, there are none in the Berlin office.'

'Can you find their names?'

'I would have to think about that.'

'While you're thinking,' Curtis shot back, 'think which of those company directors might travel abroad.'

Reuter looked uncomfortable, and Curtis thought he was touching some sort of a nerve here, as if the man had thought of a name he feared.

'One of your responsibilities is to dispense funds overseas, correct?'

'How do you know?'

Curtis's casual, 'I asked around' did not make Reuter look any more comfortable.

Curtis went for broke. 'I need a name.'

'A name?'

'The name of the recipient.' *Push!* Arthur Curtis thought. Push him hard. Don't give him time to change his mind. 'Two days,' he said. 'Meet me here. Seven o'clock.'

'It is risky.'

'Don't worry, it will be the last time I ask.'

'No more?' Hans asked, partly with relief, partly with disappointment that the money would stop. Curtis said, 'In addition to triple, I will seek authorization for a separation bonus. A thank-you.'

Greed was Reuter's middle name. Suddenly he was brave. 'But for the name you ask I will have to pay someone else.'

He was lying, bless him, Curtis thought. Reuter was high enough up in Krieg to know the name himself. Curtis said, 'O.K. If I must, I will pay your "someone else," too.' Maybe Reuter was lying. But maybe he wasn't. Hopefully, he was so grasping he would take a big risk.

On his way back to the office, Art Curtis stopped at the all-night telegraph in a railroad station to cable Isaac Bell.

WIRE AUTHORIZED FUNDS.
NAME POSSIBLE TWO DAYS.

*

Andrew Rubenoff reported back to Isaac Bell that he was very impressed by Irina Viorets.

'I'm surprised,' Bell admitted. 'I thought there was something fishy about how fast she got the job running such a big outfit.'

'The woman displays a keen understanding of the moving picture business. Not only the taking of the pictures, but the distribution and exhibition – which are absolutely vital to making a profit. Equally important, she understands that more must be done than introducing a couple of new shows with each change. The customers won't stand much longer for furbishing up of the exhibition with a few new features. The exhibitors must be able to declare that the entire show is new. "Keep your show fresh and up-to-the-minute," she told me, "and you will draw full houses."'

'Sounds like she was selling you.'

'I pretended to be an exhibitor with a string of picture show shops in Indiana.'

'That was a nice touch,' Bell said admiringly.

'Not really,' Rubenoff replied with a modest smile. 'I control houses in Detroit, Toledo, Battle Creek, and Indianapolis.'

'So you think she passes muster?'

'There are poseurs in this line who like to say that anyone can make a moving picture. That is not true, as Mr Thomas Edison is slowly beginning to learn at great expense. Similarly, not just anyone can distribute movies. Mademoiselle Viorets knows her business. Most important, she knows the *future* of the business.'

'You didn't fall for her, Uncle Andy, did you?'

'It is in my makeup,' Rubenoff replied, enigmatically, 'to be capable of admiring a beautiful woman without desiring her.'

'How did Irina learn so much about the future of the business?'

'Apparently she made one-reelers in Russia. Much as your bride does when she is not shooting her Picture World newsreels for the ghastly Whiteway.'

'But how did a Russian moving picture director learn about distribution and exhibition?'

Rubenoff smiled. 'You're your father's son, young Isaac. Always to the core.' Then he turned very serious, and Isaac Bell was reminded that Rubenoff had earned several fortunes since landing as an immigrant and appeared to be on the road to another. 'It seems to me that Irina Viorets learned about distribution and exhibition by listening carefully to someone who has manipulated a modern corporation to control the entire chain of production and marketing from top to bottom.'

'Like who?'

'Andrew Carnegie pretty much invented modern vertical integration.'

'Assuming the young lady did not sit on the old philanthropist's knee, who else? Any Germans?'

'Germans? Krupp has pretty much written the book on German vertical integration.'

'What about Krieg Rüstungswerk?'

'If not quite so large as Krupp, Krieg is better connected in the kaiser's circle. But wherever the lady absorbed her ideas, she has a clear understanding that the future of moving pictures belongs to those who control every aspect, from hiring actors to projecting the finished product in the theater – only then can we guarantee a place to see our product, and a product to see in our place.'

'Sounds like you're working at vertical integration, too, Uncle Andy.'

'From your lips to God's ear, young Isaac. But don't go blabbing it about.'

'Will you keep digging into who's behind her?'

'I've already begun inquiries,' Rubenoff replied.

'Quiet as a church,' the Van Dorn Protective Services operatives reported whenever Bell dropped by the Imperial Building laboratory where Clyde Lynds was hard at work. 'He's at it from breakfast to supper, and sometimes half the night. The man works hard as a nailer.'

'Have you seen anyone hanging around?'

'No. It's just him and us and Clyde's helpers – and you know we looked at them real close.'

'No shadows on the way home?'

'No, sir, Mr Bell. None coming in either. And the boys watching the house haven't seen a soul who looked like trouble. Do you think maybe they just gave up and packed it in?'

'I would be very surprised,' said Bell. 'Keep on your toes. And remember, the hardest part of guarding a fellow is that the attack can come anytime, night or day.'

Privately, however, Bell had to wonder. Had Krieg given up? Or were they laying back, reasoning that once he was set up in a laboratory, Clyde Lynds wasn't going anywhere until he had finished the machine, in which event they had him just where they wanted him?

28

Joseph Van Dorn arrived on the train, unexpectedly.

Isaac Bell saw by his expression that the boss doubted that his chief investigator was on the right course, although Van Dorn's opening salvo was uncharacteristically mild and somewhat oblique.

'Our friends at Dagget, Staples and Hitchcock are alarmed by inquiries from disreputable types.'

'What sort of disreputable types?'

'Some furrier and his cousin in the glove trade marched in big as day demanding to borrow money to build a plant for the manufacture of motion pictures. Thanks to your bankrolling masquerade, word's getting around the film folk that Dagget has money to lend.'

'Are you sure they weren't Krieg agents onto us?'

'I looked into them, of course. But they appear legitimate.'

'Legitimately disreputable?' Bell asked with a smile.

'That's what I just said: a furrier and a glover. How's Clyde making out with the machine?'

'He's making progress. Seems excited by a scheme to photograph the sound directly onto the movie film.'

'I hope he makes progress faster. Guarding a man night and day does not come cheap.'

'How did you make out with the German ambassador?' Bell asked.

'We danced around each other, me pretending I was merely curious about Army officers serving as consular attachés, the ambassador pretending not to wonder why I was pretending mere curiosity. I left the Cosmos Club with the distinct impression that he hasn't a clue what his consuls are up to, much less the German Army. Nor does he want to.'

'In other words, the consuls do the dirty work.'

'As I told you in Washington.'

'So nothing new from the ambassador.'

Van Dorn sighed. 'Look here, Isaac, is it possible Krieg and company have thrown in the towel?'

'No. They're biding their time.'

'Until when?'

'Until Clyde gets closer to finishing.'

'That could be years!' Van Dorn exploded. '"Several years." Clyde's own words.'

'I doubt they'll hold off that long. For now, he's working on the machine and they can wait until he's made enough progress so they'll know it really works.'

'How will they know? You've forted him up. He's surrounded with costly detectives, night and day, in the laboratory, home in bed, and the quick-march in between.'

'All they need is one spy in the Imperial Building, watching and reporting back. There are scores of employees within range of Clyde's laboratory. It would only take one to keep an eye on him – an otherwise legitimate technical fellow or a mechanician.'

'If that's the case, then Clyde Lynds is safe while he works on his machine.'

'*Temporarily* safe,' retorted Isaac Bell. 'Each time they've tried to lay hands on him it was clear they intended to take him back to Germany, where they're ready to put him to work making the machine. Now we've put him to work, so right now they're watching and waiting. What will trigger their next attempt will either be movement ahead on Clyde's part, or us lowering our guard.'

'It is very hard to keep your guard up for a long time, Isaac.'

'That is why I am investigating what Krieg Rüstungswerk is up to in America. When we find out what and put a stop to it, Clyde and the talking machine will be free and clear.'

Van Dorn sighed again. 'What if all they are "up to in America" is grabbing Clyde and his machine? It's the machine they want. If you hadn't stopped them on the ship, they'd be happily holed up in some Prussian castle while Clyde and Beiderbecke tinkered away with guns to their heads. The first the world would know was when the Germans showed talking pictures.'

'The Germans were here already,' said Bell.

'Here? What do you mean?'

'Here in America, long before I broke up the kidnapping.'

'What makes you say that?'

'Look at the operation to grab Clyde off the Limited. Back in Chicago they smuggled the Acrobat into the express car. Only thirty-six hours later in New Mexico, *halfway across the continent*, they wrecked the train and had horsemen and mounts positioned to spirit Clyde across the Mexican border and onto a train. Five to one, they had a ship waiting in Veracruz. And they organized the entire operation in the few short days after Clyde gave their Marzipan Boys the slip in New York. Don't you see, Joe? This is a gigantic outfit with a continental reach. I'll bet you *ten to one*, Krieg secretly owns American factories, farms, ranches, and hotels where their agents hole up.'

In dead silence, and in movements so lithe he seemed to flow like oil, Christian Semmler roamed up and down a stairwell concealed in the center of the Imperial Building. The hidden shaft let him enter every floor from the sub-cellar to the roof. He could watch, unseen, seeing everything. On the penthouse story, he pressed his eye to a spy hole. The cinematography stage camera operator was photographing a scene of a couple kissing good-bye in their parlor as the man went off to war.

Semmler descended three floors to watch Irina Viorets busy at her desk, female stenographers on either side, a runner hurrying notes to a telegrapher tapping in a far corner, and the telephone pressed to her ear. Though the walls that encased his secret stairwell were thick, he fancied he smelled her perfume.

Floor by floor he descended, peering through spy holes at scene shops, carpenters, and seamstresses, ranks of darkroom chemists laboring under red lights, films being loaded into canisters. He stopped to watch an entire ten-minute reel of film being presented to Imperial Company salesmen, who would take it to the exhibitors and distributors around America. All was up-to-date, all the latest way of doing things, with one glaring exception: the sound-recording studio on the fourth floor.

Christian Semmler surveyed the recording studio with

a knowledgeable eye. It was antiquated – even though the equipment was the latest available – because words and music were recorded here as feebly as they had been when Edison and his competitors first tinkered with phonographs and gramophones thirty years ago. Grim proof of *how* antiquated was the makeup of the band of trumpets, clarinets, and saxophones playing into an acoustical horn. Where were the violins? Where was the double bass? Where was the piano? Where was the tympani? Nowhere! None of those instruments could be recorded faithfully. The saxophone played for the string bass. The clarinet was supposed to fill in for the violins. Banjos attempted to keep the beat. The untutored listener of the recorded wax disc would assume that the piano had never been invented.

General Major Semmler climbed back up to the eighth floor for another look at the one man who could change that. He watched through the spy hole as Clyde Lynds's eager assistants scurried. He saw that Lynds had had a cot moved in so he could work long nights. Semmler grunted approval at the sight. The scientist who was key to surmounting the shortcomings on the fourth floor was what Fritz Wunderlich's drummer friends applauded as a 'live wire'. Lynds was working, Semmler thought with a cold smile, just as hard as if he were locked in a Prussian dungeon with a gun to his head.

Semmler glided up the stairs to his lair on the ninth floor, confident that he had Clyde Lynds exactly where he needed him to save Germany from the fatal flaw of *Der Tag*. And, despite Isaac Bell's repeated interference, the grand scheme of the Donar Plan was unfolding as it was destined to.

General Major Christian Semmler had soldiered abroad. Fighting in China and Africa, he had seen firsthand foreigners' weaknesses and their strengths, and he knew better than any other officer in the kaiser's army that Germany could never survive a war against all the world at once.

The Donar Plan – Semmler's strategy to save Germany – had sprung to life in a rainstorm at Katrinahall, the hunting lodge on the Rominter Heath that was the jewel of his wife's dowry. Kaiser Wilhelm II had come to shoot wild boar. A royal visit was a singular honor that aristocrats vied for at court. Semmler had stocked the estate with that in mind, but in fact the kaiser had always cast a warm eye on his youngest general major. He called Semmler a man's man and a soldier's soldier, and he chortled over rumors of deadly duels at school and reports of savage battles in Peking and with the Boers behind the English lines.

Semmler suspected another reason for His Majesty's favor. He was acutely aware of his long arms and simian brows. He knew that 'gorilla' or 'monkey' looks would have doomed an ordinary soldier to a stagnant career in an army that revered the handsome features that epitomized superior races and ridiculed the ugly. But the kaiser's own appearance was blighted by a birth defect – a withered arm that hung from his shoulder like a toy doll's. Perhaps two refugees from the mirror felt a kinship?

When they were driven indoors by the rain, Semmler invited the kaiser into his library and entertained him by projecting films of galloping cavalry, armored trains, the new flying machines, and the ocean-churning dreadnoughts of Wilhelm's beloved High Seas Fleet.

'Behold, Your Majesty, the newest weapon of all.'

The kaiser squinted at the screen. 'Where is it?'

'The *movies* are a weapon, Your Majesty.'

'I don't understand.'

'You know that the superior classes have always enjoyed theater and opera.'

'As they should.'

'The movies are an even bigger event in the lives of the workers. Millions crowd into *Kintopp*s and tenement cinemas. They watch whatever appears on the screen. *Mesmerized.* Imagine millions upon millions assembled daily to watch the same thing – wanting to be mesmerized; *hoping* to be mesmerized. They are ripe for propaganda.'

'Propaganda?' The kaiser had frowned. 'They boast in England that movies are a propaganda of *democracy*.'

'Movies are even better propaganda for love and hate, Your Majesty. Friendship and war. There are millions watching. They could watch your message.'

'What message, General Major?'

Christian Semmler stood face-to-face with Kaiser Wilhelm and said, 'Friendship.'

'*Friendship?* . . .'

Semmler took a deep breath to remind himself that patience was the hunter's deadliest virtue. He smothered his impulse to grip the kaiser by his shirtfront and shout that if propaganda could convince the German people to pay for a fleet of warships they didn't need, propaganda could convince anyone of anything. But he could not shout that in so many words without instantly destroying his special rapport.

'With all the respect due the power of your splendid armies, Majesty, and your navy, when *Der Tag* dawns we will almost certainly have to fight England, France, and Russia simultaneously.'

'We will win,' the kaiser said. 'Our rail lines will shuttle our armies from front to front, east to west, west to east. A two-front war holds no terrors.'

'To be sure, Your Majesty. But *three* fronts? Even Germany will be hard-pressed to fight on three fronts simultaneously . . .'

'America.'

'As you say, Your Majesty. America.'

It finally dawned on the kaiser. 'Allies!'

'Allies, Your Majesty. The movies can defeat Germany's enemies by turning them against one another. We will show *propaganda* movies that depict Germans and the immense German-American minority as America's friends and the British, French, and Russians as her enemies. Can you imagine a more powerful weapon? Germany, their friend, and England, their enemy.'

The kaiser had looked at him sharply. 'You've put great thought into this, haven't you? This didn't just pop into your mind.'

'Yes, Your Majesty. I have thought of little else for a long time. *Der Tag* must be Germany's beginning, not her end.'

Kaiser Wilhelm flung his strong arm around Semmler's shoulders.

'Do it,' he said. 'Take whatever you need.'

'I need the Army, the diplomatic corps, the banks, and the steamship lines.'

'All will serve you.'

Semmler's gifts included an unerring eye for a person's nature and desires. Instead of responding with a soldierly salute, he extended a strong man's hand. They clasped hard and stared each other in the face. 'I swear a sacred oath: I will not let you down, Your Majesty.'

But the kaiser was famously mercurial. Before Semmler could suggest they rejoin the other guns at the hunt since the rain was slackening, the kaiser's face took on a dreamy expression, and he said, with what turned out to be amazing prescience, 'Wouldn't it be fine if movies made music?'

'Music, Your Majesty?'

'Music! So that thousands watching in giant theaters could listen, too, and feel the emotion of the music. Music is key to effective propaganda. Music is visceral.'

'You are right, of course, Your Majesty, I will look into it.'

But there were few orchestras in the small theaters in most American towns. Nor would a tinny piano do much to stir emotions. He investigated the likelihood that movies themselves could make their own music and learned the sorry history of those attempts.

And then the strangest thing happened. Semmler had already set the Donar Plan in motion to show pro-German movies to American audiences. He had established the Imperial Film Manufacturing Company and was integrating exchange men and exhibitors to control film production, distribution, and exhibition when all of a sudden – like a comet roaring through the atmosphere – came news from Vienna of *Sprechendlichtspieltheater*, a talking pictures machine that actually worked.

The kaiser himself had virtually predicted it, and there it was. The invention that Beiderbecke and Lynds had named the Talking Pictures machine would transform movies into far more potent voices to persuade, cajole, and play on the emotions. Music and the human voice married to moving images would stir millions to go to war in the name of love.

Arthur Curtis got to the *Kintopp* an hour early for his appointment with Hans Reuter. The *Kino* was full already with a hundred film patrons in the narrow space, both men and women tonight, watching Sarah Bernhardt. He took his beer and wandered toward the screen, simulating a search for a closer seat while he looked for a back way out. There was none – which would make a fire a precarious proposition, and the effect of Reuter betraying him even worse.

The safer move would be to stay out of the *Kino* and nurse his beer at the bar. With an unpleasant premonition gnawing at him, Curtis emerged from the darkened theater and took a place at the bar. At six forty-five, a carpenter with his toolbox in hand and sawdust on his overalls came in, ordered beer, and drank it slowly, ignoring the entrance to the *Kino* and glancing occasionally at the street door, as if waiting for a friend. Arthur Curtis studied the man intently. The premonition grew sharp, but it took him too long to isolate the source.

The sawdust was what troubled him, he realized at last. German workmen were precise. They swept up at the end of every day. They would never step out in public covered in sawdust, even hurrying home from work, and this one wasn't hurrying. He was barely touching his stein to his lips.

Art Curtis downed his beer, nodded a casual farewell to the barmaid, and pushed through the front doors into the street. He breathed in the evening air and glanced around the bustling neighborhood of shops and tenements.

As luck would have it, Hans Reuter was early. He was walking fast, his head down, either unconcerned that he was being followed or hoping like an ostrich that what he couldn't see couldn't hurt him.

Curtis made a lightning decision and took a huge chance that his initial glance at the street had correctly picked up no shadows.

Reuter flinched as Art Curtis took his arm.

'Let's walk, instead.'

'Why?' asked Reuter. But his hunger for the money gave him no choice but to let Curtis set their course.

'We can transact our business in half a minute. Give me the name. I'll give you the money, and we can go our separate ways.' *Run* our separate ways was what he meant – in his case, straight to the French border, the hell with the office. But telling Reuter they were under observation was no way to make him take a chance.

'His *name?*'

'They call him "the Monkey."'

Isaac Bell had called him an acrobat. 'What's his real name?'

'I don't know.'

'I don't pay for "I don't know",' Curtis shot back, scanning the street ahead and behind. He saw workmen homeward bound, shoppers with groceries, couples holding hands converging on the *Kintopp*. Oddly, there were no cops.

'He's an Army officer.'

'That much I knew already.'

'You didn't know he was a *general major*,' Reuter replied smugly.

'His rank means nothing without a name,' Curtis lied. If it was true, such a high rank would narrow the possibilities to a handful.

'Would you accept a description?' Reuter asked.

'It'd better be precise.'

They were passing under a streetlamp and Curtis got a good look at Reuter's face. A confident expression matched his smug tone as he said, 'Thirty-five years old, medium height, powerful frame, blond hair, green eyes, long arms like a monkey.'

Thirty-five was unusually young for a general major in the German Army. But the rest of the description was too incongruous to be a lie.

'If you can tell me that, you know his name. There can't be two officers his age who look like that. No name, no money.'

Two men gliding toward them on bicycles took PO8 Luger pistols from the baskets attached to their handlebars, and behind him Arthur Curtis heard the carpenter burst out of the *Kintopp* and drop his toolbox.

29

Hans Reuter ran.

The bicyclists shot him down. He tumbled into the gutter. Pedestrians screamed, dove to the cobblestones, and bolted into shops. Art Curtis had already pulled his Browning. He whirled around and dropped the carpenter with a lucky shot to the chest, then spun back around and fired twice, wounding the nearest bicyclist. The man he missed returned his fire.

Art Curtis felt the hammer blow of a 9mm slug and found himself suddenly on his back, staring up at the darkening sky. If anyone had shouted *Polizei!*, he might have stayed on the ground. But no one did, and the men on the bicycles had Army pistols, and the cops had been ordered out of the neighborhood. That meant they'd been sent to kill him, which gave him the fear-driven strength to stagger to his feet. The man who had shot him looked surprised, raised his pistol, and took deliberate aim.

The Van Dorn detective did not waste precious time aiming at a target six feet away. He triggered his Browning, jumped over the body, and ran.

'You're white as a ghost, my friend,' exclaimed the old Army sergeant when Arthur Curtis collapsed onto the bentwood chair beside him.

'Too much schnapps last night.'

He kept telling himself it was only a shoulder wound, except he could feel in his lungs that the bullet, which was still lodged inside him, had done greater damage. At least it hadn't broken any bones, and for some reason there was no blood on his coat, just a tiny hole that a moth could have eaten. But it hurt to breathe and his head was spinning, and the walk to the sergeant's beer garden had nearly killed him.

'Good German lager will fix that! Waitress! Beer for my friend.'

Arthur Curtis rested until the beer arrived, tipped the stein toward the old man, and asked, through gritted teeth, 'Do you recall before you retired a general major nicknamed "Monkey"?'

The old sergeant shook his head. 'No.'

'I heard it the other day. It's such a strange nickname for a high-serving officer.'

'Well, he wasn't so high then.'

'*What?* I mean, what do you mean he wasn't so high then? Who?'

'I retired, what was it . . . six years ago? He was only a colonel, a very young colonel. What a man! What a soldier! You've never seen a fighter like him. They say he resigned his commission to fight in Africa. A guerrilla fighter with the Boer commandos.'

'Did you know him?'

'Me? A sergeant from Berlin know a Prussian aristocrat? What could you be thinking, my friend?'

Curtis gripped the table to right himself as a sudden burst of pain nearly knocked him off his chair. He put all his might into composing his voice. 'I meant, did you serve under him?'

'I only knew him by reputation. He was admired. Still is, I'm sure.'

'Why did they call him Monkey?'

'Not to his face,' the sergeant chuckled. '*Mein Gott*, Colonel Semmler would have sliced their ears off and made them eat them.'

'Semmler . . . But why did they call him "Monkey"?'

'He looked like one. Enormous arms and big brows like a monkey.' The sergeant glanced about and lowered his voice. 'Not quite the picture of the purebred Prussian aristocrat, if you know what I mean. More the sturdy peasant, like me.'

'I thought Semmler was a Prussian name?'

'Of course. And they said he's a Roth, too – buckets of superior Prussian blood, if not the superior shape. My friend, are you all right? You look at death's door.'

'What is his first name?'

'Christian.'

Arthur Curtis gathered his spirit in an effort to stand.

'I am thinking it is more than the schnapps. Bad oysters. I had a dozen at lunch. Perhaps . . . I better go – here, let me pay.'

'No, no, my friend. You always pay. You hardly touched your beer. I'll pay and finish it for you. You go home and get to bed.'

The telegraph offices in the main railroad stations were open all night. He would cable Semmler's name and description to Isaac Bell, care of the New York office, and just to be sure he would also wire it to the Van Dorn field office in Paris. He headed for the nearest station, hoping that his lurching pace would not draw attention on the well-lit streets. He paused just inside the main entrance to check in a kiosk mirror that no blood showed on his coat, and as he did, he saw across the vast hall that the police were checking the papers of the men lined up at the telegraph office. They'd be doing the same at every office open all night and, he realized with a touch of panic, at the hospitals, too. And as the night wore on and the streets and bars and restaurants emptied, they would stop any man still about.

The French border, four hundred and fifty miles west, was a fantasy. He could barely walk. Nor could he go home to his *Pension*. It was filled with busybody boarders and a nosy dragon of a landlady. Anyone who saw him in the lighted foyer would report his condition. Kicking himself for not trading the convenience of the boarding house for the privacy of a furnished apartment, and with panic rising, Arthur Curtis convinced himself that he could hole up in his office. There he could rest, regain his strength, and then light out for the border in the morning – or maybe the North Sea coast. A million and a half people lived in Berlin, and when they all rushed to work in the morning the railroad stations would be too crowded for the police to check everyone. Concentrating on placing one foot after another, he headed for the tram. They stopped running at eleven. He had time. He pulled himself aboard with a herculean effort, staggered off at his stop, managing not to fall, and walked toward his office.

A man in a macintosh was standing across the street.

Art Curtis reached deep into his pocket and closed his hand around his Browning, which had a round in the chamber and two left in the magazine. He looked for the man's partner and spotted him in a doorway. He veered off the sidewalk into the street, drawing both from their cover. They exchanged looks and moved quickly. He let them come close. When they drew their weapons – Army Lugers again – he fired twice through the cloth of his coat, dropped both men, and staggered into his building. He hauled himself up the steps, fumbled his key into his lock, pushed inside, and locked the door, wondering whether he still had the strength in his hands to reload. There'd be more of them coming any minute.

The desk lamp flared on, and he whirled to fire his last bullet.

'What happened?' asked Pauline. Her eyes were clouded with sleep, her face creased where she had rested her cheek on her sleeve.

30

'Nothing. Go home. Go on. Get out of here!'

'I'm sorry. I was doing my homework, and I fell asleep. I can't go home, my mother's friend –'

'Get out of here!' Curtis roared. The girl flinched and tears of hurt filled her eyes. Curtis started coughing. He pressed his hand to his mouth, and it came away full of blood.

'Oh my God,' she whispered. 'You've been shot.'

'Turn out the light.'

She did, instantly. 'Are they coming?'

'Soon,' he said. 'Get out. Use the window.'

She had jumped up from the chair and was standing behind his desk. He could see her silhouetted against the light in the alley. She stood stock-still.

'Quickly,' he urged. 'Get away.'

'I can't leave you like this.'

'Go!'

'Come with me.'

'I wish I could. I can't move another step, much less climb down that ladder. Go. Please go before they come.'

'I can't leave you.'

'They'll kill you, Pauline.'

She rummaged in her book bag and pulled something out. He heard the sharp click of a hammer cocking.

'What the devil is that?'

'I bought a gun.'

Arthur Curtis felt a part of himself die. This silly child, he thought, is going to stay here like I'm Sherlock Holmes and die with me, and I cannot think of a worse way for a man to leave this earth than drag a child with him.

There was only one way to get her to leave.

'Give that to me!'

She handed it over, butt first. It was a little revolver. He could feel rust on the trigger guard.

'Draw the window shade. Stand to one side as you do it. Good. OK, now. Bend the desk lamp down until it just lights the desk. Turn it on.'

It cast a dim glow.

'Let me sit there.' He lurched to the desk and sank into his chair. He shoved her pistol aside, drew his own from his coat, and laid it on the desk. 'Watch this.'

He removed the magazine and the cartridge from the chamber and took the slide and return spring from the barrel. He swabbed the parts clean with a rag he took from the cleaning kit in his desk. Then he reassembled the pistol, inserted a fresh magazine, and shoved it toward her. 'Now you do it.'

Pauline mimicked the field stripping of the little Browning, step by step. Curtis was not surprised. She was as sharp a cookie as he had ever met.

'Good. Remember, always check there's no bullet in the chamber, or you'll blow your head off by mistake. OK. Pick it up. Here's how you cock it.'

He guided her hands and saw to his relief that she was strong enough to move the slide and chamber a round. 'You have small hands, like me. It fits you fine. Keep it clean. Here's a spare clip.' He took it from the drawer. 'OK. You got fourteen bullets.'

'You're giving me your gun?'

'If anyone ever tries to take it away from you – they will, because you look like a little girl – here's what you do. You point the gun at his face. And then you look through him, like he's not there. Like you can't see him, like he's made of glass. Then he'll believe you're willing to kill him. Understand?'

She nodded solemnly.

'Still want to be a detective?'

'More than anything.'

'Starting this minute, you are a Van Dorn apprentice detective. Here's your first assignment: report to the Van Dorn field office in Paris.'

'Paris?'

'On the Rue du Bac. My old pal Horace Bronson ramrods it. He'll take care of you. He's a top man. Used to run the San Francisco office. Here. Here's money, you'll need it.' He emptied the notes from his billfold and coins from his pockets into her hands. Then he yanked open another desk drawer. 'And here's some French francs. Tell Mr Bronson you have a message for Van Dorn's chief investigator in America . . .' He tried to catch his breath. It was getting hard to get wind into his lungs.

'The message is: "Krieg Rüstungswerk GmbH's agent in America is an Imperial Army general major named Christian Semmler." Repeat that!'

Pauline repeated it word for word.

'Second half of the message: "Semmler is nicknamed 'Monkey'. He's thirty-five years old, medium height, powerful frame, blond hair, green eyes, long arms. Like a monkey." Repeat that!'

She did.

'Now get out of here.'

'But I can't you leave you.'

'A Van Dorn apprentice always obeys orders.' He clasped her face between his trembling hands and glared into her eyes. 'This is vital, Pauline. You are the only one who can solve this case and save men's lives. Go. Please, go.'

He pushed her away.

Biting her lips, Pauline put on her coat and hat and pocketed the Browning. Curtis turned out the light. To his immense relief, he heard her open the back window. He heard the fire ladder rungs creak. He listened for her footsteps in the alley, but instead heard boots pounding up the stairs.

Arthur Curtis picked up Pauline's rusted revolver and aimed it at the door, hoping it wouldn't blow up in his hand. Not that that would make much difference. But the longer he could hold them off, the farther she could run.

'Cablegram from Paris, Mr Bell.'

Bell took it with an amused smile. The Van Dorn apprentice detective who had delivered the cablegram, a slender youth in immaculate white shirt and trousers and a lavender bow tie, was aping the sartorial magnificence that the Van Dorn Los Angeles field office was famous for. All he was missing was a lavender bowler, for which he was probably banking his salary.

'Wait for my reply, please.'
Isaac Bell slit the envelope:

GERMAN POLICE REPORT ART CURTIS SHOT DEAD.
I'VE SENT MAN TO BERLIN FOR PARTICULARS.
BRONSON

31

'What's your reply, Mr Bell?'

Isaac Bell heard the apprentice as if he were calling from a rooftop. When he turned to him, the boy flinched from his raging eyes.

'Reply, sir?' he repeated bravely.

'Cable this:

    RETURN BODY DENVER.
    MY EXPENSE.
    BELL

'Write it down, son.' The tall detective turned away to hide his grief.

The boy patted his empty pockets in sudden panic.

Bell said, 'Son, never go anywhere without a pencil. If you're going to become a detective, you have to write down your thoughts and observations. What's your name?'

'Apprentice Detective Adams, sir. Mike Adams.'

'Here, Mike, use mine.' Bell lent him his pencil and gave him a sheet of paper from the desk he had commandeered.

Apprentice Adams wrote the message, read it back, and ran.

Isaac Bell turned to the window and stared down at busy First Street, barely seeing the parade of streetcars, autos, trucks, wagons, and a squad of helmeted police on bicycles.

Joe Van Dorn pushed into the office without knocking.

'I just heard. I'm sorry, Isaac. I know you liked him.'

Bell said, 'The evidence of the Acrobat's ruthlessness was right before my eyes. I saw him throw his own man into the sea to conceal his identity. What made me think he wouldn't murder Art Curtis for the same reason?'

Joseph Van Dorn shook his head emphatically. 'I saw Art once in a gunfight. Most men lose perspective when the lead starts flying. Not Art.'

'I appreciate the thought, Joe. I know Art could handle himself. Nonetheless, he was working for me.'

Van Dorn said, 'You are, of course, authorized to pull out all stops until we get who did it.'

'Thank you.'

'Until Bronson learns otherwise in Berlin, we have to presume he was gunned down by Krieg.'

'Or the German Army.'

'Don't you wonder what he learned that got him killed?' Van Dorn marveled.

'He learned a name,' said Bell.

'How do you know?'

'He cabled me the day before yesterday asking for more money. He said we'd have the money back – or a name – in two days.'

'What did you cable back?'

'"Blank check."'

'Well, if he got the name, he took it to his grave.'

'I'm afraid so,' said Bell.

'Now what?' asked Van Dorn.

'Short of a lucky break walking in that door,' said Isaac Bell, 'I'm starting from scratch.'

There was a knock at the door. The front-desk man, wearing a scarlet vest and matching shoulder holster, called, 'Mr Bell – Oh, there you are, Mr Van Dorn. Police chief's phoning from Levy's Cafe, wondering what happened to you?'

Van Dorn tugged out his watch. 'Telephone the restaurant I'll be there in ten minutes. Lunch with the chief,' he explained to Bell and rushed out, saying, 'Then I'm on the Limited to Chicago. Keep me posted.'

'Mr Bell, there's a fellow to see you. Hebrew gent. Has one of those funny caps on his head.'

'It's called a yarmulke. Send him in.'

Andrew Rubenoff marched in smiling, but when he saw Bell standing by the window, his smile faded. 'You do not look well, Isaac.'

'Lost a friend,' Bell answered tersely. 'What have you learned?'

The newly minted film-manufacturing banker went straight to the purpose of his visit.

'To my great relief,' he said, 'the so-called Artists Syndicate does not exist.'

'What do you mean?'

'I mean that a syndicate that I knew nothing about, but thought I should, is a sham. It exists only on paper. Its supposed Wall Street investors are ghosts.'

'Are you sure?'

'Positive.'

'Then who paid for Imperial Film's ten-story building?'

'I don't know yet. But it was not the Artists Syndicate.'

'Someone funneled a lot of money into Imperial.'

'To be sure. But so far Wall Street has greeted my questions about who that someone might be with a wall of silence.'

'Are the Wall Streeters protecting Imperial?'

'No, no, no. Imperial's money almost certainly comes from someplace other than Wall Street. Abroad, I suspect.'

'Germany?'

'Perhaps. But English bankers are our biggest source of foreign funds. They invest in American railroads and ranches and ore mines. Why not moving pictures?'

'And the Germans?'

'Obviously, your first interest in this is the Germans. We shall see. Not to worry, I'm just getting started.'

'I'll have our Research people nose around that, too.'

Rubenoff smiled modestly. 'I'm sure that the Van Dorn Research department will be . . . helpful.'

'How did you find out so quickly that there's no Wall Street interests in the Artists Syndicate?'

'Isaac! You are talking to Andrew Rubenoff. When the Messiah comes, he'll ask me to recommend a stockbroker.' He sobered quickly. 'I don't mean to offer false hope. Wall Street was easy. Abroad is much more complicated. I've already started, but I can't deliver such fast results.'

Bell heard the clatter of a troop of horsemen in the street, not a usual sound in downtown Los Angeles. He looked down from the window again. Twenty actors dressed as cowboys in white hats and bare-chested, war-painted Indians were trotting by, bound, it appeared, for picture taking in nearby Elysian Park. He watched them pass, his brow furrowed in thought. Then he picked up the Kellogg intercommunicating telephone.

'Send an apprentice.'

One came instantly. It was the kid wearing the lavender bow tie. 'Mike, transmit a wire on the private line to Texas Walt Hatfield. The Houston office will know where to find him.'

The kid whipped out pad and pencil. 'Yes, sir, Mr Bell. What's the message?'

> COME LA.
> SEEK EMPLOYMENT WITH IMPERIAL FILM AS
> COWBOY PLAYER.

'Go on, Mike. That's all.'

'Should I sign it "BELL"?'

'Sign it "ISAAC".'

Mike Adams ran out.

Andrew Rubenoff raised an inquiring eyebrow.

Bell said, 'Walt Hatfield rode with the Texas Rangers before he joined Van Dorn. He'll make a believable cowboy looking for work as an extra in Wild West dramas. Heck, they might make him a Western star. He looks like he was carved from cactus.'

'I presume that Texas Walt is an old friend?'

'What makes you say that?'

'Sometimes we need an old friend on the premises.'

'Maybe so. But what I need most is a crackerjack detective inside Imperial Film.'

'What can one detective do? Imperial is an enormous company with four hundred hands.'

'He won't be the only one.'

Bell wired Grady Forrer on the Van Dorn private telegraph, inquiring what progress he had made with Imperial's bankers.

The redoubtable head of the Research department wired back:

> MY BOYS ARE DIGGING DEEP.
> REMEMBER BANKS LIKE SECRETS.
> HOPEFUL MORE SOON.
> SORRY ABOUT ART. GOOD MAN.

Isaac Bell replied:

> CONCENTRATE GERMAN OVERSEAS MERCHANT
> BANKS WITH ARMY TIES. LOOK FOR KRIEG-IMPERIAL
> CONNECTION.

32

Pauline Grandzau woke up in a haystack with four tines of a pitchfork inches from her face. The steel was shiny from use and recently sharpened. Three of the tines tapered to a needle point. The fourth was bent as if the farmer had accidently hit a rock shortly before finding her in his hay.

She asked herself, What is the best thing possible at this moment?

The best thing was that her disguise worked. She didn't look like a girl. She looked like a boy, a tough Berlin factory boy in a cloth cap and a rough woolen jacket and trousers. She had traded her dress, her coat, and her beautiful hat last night with her friend Hilda for Hilda's brother's things. Five groschen from the marks Detective Curtis gave her had bought the brother's rucksack. It held dry socks, a wool jumper, an apple and biscuits (which she had already eaten), a *Strand* magazine, a map of France and Baedeker's *Paris and Its Environs* purchased in a railroad station, and Detective Curtis's gun.

Best of all, her disguise worked so well that the farmer was frightened. The haystack was behind his barn. There was a dense wood across the field, and beyond the wood were the railroad tracks, which brought tramps and gypsies and troublemakers from Berlin.

Pauline asked herself, now what? What would Sherlock

Holmes do when his disguise worked? She forced her voice low and in guttural tones asked, 'Why are you pointing your pitchfork at me?'

'Who are you?' asked the farmer. What would Sherlock Holmes do? The answer: Sherlock Holmes would observe *everything*, not just the steel tines in her face. The farmer was young, she saw. This was not the farmer, but the farmer's son.

'Who are *you*?' she demanded. 'Why are you pointing that at me? What kind of German are you? Have you no shame?'

The boy blinked. 'But what are you doing here?'

'I won't tell until you move that thing away from my face.'

He lowered the pitchfork.

Pauline climbed to her feet, taking her time, observing. His legs were short. Hers were longer. She could run faster. She saw a bulge in his jacket and white cloth poking from his pocket. It was a bundle a mother would pack. 'I'm hungry,' she growled. 'Do you have food?'

He pulled it from his pocket, and she smelled ham. It was wrapped in a piece of buttered bread. She bit hungrily into it, two enormous, delicious bites.

'Hans!' a man shouted. 'What are you doing there?'

It could only be Hans's father. And he would not be fooled.

She ran for the wood through which she had felt her way from the railroad. It was still dark, and the train she was clinging to had suddenly rumbled through a switch and stopped on a siding, shorn of its locomotive, which then had steamed back toward Berlin.

She heard the farmers shouting behind her. 'Catch him!' the father yelled. Hans was scampering as fast as he could on his short legs, and the father was limping on a cane.

Ahead through the trees Pauline saw the siding and on it the single railcar on which she had escaped from Berlin, but which the train had dropped. She ran past it and jumped onto the main line. Then she ran on the crossties until her legs ached and her lungs were burning and the blood was pounding in her head so loudly that she couldn't hear the speeding train behind her.

In Griffith Park, a wilderness in the hills north of Los Angeles, Jay Tarses complained to the petite dark-haired woman who served as his mistress and business manager, 'I want to go back to New Jersey.'

'Jersey? Are you nuts? Best thing we ever did was beat it to California. It's beautiful here. The sun has shined all day. You've already exposed eight hundred feet of film. You'll finish the whole picture before dark. And tomorrow you'll start a Western drama.'

'This is the worst day of my life.'

The City of Los Angeles had just fined Tarses twenty-five dollars because gunfire between his French Foreign Legionnaires and his Arabs abducting his heroine had frightened the elk in Griffith Park. Then his camels had stampeded a herd of horses that were not used to their smell. And now, just as his wranglers had finished rounding up the horses so he could start taking pictures again, a squad of Edison thugs piled out of a Marmon auto, itching to pull out their blackjacks if he wasn't taking pictures with an overpriced Edison camera.

The head thug, a rangy street fighter with bony fists and a Hoboken accent, saw at a glance that he wasn't.

'You think California's so far from Joisey Mr Edison don't notice?'

'Let the girls go,' Tarses told him. 'I'll take my lumps.'

'You're all takin' yer lumps this time. We're setting an example for the rest of youse independents.'

He grabbed Tarses by his lapels and held him stiff-armed for the first blow.

'Hold it!' someone shouted.

If Jay Tarses had any hope he'd been rescued, the sight of chief Edison bull Joe McCoy swaggering out of the woods disabused him of that. McCoy, the meanest Edison detective Tarses had even met, reported directly to Mr Dyer, Edison's lawyer, who enforced Trust restrictions with an iron hand. McCoy had a coal trimmer's shoulders and less mercy in his face than a cinder block.

'Mr Tarses,' he snickered. 'I would have recognized your picture taking anywhere by the camel stink.'

'Any chance of buying you off?' asked Tarses, his eyes locked on McCoy's blackjack.

McCoy raised a mighty arm. The blackjack whistled as it tore down from the sky, and the Edison thug holding Tarses by the lapels went flying sideways into a camel and fell on his face. Tarses was vaguely aware that he himself was still on his feet and nothing hurt. Aside from that, he had no idea what was going on.

McCoy handed him a calling card. Through a smudge of blood from McCoy's blackjack, Jay Tarses read:

IMPERIAL FILM PROTECTION SERVICE
'THE INDEPENDENT'S FRIEND'

'Telephone number's on the back. Operator on-station night and day.'

'You don't work for Edison anymore?' Tarses asked.

'Didn't you hear?' McCoy grinned. 'I'm a trustbuster. Just like Teddy Roosevelt.'

'What the hell is Imperial Film Protection Service?'

'"The Independent's Friend." Can't you read?'

'Friend? I'll bet. What's it going to cost me?'

'Nothing.'

'Come on, Joe. What's the big idea?'

McCoy threw a heavy arm around Tarses's shoulder. 'Jay, don't look a gift horse in the mouth. And stop asking stupid questions.'

Tarses knew he had his share of flaws, but stupidity wasn't one of them, and he said, 'Thanks, Joe.'

'Don't thank me. Thank Imperial. Well, sun's in the sky. Bet you're itching to get back to work – Say, what's your picture called?'

'The Imperial Horseman.'

McCoy tipped his hat to Tarses's pretty business manager, slung the unconscious thug over his shoulder, and carried him away.

Tarses shouted for his players to climb on their animals. 'Camera . . .'

That evening, when Tarses was paying off his extras, the one last in line drawled, 'Who were those fellers pushing you around?'

Tarses was about to tell him to mind his own business

when he recognized the extra as the tall, barbed-wire-thin cowboy with whom his costume girl had traded a French Foreign Legionnaire kepi for the cowboy's Stetson, with a promise to trade hats again over a glass of wine after work. Tarses had noticed him sitting in his saddle as if born to it, and now, close up, he saw angular bone structure in the cowboy's face that looked ferocious in the light of the setting sun.

'What's your name?'

'Tex.'

'Come back tomorrow, Tex. I'll be taking pictures for a Wild West drama.'

Texas Walt Hatfield sauntered into the Los Angeles field office, cast a withering glance at the front-desk man's fancy duds, and shook howdy with Isaac Bell.

Bell felt the tall Texan flinch.

'What happened to your hand?'

'Busted it falling off my damned horse. Camel spooked him.'

Bell was astonished. There was no finer horseman in the West. 'When's the last time you fell off a horse?'

'Unless you mean shot off,' Texas Walt drawled, 'Ah was three years old, and he hadn't been broke yet.'

'Did you catch up with Joe McCoy?'

'Yup. Like Tarses told me, used to thug for Edison – McCoy called it "engaged by Mr Edison's legal department". Quit or got fired, Ah couldn't tell, came out here, and hired on with Imperial Protection. McCoy claims they've been whupping the heck out of the Edison Boys.'

'I just saw a bunged-up bunch headed back East on the train,' Bell said. 'McCoy have any inkling what Imperial Protection's all about?'

'He's not a talkative feller. Though near as Ah can gather, he himself's on the level.'

'Are they?'

'All I know is they ain't asking for protection money. But if it's not a racket, why is Imperial taking the independents' side in the Trust war? Kindness of their hearts?'

Bell said, 'I suspect that the truth is printed on their calling card.'

'"The Independent's Friend?" How you figure that?'

'If an outfit that distributes and exhibits moving pictures befriends all the independents, they can rent out a lot of films.'

Texas Walt shoved his Stetson back on his head. 'Like the cattle broker buying up every herd at the railhead.'

'And the meat packer in Chicago buying by the train-load. The Independent's Friend could control the distribution and exhibition of all the independents' moving pictures.'

'You're sure they're the same Imperial as the outfit you're tracking?'

Bell nodded emphatically. 'Larry Saunders got the Los Angeles exchange to trace their telephone number back to the Imperial Building.'

'And you're sure Imperial Film's a blind for something else?' Hatfield asked.

'That's what we're going to find out,' said Isaac Bell.

'Reckon you want me to continue riding for Tarses?'

'No. I want you inside that building. They've got cinematography studio stages up in the penthouse. Audition at Imperial to get a job acting inside.'

'Acting jobs ain't all that easy to tie on to, Isaac. There's men and women lined up everywhere they're taking pictures.'

'You have a leg up, Walt. You look like you should be in pictures. And you've already worked in a couple. Get inside Imperial first thing tomorrow.'

Texas Walt hesitated.

'What's wrong?' asked Bell.

'Well, I don't want to leave Tarses in a lurch.'

'Tarses? What does Tarses have to do with the Talking Pictures case?'

Texas Walt scuffed the carpet with his boot. 'Fact is, he's talking about me playing a bigger part.'

'Why don't you ask Mr Van Dorn for a leave of absence?' Bell asked in a quiet, silky manner that Texas Walt Hatfield misinterpreted.

'Think the boss would go for that?'

'After we crack the case.'

Texas Walt worked a deep groove into the carpet. 'Sorry, Isaac. I didn't mean to say I won't take home the gal I brung to the dance.'

'Appreciate it,' said Bell. 'Here's where we stand: I've got the boys watching Clyde on the eighth floor of the Imperial Building; I want you up top in the roof studios. I've seen Mademoiselle Viorets's office on the seventh, and I'm heading now to the fourth floor where they do the recordings.'

'How you fixin' to get in?'

'I already am in.'

The tough nuts in fancy uniforms who guarded the Imperial Building lobby were not exactly friendly toward Isaac Bell, but he had visited Clyde Lynds often enough that they acknowledged a familiar face and greeted him by name.

'Afternoon, Mr Bell,' said the doorman, then spoke sharply to the well-built men crowding behind Bell who were carrying musical cases for horns, saxophones, a clarinet, a violin, and a double bass. 'Wait right there, gents! I'll be with youse in a minute.'

'They're with me,' said Bell.

'All of 'em?'

'Mr Lynds requested a band.'

'Open those cases.'

'Gentlemen,' Bell said mildly, 'they're jumpy here. Show him your instruments.'

Hinged open, the cases revealed shiny trumpets and saxophones, clarinets, a little violin, and an enormous string bass.

'Fourth floor,' Bell told the glowering elevator operator, who glanced for the OK from the chief doorman before delivering them to the fourth floor.

Clyde Lynds was waiting impatiently in the recording room. 'What took so long?'

'Nervous doormen thought the boys were smuggling Gatling guns.'

'Idiots — All right, boys, sit yourselves around that

recording horn. Violin closest, trumpet over there, saxophone and string bass back there.'

'Where you want me?' asked the clarinetist, a nattily dressed wisp of a fellow whom Isaac Bell had last seen in Idaho separating two bank robbers from their shotguns.

Clyde said, 'Stand behind the violin and wait to come in until I tell you.'

The string bass player, most famous at the Van Dorn Detective Agency for infiltrating San Francisco's corrupt police department, blew A on a pitch pipe to start the tuning process.

Clyde said, 'When making acoustic recordings of music, we have to replace the violins with horns and clarinets and reinforce the string bass with a bass saxophone and the drums with banjos. One of my goals is to replace the acoustic mechanical systems invented by Edison. Edison machines can't record strings and drums and can't record piano, which is really just a bunch of strings and drums. It comes out flat and tinny.'

Isaac Bell glanced over his shoulder. He had an eerie sense that someone was watching him. But the only people he saw were Clyde's assistants coming into the room carrying a box trailing wires. While they began attaching the wires to a disc-cutting machine, Bell went to the door and looked out. The corridor was empty, but the feeling persisted that he was under observation.

Clyde's helpers lugged in a wooden box on top of which stood a thick round disc peppered with holes. They placed it next to the horn. 'This is a carbon microphone, like you'll find in a telephone, only much bigger. Inside this box is an electrically charged glass vacuum valve that will amplify and regenerate what the microphone hears. It is my theory that an electric recording will add an octave of sound reproduction so that we can record violins, and hopefully one day, the piano. Eventually I'll make a microphone that lets the sound wave be lazy, unlike Edison's microphone, which demands lots of work. By the time the sound comes out of Edison's horn it's exhausted, just like some poor laborer. OK, why don't you boys tune up while they finish hooking up wires?'

Clyde joined Bell at the door, and they stepped down the hall into a soundproof room that Clyde had built next to the recording studio. It had a window made of multiple layers of glass that looked out on the musicians. There was an enormous tin gramophone horn on a wooden box, which, Bell noticed, had wires trailing out of it and through the wall into the recording room.

He asked, 'What's this about cutting a wax disc? I thought you were putting the sound straight on film.'

'One thing at time. First I have to make a clear electrical recording. There's no point in putting acoustically recorded sound on the film if I can't play it back loudly enough for an audience to hear in a big theater.'

'When do you think you'll be able to?'

'Listen to this.' Clyde closed a knife switch on the box that held the horn. The horn emitted the discordant cacophony of the musicians tuning violins and banjos. Bell listened carefully, trying to distinguish between the different instruments he was watching through the window. 'I can't hear much difference between the violin and the clarinet.'

'The fact that you're hearing the violin at all tells me I'm on the right track.' Clyde opened the switch, and the noise stopped. 'You can tell Mr Van Dorn that we can sell a version of this microphone to Alexander Graham Bell to make longer long-distance telephone calls. Like from here all the way to New York.'

'I'll tell him,' said Bell, adding drily, 'I'll also tell him that it sounds like we have a long way to go.'

'I had a better one made, but someone stole it.'

'Stole it? Who?'

Clyde shrugged. 'I don't know. I came in yesterday morning, and the best one I'd made yet had disappeared. None of my boys saw anything. And neither did yours.'

'Do you think someone sneaked in while you were sleeping?'

'I went back to the house to get a bath and a full night's sleep. The cleaners might have tossed it out with the garbage, but they claim they didn't.'

Isaac Bell was troubled that he could not tell for sure whether the young scientist was speaking the truth or making excuses for slow progress. He said, 'I'll post a man in here, overnight, when you're not here.'

'I don't leave often.'

'I know. Mr Van Dorn is impressed by your dedication. Have you heard anything new to do with Imperial?'

Clyde Lynds had made many friends, as was his wont, while wandering the halls and riding the elevators while pondering the knotty science behind his Talking Pictures machine. He shared Bell's suspicion of the mysteriously wealthy company. 'I met an Imperial director who's taking pictures outside. He got the job 'cause he's pals with somebody high up in the company. He might know something. Or he might be just another hired hand.'

'What's his picture called?'

'*The Brewer's Daughter.*'

'What's it about?'

'The hero marries a German immigrant's daughter, and they live happily ever after.'

'I'll look into it.'

33

Isaac Bell dabbed a mixture of black shoe polish and Pinaud Clubman Wax on his mustache, stuffed his distinctive golden hair under a leather flying-machine helmet, and pulled a big set of birdman goggles over his blue eyes. Then he mounted a shiny black Indian motorcycle and roared up Second Street, weaving in and out of streetcars, autos, trucks, and wagons at breakneck speed. The machine was the brand-new model with an automatic oil pump, a two-speed transmission for lightning starts, and a springy front fork that Bell hoped would help in the jumps.

Leaning into a turn, he cut along the Southern Pacific Railroad tracks toward Aliso. He careened onto Aliso, headed straight for an intersection occupied by an enormous red brick brewery and its bottling plant, and poured on the speed. Closing fast on the brewery, he saw a canvas sign hanging above a roped-off empty lot that read:

IMPERIAL FILM
'THE BREWER'S DAUGHTER'
Extra Players Wait Here

A huge crowd of costumed extras milled around the lot: mustachioed villains, helmeted cops, fat men bulging in loud suits, and dozens of dust-caked cowboys – many twirling lassos – numerous circus clowns, and no less than three female trick riders in buckskin standing on their saddles. Texas Walt was right. Competition was tough. Everyone in Los Angeles wanted to be in a movie. To get the job, you had to stand out.

Bell spotted the camera operator at the brewery's ornate iron gates, cranking at full speed. The camera was flanked by a director with a megaphone and a blazing bank of Cooper-Hewitt lamps. A Pierce-Arrow limousine rolled in front of the gates. A beautiful actress in evening clothes stepped from it into the glare of the Cooper-Hewitts.

Isaac Bell twisted his throttle and kicked the Indian into first gear. Hunkered low over the handlebars, he headed for a long ramp down which motortrucks and horse-drawn beer wagons were exiting the brewery's second story. Dodging trucks and horses, he leaned into a sharp turn, raced up the ramp, and leaned into another. The Indian's motor screamed in protest as his wheels left the pavement.

The motorcycle took to the air, flew from the top of the ramp, and soared over the hood of the Pierce-Arrow. Clearing the auto by a whisker, Bell banged down hard on the cobblestones and skidded to a rubber-scorching halt in front of the camera.

When he saw that the startled camera operator had kept his wits about him and continued cranking, Bell extended his gloved hand to the beautiful woman with a courtly bow. The actress took it, covering her surprise, as if assuming Bell was a part of the film no one had told her about.

'What the hell are you doing?' the director yelled.

'Came for a job,' said Isaac Bell, mimicking the tone of a country man trying his luck in the big city.

'Are you crazy?'

'I hear you got a chase coming up in this *Bride of the Brewery* show you're taking pictures for.'

'It's called *The Brewer's Daughter* – hey, hold on a minute! Where'd you hear I have a chase scene?'

'Feller in the business told me.'

Among the acquaintances Clyde Lynds had met in the halls was this Imperial director, who had boasted to Clyde he was planning to have the couple elope on a bicycle chased by brewery trucks and wagons spilling barrels.

'Where's he work?'

'Works for Mr Griffith.'

The director beamed proudly. 'D.W. heard I'm doing a chase scene?'

'That's what the feller said.'

'Did Mr Griffith mention anything specific about it?'

'"If I was filming it, I'd use something more exciting than a bicycle."'

The director's face fell. Then he got truculent. 'Oh, I get it. You think I need a lunatic on a motorcycle.'

Isaac Bell pointed at the camera. 'Look at the pictures that camera just took. Then tell me I'm not the best motorcycle rider in the movies.'

A Bremserhäuschen – a brakeman's van, which Detective Curtis had told Pauline was called a *caboose* in America – sat by itself on a lonely track siding. It had high spoked wheels like a freight wagon, a cupola above one end, three square windows, a tin chimney, and ventilators in the roof, which the wind was spinning. She saw a door in the middle and two more on the platforms in front and back.

It was starting to rain again. Night was falling. Pauline was cold, hungry, and still hundreds of miles from France. What, she asked herself, is the best thing possible at this moment?

None of the windows showed lights, and no smoke rose from the chimney.

No one was around. All day she had been surprised by the emptiness of the countryside the train tracks traversed. Germany's population had grown enormous, even in her short lifetime. She had expected the freight trains to take her through busy cities and bustling suburbs. Instead, they trundled past farm after farm and more animals than people. It was an unexpected piece of good luck – this empty caboose. It would be dry inside, and out of the wind. There might even be food.

She checked for the tenth time that no one was near, then sprinted as fast as she could across a muddy field and climbed a short ladder onto the back platform. The door was locked. She climbed down, walked along the siding, and tried the center door. Locked. She went to the front of the caboose, climbed up, and discovered that door locked, too.

She was so cold she began shivering. The cupola! Maybe it had a hatch they'd forgotten to lock. A ladder was attached to the side. She climbed the wet metal rungs, scrambled along the roof, and knelt to inspect the cupola. There was no hatch in its roof, but then she discovered the entire roof was a hatch that hinged open and no one had locked it. She lowered herself down a ladder into near darkness, closing the roof hatch to keep out the rain.

She felt around until her hands brushed a lantern and a box of matches. She was afraid to light it because someone might see. But then she thought, the brakemen sleep in here when they are not working. She was right. The windows had curtains. She felt her way around, drew the curtains shut, located the lantern again, and lighted its wick.

She looked around in amazement.

It was neat and cosy as a dollhouse. It had sleeping bunks along the walls with warm blankets and a little kerosene stove with a teakettle, and she suddenly realized she would give anything for a warm drink. The kettle had water in it. She struck a match to the kerosene, and while the water heated she found a tin of tea and another of sugar. When she found a jar of blackberry jam, she thought she would cry with happiness.

She was spooning the jam from the jar when her active gaze fell on a map of the railroad system that covered one wall. She saw why the route was lonely. The tracks ran in a remarkably straight line southeast from Berlin, through Güsten, Wetzlar, and Koblenz to Metz, in Alsace-Lorraine. The *Berlin-Metzer Bahn* bypassed cities like Leipzig and Frankfurt in favor of a direct route. This was what people called the *Kanonenbahn*, the Army's strategic railway, built with gentle curves and easy grades to transport cannon and soldiers quickly to the border to defend against French invasion. Looking east on the map she saw similarly straight lines radiating from Berlin across Poland to hold the Russians at their border.

Sipping hot tea, the first warm drink she had had in two days, Pauline traced her route from Berlin and saw with a sinking heart that she had a long way to go. Suddenly a train whistle blew. It was coming from the east, headed toward France. She doused the lantern, unlocked a door, jumped to the siding, and hid behind the caboose in hopes of hopping onto the approaching train. She had done this twice already and had survived it only because Detective Curtis had turned unusually talkative one evening when she couldn't go home. He had told her that when he was her age 'riding the rails' older hobos had taught him to jump on the front of a moving railroad car, not the rear. If you fell from the front, you fell to the side. If you fell from the back, you fell under the train.

She crouched on the embankment, shielding her eyes so as not to be blinded by the locomotive's headlight. It sounded like it was coming too fast, but the instant the locomotive passed she ran alongside, scrambling to catch onto a boxcar ladder. She tripped on a tie and fell, rolled down the embankment, and jumped up. Too late. It was racing by.

Dejected, she went back inside the caboose, wrapped herself in blankets, and fell asleep on a hard mattress. Utterly exhausted, she slept without moving. Deep in the night she dreamed something was shaking her, but it stopped. Later she dreamed she was on a tram rolling along a Berlin street, lurching as it switched tracks. The tram stopped. Later it started again.

Suddenly she sat up, wide awake. The caboose was moving. She jumped to a window and pulled back the curtain on a blur of lights. The caboose was passing through a town at sixty kilometers an hour, attached to the back of a train that was picking up speed.

West to Paris?

East to Berlin?

She heard a rattling at the door, louder than the clatter of the wheels. The brakemen who had coupled the caboose to the train were unlocking the door.

Irina Viorets and Christian Semmler were watching Imperial's latest film projected on a screen in Semmler's ninth-floor apartment before showing it to their distributors. It ended with a bang-up chase involving brewery trucks dropping beer barrels, a puffing locomotive, and a motorcycle that jumped the barrels and landed beside a Pierce-Arrow limousine. A bride in a flowing wedding dress jumped out of the limousine and jumped onto the motorcycle, which raced off, pursued by beer trucks, careened onto railroad tracks, and was chased by a train.

Suddenly Semmler leaned forward and stared hard at the flickering screen.

'Who is that motorcyclist?'

'I hope it's an extra and not a good actor,' answered Viorets. 'He's not going to live long.'

'He looks like Isaac Bell.'

34

'How can you tell under those goggles?'

'The way he straddles the machine.'

'But Isaac Bell is a Connecticut insurance executive. It can't be Bell.'

'Of course not,' Semmler mused. 'I can't imagine an insurance man pursuing such a dangerous line of work.'

The picture ended happily with the eloping couple married in a Lutheran church and boarding a Hamburg-America ocean liner for a honeymoon in Germany.

'Irina, I want you to engage Marion Bell.'

'Bell's wife?'

'How soon can you get her here?'

'Tomorrow, if she's willing. She's visiting her father in San Francisco.'

'She should make our history of the western railroads.'

'Why her?'

'I'm betting she's ready to make something big.'

Irina Viorets looked at Semmler sitting in the shadows. The German general was a strange one up to stranger things, but he often had good ideas. He knew what he was up to in the moving picture business. *The Iron Horse*, Imperial's history of the western railroads, would be an ambitious two- or three-reeler. Marion Morgan would bring a topical filmmaker's sensibility to the story and all the skills necessary to take pictures of real events out-of-doors.

'I'll telephone her long-distance. I just hope she hasn't engaged with Preston Whiteway already.'

'Tell her if she'll leave Whiteway she can have a fleet of locomotives at her disposal. Promise her you'll put Theda Bara, King Baggot, and Florence Lawrence under contract.'

'She's not the type to walk out on *her* contract.'

'Tell her she can tie Billy Bitzer and his camera to the front of a locomotive if that will make her happy. Just get her here! Immediately.'

'I'll telephone San Francisco.'

'And then you get busy writing a scenario that features handsome German-Americans working on the railroad.'

'That much,' said Viorets, 'I had already figured out.'

Semmler barred the door when she left.

For a man who was supposed to be a wealthy insurance executive, Isaac Bell had, too many times, appeared at exactly the wrong moment with a gun in his hand. Now he was pretending to be a movie extra – in an Imperial film, no less.

Semmler had already wondered about Bell. Transmitting on the Los Angeles German vice-consul's private wire, he had ordered the New York consul general to investigate Dagget, Staples & Hitchcock. The Hartford insurance company was genuine, the consul general had reported back, and Isaac Bell was listed as a partner.

Semmler was not convinced. The Leipzig Organ & Piano Company appeared genuine, too. And who was more 'one of the boys' than Leipzig's well-liked American sales representative, Fritz Wunderlich?

Isaac Bell had stopped him from kidnapping Lynds

and Professor Beiderbecke from the *Mauretania*. Isaac Bell had stopped him from taking Lynds off the Golden State Limited. And now a man who looked very much like Isaac Bell was pretending to be a moving picture stunt performer. He would find out whether it was Bell.

But until he knew for sure, General Major Christian Semmler wanted Isaac Bell's wife in easy reach.

At the sound of the brakemen unlocking their caboose door, Pauline snatched a blanket and scrambled up the ladder, out the hatch, and onto the roof just as they burst in complaining about the cold. The wind of the speeding train's passage hit her like a fist. It smelled of coal smoke and rain. Across the forests and farmland, black clouds blacker than the locomotive's smoke filled the sky. She crouched behind the cupola, seeking shelter.

What would they do when saw her tea mug and the jam jar?

The train was moving too fast to jump off, and the roof was too high even if it weren't moving.

She looked back. The sky was gray.

She looked ahead. Under lowering clouds, the train looked like a long dark snake. Sparks flew from the distant locomotive. It was the fastest yet that she'd ridden on. In the dull morning light seeping from the storm clouds, she saw why. It was a military train. Flat cars bore either a single long cannon, or two-wheeled artillery caissons. As the train swept through a long curve exposing its side, she saw livestock cars, which would be carrying the artillerymen's horses, and passenger cars, which would be packed with soldiers.

What was the best?

Hope? A hope that they would assume tramps had broken in to steal food. How did the tramps leave through locked doors? The cupola hatch? Hope was the best she could conjure, hope that the brakemen did not read Sherlock Holmes.

Bolts of lightning pierced the clouds. She felt an icy breath of cold wind. She tugged the blanket she had taken around her shoulders and prayed for a miracle. But, answering her worst fear, the hatch began to rise. A brakeman was climbing up to look to see if a tramp was hiding on the roof.

Suddenly thunder shook the caboose, and rain pelted down.

The hatch slammed shut.

A bolt of lightning struck the locomotive. The thunder crashed again and again as if Donar himself had noticed the train and didn't like it. But she was the luckiest girl alive: the thunder god had saved her from the brakeman.

Another bolt of lightning struck, blanketing the locomotive with blue fire. It slowed abruptly, and the train clanged to a stop with a crash of banging couplers.

Balls of electric fire spewed from the locomotive's wheels and leaped to a tree beside the tracks. The tree flew to splinters when its sap exploded in a burst of superheated steam. Pauline saw green fire race toward her along the boxcar roofs, and she felt the incipient tingle of electrical shock. Clutching her precious rucksack, she scrambled down the ladder and ran into the woods.

*

Isaac Bell caught Marion in his arms as she stepped off the Coast Line Limited from San Francisco. They kissed, and they kissed again. Bell seized her bag and gave the porter her trunk check, the name of their hotel, and a large tip.

'Mighty generous, sir.'

'I am happy to see my beautiful wife.'

'Hard to imagine you wouldn't be, sir.'

They kissed once more. 'Andrew found us a house to rent near his place on Bunker Hill,' Bell told Marion. 'Until it's ready, I booked rooms at the Van Nuys.' They walked hand in hand off the platform.

Bell asked, 'What was your first thought when Irina telephoned and offered you this job?'

'Joy. I'd get to see you.'

'And then?'

'I thought that *The Iron Horse* would be very challenging. It's a big story to pack into three reels, and I thought right away that maybe I can persuade Irina to take a chance on four.'

'And your next thought?'

'Do you really want to know?'

'Yes.'

'Well, it's somewhat technical, but I was thinking I want to revive the old-fashioned "traveling pictures" they used to take years ago, where the camera moves alongside the action. They've fallen out of favor. Everyone is in love with presenting close-up figures. But with handcars available to glide the camera on a smooth track, and the fact that I want to start the scenario before the western railroads with galloping Pony Express riders and stagecoaches – You see what I mean, it's technical, but that's what I was thinking.'

'Did you wonder why Irina hired you?'

'No.'

'You weren't at all surprised?'

'There are many women in the movie business, but more men, and I've found that women do like to work with women. Also, she knows that I've made topical films, so I'm comfortable taking pictures on the fly. Why do you ask?'

Bell smiled. 'I believe you know my feelings about coincidences.'

'You dislike them, intensely.'

'Irina works for a firm that has caught my interest in the Talking Pictures case.'

'Imperial. Where you have Clyde set up.'

'But Imperial turns out to be something of an enigma. They're spending a lot more money than they earn. No one knows where they get the money. They've raised an army of private detectives who are driving the Edison bulls out of Los Angeles.'

'That's wonderful!'

'They seem to be doing it to court the independents.'

'That's a brilliant way to ensure plenty of fresh product.'

'And suddenly they're offering my wife a job. I have to wonder.'

'Oh. Well, put your mind to rest on that score. Irina didn't telephone to offer me the job.'

'She didn't?'

'She telephoned wondering when I might be coming to

Los Angeles and to say hello and to ask my recommendation for someone to take pictures for *The Iron Horse*. I mentioned a few people who I thought would be up to it – Christina Bialobrzesky, for one. You remember her?'

'The "Polish countess" with the New Orleans accent.'

'Irina thanked me, and then just as we were saying good-bye, almost as an afterthought, she asked would I have any interest in it.'

'Why didn't she ask you first?'

'She assumed I was tied up with Preston. I assured her I was not. At any rate, to make a long story short, here I am – a genuine coincidence.'

'I am relieved to hear that,' said Isaac Bell. 'But just to be on the safe side, how would you like to be a genuine detective?'

'Under you?'

'So to speak,' Bell returned her smile.

'What would it entail?'

'Keeping alert – with an eye to your own safety – to note anything out of the ordinary.'

'I must say that everything Irina told me about *The Iron Horse* was absolutely what I would expect of a firm that is making moving pictures.'

'I want to know what they are doing in addition to making moving pictures.'

The Van Dorn Detective Agency's Los Angeles field office was located in a two-story warehouse on Second Street on the edge of a section devoted to lumber, hardware, machinery, and paint. While the Los Angeles detectives longed loudly for as stylish an address as their counterparts enjoyed in New York, Chicago, and Washington, their comings and goings went unobserved by the wrong element thanks to a variety of entrances through back alleys and neighboring businesses.

Texas Walt Hatfield sauntered in, flicking sawdust off his boots with his bandanna, as Isaac Bell arrived scraping metal shavings off his. Both men were dressed to work in guise, Hatfield in cowboy gear and Bell in flying machine helmet and goggles, with a wide motorcycle belt cinched around his waist.

Hatfield reported nothing new or suspicious in the penthouse cinematography studio stages atop the Imperial Building. Bell had little to add. The picture taking for *The Brewer's Daughter* had been wrapped up this afternoon, and he had already been offered another job by the same Imperial director on an as-yet-untitled picture involving a motorcycle and a runaway freight train.

'Let me ask you something, Walt.'

'Shoot,' said Walt, suddenly all ears because Isaac Bell did not usually preface questions with 'Let me ask you something'. Something out of the ordinary was on the chief investigator's mind.

'At any time when you are up in that studio, did you get a funny feeling?'

'What sort of funny feeling?'

'That you were being . . .' Bell stopped talking and looked the tall Texan in the face. This was not a question he would ask most detectives. But Walt Hatfield was a natural-born hunter who had been raised by Comanche Indians. Of the Van Dorns Isaac Bell had worked with,

Hatfield was by far the most sensitive to his surroundings.

'Watched?' asked Hatfield.

'You did, didn't you?'

'Shore did feel watched, now that you mention it. Didn't pay it much mind at the moment, what with fellows cranking cameras.'

Bell's eyes were suddenly burning.

'You, too, Isaac?'

'I had a feeling.'

'Where?'

'The recording room on the fourth floor.'

'How about in Clyde's laboratory?'

'Possibly there, but not as strong a sensation.'

'Reckon someone's peeping through a judas hole in the room next door?'

'One way to find out.'

Bell stepped across the hall to see Larry Saunders, the recently promoted head of the Los Angeles office. Saunders, a trim, stylish man, wore a white linen suit like Bell's, for the warm city. But unlike Bell's, which was artfully tailored to conceal a good-sized automatic and a spare magazine, with room for a sleeve gun and pocket pistols when the occasion called for it, Saunders's suit was cut so tightly that the Los Angeles detective would be hard-pressed to hide a weapon larger than a stiletto. Saunders's hat rack held a white derby and several silk scarves. The derby, Bell hoped, had room for a derringer. Saunders's patent leather pumps certainly did not.

'Larry, who would you recommend I send over to City

Hall to inspect the architect's plans for the Imperial Building?'

'Holian.'

'I think I've met him. Big-in-the-belly fellow who looks like a saloonkeeper?'

'He's the one, though I've seen Tim do a credible job of imitating a brothel bouncer, too.'

'I don't want this getting back to the owner of the building.'

'Don't you worry, Mr Bell. Holian's got the city clerks eating out of his hand. There isn't a body buried in Los Angeles he couldn't jab with a spade. They'll do as he asks and do it with a smile.' Saunders rubbed his mustache, a pencil-thin affair that Texas Walt had likened, privately, to a 'dance hall gal's eyebrow', and said, 'It wouldn't hurt if Holian could share a little wealth while he's poking around.'

'Charge as much as he needs against the Talking Pictures account. Tell him I want layouts of the fourth floor, eighth floor, and penthouse — every room and every closet.'

35

Isaac Bell received a long, speculative report from Grady
Forrer by telegraph, which was a hundred times faster
than mail but lacked the subtlety and precision of a letter
and offered little opportunity for the give-and-take of a
conversation by telephone. Clyde Lynds had claimed that
his electrical microphone would one day spawn devices
for amplifying feeble electrical currents for long-distance
telephones to span the continent. That day could not
come soon enough for Isaac Bell.

Back and forth he and Grady Forrer transmitted on the
Van Dorn private wire. The upshot was that Grady had
turned up the name of a private German merchant bank
– *Hamburg Bankhaus* – which the Research department
suspected of funneling money to Imperial Film.

POSITIVE?
REASONABLY.
KRIEG-IMPERIAL CONNECTIONS?
NOT YET.
KRIEG-HAMBURG BANKHAUS CONNECTIONS?
NONE YET.

Isaac Bell telephoned Andrew Rubenoff, filled him in
on Research's suspicions, and asked, 'Is the Bank of Hamburg a real bank or a sham?'

'Where did you hear about Bank of Hamburg, if I may ask?'

'Van Dorn Research.'

'I am impressed,' Rubenoff answered. 'I doff my hat to them. Hamburg Bankhaus is not widely known outside professional circles.'

'I'll pass on the compliment. Is it real or a sham?'

'It's real. They're very active in German enterprises doing business in America. First among their enterprises, they're the principal lender to the Leipzig Organ and Piano Company.'

'The piano shops?'

'You've seen them. Leipzig Organ has expanded hugely in America – opening all sorts of branches to sell parlor pianos. Funny you should ask, though.'

'Why is that?'

'I was just in one of their shops the other day trying to buy sheet music. But they were sold out of "Ah! Sweet Mystery of Life".'

'It's very popular.'

'When a music shop is sold out of a brand-new Victor Herbert song, something is terribly wrong with the shop.'

'Or the publisher.'

'The publisher will blame the shop, of course. Either for not ordering enough or not paying their bills. Though in this instance they may be right. The shop had a very poor selection. The most recent I could find was "I Love My Wife; But, Oh, You Kid!". That's been around so long the paper was turning yellow.'

'How were their pianos?'

'Decent enough, for uprights. Good German quality.'

Bell asked. 'Where is Leipzig's headquarters?'

'Leipzig. As their name would suggest.'

'I mean here in America.'

'They'd have a sales rep.'

'How do they conduct business?'

'The representative will be a top man on commission. He'll conduct any business that has to be done here. The rest will be handled in Leipzig.'

'Leipzig wouldn't be owned by Krieg, by any chance?'

'I doubt they'd borrow money from Hamburg if they were. They'd have access to better rates of interest through Krieg.'

Bell pondered his next move.

'Uncle Andy, tell me about pianos.'

The Leipzig Organ & Piano Company's plate-glass front window was sparkling clean, Isaac Bell noted as he hurried along the sidewalk. Sheet music shortcomings aside, from the sidewalk at least the shop had nothing to apologize for. He stopped, peered through the glass, pulled his watch from his pocket by its heavy gold chain, pretended to check whether he had time to spare, and went inside.

Sturdy upright pianos lined the walls, each bearing the name Leipzig in gold leaf. Revolving mahogany racks of music flanked a glass-topped counter displaying metronomes and hymnals.

A salesman got up from his desk by the back door. He was a middle-aged German with a military bearing and a cold manner. 'Yes?' he demanded.

'I am shopping for a piano for my niece, who has impressed her teacher.'

'Ve have vaiting list for new orders.'

'How long will that be?'

'It is difficult to tell.'

'A month? Two months?'

'More like six months to a year, sir. Our pianos are made carefully. Very carefully.'

'Are they strung with music wire made by Stahl- and Drahtwerk?'

The salesman's jaw tightened.

'Or,' asked Bell, 'are the strings from Moritz Poehlmann of Nuremberg?'

The saleman stared straight ahead, his gaze locked on the knot of Isaac Bell's four-in-hand necktie. At last he said, 'I do not know that. But our plates are of cast iron.'

'I would hope so,' said Bell. 'Would you play a few of them for me? Let me hear the difference.'

'You may play them, sir.'

'Ah, but sadly I do not. So if you would play for me . . .'

Again, the tight jaw. Finally, he said, 'It is not possible.'

'A man who sells pianos can't play them?'

'I have injured my hand.'

'I'm so sorry. Could I trouble you to telephone your sales representative.'

'Vat for?'

'I would like to ask whether I could buy an instrument sooner than six months.'

'He is not near.'

'Well, perhaps your head office could help me.'

'No.'

'Then I wonder could I have your representative's address that I might write him myself.'

'He is traveling.'

Bell stepped to the windows and stood there for a long moment.

Suddenly a stylish crowd of free-spirited young men and women came along the sidewalk and burst in the door. Gaily hailing the salesman, all talking at once, they took a long time to explain they needed to rent a piano for a party tonight. Informed that the shop did not rent pianos, they laughed.

'Then we'll buy one.'

'We'll pool our cash.'

'I've got Dad's check. I'll buy it.'

'How about that one?' a girl cried, and they gathered around it, two of them plopping down on the bench, throwing open the key lid, and pounding out a ragtime duet.

The salesman kept saying, 'Not for sale. Not for sale,' and when he had at last showed the buoyant mob out the door, he discovered that the tall golden-haired gentleman hoping to buy a piano for his niece had slipped away in the confusion.

Good riddance, he thought, and locked the door.

'Nicely done,' Isaac Bell told the Los Angeles field office apprentices and secretaries and their girlfriends and boyfriends. 'You were thoroughly authentic "gilded youth" on a lark. That poor salesman never knew what hit him.'

'Did you find what you were looking for, Mr Bell?'

All eyes locked on the Van Dorn Detective Agency's legendary chief investigator.

'With your help, I found a letter in his desk and a business card. The Leipzig Organ and Piano Company is represented by a traveling man named Fritz Wunderlich who collects his mail in Denver at the Brown Palace Hotel.'

Isaac Bell telegraphed Van Dorn field offices around the country to cover Leipzig's other piano shops to see what they could pick up. Those large enough to maintain apprentices would instruct them to pretend to be shopping on behalf of their school or church. Agents in smaller one- and two-man outfits would shop, as Bell had, for nieces and daughters.

Bell himself boarded the flyer to Salt Lake City, changed trains a day later to the Overland Limited, arrived in Denver early the next morning, and walked the short distance up Broadway to the Brown Palace Hotel, a favorite haunt. He knocked on a door just inside the main entrance. Omar P. Armstrong, the Brown Palace's managing partner, invited him to breakfast.

As they walked across a vast marble and cast-iron atrium lobby where tier upon tier of balconies soared to a skylight one hundred feet above the carpet, Bell asked, 'Have you ever met a salesman named Fritz Wunderlich?'

'Fritz? Of course.'

Bell had journeyed to Denver expecting no less. Omar P. Armstrong knew everyone worth knowing west of the Mississippi. 'Have you seen him lately?'

'He's here every two or three weeks.'

'What's he like?'

'Pleasant enough fellow,' Armstrong replied with a neutral smile.

Isaac Bell was fully aware that any man who managed a grand hotel had to be as observant as a whale-ship look-out and as discreet as the madam of a first-class bordello. Omar's studiedly disinterested expression said that if Isaac Bell wished to inquire about Brown Palace guests but still be known as an innocent insurance executive, that was Bell's business but Omar P. Armstrong wasn't born yesterday.

'Have you known him long?'

'If you are interested in Herr Wunderlich, why not ask his friends?'

They paused in the entrance to the dining room. The Brown Palace's guests were breakfasting at tables set with snowy linen, gleaming silver, and fine china. Omar nodded in the direction that Bell suspected he would. At a table placed in the alcove of a tall window, three well-dressed, barbershop-pinked salesmen were in animated conversation.

'If you like, I can introduce you.'

Bell grinned. 'Did you ever meet a drummer who needed an introduction?'

He walked straight to the salesmen's table. 'Morning, gents. Isaac Bell. Insurance. May I join you?'

They took in his hand-tailored suit, polished boots, and confident smile.

'Sit down, brother. Sit down. Waiter! Coffee for Mr Bell – or something a mite stronger, if you're so inclined.'

'Coffee will be fine. Long day ahead.'

They shook hands around and introduced themselves, a rep for the Gillette Safety Razor Company, a Loco-mobile salesman, and a traveler in the cereal line. The

Locomobile man said, 'Mr Bell, stop me if I'm wrong, but don't you drive a Locomobile?'

'I thought I recognized you, Jake,' said Bell. 'We met in Bridgeport when I was picking her up at the factory.'

'Red one, if I recall?'

'Red as fire.'

'How's she running?'

'Like a top. Small world, isn't it? I ran into a traveling man the other day. We got to talking about autos, and when I told him about mine he mentioned he knew a fellow who handled the line. That could have been you.'

'Probably was me. What's his name?'

'German fellow. Fritz Wunderlich.'

'Fritz! Yes, we just saw him in – Where'd we see him?'

'Chicago?'

'Chicago it was. Isn't he a character? *"Mit schlag"*!'

'"Time is money."'

'"Eight days in the veek."'

'Pretty good salesman, I gather,' said Bell.

'Valuable man. No question. Valuable man.'

'Lucky for him he's got that smile,' the cereal salesman chortled.

'What do you mean?' asked Bell.

'Well, you know . . . Fritz is a heck of a worker, but he sort of looks like a monkey.'

'Sort of?' snickered Jake. 'I'll say he looks like an ape in the jungle.'

'You mean his long arms?' asked Bell.

'Arms like a monkey. Face like one, too.'

'He didn't really look like a monkey,' Bell protested, mildly.

'He does to me.'

Isaac Bell drew his notebook from his pocket and opened his Waterman fountain pen. 'No. Fritz looks more like this.' He tried to draw a man's face with a prominent brow. 'Sort of like this. I'm not much of a hand at drawing.'

The cereal salesman took out his order book and his pen. 'No, more like this.'

'Neither of you can draw worth a darn,' laughed the Gillette man. He opened his order book and moved his pen over it, laboriously. 'He looks like this.'

The cereal salesman disagreed vehemently, and Bell said, 'Not one bit like that. How about you, Jake?'

Jake, the Locomobile man from Bridgeport, took out his book. Isaac Bell watched, holding his breath. Jake was his last chance to get a sketch that resembled Fritz Wunderlich. Surely one of the men at the table could draw. Jake, it turned out, possessed a modicum of artistic talent.

'Like this,' said Jake. He drew in a few quick lines a simian face with long cheeks and deep-set eyes. Then he turned his pencil on the side and shaded in a heavy brow.

The others stared. 'You got him just about right, Jake,' one marveled. 'That's Fritz. Darned near.'

'I think you're right,' Bell ventured, looking to the cereal salesman for confirmation.

'He sure does.'

'Well, I'll be, Jake's an artist.'

Jake beamed.

'Could I see that?' asked Bell, picking it up and studying it by the light of the window. 'Yes, I believe that's what he looks like. You're a real artist, Jake.'

Jake flushed with embarrassment. 'Naw, not really. I just started out in the design shop, before I started selling. You really think it's good?'

'Sure do. Mind if I keep it?'

'You ought to pay for it,' laughed the man from Chicago. 'It's a piece of artwork.'

'You're right,' said Isaac Bell, reaching for his wallet. 'How much?'

'No, no, no.' said Jake. 'Go on, you take it.'

'OK. But when I need a new auto, I'll know who to come to.'

'Just don't show it to Fritz,' the cereal man laughed.

'It don't matter he looks like that,' said Jake. 'Fritz's got that smile, and folks just buy anything he sells.'

'I don't know about that,' said the man from Gillette.

'What do you mean?' asked Bell.

'Eh, you're always going on about that,' the cereal sales rep protested. 'Fritz is a valuable man.'

'About what?' asked Bell.

'Those shops his firm supplies. I just don't see them selling that many pianos or sheets of music, for that matter. It's not a well-run business. From what I've seen.'

'They've got a fancy-looking shop in Los Angeles,' said Bell.

'Well, you just try buying a piano, you'll find a waiting list as long as your arm.'

'Or Fritz's arm,' Jake said, and the table roared.

'Where's Fritz now?' asked Bell.

'Hope he's not at the next table listening to this,' said Jake, and the others looked around uncomfortably.

'I'm trying to remember when I saw him,' Bell persisted.

'Must have been two weeks, maybe more. Time flies. Anyone seen him lately?'

'I thought in Chicago, he said he was going to Los Angeles.'

Isaac Bell took Jake's drawing of Fritz Wunderlich to the Denver Post Building and paid a newspaper sketch artist to make him copies. He took them to the train stations. The Van Dorn Detective Agency had warm relations with the express companies, as the detectives often cadged rides on express cars, whose messengers were glad of another dependable gun. By noon the copies were headed around the continent, courtesy of Adams Express, American Express, and Wells Fargo, to the field offices covering German consulates in New York, Boston, Chicago, Cincinnati, St Louis, San Francisco, and the vice-consul's mansion in Los Angeles.

In Jersey City, New Jersey, a short, round Van Dorn apprentice from the New York field office named Nelson Mills found himself wishing he had broken the agency rule that forbade apprentice detectives to carry guns. The baby-faced Mills had just finished his first 'solo' assignment, an investigation of the Leipzig Organ & Piano shop in the Heights neighborhood. Scanning his notes as he hurried to catch the Hudson Tube back to Manhattan, he composed in his mind the first sentence of his report – 'A yearlong waiting list for pianos, no organs, and sheet music from 1905, conspire to indicate that the Leipzig Organ and Piano Company is a false front for a nefarious business as yet unidentified.'

Suddenly he remembered that Detective Harry Warren

had advised him that using one word instead of three was the best way to get the bosses to read his reports. Mills drew mental Xs through 'conspired to indicate', to be replaced with 'suggest', and was debating deleting 'nefarious' when he bumped into a big fellow on the sidewalk.

'Excuse me. Sorry.'

Nelson Mills got a fist in his face for his apology.

The young man fell on his back on the pavement with blood pouring from his nose. He was shocked by the speed of the attack. The pain was ferocious. His eyes were blinded by tears. He sensed more, then saw the man who punched him looming over him, and he started to ask 'Why?'

The man snatched Nelson's notebook out of his hand and ripped apart the pages, scattering the pieces on his bloody shirt. 'Hey, that's my –'

A heavy boot smashed into his side. Pain seared his ribs, and Nelson realized too late to save himself that there were two of them. They kicked him repeatedly.

36

Isaac Bell found a stack of angry telegrams waiting for him in the Los Angeles field office. Van Dorns in Cincinnati, Chicago, Ohio, and Jersey City reported their apprentices were beaten up on their way back from investigating Leipzig Organ & Piano shops. Two young men were in the hospital, and one boy in Jersey City had already been given last rites while his family sat vigil at his bedside.

Enraged detectives demanded permission to arrest the shop clerks. But in rapid exchanges of wires, it became clear to Isaac Bell that there was no proof to charge the clerks. The attacks had occurred in streets and alleys far from their shops.

As chief investigator, the best Bell could do was wire a reminder of Van Dorn's standing orders regarding thugs and hoodlums who assaulted private detectives, when they had been positively identified beyond any doubt:

DISCOURAGE PERPETRATORS FROM
REPEATING ATTACKS.

Larry Saunders stuck his head in Bell's office door. He had blueprints rolled under his arm. 'How was Denver?'

Bell handed him the Locomobile salesman's sketch. 'Give this to the boys covering the vice-consul's mansion.

Wunderlich is real. No one's seen him lately. What did Holian learn at City Hall?'

Saunders unrolled blueprints on Bell's desk. They anchored them with sidearms. 'Fourth floor. Eighth floor. Penthouse. I don't see where you'd put a judas hole. Public rooms and open stairways. Maybe this storage closet on the eighth.'

Bell studied the blueprints and agreed that spy holes weren't likely.

Saunders said, 'Thing is, Holian thought the clerk he borrowed these from was acting a little jumpy.'

'What did Holian make of that?'

'Maybe the clerk knew something more he didn't want to say. Holian wants to nose around a little. I told him I'd take over.'

Bell looked at Saunders, inquiringly.

Saunders said, 'The clerks know that Holian is a Van Dorn. They don't know me from Adam.'

'Go to it,' said Isaac Bell.

As Saunders hurried out, the front-desk man came in. 'Southern Pacific Railroad express car messenger just delivered this, Mr Bell.'

It was a small package wrapped in brown paper. It was heavy for its size, and it smelled of machine oil. Bell weighed it speculatively. 'Did you happen to recognize the messenger?'

'Sure did. Benson's been with the line for years.'

'Then we can presume it's not a bomb?' Bell asked with a smile and sliced it open with his throwing knife. Inside was a wooden box. He opened it. Nestled in cotton packing was a small steel-colored tool.

'What is that, Mr Bell?'

'Cutting pliers.' There was a note from Mike Malone, in a big, open scrawl. 'Sorry it took so long. Small was the hard part. Hope you like them.'

'Never seen them that little,' said the front-desk man. 'Think they work?'

Mike had included a short length of braided cable. Bell slipped the jaws around it and squeezed the handles. The wire parted with a sharp *pop*.

Pauline Grandzau jumped off a freight train at the ancient fortress city of Metz, fearing the guards in the rail yard. She skirted the overgrown ramparts, shielded from policemen and busybodies by thick brush and tall trees, and followed on foot the ruins of an even older Roman aqueduct, which the brakemen's map had shown paralleling the tracks all the way to the Moselle River. She covered many miles in the failing light, guided by square heaps of stone and occasional lonely rows of two, three, or more arches still standing.

Suddenly barking dogs charged from a Jouy-aux-Arches farmhouse. Terrified, she scrambled onto the Roman stonework to escape them and climbed to the top of the archway, where she gnawed the last of the cheese she had stolen in Koblenz, fell asleep, and woke at dawn, forty feet above the ground, with a long view across the river.

France, made bright red and gold by the sun rising behind her, looked like heaven.

Even the cold rain that pursued her across Germany had finally stopped, as if it would not dare fall within sight of the border. Perched atop the aqueduct, she saw a gently rolling landscape. The red-tile rooftops of Novéant-sur-Moselle clustered along the Moselle, then gave way to scattered farm fields, woods, and vineyards. A suspension bridge traversed the river. Farther west, beyond her field of vision, would be the town of Batilly, where she would find the French railroad station. With forty francs of Detective Curtis's money to buy a ticket, she could dream of riding in comfort the two hundred miles to Paris.

Then she saw two flags run up the pole on the roof of a building at the far side of the suspension bridge. The red, white, and black rectangle of Imperial Germany and the swallowtail of the Customs Service marked Germany's last outpost, a frontier customhouse. Anyone crossing the bridge by train or on foot or on a bicycle would have to show their papers.

She looked beyond the town, up and down the river and the farmland and woods around it. Flat floodplains bounded the Moselle. The plain on her side was broad. On the west side, where she had to go, it was narrower and rose abruptly to a line of hills. Atop the highest hill, a mile west of the Moselle, sprawled the grim stone parapets of Fort Driant, whose giant guns dominated the Moselle Valley. They were Metz's first defense against French attack from the southwest and it struck her suddenly that she was abandoning her homeland to escape to the land of the enemy. But she wasn't really escaping, nor was she abandoning her country. She was doing the job of a private detective, serving the agency and a client who deserved her help, and avenging Detective Curtis. But only if she made it to Paris.

What was the best she could imagine? What could she see?

On both sides of the river, the banks sloped gently to the water. *Opa* Grandzau, the grandfather who had taught her to ski in the Alps, had also taught her how to swim in icy mountain lakes. The Moselle looked warm and lazy by comparison. She picked a route across from her vantage, spotting the narrowest stretch of the river where she could walk unseen out on a wooded point of land that jutted into the water.

When Pauline had chosen her route, she worked her way down the stones of the aqueduct, marveling as she descended how she had survived the climb last night in near darkness. Fear, it seemed, could have the most wonderfully concentrating effect on both mind and body.

She headed west from the bottom of the arch, through the woods, keeping the dappled early sunlight on her back. She crossed narrow lanes rutted with wagon wheels, scrambled over the railroad tracks after making sure no trains were coming, and darted over open fields, praying no farmer would see her running.

She found the wooded point of land and pressed ahead, glimpsing water through the trees on both sides, and soon found herself on the gentle bank. Two difficulties not apparent from the top of the aqueduct were starkly evident at the water's edge: the narrowing of the river made the water race fast, and the strong current would sweep her into the wider stretches downstream. And if someone were to look in her direction from the suspension bridge or the houses at the edge of the town, he might see her swimming.

She had to cross in the dark.

And she needed a raft.

She scoured the woods for fallen limbs, which were few and far between as the farmers probably gathered them for firewood. It took two hours to heap up enough fallen wood to make a raft big enough to cling to while she floated in the dark and big enough to carry her rucksack.

From her rucksack, Pauline took her extra socks. She explored them with her fingers until she found a break in the wool and then unraveled the yarn from which they were knitted, carefully coiling it so it would not tangle. Then she laid the wood out in a square, laid a second layer of branches criss-crossing the first, and lashed the pieces together at each intersection. She ran out of wool and had to unravel another pair of socks before she could finish. When she was done, she had an alarmingly flexible square raft, four feet by four feet, which she knew would never hold her weight but hoped would help her float. Now she had to wait hours for dark. She was hungry. Starving. A rabbit hopped close by. She was holding a last stick she was thinking of adding to her raft. She looked at the rabbit and thought, Not that hungry. She closed her eyes and tried to sleep.

She awakened cold. The sun had set. Shivering, she took all her clothes off. She stuffed them and her shoes in the rucksack and tied the sack to the raft, positioning the top opening high up in hopes of keeping Detective Curtis's gun dry. Then she dragged the raft out of the woods and down the sandy river-bank, trying to move it gently so she wouldn't break any of the yarn lashings.

Lights from the town reflected on the river's rippling

surface – but at least if the current did push her off course, she would drift away from the town. She waded into dark water. It was cold. She dragged the raft after her. Suddenly it was afloat, light and easily moved. The current nearly yanked it from her hands. She held on tight, took a step into deeper water, and the raft rushed downstream, dragging her with it.

The lights were a godsend. Without them she would have had no idea where the current was taking her. But they served like the North Star, and she clung to the sight of their fixed point with every circle the current whirled her in. The raft seemed to draw the river's ire, presenting something for the water to grab. But if she let it go and tried to swim across the river it would take her clothes, her money, and the gun, so she held tight and forced herself to be patient. The current had to ease where the river widened. It had to.

The lights seemed very far away when she felt the current slacken abruptly, and she judged by their position that the current had pushed her partway across the river, even as it had dragged her downstream. She let go with one arm and began to paddle and kick. The exertion warmed her. Shortly she saw the loom of the far bank, and soon after, when she kicked she hit bottom. She stumbled out of the water, freed her rucksack, dried herself off with her jacket, and put on her clothes, shoes and socks.

She wasn't in France yet, but she was close.

There were stars in the sky. The immense Fort Driant on the hilltop blocked them to the north. To walk west, she kept the fortress to her right. Soon she spotted the real North Star. She kept it to her right and eventually, when the fortress was behind her, she came to a fence in a field, far from any road. She slipped through strands of barbed wire and started walking in the general direction of Paris, steering clear of farmhouse lights and cocking her ears for the train whistles that would lead her to the railroad station at Batilly.

37

'Lights!' the director of *Hell's Bells* shouted into his megaphone.

The dynamo roared. The Cooper-Hewitts blazed.

'Camera! . . . Speed!'

Isaac Bell, clad in what had become his trademark black costume, flying helmet, and goggles, twisted his grip throttle, revving his motorcycle.

The camera operator cranked to speed.

The director took one more look. The locomotive was in place on a raised track bed rented in a remote corner of a Southern Pacific freight yard. Smoke and steam gushed from its stack. The engineer leaned his head and shoulders out of its cab. A giant electric fan just outside the camera's field of focus blew the smoke and steam the length of the locomotive and parted the engineer's long beard, making it look like the locomotive was speeding down the track.

Isaac Bell's motorcycle spewed white smoke from its exhaust pipe. Out of the corner of his eye he saw Marty, the skinny little Imperial Film mechanician who had tweaked the V-twin engine to make smoke, watching intently. The mechanician gave him the thumbs-up and hurried away, his job done.

Bell twisted his throttle wide open and slapped his clutch lever.

The motorcycle tore into the lights, its exhaust streaming an arresting picture as Bell raced tight circles around the locomotive, jumping the machine into the air every time he crossed the humped train tracks at forty miles per hour. On his fourth landing his front wheel felt wobbly. The camera operator was still cranking. The lights still blazed. Bell poured on the gas for one last jump.

The wheel fell off.

The motorcycle crashed down on its front fork. The rear end left the ground, pivoted straight up, and catapulted Isaac Bell over the handlebars.

Bell flew through the air – skull first – at the locomotive. He tried to tuck into a somersault to fend off with his boots instead of his head, but he was flying at forty miles an hour. As he hurtled, time seemed to stop for the tall detective. It looked as if suddenly the operator were cranking more slowly, resting his arm, and slowing the film. Bell saw the ground pass lazily under him. He saw the Indian standing on its front end with its back wheel spinning in the air, saw the camera itself, perched on its sturdy tripod, saw the wind fan, saw the company of actors, stagehands, grips, and horse wranglers all watching as if nothing were amiss and men performing stunts on motorcycles flew at locomotives every day.

The steel behemoth filled his vision, black as night and big as the sky. An instant later, he smashed into it. A startlingly sharp pain in his ankle told him that his somersault had saved his skull. He bounced off the boiler, fell to the rail bed, and tumbled down the ballast embankment, raking arms and legs on the crushed stone.

Sprawled, dazed, in the dirt, he heard people yelling.

He sat up to put everyone's mind at ease. Everything hurt, but he thought he would be able to stand in another minute or two.

The yelling stopped – except for the director who was still calling through his megaphone, 'That was terrific! Let's do it one more time!'

Isaac Bell climbed painfully to his feet, walked unsteadily to the wrecked motorcycle, knelt down, and inspected it.

He felt in his jacket that his Browning was still in its holster and moving freely. Thanks to his lightning-fast reflexes, he had just survived the Los Angeles version of the Cincinnati, Chicago, and Jersey City attacks on Van Dorns who shopped in the Leipzig Organ stores.

'Hurry it up,' the director shouted. 'We're losing the light.'

'Soon as you get me a new machine,' said Bell as he limped off in search of the mechanician who had tuned his motorcycle.

The *Hell's Bells* company had established a temporary machine shop in an abandoned caboose on a rusty siding. Ignoring the pain in his ankle, he mounted the ramp the mechanician had laid to wheel the motorcycle up and down, and entered the gloomy interior in a sudden rush.

'Marty,' he asked in a low and dangerous voice. 'Tell me who took a hacksaw to my front axle.'

Marty did not reply.

Bell found him on the floor behind his workbench, his eyes bulging wide open, fixed intently on nothing. Bell lighted a lamp and looked at him closely. The mechanician had been garroted with a wire that had cut his head half off his neck. It looked like the Acrobat had silenced his accomplice with the same thin cable he had wrapped around the neck of the Golden State Limited express messenger he had murdered in New Mexico. It was also the same cable he had used to vault over the locomotive and to 'fly' from the *Mauretania*'s boat deck.

Isaac Bell spoke out loud, addressing the Acrobat as if the murderer were still in the caboose.

'I am worrying you,' he said, reviewing in his mind the many strands of his investigation and wondering which had alarmed the murderer. 'I am making you afraid.'

The Acrobat apparently saw those strands as forming a net. Which ones? Bell wondered. Which of the many strands had spooked him?

Grady Forrer was pursuing a Hamburg Bankhaus–Imperial Film connection. Andrew Rubenoff had connected Hamburg Bankhaus to Leipzig Organ & Piano and was now hunting Imperial's foreign bankers. The Van Dorn field offices had exposed Leipzig Organ for a sham. Bell himself had tracked Leipzig's Fritz Wunderlich to Denver, and now the men watching the consulates had the German's likeness. Joe Van Dorn was working his Washington, DC, contacts to establish German consulate connections. Larry Saunders was probing City Hall for the Imperial Building floor plans. Texas Walt had covered Imperial Protection and was currently employed as an extra inside Imperial's penthouse studios.

If the Acrobat had ordered the murder of Art Curtis in Berlin, then he knew the Van Dorns were after him. The attacks on the Van Dorn apprentices confirmed that. But today's sabotage of Bell's motorcycle indicated that the

Acrobat had penetrated Bell's 'insurance man' disguise, too, and saw him either as aligned with the Van Dorn Detective Agency or an actual agent of the outfit.

'I still don't know what you're up to. But I'm closer than I think.'

Then it struck Bell hard. If – as seemed likely, though not close to proven – Imperial Film was mixed up with the Acrobat and Krieg Rüstungswerk, then Marion's job at Imperial was no coincidence, but rather the Acrobat's cold-blooded ace in the hole.

Bell rode the Angels Flight funicular railway two blocks up a steep grade to the residential neighborhood on top of Bunker Hill, where he had rented a mansion after Marion took the job Irina Viorets had offered at Imperial. Concealing his limp, he climbed the back steps and bounded into the kitchen.

'Just in time for our first married home-cooked meal,' Marion greeted him. 'Oh, Isaac, what a wonderful day this is.' She hugged him hard and kissed him. 'Would you like a cocktail for whatever you've done to your poor foot?'

'I'll mix them,' Bell smiled, ruefully, reminded forcibly that if women were more observant than men, then women who made movies missed absolutely nothing.

Marion's eyes were ablaze with joy. 'It's like I died and went to heaven. Irina gives me anything I want – locomotives, Pullmans, mule trains, Conestoga wagons. She even got me Billy Bitzer to operate the camera.'

'Congratulations.'

'Billy brought Dave Davidson, his number one assistant, to operate the second camera. So I have the two best operators in the business. And to top it all off – do you remember Franklin Mowery?'

'The old bridge builder. Of course. He worked for Lillian's father.'

'Franklin retired out here. I invited him to where we're taking pictures to answer my research questions. He's a walking encyclopedia of railroad history, having been there for most of it. Fabulous stories. And here's the best part: Dave Davidson has a portrait painter's eye; he took one look at Franklin's granite profile and, without saying a word, just started cranking the camera, pretending he was adjusting it or something. Later he showed me twenty feet of Franklin Mowery. The camera absolutely *loves* him. So I'm putting him in the picture – Oh, Isaac, I'm so excited!'

'Indeed,' said Bell, wondering, How can I ask her to leave this job on a suspicion?

'Don't worry,' she said, 'I warned Franklin Mowery that you are working in disguise and not to reveal that you're a Van Dorn.'

'It probably doesn't matter by now.'

'Is that what happened to your foot?'

'My ankle got off easy compared to my motorcycle,' said Bell, and told her what had happened. Then he laid out the strands of the Talking Pictures investigation one by one, from Grady and Rubenoff to his and Texas Walt's fruitless spying inside Imperial. 'Having failed to kill you,' asked Marion, 'what do you suppose he'll try next?'

Isaac Bell looked his beautiful wife in the eye. 'You tell me.'

'I know what you're thinking, Isaac. You're worried that I'm somehow in danger because I'm "coincidentally" taking pictures for the same company where you installed Clyde Lynds, and now you are having second thoughts.'

'I couldn't put it better myself,' said Bell. 'Something is amiss at Imperial.'

'But I can't believe that Irina would be part of anything that would hurt me. Besides, you don't *know* that Imperial isn't on the up-and-up.'

'Imperial's finances are deeply suspect.'

'*Everyone's* business finances in moving pictures are deeply suspect. It's a brand-new business. Nobody knows what's really going on. We're all making it up as we go along. That's why the bankers lend money for only one picture at a time.'

'Are you sure you've noticed nothing unusual while taking pictures for *The Iron Horse*? Nothing out of the ordinary? Nothing different than you'd expect or have seen on other jobs?'

Marion pondered his question. 'Only one thing. There's a film-stock shortage. Everyone in Los Angeles is talking about it. For a month or so, film's become hard to get and very expensive. Yesterday, Billy and Dave came to me with long faces. Their stock was old. It smelled awful, and they said the pictures would be terribly overexposed. I telephoned Irina. In less than one hour a truck raced up with more than we could use of the most pristine stock you could ask for. It was precisely perforated and smelled fresh as a meadow. You should have seen Billy and Dave rubbing their hands like Silas Marner counting his gold.'

'Where did it come from?'

'It was Eastman Kodak stock, straight from the factory.'

'But Imperial is independent. Eastman made a deal with the Edison Trust: they won't sell to independents.'

'Where they got it, I don't know. But for Imperial, at least, there is no shortage.' Anyway, if you'll limp into the dining room, I'll bring dinner.'

'What is our first married home-cooked meal?'

'The same as our first-ever home-cooked meal. Do you remember what I made you?'

'I remember you invited me to dinner and cooked pot roast and vegetables. It was splendid, though I have a vague memory that we got sidetracked before dessert – Marion, I'll bet you've some cowboys in *The Iron Horse*.'

'Bunkhousesful.'

'Got room for one more?'

'Texas Walt?'

Bell nodded. 'Just to be on the safe side.'

'If that will make you feel better, of course.'

'I would feel much better knowing my good friend the deadly gunfighter was looking out for you.'

Marion smiled. 'Walt may not be a deadly gunfighter much longer. Movie people are all talking about "the tall Texan" playing cowboy parts. Some people think he could be a star.'

'Please don't turn his head until we're sure you're safe and sound.'

38

Pauline Grandzau had been memorizing the St Germain section of her *Baedeker* on the train when suddenly she had to run from a gendarme who demanded her papers at a station stop. The last few miles of what should have been a twelve-hour train ride stretched to another full day clinging to the underside of a slow-moving coal car that finally dumped her near an open-air market in Paris in the rain. Thanks to the tourist guidebook and the foldout map, she found the Rue du Bac as night fell, climbed a steep flight of stairs, and staggered into the Van Dorn Detective Agency's Paris field office, exhausted, wet, and hungry.

An enormous man seated next to a bright light asked, 'What do you want here, miss?'

At least that's what it sounded like. He spoke French. She did not. But she saw in his eyes what he assumed: a street urchin with dirty hands and face and stringy braids and a snuffling nose had sneaked into the building either begging for money or running from the police.

He asked her again. The light was so bright it was blinding her. He stood up, and the entire room, which had a linoleum floor and a desk and a chair and an interior door that led somewhere, started spinning.

'Is this the Van Dorn Detective Agency Paris field office?' she asked.

He looked surprised she spoke English.

'Yes, it is,' he replied with an accent like Detective Curtis's. 'What can I do for you, little lady?'

'Are you Detective Horace Bronson?'

'I'm Bronson. Who are you?'

Pauline Grandzau pulled herself up to her full five feet two inches. 'Apprentice Van Dorn detective Pauline Grandzau reporting from Berlin.'

She tried to salute, but her arm was heavy, and her legs were rubbery. She saw the linoleum rushing at her face. Bronson moved with surprising speed and caught her.

'Cable from the Paris field office, Mr Bell.'

It was from Bronson.

It was long and detailed.

Isaac Bell read it twice.

A hunter's gleam began burning in his eyes. A smile of grim satisfaction lighted his stern face like the sun glancing off a frozen river, and he vowed to Fritz Wunderlich, to Krieg Rüstungswerk, to Kaiser Wilhelm II, and especially to Imperial Army General Major Christian Semmler that Van Dorn Detective Arthur Curtis had not died in vain.

BOOK FOUR

Lights! Camera! Speed!

39

'Telegrapher! On the jump!' Isaac Bell summoned the man who sent and received Morse code on the field office's private telegraph.

'Wire Mr Joseph Van Dorn: "Inquire US Army and State Department German General Major Christian Semmler. Show them Wunderlich sketch."

'Wire Research Chief Grady Forrer, New York: "Who is German General Major Christian Semmler? Obtain photograph or newspaper sketch."

'Cable Horace Bronson, Paris Office: "Who is German General Major Christian Semmler? Obtain photograph or newspaper sketch."

'Wire Detective Archie Abbott, New York: "Ask Lord Strone about German General Major Christian Semmler. Show Wunderlich sketch."

'Send them. On the jump!'

Of the responses that flooded in over the next twenty-four hours, the one that intrigued Bell most came from the boss. Joe Van Dorn had discovered that General Major Semmler was married to Sophie Roth Semmler, the sole heiress of the Krieg Rüstungswerk fortune. Such wealth and power explained the lone operator's ability to operate far more independently than a typical German Army officer.

But Joseph Van Dorn's informants in the Army and diplomatic corps knew almost nothing else about Semmler. The general major did not seek the limelight. A US Army observer in China had heard that Semmler had established an excellent war record in the Boxer Rebellion. A retired embassy attaché had repeated rumors of a fearsome reputation in the South African War, when Semmler had supposedly led rebel Boer commandos behind British lines. But as none of Van Dorn's informants among the diplomats and soldiers had actually met Semmler, the sketch of Fritz Wunderlich proved useless in Washington.

Grady Forrer's researchers had hunted in vain for photographs or newspaper sketches. Not unusual, Grady pointed out: only if Semmler had been a prominent member of a visiting German party or an attaché to the kaiser's embassy would American newspapers have taken note of the soldier.

Bell hoped for more from Bronson in Paris as he would have access to European papers and magazines. But Bronson cabled of the same dearth of images. Even the new man in Berlin could find no photographs or sketches in the German press. Considering how military men were lionized in Germany, it seemed that Christian Semmler went out of his way not to court publicity.

Bell was disappointed, but hardly surprised. As a private detective who habitually avoided cameras, he expected no less of a soldier experienced at behind-the-lines guerrilla warfare. Nonetheless, he had learned that Semmler was rich. And he was independent, which Bell had already guessed. But if the thirty-five-year-old, powerfully built soldier and spy had green eyes, blond hair, and long arms 'like a monkey', no one had yet matched his face to the sketch of Fritz Wunderlich, so they were no closer to proving whether Semmler and Wunderlich were one and the same.

'That is an unfriendly gate,' said Lillian Hennessy Abbott, braking her big red Thomas Flyer Model K 6-70 to a stop in front of it. 'Do you suppose it's locked?'

'I was told it would be,' said Archie.

Attached to tall stone pillars, the double gate that blocked the road into the Earl of Strone's Greenwich estate was made of heavy wrought-iron bars painted black and looked, Archie Abbott thought, very much locked.

He stepped down from the big touring car in which they had driven up to Connecticut and paused to steady himself on the fender. Lillian had gone out of her way to drive smoothly, having deliberately chosen the auto for its long wheelbase, instead of her beloved Packard Wolf racer, but the roads had been hellish.

'Are you all right, Archie?'

'Tip-top.' He hinged out a blade of spring steel from what looked like an ordinary penknife and worked the lock open. He swung the two halves of the gate wide enough for the auto. Lillian drove through, and Archie locked it behind them.

'Drive on.'

A quarter mile along a curving driveway paved with crushed slate, they saw a sizable mansion of brick decorated with stone in a style that reminded Archie of Henry VIII's palace at Hampton Court.

The thick, wooden front door had no knocker. To save his knuckles, Archie banged on it with the butt of the Navy Colt .45 automatic he had taken to carrying since being shot nearly to death. When he heard the door being opened, he smoothly holstered the weapon and drew a calling card from his vest.

A strapping butler – a retired sergeant major, by the look of him – who had been stuffed into a swallowtail coat peered out with an expression that was less than friendly.

Archie proffered his card. 'Be so good as to inform His Lordship that Archibald Angel Abbott and Mrs Abbott are here for tea.'

'I am not aware you're expected, sir.'

'We sailed on the *Mauretania* with His Lordship. He invited my wife to drop in if we were ever in the neighborhood. We are in the neighborhood.'

The butler took in the sight of Lillian behind the wheel of the Thomas. She had removed her dust hat and veil. Her blond hair shone in the sun, and her eyes gleamed like sapphires. It occurred to the butler that the next time he clapped eyes on a smile like hers it would be on the far side of the Pearly Gates. 'Please come in, sir. I will inform His Lordship.'

'I will collect my wife.'

As he helped Lillian out of her auto, Archie said, 'I feel vaguely like a procurer.'

Lillian kissed him on the lips. 'And you would be so good at it. Fortunately for me, you have other talents. Are you sure you're all right?'

'I am alive and in love on a beautiful day in the country.'

Strone was in tweed. He had a shotgun draped over his arm. 'Lovely to see you again, my dear,' he said to Lillian. To Archie he was brusque. 'Just going out for a tramp about the marsh. Come along if you like.'

He put a deerstalker on his head and led the way at a quick pace down a garden path and over lawns, heading toward a vast marsh that disappeared in the haze of the Long Island Sound.

'I was under the impression that my front gate was locked.'

'We locked it on the way in,' said Archie.

Lillian said, 'Let's walk slowly. My husband is recovering from an accident.'

'Terribly sorry. Of course we'll slow our pace. What sort of accident, Abbott?'

'I bumped into a Webley-Fosbery.'

Strone stopped walking and looked at Archie. 'Hmmm. You never mentioned that on the boat.'

'Automatic revolvers never make for wedding small talk.'

'I say, are you in the insurance trade like your friend Bell?'

'Isaac Bell and I will remain in the insurance trade as long as you remain "retired".'

A smile twitched Strone's red cheeks and gray mustache.

'One does not step out of retirement willy-nilly.'

'What if I gave you a good reason?'

'I pride myself as a man open to reason. Though one man's reason could be another man's poison.'

'Then I won't give you a reason. I'll give you a name.'

'A name?'

'Semmler,' said Archie, who observed nothing on Strone's face move except his pupils, which narrowed momentarily.

'Can't say it rings a bell, old boy,' Strone lied.

'Christian Semmler.'

'No. I don't believe –'

'Colonel Christian Semmler. The rank he held when you were stationed in South Africa.'

'Where did you get the notion that I was stationed in South Africa?'

'*Oberst* Christian Semmler, as our German friends addressed him.'

'I don't have German friends.'

'Lately,' said Archie, 'I've been dropping mine. Semmler has been promoted several times since the South African War. He is currently a general major.'

Strone abruptly dropped all pretense of ignorance. 'Yes, I know.'

'He is plotting in America.'

'Plotting what?'

'We don't know.'

Strone's jaw tightened. 'He is a slippery, nervy bastard. He was as cold-blooded an operator as any we encountered, harassing our columns, sniping our pickets. And God help the scouts he waylaid. He made the Boers seem sweet as schoolboys.'

'Would you recognize him if you saw him?'

'I only saw him once. And only through a glass at a great distance.'

'Lillian?' said Archie.

Lillian pulled a notebook from her long duster and opened it to the sketch of Fritz Wunderlich.

'Did he look like this man?'

Strone took wire-frame spectacles from the folds of his shooting clothes and studied the copy of the salesman's sketch. 'This man is older,' he said at last. 'Of course it's been, what?'

'Nearly ten years,' said Archie. 'How far away was he?'

Strone looked across the marsh in silence, his mouth working, his eyes bleak.

Archie and Lillian exchanged a glance. Archie gestured for her to say nothing.

'One thousand yards,' Strone answered at last. 'We thought we were safe from his rifle at that range and that we could ride closer. And, of course, he was just one man alone . . . What made you come to me?'

'Isaac Bell had a feeling you were more than you appeared to be. He was right. When we dug deeper, we learned that you were decorated in that action.'

Strone flushed angrily. 'Ruddy nonsense.'

'What do you mean, nonsense? You received the Distinguished Service Order.'

'I mean *nonsense*. Semmler lured us onto a bridge he had mined with dynamite. He sniped the wounded with rifle fire. My DSO was awarded to the only man that murderous swine missed.'

Isaac Bell rounded up Texas Walt Hatfield and Larry Saunders and a crew of Saunders's handpicked men for a powwow.

'Information from Art Curtis and his Berlin apprentice,

expanded upon by Archie Abbott and the Research department, proves that the murderer we called the Acrobat, the drummer Fritz Wunderlich, and German Imperial Army General Major Christian Semmler are all one and the same. In addition, Mr Van Dorn has established that General Major Christian Semmler is not only Krieg Rüstungswerk's agent, but also a principal. To put it bluntly, he married the boss's daughter.

'Semmler's alias, Fritz Wunderlich, flew the coop when he caught wind of our visits to his shops and my calling on his hotel in Denver. Before we congratulate ourselves on Wunderlich's loss of a string of shops that gave him and his accomplices safe passage around the continent, remember that the German consulates offer General Major Semmler even safer places to hide, get money, rest, eat, and sleep. Tracking Semmler will not be like tracking an ordinary criminal to his hideout. As much as we might enjoy it, we cannot smash open the doors of a sovereign nation's consulates.

'I had already expressed copies of this "Wunderlich" picture to every field office covering a German consulate in New York, Chicago, St Louis, San Francisco, and the vice-consul's office here in Los Angeles. Now I've informed them it's a likeness of Semmler.'

'Isaac Bell's voice resonates with confidence,' said Christian Semmler. 'Listen!'

He thrust the telephone earpiece at Hermann Wagner.

Wagner, sick with fear, took it with a trembling hand. The Berlin banker had seen the Donar leader's face for the first time tonight. He had speculated that the mysterious leader might be Semmler, mainly because of rumors about the kaiser's affection for the officer they called the Monkey. The heavy browridges, the massive protruding jaw, and the gangly arms were frightening confirmation. The leader was indeed the kaiser's favorite, General Major Christian Semmler. For some reason Semmler had allowed him to see his face, and Wagner feared that Semmler intended to kill him when he was done.

'Listen to him!'

Wagner pressed the telephone to his ear.

He and Semmler were hunched across from each other over a table in the cellar of Germany's Los Angeles vice-consul's mansion. The vice-consul was upstairs, aware in only the most general terms of the use they were putting his building to, and probably deeply relieved that he had been forbidden entry to his own cellar.

The telephone was one that Christian Semmler had had connected via the vice-consul's private line to a microphone he had stolen from Clyde Lynds and had paid an electrician to hide in the Van Dorn Detective Agency. Like an innkeeper tapping a keg of lager, Semmler had laughed as he explained the eavesdropping system to the disbelieving Hermann Wagner.

It seemed like a miracle. More than a miracle, it seemed impossible. But Wagner could actually hear Isaac Bell speaking to his private investigators even though a full two miles separated the Van Dorn Detective Agency from the German consulate.

'You hear?'

'A little. Not very well.'

'I know that!' snapped Semmler. 'Lynds's microphone

is not thoroughly perfected yet. But he's on the right track, and if you listen closely, you can hear the confidence in Bell's voice. Why shouldn't he sound assured? He's learned so much these past several days.'

'Yes, he has,' Wagner agreed nervously.

'Events do not always unfold as we plan them,' said Semmler. 'It is the nature of plans, and events.' He looked up and his green eyes sparkled with amusement. 'I recall one night on the high veldt, when three British Tommies cornered me, my escape went according to plan. But no sooner had I killed them than I was seized by my arm and dragged to the ground. I could hardly believe it. I was attacked out of nowhere by a lion! A lion! The beast was attracted by the scent of the Tommies' blood.'

Semmler reached across the table and laid a powerful hand on Hermann Wagner's arm. 'Relax, Herr Wagner, you look terrified.'

'I *am* terrified,' the banker admitted. 'You warned me on the *Mauretania* never to look on your face. Tonight you show me your face. What am I to think but the worst?'

'Do not worry. You are valuable alive. I still need you. I need you more than ever. There is much to be done.'

'What can be done? Bell is onto you. And he's closing in on Imperial Film.'

Semmler snatched the telephone from the banker's hand and listened. A brilliant smile filled his strange face. It brightened his eyes and spread his lips, but bright as it was, Wagner thought, it looked cold as distant lightning.

'Bell,' said the leader of the Donar Plan, 'would sound less confident if he knew we could hear him.'

40

'Mr Bell, could I see that picture again?'

Isaac Bell handed the Wunderlich sketch to a Los Angeles Van Dorn disguised in the patched clothing and dark glasses of a blind newspaper seller. The detective took off the glasses and studied the sketch.

'You know, he didn't look quite like this. But it *could* have been him.'

'*When?*'

The blind newsie opened his notebook and read dead-pan: 'Individual possibly resembling Mr Bell's sketch of Fritz Wunderlich entered German vice-consul's residence Saturday at ten past eight. Detective Balant decided it wasn't him.'

'Ten past eight this evening?'

'Yes, sir.'

'When did he come out?'

'Didn't.'

Every detective in the room reached for his hat. Bell was already at the door. 'He never came out? Are you sure?'

'I covered the front door, right across the street from my newsstand. When I needed relief to come here, Patrolman Joe Thomas, who lends us a hand, promised to cover till I got back.'

'Come on, boys, let's have a look.'

They piled into two Ford autos and raced across town.

Larry Saunders asked Bell, 'Is there any way we can get inside the consulate?'

'Not without setting off an international hullabaloo.'

Bell ordered the cars stopped a block from the residence of the German vice-consul, who had been recently appointed by the San Francisco consul general. 'Wait here. I don't want them looking out their window at half the detectives in California.'

He walked down the block and stopped at the 'blind newsie's' newspaper stand. The cop, Patrolman Joe Thomas, was seated inside, yawning. 'Van Dorn,' said Bell, picking up the evening edition of the *Los Angeles Times* to shield the act of showing the sketch. 'Have you seen this fellow come out of the consulate?'

'You just missed him,' said the cop. 'Lit out of there like the house was on fire.'

'Isaac Bell will confront you,' Christian Semmler warned Irina Viorets. 'Be prepared.'

'I *am* prepared.'

'I would recommend that you act both disbelieving and fiercely defiant.'

'I said I am prepared.'

'I would play the J. P. Morgan card if I were you.'

'I intend to.'

'It would not be an exaggeration,' Semmler smiled, 'to say that the life of your "prince" hangs in the balance.'

She did not have long to wait. The lobby guards telephoned on the Imperial Building's Kellogg system.

'Of course,' she said. 'Send Mr Bell straight up.'

She told her secretaries, 'No interruptions.'

Bell came in briskly, tall and lanky and handsome as ever, even with his face so stern.

'Isaac,' she teased, smiling as she rose from her desk to greet him, 'you look as if you exited your bed from the wrong side this morning.'

'Irina, your "investors" are Hamburg merchant bankers funneling money from the Imperial German Army.'

'That is not true.'

'The bank goes by the name Hamburg Bankhaus.'

'Isaac, please. You're being silly.'

'The operation is run by your boss, a German general major named Christian Semmler.'

She looked him boldly in the eye. 'I know no Christian Semmler. Imperial Film is a going concern. We are building a great national enterprise to produce, distribute, and exhibit moving pictures.'

Bell did not give an inch. 'If you don't know Christian Semmler, then to whom do you report?'

'I report to the head of the Artists Syndicate.'

'There is no Artists Syndicate. It's a sham.'

Irina Viorets let the silence build between them. Then she sat behind her desk and picked up a long silver letter opener and twirled it slowly in her fingers, pointing it first at Bell, then back at herself, then again at Bell.

He broke the silence. 'The Artists Syndicate is a sham. It does not exist.'

'That will come as a surprise to the man who heads it.'

'*What?* Who?'

'Singleton Brooks.'

She saw that Isaac Bell was puzzled and thrown off. It

was almost as if he knew the name, which was the one thing she had not expected. But that appeared to be precisely the case. Bell actually knew the man. All the better, she thought, relief flooding through her. A good plan – a plan to derail Bell's suspicions – had unexpectedly gotten even better. Her prince's luck had turned. She could feel it in her soul.

The name Singleton Brooks was familiar to Isaac Bell, but he couldn't recall why. Then it struck him. He remembered an unpleasant interview on Wall Street in the course of the Wrecker investigation.

'Singleton Brooks works for J. P. Morgan.'

Irina staggered him with a beautiful smile and a smug, 'I believe that Mr Morgan is not a sham.'

'I will have people in New York check on Mr Brooks.'

'No need. Mr Brooks arrives on the Golden State Limited tomorrow night. You can meet him at the station and ask him face-to-face . . . Is there anything else, Isaac? If not, please convey my warmest regards to Marion.'

Isaac Bell recovered with a smile, shook Irina's hand, and left the building. It appeared that Christian Semmler has laid his groundwork even more thoroughly than he had imagined.

He went straight to Bunker Hill, rode up on the Angels Flight, and burst into Andrew Rubenoff's mansion. Rubenoff was at the piano, singing 'That Mesmerizing Mendelssohn Tune'.

'This Berlin fellow has a knack.'

'Does Singleton Brooks still work for J. P. Morgan?'

'Last I heard. And I would have heard if he had left.'

'Irina Viorets claims that Brooks represents Artists Syndicate, which you said didn't exist.'

'I never said it would *never* exist. It did not exist when I inquired. Perhaps it exists now.'

'What the heck is going on?'

'Morgan's shipping combine is taking a bath. International Mercantile Marine has been sorely used by the British government and the American Congress. Perhaps he sees an opportunity in Imperial Film. However it was financed aside, Imperial is poised to seize a controlling interest in much of independent film manufacturing, distribution, and exhibition. That's the sort of meat Morgan feasts on.'

'But Krieg and the German Army –'

'Things change, Isaac. Events do not always unfold as first planned.'

The bookcase in Irina Vioret's office slid open on silent, ball-bearing tracks. Christian Semmler emerged from his stairwell. 'Tomorrow night,' he said, 'after the *Iron Horse* company returns from taking pictures, I want you to ask Mrs Bell to do you a favor.'

'What sort of favor?'

'I overheard our bloody director upstairs threatening to quit – just when they finished building the ship and pier.'

'Why?'

'He says the scenario won't work. Something about the searchlights in the dark. I want him fired tomorrow. Then I want you to ask Mrs Bell to help you by staying late to take pictures for his immigrant arrival scenario so the carpenters can clear the ship and pier and build her *Iron Horse* stage set.'

'What if she says no?'

'You know as well as I do that Marion Bell will not say no to anything that would help her production. Nor would she miss an opportunity to take pictures in the dark by the glare of searchlights. She will rise to the challenge. Particularly when you can tell her that the original director quit because he wasn't up to it.'

Irina Vioret's dark eyes filled with anxious foreboding. 'What are you going to do to her?'

'Nothing! *Gott im Himmel,* what are you thinking, woman? I promise you I will do nothing to derail the success of *The Iron Horse.* Just make sure that damned cowboy has gone before you ask her.'

41

Minutes before Isaac Bell went to La Grande Station to meet Singleton Brooks's train, Los Angeles field office chief Larry Saunders reported that the city records clerk, who Saunders had hoped would admit to the existence of a secret set of blueprints for the Imperial Building, had been crushed to death under an Angels Flight funicular railway car.

'The cops say he got oiled and tried to walk up the tracks. But being they are so steep, I'd expect that stunt more of a drunken sailor than an overweight, middle-aged file clerk. I'm sorry, Mr Bell, he was my best shot, but I'll keep trying.'

Bell thought hard. Then he said, 'Larry, I want you to take personal charge of the Van Dorn Protective Service men guarding Clyde Lynds starting right now.'

The dandified Saunders asked why.

Isaac Bell replied in a manner that left no latitude for debate: 'Because I have a very strong feeling about tonight.'

Then Bell switched tactics at La Grande Station.

Singleton Brooks's Limited was due in at nine. Instead of simply walking up to Brooks and challenging him, Bell decided to have the J. P. Morgan executive followed first. Where he went might reveal a lot. He believed that Brooks might lead him to Christian Semmler – or did he merely hope? Regardless, Brooks would likely recognize Bell. Even if Bell disguised himself in his black motorcycle costume, the odds were Irina had alerted him to Bell's suspicions.

So Bell had ordered Texas Walt Hatfield to do the primary tracking, and Texas Walt was ensconced in a saloon just outside the station's main entrance. Bell would point out Singleton to him. Bell had another Van Dorn standing by in an Oldsmobile taxicab in the event that Singleton was picked up in an auto, while Balant, the blind newsie, transformed tonight into a gawking tourist, would follow the New York banker if he boarded a streetcar.

Van Dorn Detective Chuck Shipley, a young, eager-to-prove-himself transfer from the Kansas City office, sat inside the blind newsie's stand wearing a cap rented from a rooming house neighbor who made a living hawking newspapers on the street. Mr Saunders had encouraged Shipley to get a nickel-plated changemaker to hook over his belt, enhancing his disguise. But Detective Balant had forbidden him to wear dark glasses, explaining, testily, that even if the Germans inside the vice-consul's mansion were stupid – and there was no evidence they were – they would still wonder why the recently installed newsstand on their corner employed only blind men.

'In other words, Chuck, get your own disguise.'

Along with the cap and the changemaker, Shipley affected a severe limp, but seated behind the counter it was hard to show it off, as the only time he got to step out was when the trucks arrived with fresh editions. But here came one now, bearing bundles of the *Los Angeles Examiner*. The driver stayed behind the wheel. The helper slung a bundle under his arm and brought it around to the side, blocking the door so Chuck Shipley couldn't get out to strut his limp.

'Where's the blind guy?'

'He's off tonight. His old man got sick.'

'Here, I got something for him. You give it to him.'

'What is it?'

'Look here.' The helper was holding something below his knees. Chuck looked. He saw nothing but the helper's hand, which suddenly formed a fist encased in brass knuckles that traveled at his jaw like a rocket. Caught flat-footed, Chuck saw fireballs of different colors and then nothing but night.

The helper stretched Shipley out on the floor and grabbed more bundles from the truck to cover the body.

Then the *Examiner* truck pulled across the street and stopped in front of the German vice-consul's mansion. Six powerful men in a variety of slouch hats and loose-fitting suits of clothes exited the mansion by a basement door. Most wore short beards; all had the blue-eyed, strong-jawed features of the South African Dutch. They piled into the truck, which drove straight to the Imperial Building. The six entered the lobby by the side entrance. The doormen greeted them warmly, like old comrades-in-arms.

The Golden State Limited rumbled into La Grande Station on time.

From a distance, Bell spotted a familiar short, compact figure jump impatiently from the stateroom car that

313

Research had determined was Brooks's. Brooks pushed through the crowd on the platform and through the arrival hall to the front of the station.

Bell gave Texas Walt the nod. Brooks hopped into a taxi. Walt eased into the Oldsmobile, and the Van Dorn driver trailed Brooks's taxi away from the station. Balant, waiting by the streetcar track, hailed another taxi and tore after them.

'Mr Bell. Mr Bell.'

Bell recognized the out-of-breath Van Dorn messenger running up to him.

'Best to keep your voice low, son, while engaging a colleague on duty,' Bell cautioned, mildly. He took the messenger's arm. 'Walk along with me while we try to notice who took notice . . . What do you make of that fellow in the straw hat? Is he watching us? . . . Oh, there he goes with that lady kissing him. Otherwise, we're clear. What's the message?'

'Telephone Mr Clyde Lynds soon as you can.'

Bell hurried inside the train station and telephoned the laboratory. Clyde Lynds sounded even more excited than the messenger. 'Come see. I've synchronized sound and pictures.'

'I'll be right there.'

But as Bell exited the station to race to the Imperial Building, he bumped into Texas Walt.

'What are you doing here? Did you lose Brooks?'

'Nope.'

'Where is he?'

'Stopped in Levy's Café for supper. Balant's watching him.'

'Cover him closely. I'll be at the Imperial Building.'

'Can't.'

'Why not?'

'Guess who he's eating supper with?'

'Irina Viorets.'

'Nope. He's eating with a fellow who'll spot me in a second.'

'Who?'

'The feller who directed me in those Western dramas, the Pirate King himself, Jay Tarses.'

Bell shook his head in disbelief. 'I figured Brooks would meet Irina first thing. And I hoped he would lead us to Semmler. What's he doing with Tarses?'

'Balant took a table near 'em. We met up in the alley outside the facilities and Balant told me that Tarses mumbles too quiet to hear, but he heard Brooks jawing up a storm.'

'About Imperial?'

'No. J. P. Morgan is fixing to start a moving picture factory, and he wants Tarses to run it for him. Brooks is troweling it on thick about how much they need Tarses. Tarses is watching him like a snake. So it don't sound to me like Brooks came to Los Angeles to visit Imperial. He's come out here to grubstake a new outfit.'

'Maybe he's meeting Irina tomorrow,' Bell said with little confidence.

'Hell, Isaac, why don't I just walk in and ask him straight off?'

'I'll do it. I know Brooks slightly, and I want to watch to see if he's lying.'

'You want me to back you up?'

'I think between Balant and me,' Bell answered drily, 'we can handle one back-East banker . . . Walt, would you do me a favor?'

'Shore, Isaac. What do you need?'

'Get an auto and park outside the house we took up on Bunker Hill.'

'Keep an eye on Marion?'

'I'd appreciate it.'

'You want me to go in the house?'

'No, she's up so early, she's probably sleeping by now. Just watch from outside.'

Bell hurried to Levy's Café. Many of the tables were empty as the late second seating was finishing up. Boot heels clicking on the tile floor, he strode straight to the table where Tarses was listening to the Morgan banker with an expression of unconcealed suspicion. Bell pulled up a chair. Tarses looked up, remembering Bell but not quite sure why. Singleton Brooks, too, recognized Bell, and the banker turned out to have a very fine memory.

'Detective Bell. What are you doing here?'

'My question exactly,' said Isaac Bell. 'Why are you dining with Mr Tarses instead of Mademoiselle Irina Viorets?'

Jay Tarses's face darkened, as if his suspicions had all been confirmed. 'Why didn't you tell me you were talking to Imperial, too?'

'I am not talking to Imperial. I told you, I came all the way out here specially to talk to you.'

'Oh, yeah? Then why are you meeting Irina Viorets, who happens to run Imperial?'

'I'm not,' Brooks protested. 'I don't know the woman.'

'You know who she is.'

'Of course I know who she is.'

Tarses looked at Isaac Bell. 'Mr Bell, what is it about moving pictures that rewards the worst and punishes the best?'

'What, sir, are you implying?' demanded Brooks.

Isaac Bell said, 'Hold on, gentlemen, I owe you an apology. Answer one more question, Mr Brooks, and I will be able to assure Mr Tarses that you are on the level. Do you represent the Artists Syndicate?'

'I don't even know what the Artists Syndicate is. And whatever it is I certainly don't represent it.'

'And you don't know Mademoiselle Viorets?'

'I know who she is. I do not recall ever meeting her.'

'You would,' said Tarses. 'She's a looker.'

'I am a married man,' Brooks said stiffly.

Bell stood up. 'Further proof that he's on the up and up, Mr Tarses. Sorry to have interrupted your supper.'

'Mrs Rennegal,' Marion said to her favorite Cooper-Hewitt operator. 'We are supposed to be laying a scene on a pier beside a ship on a foggy night in the spooky glare of searchlights. This looks like a romantic candlelit dinner for two.'

'But Mrs Bell,' said Rennegal, climbing wearily down the ladder from yet another adjustment of the Cooper-Hewitts hanging high in the flies over a stage decorated to depict the immigrants' landing at Ellis Island, 'Mr Bitzer and Mr Davidson keep complaining the searchlights over-expose their film.'

'That is why I sent Mr Bitzer and Mr Davidson out for a late supper – before I shot one of them – so you and I can try some other stunts to light this scene.' Davidson had joked that tossing spare actors off the roof carrying cameras to film their own fall in the general direction of the life net would be easier than faking a foggy night scene in the studio, while providing bigger thrills for the exhibitors.

'What if we painted the side of the ship a darker color?'

'I'm really sorry, Mrs Bell. I can't stay any later. My husband is working the graveyard shift, and there's no one to stay with the baby.'

'Go. Thanks for staying as long as you could. I will figure it out. See you at *The Iron Horse* in the morning. We will try this again tomorrow night. The sooner we're done, the sooner they can knock down this ship and put up our locomotive. Good night, dear. Thank you. Good night, *everyone*. Thank you all.'

Rennegal, her assistant, and the stagehands and electricians trooped into the elevator, chorusing, 'Good night, Mrs Bell.'

The elevator hummed down to the lobby, leaving her in a silence. Marion paced the empty stage. What if, she wondered, she got rid of the smoke? Did it soften the light or make it brighter?

She really had to go home and rest up for tomorrow. But as tired as she was, she could not stop thinking.

She opened the door in the glass north wall of the penthouse and stepped outside, onto the narrow terrace. A chilly breeze from the mountains plucked at her blouse. She hugged herself for warmth and peered over the parapet down at the tiny circle of the life net a hundred feet below.

Lighted by the spill from the windows of the first-floor film exchange, the canvas gleamed like a silver dollar. Marion studied it intently. There had to be a way to depict the beams of the searchlights without washing out the surrounding darkness.

'Welcome, Bittereinders,' Christian Semmler greeted the fighters he had summoned from the vice-consulate. These six had been the last of the so-called *Bittereinders*, holdouts who had refused to surrender when the British defeated the Boers' regular armies and had fought on, extending the last days of hostilities by harassing slow-moving British columns, cutting their lines of communication, and killing sentries.

In the decade since the lost war, they had wandered, fighting for pay in the remote parts of the world where disciplined mercenaries fetched a premium. Ten years of such work had seasoned them into quick and nimble gunmen intimately familiar with up-to-date weapons, who were brave when they had to be and feared no one. But Semmler gave them pause. Some had seen him in action. All knew him by reputation. Each vowed privately that he would do exactly what the strange-looking German demanded – for despite his dazzling smile, he carried himself in a light and fluid way that promised sudden violence of memorable speed and ferocity.

He issued weapons, heavy-caliber American revolvers, clean and oiled, and short lengths of dynamite with fuses attached.

He showed them a map of the escape route from a secret exit out of the Imperial Building to a boxcar in the nearby Southern Pacific freight yards, where a special had steam up to shuttle them to the harbor at San Pedro and a ship ready to sail. Then he showed them blueprints of the building.

'We will survey the recording studio through this judas hole. After we locate our targets, we will enter through this wall, which slides open to the right.

'We will take the machines down these this hidden stairs. Once outside the building we will throw these quarter sticks of dynamite through the windows of the film exchange.'

One of the Boers held the quarter stick disdainfully between two fingers. 'What will this little piece do other than make a loud noise?'

'The film stock is highly flammable. When the dynamite ignites it, it will burn the building to the ground.'

Semmler was a guerrilla fighter at heart, which made him a realist. He sensed that Isaac Bell was tightening a noose around his neck. The cold truth was that a single piece of bad luck – Isaac Bell appearing on the *Mauretania*'s boat deck at precisely the wrong moment – threatened to run the Donar Plan off the rails. Everything that had gone wrong since could be traced to that night on the ship, and it was only a matter of time until the private detective exposed the Imperial Film scheme to spread pro-German propaganda.

But the Imperial Film system of manufacturing, distributing, and exhibiting propaganda movies was only a device. Better that he destroy it himself, incinerating all connections to the German Army. The volatile moving picture business would welcome a new 'Imperial Film' by whatever name and under whatever pretense. The key to the Donar Plan was still the Talking Pictures machine that would make the moving pictures irresistible.

With Talking Pictures in hand, he could still implement his original goal of using propaganda to divide Germany's enemies. Killing three birds with one stone, he would take his revenge on Isaac Bell, destroy all evidence, and escape home to Germany with the propaganda tool he needed to start anew.

He beckoned his fighters closer. 'Pay strict attention to this photograph.'

Christian Semmler showed the fighters a picture of Clyde Lynds that had been snapped by an Imperial publicity photographer when the scientist visited the penthouse studio stages.

'Not one hair on the head of this scientist is to be disturbed. He is the sole purpose of this raid. So mark well where he stands when we raid the studio. We will take him and his instruments – him unharmed, his equipment intact. Is that clear?' He looked each man in the eye until he answered, 'Yes, General.'

42

Isaac Bell telephoned Irina Viorets.

'I was hoping you were working late,' he said when she answered.

'I am always working late.'

'I met Mr Brooks.'

Irina Viorets surprised him. She said, 'Then you know I lied to you.'

'Why?'

'I think you should come to see me. Now.'

'All right. Tell the doormen to let me in.'

'No. Not here. I'll meet you on the street.'

Impressed by Isaac Bell's cold confidence that events were coming to a head, Larry Saunders had shed his tailored jacket for a still-stylish but more loosely draped garment with room for a Colt .45 in a shoulder holster and a couple of pocket pistols. And just to be on the safe side, he brought with him his top man, the formidable Tim Holian, who was the only detective in the field office who didn't care how he looked and slouched about the city in a disreputable-looking sack coat bulging with firearms.

When they got to the Imperial Building, they found that Clyde Lynds and his Protective Services guard had descended from the laboratory to set up camp in the soundproof fourth-floor recording studio, and they joined them there.

The detectives were edgy as the evening began, but when Clyde Lynds suddenly demanded a messenger to find Isaac Bell so Lynds could report to Bell, even Saunders and Holian were swept up in the scientist's excitement.

Detectives, Protective Service operatives, and Clyde Lynds gathered around Lynds's machine, which was projecting a moving picture on a white wall that served as a screen. Mounted on both sides of the makeshift screen were stacks of phonograph horns.

'Listen to this!' shouted Lynds.

His face alight with glee, Lynds grabbed the handle of an electrical switch and pulled it toward him.

A woman's voice came from the horns. She sounded hoarse and far away, but every eye in the room fixed on the image of her lips, which moved in precise synchronization with the words she was speaking.

Larry Saunders felt his own mouth drop open in amazement. It was an arresting sight. 'Wait till Bell sees this. It's like she's alive.'

Clyde Lynds grinned with pride. 'We're getting there,' he said. 'We're on our way.'

The wall on which the woman talking was projected moved.

Clyde Lynds stared in puzzlement.

The wall was sliding to his left, revealing darkness behind it that seemed to swallow the moving picture. And suddenly the woman's face vanished, and where it had been was the smile of the German whom the Professor had named the *Akrobat*.

43

Men with guns in their hands flanked the Acrobat.

Larry Saunders and Tim Holian stepped in front of Clyde Lynds, shielding him as they reached for their pistols. Saunders whipped his Colt from his shoulder holster with blinding speed.

Christian Semmler's gunmen fired as one. Six shots exploded in deafening thunder. The chief of the Van Dorn Detective Agency's Los Angeles field office fell dead with six bullets in his chest.

Their second volley dropped both Protective Service men, who had been so startled by the raid that they were still reaching for their weapons. The guns wheeled toward Tim Holian, whom they had been afraid to fire at because he was next to Clyde Lynds. Holian took full advantage of the two-second respite. Standing tall, pistols flaming in both hands, he stalked the raiders. One *Bittereinder* went down, and another fell back with a cry of pain. Four returned Holian's fire. The big detective tumbled across the laboratory, and crashed into a table, splintering it.

Clyde Lynds ran. The Acrobat leaped over the fallen men's bodies and bounded lithely after him, catching him by the arm. He drew him close in a powerful grip, squeezed until Lynds groaned in pain, and glared in the frightened scientist's eyes. 'I have you, Herr Lynds. Do not struggle, or I will hurt you. Where is the Talking Pictures machine?'

'You're looking at it,' Lynds said sullenly.

'That is the part for showing the Talking Pictures,' Semmler said, gesturing for his men to pack it down the stairs. 'Where is the part that manufactures it?'

He squeezed harder, crushing muscle against bone. Gasping, Lynds led him to a camera on a tripod.

'This is for pictures,' said Semmler. 'What captures the sound?'

Lynds nodded mutely at a carbon microphone on a tall wooden box.

Semmler said, 'Lastly, where is the machine for imprinting the sounds on the film?'

Clyde Lynds sagged in Semmler's grip. The monster knew everything. It was as if he had been watching over his shoulder. Pain bored through his arm as Semmler shook him like a terrier. 'Where?'

'Upstairs in the lab.'

Semmler was relentless. Squeezing harder, grinding Lynds's flesh agonizingly against bone, he asked, 'Where are your plans?'

Clyde Lynds realized with a sinking heart that, having been outfoxed in the past, the German was too suspicious to be fooled again. 'There!' he gasped, indicating a satchel full of drawings and schematics. That seemed to appease the Acrobat, Lynds thought, but he soon realized he was wrong.

'Let's go!' Semmler dragged him toward the opening that had appeared so suddenly in the wall.

'Where?'

'Up to the laboratory for your imprinting machine, then home to Germany.'

'Germany's not my home,' Lynds protested.

'It will be your home until your machine is made absolutely perfect.'

The Gopher gangsters back in New York had taught Clyde Lynds their favorite fighting trick. They had done it as a joke, thinking he was an overeducated sissy boy, but, craving their respect, he had learned it anyhow. With nothing to lose, he tried it now, so unexpectedly that he startled even the Acrobat. Springing off his toes he butted his forehead against the big German's massive jaw. In the split second that the grip on his arm eased, Lynds wrenched free and ran. He stumbled over Larry Saunders's body, arrested his fall with one hand, and scooped up a fallen pistol.

Clyde Lynds heard a shot.

The sound seemed to come from a great distance, and he heard it long after he realized that his legs had stopped moving and that the shot had hammered him to the floor. He tried to sit up. He saw the man who had shot him, a yellow-bearded Dutchman in a slouch hat, still holding the gun and violently shaking his head. The Acrobat was standing close behind the man, his face contorted with rage and stupendous effort as he yanked a garrote around the Dutchman's neck so tightly that it sawed through flesh.

'Take everything to the train,' Semmler ordered his remaining men. 'I'll go up to the laboratory.' He threw the Boer's body out of his way and knelt to pick up Clyde Lynds to have him identify the correct imprinting machine. The scientist had lost consciousness. Air bubbled bloodily from his chest, and Semmler could see that he was mortally wounded.

Again cursing the trigger-happy fool who had shot Lynds and remembering how Lynds had tricked him in the past, Christian Semmler searched the dying scientist's clothing. He found tucked beneath his shirt a flat object carefully folded in a wrapping of oilskin. He opened it and found a single sheet of heavy parchment paper. To his joy, written on it in a fine, clear, miniature hand were diagrams and schematic drawings annotated with mathematical formulas.

Semmler rewrapped it with reverent care in the waterproof oilskin. Surely this was the cagey Lynds's true plan for the Talking Pictures machine. Why else would he have wrapped it so carefully? Why else would he hide it? Semmler slipped it inside his own shirt. He would take it, along with the satchel full of plans and the machine itself, back to Germany and let the scientists determine which was real.

Isaac Bell spotted Irina Viorets standing just at the edge of the light drifting down from a streetlamp. She was craning her neck, staring up at the top of the Imperial Building. Her coat was too heavy for the mild climate. At her feet was a carpetbag.

'You look,' said Bell as he came up behind her, 'like a woman leaving town.'

She turned to the sound of his voice. Her eyes were bright with tears. Her voice trembled. 'Do not speak,' she said. 'I will speak.'

Bell listened with some skepticism and then growing

sympathy as she told him how her fiancé was locked in Semmler's Army prison in Prussia. 'Semmler says he's a fool. But his cause is right. His dreams are just. I know, now, that he was not meant to survive in the world in which he chooses to fight. I am his only hope.'

'Irina, why are you telling me this?'

'Because maybe if you kill Semmler, perhaps, just perhaps, there will be no one else to order them to kill my prince.'

'I'm a private detective, Irina. I'm not a murderer.'

'I know that, Isaac. But if you confront Christian Semmler, only one will survive. Call it what you want. Self-defense. I don't care. You are my only hope.'

'To confront him, I have to find him.'

'I will tell you how to find him. There is a secret stairwell that rises from the basement to the penthouse. He roams it. He spies from it. On the ninth floor he has his own hidden quarters. Now you can find him.'

'Where is the basement entrance?'

'Do you recall the life net that I showed you behind the building? For the actors to jump in?'

'Yes.'

'There is a trapdoor directly under it.'

'Why tonight?' Bell asked. 'Why did you tell me tonight?'

'Because I have done a terrible thing, and only you can save me from it.'

'What?'

'Semmler asked me to make sure that Marion is in the building tonight.'

'She's here? She can't be. She's home.'

'I put her to work, last minute, taking pictures in the

roof studio. She's up there now. Where he wanted her. I am so sorry, Isaac, but my –'

Bell whirled away and ran full tilt down the block and around the corner. He saw an International truck pulling away from the gate in the wooden fence that surrounded the vacant lot behind the building. One of the uniformed lobby doormen was standing guard at the gate and moved to stop him.

'Where the hell you think you're going?'

Bell hit him twice, continued through the gate, and ran past the temporary outdoor studio stages. He saw the life net in the light of a nearby window. The canvas was stretched between springy ropes, five feet above the ground. Bell ducked under it and found the trapdoor. Oddly, it was open.

Isaac Bell climbed into the hole and down a steel ladder affixed to a concrete wall. At the bottom, he saw light at the end of a narrow hall and ran toward it, drawing his Browning. The hall ended at a dimly lit narrow stairwell. Steps spiraled tightly upward into the highest reaches of the building. Bell bounded up them, the sound of his boots muffled by rubber tile.

At an abbreviated landing at the top of the first flight, he saw several twelve-inch-square doors set in the walls at head height. He jerked one open. It covered the judas he had suspected was there. The spy hole took in the lobby. He saw four doormen blocking the front door, the stairs, and the steps to the theater. The elevators were open, their lights off, out of service.

Bell opened the judas hole cover on the opposite wall. The film exchange was empty at this late hour, and a steel scissors gate was closed across the motorcycle messengers' entrance. Irina had given him the only way to breach the building's defenses.

He climbed another flight and ran face-to-face into Detective Tim Holian. Holian shambled past him, bleeding from bullet wounds in his arms and legs, white with shock, and muttering, 'Hospital, hospital, gotta get to the hospital.'

Bell thought fleetingly that Holian had to be one of the luckiest men alive to survive a fusillade of gunfire with only flesh wounds.

'Where's Saunders?'

'Dead. All dead.'

Bell pounded up the stairs. At the fourth flight, the wall had disappeared, having been slid aside into a pocket. He stepped through the opening and stared in horror. The recording studio was a slaughterhouse.

Larry Saunders lay dead on the floor. Two men Bell didn't know lay dead, revolvers locked in their fists, slouch hats fallen beside them. A third man had been strangled and bore the bloody gouge around the throat that was the Acrobat's signature. Then he saw Clyde Lynds sprawled on his back, his chest covered in blood, his face drained of color.

'Clyde?' Pistol in hand, Isaac Bell knelt beside him. He saw immediately that the brash young scientist was not long for this world, and he had a horrible feeling that he had let him down.

Clyde opened his eyes. 'Say, Isaac,' he whispered. 'You didn't make the rescue this time.'

'I'm sorry I got you into this,' said Isaac Bell. 'I wish I had insisted you take your chances with Edison.'

'At least Edison wouldn't kill me.'

'Did they take your machine?'

Clyde answered slowly, in a whisper so faint that Bell had to move within inches to hear him. 'They took a jury-rigged contraption I slapped together with baling wire. It will drive their scientists nuts. Joke's on the Acrobat. I fooled him again. And I kept the new plans – Isaac!'

'What?'

'You have to take care of the plans.'

'I will.'

'You have to promise.'

'I promise. Where are they?' Bell asked.

'Right here.'

'Where?'

Clyde raised his hand as if to point at his head as Bell remembered he had on the *Mauretania*, claiming he held it in his mind and only needed time and money to finish Talking Pictures. A lot of good that would do. They would die with him this time. But instead Clyde was reaching to pat his chest, then hastily to cover his mouth. He coughed, a harsh sound that wracked his body head to toe. The cough ended abruptly with a sudden intake of breath and a long sigh, and before Clyde Lynds could tell Isaac Bell where he had put his plans, the young scientist was dead.

Bell closed Clyde's eyelids and spread a handkerchief over his face. Mindful of his promise, he searched Clyde's clothing.

'Looking for something, Detective?'

44

The Acrobat was speaking directly behind him. His English was fluent, his accent light.

'Place your pistol on his chest.'

Isaac Bell laid the Browning on Clyde's chest and raised both hands. As his right hand passed his head, he whipped his derringer from his hat, spun around, and fired both barrels in the direction of Semmler's voice. The slugs clanged through a tin acoustical horn.

The Acrobat laughed.

Now Bell saw him on the far side of the room, a man with hair as gold as his and green eyes bright as emeralds. He was standing behind a disc microphone mounted on a wooden box, smiling the 'Fritz Wunderlich' smile that the drummers had raved about. The sketch had failed to capture the magnetic power of his presence. Nor were his thick brow and massive jaw monkey-like. Isaac Bell thought that Semmler, the Acrobat, looked like the work of a brilliant sculptor more enchanted by the structure within his stone than by the surface. The word 'mighty' sprang to Bell's mind. There was a quality to the man of power that made him seem larger than life.

Semmler returned Bell's inquiring gaze, and his smile broadened and his eyes brightened. Bell was reminded of Art Curtis – though six inches shorter than Semmler and round instead of rangy, Art had possessed a similarly compelling smile. Art had been a fighting man, too, and his eyes could turn cold. But Semmler's eyes were of a different order, as cold and empty as the stars.

His hands were hidden behind the box.

Bell could not see if he was holding a weapon.

'Clyde's microphone is quite effective, don't you think? You thought I sounded real.'

'You sounded like a murderer.'

'I am not a murderer,' Semmler replied, with such conviction that Bell knew he was confronting a madman. 'I am a soldier for my country and my kaiser.'

Bell gathered his legs to spring. 'That insults every soldier who ever served. You murdered eight men starting with your own accomplice on the *Mauretania*.'

'None would have died if you had not interfered,' Semmler shot back. 'Every death is on your head.'

Bell surged to his feet and rushed the Acrobat in a burst of fluid motion.

Semmler raised a Webley automatic pistol and leveled it at Bell's chest. 'I load hollow-point .455s. I'm told that your friend Abbott will never fully recover from his encounter with a "manstopper".'

Bell stopped, reluctantly.

'We will leave the building,' Semmler said. 'Walk ahead of me. Lead the way downstairs.'

Bell had no choice but to do as the Acrobat demanded. But at least with every step down the stairs, he was drawing Semmler farther away from Marion. They descended four flights to the lobby and another to the cellar. Semmler indicated the narrow hall and switched positions when they reached the ladder to the trapdoor.

'I'll go first,' he said, backing agilely up the ladder, covering Bell until, crouched under the life net, he beckoned with the Webley for Bell to come up next.

When the detective climbed out, Semmler said, 'Feel around at the foot of the wall. There's some loose bricks. Pick one up.'

Bell stepped from under the canvas life net and two paces to the wall of the building, crouched down and felt in the dark until he found a brick. Glad of another weapon, he stood with it in his left hand. His right was reserved for his throwing knife, which he would draw from his boot the instant he saw a chance.

Semmler said, 'Your interference ruined years of meticulous planning. It cost me time and treasure and dimmed my star. Promises made to my kaiser, my army, and my family have all been broken. I will redeem them now that I have Talking Pictures in hand. But it did not have to take so long.'

He gestured with his pistol. 'Before you get any silly ideas about braining me with that brick, throw it through that window.'

Bell raised the brick, watching Semmler's posture for signs of the split second of distraction he needed to go for his knife. But Semmler was watching closely and with sublime confidence in his mastery of the situation. Bell tried another tack. 'Meticulous planning for what? I am mystified. What is it you want?'

'I want to save Germany from well-meaning fools. Throw the brick.'

Bell tried again. 'What –'

Semmler trained his gun at Bell's chest. 'Throw the brick or convalesce with Abbott.'

Bell threw the brick at the lighted window. The glass shattered, and shards fell from the frame, widening a jagged hole.

'Here's your next choice: either keep dogging my steps or try to save what is dear to you.'

Christian Semmler raised his free hand for Bell to see. Between his thumb and forefinger he held a book of safety matches. Beneath the matches, cupped in his big palm, was a dark cylinder, which looked to Bell in the uncertain light from the broken window to be a small chunk sawed off a stick of dynamite and fitted with a fuse and detonator. Semmler manipulated his fingers with the dexterity of a magician. He lighted a match and touched the flame to the fuse.

It caught with a shower of sparks. Semmler lobbed the dynamite through the broken window. Bell heard it hit the floor. There was a moment of silence, then a loud explosion. Bright white-orange flame suddenly lit the spot outside the window where they were standing, making it bright as day.

Christian Semmler looked Isaac Bell in the face.

'I could have simply shot you. But I prefer revenge. So it is up to you to choose, Chief Investigator Bell. Shadow me like a good detective or jump down that trapdoor like a good husband and climb to the roof in hopes of leading your lovely wife out of the fire before she burns to death. If the stairs are too thick with smoke, you can always jump from the roof in hopes of landing on this life net. We've yet to persuade the actors to try it, and I regret that I don't have time to watch your landing. Go ahead. Choose!'

Isaac Bell spun on his heel, dove under the life net that concealed the trapdoor, and vaulted himself feetfirst through the opening. As his foot grazed the top rungs of the ladder, he pulled his throwing knife from his boot and, without wasting a step of his swift descent, flung it overarm at Christian Semmler's throat.

Isaac Bell's blade streaked through the air like a silver bolt of electricity.

Superhuman speed saved the Acrobat from instant death.

But no power on earth could save his face.

Bell's knife pierced his cheek and his tongue and rasped against his teeth.

Desperate to reach Marion in time, Bell had not lingered to watch.

But as he dropped off the bottom rung of the ladder and whirled toward the narrow hall that led to the stairs, he heard Semmler scream. Loud with dismay, shrill with pain, and sharp as a clarinet, the sound suddenly thickened, gurgling hollowly, drowned in blood.

45

Delicately, but shaking with the effort, Christian Semmler pulled the smooth blade from his flesh. The pain threatened to knock him off his feet. He staggered to the life net, propped an elbow on it to keep his balance, and spewed a mouthful of blood. Then he slashed his coat sleeve with the razor-sharp knife. Spitting more blood, he wadded the cloth, stuffed it in his mouth, and bit down hard to staunch the wound.

He had to get moving. He had to get away. Fire engines were coming. He was afraid he would pass out. But a second explosion blowing glass from more windows galvanized him with the realization that the fire was spreading so fast that if Isaac Bell somehow did manage to reach the roof ahead of the flames, he and his bride's only way down was to jump to the life net.

The Acrobat's sudden laughter lanced pain through his face, but he couldn't help it. It was such perfect justice for all Bell had done to him. With Bell's own knife, he slashed the ropes that held the net.

White smoke seeped into the secret stairwell. The acrid, tarry stink of nitrate gas clawed at Bell's lungs. As he raced by the film exchange, a judas hole cover blew open and hot flame shot through the spy hole like a fiery arrow. Bell ducked it and kept climbing, bounding three steps at once, pursued by smoke and fire. He passed the opening to the recording studio. The fire was there ahead of him, licking the bodies, having leaped up an elevator shaft or another stairway, and he prayed that Marion had not left the temporary safety of the rooftop studio in a doomed attempt to descend.

At the fifth-floor landing, when he was halfway to the top of the building, the flames feeding on the hundreds of reels in the film exchange far below breached a vault and detonated tons of film stock stored inside. The explosion shook the stairs under Bell's feet. A shock wave traveled up the shaft and lofted him off the rubber treads.

He tumbled down half a flight of stairs, clambered to his feet, and ran harder, climbing past Irina's office on the seventh floor, Clyde's laboratory on the eighth, and Semmler's lair on the ninth. After one more flight he was at the top, gasping for breath and stymied by walls on every side. He yanked open a judas door and saw a studio stage in semidarkness, with a looming shadow of a ship and towers bearing Cooper-Hewitt light banks. Silhouetted against a lurid sky, Marion was stepping through the door in the northern glass wall, climbing out on the terrace that overlooked the life net.

Bell shouted. The wall was thick, and she could not hear him.

Remembering the sliding fourth-floor wall, he spotted the bulge where the wall thickened to make room for the pocket. He looked for a lever but saw none. He flattened his palms against it and tried to slide it, which had no effect. Then he saw what looked like an ordinary electric light switch on the floor molding. He moved it and the wall glided aside.

'Marion!'

A second explosion rocked the building.

Bell ran the length of the studio stage, dodging wires and camera tracks, and tripped over a sandbag counterbalancing a fly lift. He rolled to his feet and pulled open the door in the glass wall. Marion was climbing the steps that had been built in hopes of one day convincing an extra to try the life net.

'Marion!'

'*Isaac?* Oh my God, it's you. Hurry! All the stairs are blocked. The elevators won't come. We have to jump.'

Bell bounded up beside her and held her close, overwhelmed with the relief of finding her alive. The net appeared even smaller than it had when he last saw it from here. Flames leaping from many windows were lighting it clearly. There were dark splotches on the white canvas that he hadn't noticed before.

'They built it strong enough for two,' said Marion. 'Irina wanted a "Lovers' Leap".'

'We have to hold each other tight, or we'll smash into each other when we bounce.'

'Thank God, you're here. I didn't know if I had the courage to jump.'

'What is that dark color? Those splotches?'

'They shine,' said Marion. 'Like liquid.'

A third explosion shook the building. It felt as if it were swaying in an earthquake. Bell, staring down at the net, puzzling over the splotches, saw great torrents of fire thrusting from windows on the sixth floor. They had moments to jump before the building collapsed. 'I'll be right back,' he said. 'Don't leave without me.'

'We can't stay here, General Major,' Hermann Wagner pleaded with Christian Semmler.

A fire engine thundered up the street, pulled by two bay horses, and from the opposite direction came police on bicycles.

Wagner's chauffeur, who kept turning around to stare anxiously, opened the glass that separated the passenger compartment. 'We're blocking the gate. We have to move.'

'Wait!' said Semmler, his voice muffled by the blood-soaked coat sleeve he pressed to his face. 'Do not move this auto.'

'But they will see that you were wounded, General Major.'

Semmler did not deign to reply to the obvious, saying instead, 'Wounds and war march in lockstep. That is the reason I ordered you to stand by. Don't disappoint me – Look!' Semmler pointed at the parapet of the Imperial Building. The flames, fanned by a stiffening wind, were shooting higher than the roof. Suddenly something moved in front of them. A man in white teetered on the parapet. 'See! There he goes!'

Smoke obscured the figure. Then he separated from the parapet, as if he were pushing off with all his strength to clear the building, and fell through the air.

'I think it's both of them.'

'My God, it is.' Hermann Wagner held his breath. It

seemed that it took them forever to plunge past the burning windows. How afraid they must be that they would miss the tiny net. What would they do if they saw that they were falling off course? To Wagner's immense relief, the poor couple did not miss the net. They landed dead center. But instead of bouncing back up in the air, they smashed through it to the ground.

'Bull's-eye,' said Christian Semmler.

'The net collapsed,' cried Wagner. 'It didn't hold.' He stared at the wreckage, but, of course, no one moved from it. How could they? A moment later a section of the building's wall gave way and thundered down, burying their remains under tumbled bricks.

The first team of fire horses clattered alongside the auto.

'Drive!'

Wagner's chauffeur almost stalled the motor in his haste to get away.

'Where now, General Major?' asked Wagner, staring back over his shoulder at the burning building, and grateful that the wooden fence blocked his view of where Bell and his wife had died. 'To the freight yard?'

'Take me to a doctor. While he sutures this, charter a special to New York. We are done in Los Angeles. For now.'

Christian Semmler sounded remarkably pleased, Wagner thought, for a man who had seen his entire enterprise go up in smoke. And he displayed a God-like indifference to his grievous wounds. God-like, or machine-like – it was as if he didn't feel pain.

Semmler noticed him staring. 'Of course it hurts,' he said, spitting blood so he could speak. 'You should pray you never feel anything like it.'

'We're running out of rope. Hang on! I'll see what I can do.'

Isaac Bell let go of the last inches of a seventy-foot-long string of Cooper-Hewitt light cables and stage fly ropes he had knotted together, and dropped ten feet to the roof of the Imperial Moving Picture Palace marquee that sheltered the sidewalk in front of the building. He landed on stinging soles and looked up. Flames were gushing from windows they had descended past moments ago.

'Let go. I've got you.'

Marion slid down to the end of the rope, shredding the little that remained of her gloves, and opened her hands. Bell caught her in his arms, swooped her to a gentle landing, and held her tightly for a grateful moment.

The clatter of hoofs and the throb of steam pumps heralded the arrival of the fire department. 'Firemen!' Bell called down to them. 'Did you boys happen to bring a ladder?'

'I still can't sleep,' Marion whispered, 'I keep seeing that sandbag burst on the ground. That could have been us.'

Bell held her close. 'But it wasn't us. Don't worry, we're fine.'

Marion laughed. 'I'm not worried. And I know why I can't sleep. It feels so wonderful to be awake – Isaac, thank God you saw his blood on the net. But what made you think he cut the ropes? I'd have thought he would have run for his life, particularly if he was so badly wounded as to be bleeding like that.'

'He's a killer. He calls himself a soldier, but he is first a killer. In fact, I'll bet he waited to watch us hit bottom.'

'When he finds out you tested the net with a sandbag, he's going to be badly disappointed.'

'He's going to be more than disappointed,' Bell promised grimly, climbing out of bed and kissing her good night. 'Sleep tight.'

'Where are you going?'

'New York.'

'Why New York?'

'Christian Semmler's got what he came for. He's going back to Germany.'

'How do you know?'

'He asked me, mockingly, "Looking for something?" I was searching Clyde's body because Clyde told me as he died that he had kept the real plans. Doesn't "Looking for something?" sound like Christian Semmler already found them?'

Marion sat up. 'And since he asked when he saw you searching Clyde, that means he found them in Clyde's clothing.'

'Meaning he can carry them in *his* clothing.'

Bell dressed hastily. He filled his pockets, holstered his spare Browning in his coat and a fresh throwing knife in his boot, and reloaded the empty derringer he had managed to palm without the Acrobat noticing.

'From the sound of his scream, I'd say he's sporting a good-sized bandage. In fact, I'm hoping he needed stitches. Lots of them.'

'But how do you know he's going to New York?'

'I don't for sure, but it's a good bet. If Clyde's plans were on his person, then Semmler's traveling light. And if he's traveling light, the fastest way home to Germany is a train across the continent and a boat from New York.'

46

Joseph Van Dorn welcomed Isaac Bell to the New York headquarters with words that Bell could have construed as compliments were it not for the thunderclouds on the boss's face.

'Excellent reasoning,' said Van Dorn. 'Downright intriguing, even: traveling light, swathed in bandages, a murderer responsible for the deaths of two of my best agents races fleet-footedly across the continent, having stolen the plans to a revolutionary machine in which I have invested heavily, and boards a steamship for Germany. Our investigative agency pulls out all stops: we cover every Limited train station between Los Angeles and New York; we pull every wire we have in the government to obtain passenger manifests from eastbound German and French liners; we shake hands with the devil – currently masquerading as a British earl and military intelligence officer – to obtain the passenger lists of British ships; we canvas shipping clerks to watch for a man who fits Semmler's description booking passage to Europe; we pay enormous sums of money to policemen and customs officers to help watch those ships when our forces are stretched to the breaking point. And who do we find?'

'No one, yet,' answered Bell.

'Did it ever occur to you that he might have gone the

other way and boarded a ship in San Pedro, in which case he is now steaming hell-for-leather toward the Panama Canal?'

'A Talking Pictures machine is doing just that,' replied Isaac Bell, 'aboard a German freighter, which will reach the canal in ten days. After they traverse it they will likely load the machine onto a warship. The Imperial German Navy has a squadron stationed off Venezuela.'

'*What?*' exploded Van Dorn. 'He has the *machine*? How do you know that?'

'Tim Holian and his boys traced it and a gang of gunmen from the Los Angeles Southern Pacific freight yard to San Pedro and onto the ship. Holian is positive that Semmler wasn't with them.'

'I was told that Holian was shot four times.'

'Apparently it didn't take. Flesh wounds.'

'Well, he had flesh to spare, last time I saw him. So they have the machine?' Van Dorn smiled and stroked his beard. 'I think I can pull a wire or two in the Canal Zone and have that freighter held up.'

'No, sir,' said Bell.

'What do you mean, "No, sir"? Why not?'

'Clyde switched machines. He gave Semmler a contraption that will cause them no end of confusion. Better to let them take it to Germany.'

'Where's the right one?'

'Burned up in the fire.'

'Destroyed,' Van Dorn said, gloomily.

'Except for the plans.'

'Which General Major Semmler has.'

'I'm afraid so.'

Van Dorn sighed. 'What about that Russian woman, Isaac? Might she not be helping him?'

'She vanished. The Los Angeles office is hunting, but she's nowhere to be found.'

'So she could be with him.'

'Highly unlikely. She betrayed him, hoping I would kill him.'

'A sentiment echoed warmly in this office, Isaac. Unfortunately, first you have to find him. I saw in the wires you exchanged at your train's station stops that you think Semmler may have chartered a special.'

'So far nothing's turned up,' said Bell. 'The difficulty is, even though we're watching the German consulates like hawks, his private contacts, German businessmen or commercial travelers, could have chartered it for him.'

'So the long and short is that General Major Christian Semmler, Imperial German Army, Military Intelligence, could be sleeping upstairs in one of the Knickerbocker's palatial suites directly over our heads.'

'I would not rule that out,' Bell admitted. 'He is a guerrilla fighter – a behind-the-lines operator. But we can hardly roust every guest in the hotel without management taking notice and terminating our lease.'

'You are remarkably flippant for a detective who has no idea where his quarry is.'

'He is either in New York or still on his way to New York, and he's going to board a ship to Europe.'

'You sound awfully sure for a detective with no facts.'

'I have more irons in the fire.'

'Other than the obvious advice to keep an eye peeled

for doctors, I saw no talk about "more irons" when I read your wires.'

'Not everyone talks by electricity,' said Bell. He reached for his hat.

'What does that mean? Isaac, where in hell are you going?'

'Harlem.'

The Monarch Lodge of the Improved Benevolent and Protective Order of Elks offered a home away from home on West 135th Street to Pullman porters laying over in New York. A man could get a decent meal and sleep on a clean cot. Or he could smoke in a comfortable chair in a big parlor and swap tales, both true and fanciful, with friends from all across the United States who served on the trains. It was true that the *white* Benevolent and Protective Order of Elks was suing the Negro Elks to stop them from using a similar name, but the Monarch Lodge remained, for the moment, a sanctuary. No one there would shout 'George' to demand service, as if a black man didn't have his own name. In fact, a white man crossing the Negro Elks' threshold was extremely unlikely, which was why everyone looked up when a tall white man in a white suit knocked at the door, took his hat off as he stepped inside, and said, politely, 'Excuse me for interrupting, gentlemen. I'm Isaac Bell.'

Heads swiveled. Many stood to get a better view of him. They knew the name. Who didn't? One dark night – the story went – when the Overland Limited was highballing across Wyoming at eighty miles per hour, a passenger named Isaac Bell who had won a big hand in a poker game had tipped a porter one thousand dollars. The Pullman porter might be the highest-paid man in his neighborhood, but he still had to work two years for a thousand dollars, and few in the Elks parlor had believed the tale until they saw him standing there.

Bell said, 'I wonder if I might speak with Mr Clement Price – Oh, there you are, Mr Price,' and when Clem stepped forward, Bell thrust out his hand and said, 'Good to see you again. Did you have any luck?'

'Just walked in myself,' said Price, a fit young fellow with an eye for the ladies, whom the others were a little wary of. Clem kept talking about how everybody would be better off forming a labor union, which leveler heads feared would provoke the Pullman Company to fire every last one of them, as it had done numerous times in the past.

Price addressed the room. 'Mr Bell has his eye out for a yellow-haired, green-eyed gentleman riding to New York wearing a fresh bandage on his head or neck. Such a gentleman was seen in Denver and someone similar-looking might have passed through Kansas City, but no one I saw in Chicago had seen him when Mr Bell asked me yesterday.'

'Bandage?' echoed a sharp-eyed older man, who looked Bell over carefully and asked with a smile, 'Like he ran into something?'

'Me,' said Bell, to knowing winks and laughter.

'Is he riding in the open section or a stateroom?'

'Stateroom, almost certainly,' said Bell.

The men exchanged glances, shook heads, shrugged.

'Not that I've seen.'

'I just got off from DC. Didn't see him.'

'He's traveling from the west,' said Bell. 'Though he could be plying a circuitous route.'

'I just come in from Pittsburgh. Didn't see him. Didn't hear anyone mention him, either.'

'He would have stood out, aside from the bandage,' Bell answered. 'He has unusually long arms. I was really hoping his appearance would have caused some talk. Long arms, heavy brow. And a bright smile that could sell you ice in Alaska. Here. Here's a sketch.'

They passed it around, shaking their heads.

'Would have stood out, if folks had seen him,' the porter in from Pittsburgh ventured.

Bell said, 'It is possible that he's traveling with someone else. Possibly a doctor.'

'Doctor?'

'For his injury.'

'Well, funny you should say doctor, Mr Bell.'

'How's that?' Bell asked, eagerly.

'I saw two men like you're saying, but they weren't on a Pullman. Least not a scheduled one.'

'He could have chartered a special.'

'It was a special I saw. Out in New Jersey, in the Elizabeth yards. They were walking by a special that had just pulled in. I thought they were tramps, but they could have got off the special. And the other fellow was carrying a little bag, that could have been a doctor's bag.'

'Was he wearing a bandage?'

'I don't know. But when you ask, I realize he had his collar turned up and his hat pulled low.'

'Yellow hair?'

'Hard to tell under that hat – big old slouch with a wide brim pulled down low.'

'Did you notice whose special it was?'

'I think she was private. I just wasn't paying much mind.'

'I don't suppose you saw the engine number?' said Bell.

'Sorry, Mr Bell. Wish I had. Mr Locomotive was pointed the other way.'

'It is strange,' Bell told Archie, 'to think it was Semmler whom the porter saw in the Elizabeth yards. If he crossed the continent on a special, why did he get off way out in Elizabeth?'

Archie agreed. 'You would think he would take his train closer to the steamship docks. Step from the privacy of a special train to the privacy of a First Class stateroom.'

'Once on the boat, he takes his meals in his room. No one sees him till he lands in England or France or Germany – First Class and private all the way from Los Angeles to Berlin.'

'So why did he get off in the Elizabeth yards?'

Bell pulled a regional map down from the ceiling of the Van Dorn library. 'He could go anywhere from Elizabeth. Newark has a German community. The German steamers dock at Hoboken. Or he could catch the train or the tubes into Manhattan. Lots of choices.'

'But not so private and not First Class.'

Bell raised the map, spun on his heel, and stared at Archie, his eyes alight with sudden realization. 'But Christian Semmler did not arrive in America in First Class.'

'What do you mean?'

'He did not disembark from the *Mauretania* with the First Class passengers at Pier 54.'

'He wasn't a passenger,' said Archie. 'He did not intend to sail on the *Mauretania*. He would have taken Clyde and Beiderbecke off the ship in Liverpool Bay if you hadn't stopped him.'

'He crossed the ocean in the *Mauretania*'s stokehold and landed on a coal barge without leaving a trace of his arrival. What if he goes back the same route? No one in the black gang is going to question a knife wound. I'll bet half the trimmers who return to ship are bunged up from bar fights and saloon brawls. So while we're canvassing ship lines, ticket clerks, and customs agents, Semmler will leave the United States the same way he came.'

Bell grabbed the Kellogg's mouthpiece. 'Get me Detective Eddie Tobin. On the jump!'

47

Van Dorn Detective Eddie Tobin, whose lopsided face and drooping left eye were the result of a brutal beating inflicted by the Gophers when he apprenticed with the gang squad, was from Staten Island, a faraway, isolated borough of the city. His family, an extended clan of Tobins, Darbees, Richardses, and Gordons, ran oyster boats out of St George on the northeast tip of the island. Many of the small, flat, innocent-looking vessels were used to tong oysters. But hidden below the decks of some were powerful gasoline engines enabling them to outrun the harbor squad while smuggling taxable goods, ferrying fugitives away from the police, pirating coal, and retrieving items of cargo that fell from the docks. Young Eddie was honest, despite the childhood spent roving with opportunistic uncles and felonious cousins, which made him an invaluable guide to the immense and sprawling Port of New York.

Isaac Bell asked Eddie where the coal barges that bunkered the Cunard liners at the Chelsea Piers might come from.

'Perth Amboy, Joisey, down where the Arthur Kill and the Raritan enter the Bay.'

'Do you know anyone in the coal yards?'

'Sure.'

'What's our fastest way down there?'

'Boat.'

'Is your Uncle Donny out of jail?'

'He'd be glad of the job. Poor old guy's got his boat tuned up but nothing to do, seeing as how the harbor squad is shadowing him.'

Eddie Tobin telephoned a Tomkinsville saloon, where a boy was sent running to the docks. Bell and Eddie caught the Ninth Avenue El down to the Battery. They waited at Pier A, at the tip of Manhattan Island, trading gossip with New York Police Department harbor squad roundsman O'Riordan, whose steam launch was bouncing alongside on the chop stirred by the wind and passing boats.

Eying the waterborne traffic, Bell was struck by the near impossibility of their task. The Acrobat had his pick of seagoing ships getting ready to sail – American and British liners and freighters up the west side of Manhattan, German and French boats across the river in Hoboken, and hundreds across the Lower Bay in Brooklyn – all attended by hundreds of barges and lighters. Every few minutes, the thunder of a steam whistle announced another ship putting to sea.

Roundsman O'Riordan's eyes suddenly narrowed warily. Donald Darbee's square-nosed oyster scow was closing on his pier. 'Our ride,' Bell explained, slipping the cop a couple of bucks. 'Good to see you again, Roundsman. Say hello to the captain.'

Six months of regular hours, square meals, and no booze had done Uncle Donny a world of good. 'You look ten years younger, sir,' Bell greeted the scraggly old waterman. 'I'll bet the girls are chasing you with a net.'

'Where you want to go?' Donald Darbee growled.

It was fourteen miles down the Upper Bay, through the Narrows, and down the Lower Bay. Hugging the Staten Island shore, passing string after string of tugboat-drawn barges – southbound empties riding high, full ones with decks awash northbound – they rounded Ward Point below Tottenville, crossed the Arthur Kill, and landed in an immense, windswept coal yard where Lehigh Valley hopper trains from the Pennsylvania mines unloaded into the barges that supplied the steamship piers.

A black coal dumper made of steel girders towered over the water and dominated the sky, and Isaac Bell saw that, unlike the backbreaking process of bunkering the ships and stoking their furnaces by hand, here the coal was moved by modern machines. A sloping pier rose to the dumper. On the pier were tracks for the hopper cars. A cable-driven 'pig' between the rails clanked tight to a car's coupler and pushed it up the incline onto a platform on top of the dumper. Positioned beside a gigantic funnel, the entire railroad car was then tilted on its side. Tons of coal spilled out of the car and thundered into the funnel, which directed it through a huge nozzle into a waiting barge. As soon as the barge was full, tugboats whisked it away and nudged an empty into its place. The only handwork was performed by the barge's trimmers, who leveled the load, spreading the coal with shovels and rakes.

A trimmer suddenly fell off a barge and splashed into the water.

Ropes were thrown and ladders lowered, and within minutes the worker was hauled out, soaking wet and retching on the dock.

The foreman showing Bell and Eddie Tobin around

groaned, 'They're usually drunk, but not this drunk. But Pete Lampack suddenly struck it rich. He's been buying drinks for the house for two days.'

Bell and Eddie Tobin exchanged a glance. 'Who is Lampack?'

'Damned fool trimmer on the boats.'

'How did he strike it rich?' asked Bell.

'Who knows? Picked the right horse, aunt died, or some undeserved thing.'

Eddie asked, 'Where's Lampack? Still at the saloon?'

'Naw, he finally ran out of dough. It's back to work for him. He ought to be on one of those empties.' The foreman indicated the barges lined along the pier awaiting fresh loads.

'I want to speak with this fellow,' said Bell.

Money had already passed between the Van Dorns and the coal yard foreman. From a grimy sheet of paper pulled from inside his derby, the foreman determined that the barge being trimmed by Pete Lampack was next in line to be refilled. 'Just back from our best customer. She burns a thousand tons a day.'

'*Mauretania?*' asked Bell.

'We love the *Maury*. Gobbles coal like it's going out of style, and you could set your watch by her: six thousand tons every two weeks.'

'Is Lampack's barge going back to the *Mauretania*?'

'Nope, she's full up. Ought to be sailing just about now.'

Bell nudged Eddie Tobin, and the two detectives ran out on the coaling pier, climbed the incline under the shadows of the dumper, and looked down. 'I don't see no trimmer,' said Eddie.

'What's that in the corner?'

'Just some coal stuck there.'

Bell ran to the steel ladder affixed to the girders.

'Look out, you idiot!' yelled the workman who manipulated the levers that tipped the cars and aimed the dumper nozzle.

'Tell him to wait,' Bell shouted.

Eddie jumped to the controller's shack. 'Hold on a sec.'

'I got fifty barges waiting. I'm not stopping for that fool.'

Eddie opened his coat. The operator saw the checkered grip of a Smith & Wesson and said, 'Think I'll go have a smoke.'

Bell slid thirty feet down the ladder and landed on the pier beside the barge. Eddie was right. It was a heap of coal jammed in the corner of the barge. The breeze swooped down and blew grit. Cloth shimmied. Bell dropped into the barge and scattered coal with his hands. The trimmer lay under it, with the red ring of Semmler's garrote around his throat.

'Mr Bell!'

Bell looked up. Eddie Tobin had climbed to the top of the dumper, where he could see over the low buildings of Tottenville that blocked their view of the harbor.

'*Mauretania*! She's coming out the Narrows.'

48

The thunder of the liner's whistle – a stentorian warning that she would stop for nothing – carried for miles. Isaac Bell heard it as he ran to the dock where Darbee had tied his oyster boat.

Seeing him coming, the old man fired up his engine and cast off his lines.

'Who's chasing you?'

'Can you catch up with the *Mauretania*?'

The oyster boat soared away, trailing white smoke. They rounded the point and there she was, the largest and fastest ship in the world, emerging from the Narrows, six miles away, steaming down the Lower Bay, billowing smoke from the forward three of her four tall red-and-black stacks. Darbee steered a course to intercept the giant at the mouth of the harbor where the channel passed close to Sandy Hook.

'Is little Eddie OK?' he asked over the roar of his motor.

'He's fine. No time to wait. Can you catch the ship?'

'I can probably catch her, but what do I do with her when I do?'

'Put me aboard.'

'Can't. Pilot door's much higher than you can reach from my deck.'

'I'll throw a line.'

'They ain't gonna catch it.'

'Do you have any grappling hooks?'

'Cops took 'em. But even if you threw a grappling hook, they'd just cut the rope and yell down, "Next time, buy a ticket".'

Isaac Bell saw a black steam launch trailing the Cunard liner. Its masts were draped with signal flags. 'Is that the pilot boat?'

'If it ain't, that New York pilot is going to Europe.'

'Can you put me aboard it?'

'I'll let you do the talking.'

Darbee altered course slightly. After fifteen minutes of pounding across the Lower Bay, they passed under the immense overhanging stern of the *Mauretania* and veered alongside the pilot boat. There were several pilots on board – some waiting to be put on incoming ships, others just retrieved from outbound vessels – and they eyed Darbee's oyster boat warily.

'Now,' Bell shouted.

Darbee steered alongside the lowest part of the afterdeck. Even the pilot boat was considerably higher than the oyster boat. Bell jumped, got his arms over the gunnel, and pulled himself in. 'Van Dorn!' he shouted. 'Boarding *Mauretania*.'

One hour into his shift in the No. 4 boiler room, Christian Semmler feared that his perspiration would penetrate the oilskin that protected the Talking Pictures plans. He was sweating like a pig. The other stokers had long ago stripped off their shirts.

The stoking gong gave the signal to shut the door of

the furnace into which he was scooping coal. He dropped his shovel and looked in the half-dark, clanging madness for a hiding place that was safer than his soaked clothing. Knowing he had only seconds before a gang boss or an engineer officer shouted for him to get back to work, he stumbled into a coal bunker. Parnall Hall and Bill Chambers were shifting coal to the front.

'Stand watch!' he ordered, and when they turned their backs, he stuffed the flat oilskin into a narrow slot between the side of the bunker and a frame where it would be safe until the end of his shift. A stoking gong rang.

'You're up!' Hall warned, and Semmler darted back to the fire aisle, scooped up a shovelful of coal, and spread it on the flames. The pace was accelerating as the ship forged into the open ocean, gaining speed, and the bells rang faster. A door shut. Another opened. Semmler bent to scoop from the pile the trimmers had dropped at his feet. Someone stepped on his scoop.

He looked up.

'Leaving town, General?' asked Isaac Bell.

Bell feinted a hard right, and when Semmler slipped the phantom punch with his usual speed, Bell was ready to hit his jaw with a left, which tumbled the German across the fire aisle. Semmler crashed into a hot bulkhead and stood swaying, trying to shake off the effect of the heavy blow. He had a long coal-blackened bandage on his cheek.

Bell was already moving in on him. He feinted again, this time with his left, and landed a right to the jaw. Semmler went flying. He skidded along the fire aisle, bounced off a stoker scrambling out of the way, and regained his feet. The blow had knocked the bandage from his face, revealing a long string of finely fashioned sutures. Bell threw another punch. This was not a feint. The Acrobat fell again.

Bell drew his pistol to make the arrest.

Down the aisle, a furnace door opened. In the sudden flash of red coals Bell saw, from the corner of his eye, a ten-foot steel slice bar arcing at his head, and he realized that Semmler was not alone. It was too late to dodge the bar. But if it hit him, it would splinter bone. Bell hurled himself inside the arc, straight into the arms of the coal trimmer swinging it. The bar slammed into the furnace, ringing like a giant chime. The man who had swung it made the mistake of holding on to it, and Bell took full advantage, pounding his torso, doubling him over.

The timing gong sounded. Another door flew open. In the flash of coals Isaac saw a shovel flying at his head, and he realized, even as he ducked, that the trimmer he had doubled over was not alone either. The shovel missed his head, but it knocked the Browning out of his hand. The man who had thrown the shovel charged Bell, swinging his fists and catching the tall detective off balance.

Bell rolled with one punch but caught the next one square in the face.

His feet flew out from under him, and he went down hard, slamming onto the steel deck with an impact that shook him to the core. He was vaguely aware that the rest of the men on the fire aisle were fleeing from the battle. He heard an engineer shout, 'Leave 'em to it.'

Watertight doors ground shut, and he was alone with the three of them.

'Knife in his boot,' shouted Semmler.

Bell saw where his gun had landed and scrambled for it. The trimmer who had scored with his fist lunged for it, too. Bell got to it first, barely managing to grab the barrel, and when he saw that the trimmer would have his hand on the butt before he could stop him, Bell flipped it into an open furnace.

Then he went for his knife, but he was still too slow. The man yanked it from his boot, stood up, and kicked Bell in the chest, and as Bell rolled away from the next kick he saw the shadow of the trimmer he had doubled over loom above him like a maddened grizzly. Bell felt his hand brush a lump of coal. He picked it up and threw it with all his strength. It struck the 'grizzly' a glancing blow that knocked him backwards into Christian Semmler, who shoved him back at Bell, shouting, 'Pick him up!'

Still on his back, Isaac Bell kicked out at the trimmer, who was lurching at him. The man dodged and grabbed Bell's foot. As Bell tried to break free, the other trimmer seized both his wrists. Before the detective could break his powerful grip, he was suspended between the two by his arms and legs.

Semmler jumped to the nearest furnace and opened the door.

49

'Here,' Semmler shouted. 'In here.'

Bell could see the bed of coals glowing yellow. Red flame rippled over their incandescent surface. From six feet away the heat was unbearable, and as they dragged him toward it, it grew hotter. A corner of Bell's mind stood aside as if he were looking down on the tableau of the trimmers holding him and the Acrobat urging them on. They would not be able to fit him through the furnace door sideways. They would have to feed him into the fire either head- or feetfirst. They would have to let go of his arms or his legs to align him. But to let go would be to let him fight back, and so before they let go, they would have to incapacitate him by breaking some bones.

'Headfirst!' said Semmler, picking up a slice bar. He raised it high, his eyes fixed on Bell's arms.

For a single heartbeat the men holding him were distracted by having to maneuver in the cramped space. Isaac Bell contracted every muscle in his body, ripped one leg and one arm free, and exploded in a flurry of kicks and punches. A kick caught the trimmer who was holding his other leg in the face, cracking his nose, and he let go with a cry. Bell's fist landed solidly. The man who had been holding his arm fell backwards. His head struck the rim of the firebox opening, and he screamed as his hair burst into flame. Desperately trying to escape the fire, he banged his brow on the rim of the furnace mouth and fell deeper into the coals, his head in the furnace, his body thrashing on the deck.

Bell was already trying to roll beyond the range of Semmler's slice bar, which hit the deck an inch from his head, scattering sparks. He leaped up and dodged a wild swing, then rounded unexpectedly on the trimmer whose nose he had broken, who was creeping up behind him, and dropped him with a punch that smashed his jaw.

He spun around, reeling on his feet. 'Just us, Semmler.'

Christian Semmler flashed his dazzling smile. 'First you'll have to catch me.'

He crouched, sprang up, caught the bottom rung of the ladder that rose up the ventilator shaft that shared the interior of the No. 4 funnel, and pulled himself up effortlessly. Bell jumped for the ladder and went after him. It was 220 feet to the top of the stack, and in the first hundred Bell realized he would not catch the man until he ran out of ladder. For if anything rang true about Semmler's nickname, he climbed like a monkey.

Nearing the top, Bell saw daylight silhouette Semmler, who was clinging to the upper rim of the funnel. Smoke from the three forward funnels was streaming over him blackening his face and hair. His green eyes gleamed eerily within that dark frame. Then his teeth flashed.

'Thank you for joining me,' he smiled. 'Now I have you where I want you.' He folded back his sleeve, revealing the leather gauntlet that held the braided wire with which he had strangled so many. It was Bell's first close look at it, and he saw a lead weight on the end of the cable. Semmler straightened his arm suddenly, and the weight drew six feet of wire from its spool and wrapped it around one of the steel stays stiffening the funnel top.

Bell lunged suddenly and reached for the man's foot.

The Acrobat moved just as swiftly, eluding Bell's grasp and launching himself off the ladder to the other side of the ventilator shaft, where he hooked an elbow over the rim and smiled down on Bell.

'The man who falls two hundred and twenty feet to the bottom of the ship will not be the man who learned to fly in the circus.'

With that, Semmler used his elbow to flip over the rim and disappear.

Bell climbed to the top of the ladder and jumped across the ventilator. He caught the rim with both hands, pulled himself over the top, and peered down through hot smoke into the soot-blackened uptake that exhausted No. 4 boiler room's furnaces. As it shared the funnel with the ventilator they had climbed up, it was only ten feet in diameter.

Semmler crouched with bird-like grace on a foothold several feet down.

'Now when you fall,' he taunted, 'you will fall into the furnace.'

Bell surveyed Semmler's new position. The foothold, a steel shelf less than a foot deep, circled the entire uptake. There were handholds welded just beneath the top rim, and Semmler's eyes blazed again as he chose his next landing. The cable shot from his gauntlet, snagged a handhold, and the Acrobat flew, while launching a deadly kick at Bell's head.

Isaac Bell jumped at the same time, landed beside him

on the foothold, grabbed the nearest handhold, and punched Semmler in the stomach as hard as he could, staggering the man. 'I was in the circus, too.'

But he had not reckoned with Semmler's superhuman speed, nor his capacity to shrug off pain. In a move too quick to anticipate, Semmler flipped the cable off the rung and around Isaac Bell's neck.

Bell drove punch after punch into Semmler's torso, but even the hardest blow did nothing to relieve the pressure that was suddenly cutting blood and air from his brain. White lights stormed before his eyes, and he felt his strength ebb. A roar in his ears smothered the pounding of his heart. Gripping a handhold with the remaining strength in his left hand, he rammed Semmler with his knee, and the German slipped from the foothold. The only thing that kept him from falling was the wire stretched between his wrist and Isaac Bell's neck.

With the man's entire weight hanging from his throat, Bell could barely see. He felt as if he had not drawn breath in a year. His hand was slipping.

'Interesting situation, Detective. When you die, I'll fall. But you'll die first.'

'No,' gasped Bell. His hand moved convulsively.

'No, Detective?' Semmler mocked. 'No deeper last words, than "no" before we plunge into the fires? Speak now or forever hold your peace. What was that, you say?'

'Thank you, Mike Malone.'

'Thank you for what?'

'Cutting pliers.' Holding on with the last of the strength in his left hand, Bell jerked his right hand, and the tool slid out of his sleeve into his palm. He closed his fingers around the handles and squeezed with all he had left in him.

The cable snapped.

Isaac Bell's last sight of the Acrobat before he vanished down the *Mauretania*'s stack was the astounded light in his eyes.

50

Arriving at the Berliner Stadtschloss in a triumphal mood, Hermann Wagner handed his top hat to the palace maid attending the commoners' cloakroom and proceeded upstairs to Kaiser Wilhelm II's private throne room, where a small, select company of high-ranking soldiers, industrialists, and bankers – the elite of the elite – had been summoned to observe the final demonstration of a device that the kaiser himself had proclaimed the epitome of German achievement.

A pair of generals flaunting gruesome dueling scars looked down their noses at the banker. Wagner serenely ignored the scornful aristocrats and took great pleasure in watching their expressions change when the kaiser marched straight to Hermann Wagner and shook his hand, shouting, 'Behold a true German patriot. Wait till you see what he has made happen. Begin!'

Lackeys rushed in with a moving picture screen, acoustic horns, and an enormous new film projector. The lights were dimmed. His Majesty the kaiser sat on his throne. The company stood and watched a moving picture of Kaiser Wilhelm himself striding into this very room with his favorite dachshund tucked under his arm.

When the monarch on the screen opened his mouth to speak and his words poured mightily from the acoustic horns, the expressions on the generals' scarred faces, thought Hermann Wagner, were priceless. The worm had turned. Soldiers were no longer the only ones whose magic enchanted the kaiser.

'*Der Tag!*' spoke the kaiser's image, easily heard over the clatter of the film projector. '*Der Tag* will be Germany's beginning, not her end. Victory depends not only on soldiers.'

Hermann Wagner closed his eyes. He knew these words by heart. He had edited the film, having discovered a knack for such things, and in a brilliant touch, when the kaiser had proclaimed his piece, the dachshund would bark at the camera and the kaiser would pat his head. Millions would smile, touched that the kaiser loved his pets as much as any ordinary German.

'Victory also depends on Germany persuading our allies to join the war on Germany's side. One by one, Germany will destroy –'

Laughter interrupted the kaiser's words – nervous laughter, which was choked off abruptly.

Wagner opened his eyes and saw to his horror that even as the kaiser's words issued from the horns, the picture showed his dachshund barking at the camera. But that couldn't be. The dog was supposed to bark after the kaiser had finished speaking. Somehow the sound and the picture had jumped apart.

The kaiser leaped from his throne and stormed out, trailed by his generals.

Hermann Wagner stood frozen with disbelief as the company melted away. How could it have gone so wrong? Left alone, he plunged blindly toward the doors, the Donar Plan a failure, his career destroyed.

A palace maid ran after him. 'Your hat, Herr Wagner. Your hat!'

She was a tiny little thing with gold braids. Polite even on the worst day of his life, the gentle Hermann Wagner thanked her with a compliment – 'What a sharp-eyed girl you are' – and even tipped her a silver coin.

'Thank you, Herr Wagner.'

Moments after she curtsied her thanks, Detective Pauline Grandzau slipped out of the palace to cable the good news to Chief Investigator Bell.

Epilogue

After the Great War
Newcastle upon Tyne

The Widow Skelton had taken up with the Widower Farquhar, which pleased everyone in Newcastle upon Tyne except the priest. Mrs Skelton, who had served as a nursing sister in the Boer War and a matron of military hospitals in the Great War, and was still a raven-haired beauty, owned the Marysmead Arms, a popular pub in the shadows of the Swan Hunter shipyard. Mr Farquhar was admired as one of 'nature's gentlemen', a master craftsman and head foreman at the Swan Hunter furnace works where the legendary Cunard flyer *Mauretania* – which still held the Blue Riband for the fastest on the Atlantic – had returned to her launching place to be converted to burning oil instead of coal.

'I brought you something,' said Mr Farquhar, coming home from his shift on a wet, blustery evening to their flat above the pub.

'There's no need,' she said, though pleased. 'You should save your money.'

He thrust an oilskin-wrapped packet in her hand. 'It didn't cost a penny.'

'I'm not surprised.' It was grimy with coal dust.

'Aren't you going to open it?'

371

He showed her where he had already unfolded one end. She peeled back the oilskin and found a fancy envelope.

'What is this?'

'The lads found it behind a coal bunker. It must have been there for years. See what's inside.'

'You didn't look, yet?'

'No, I saved that for you.'

She turned back the flap and pulled out a thick sheet of lavishly decorated parchment paper. Mr Farquhar rested a hand on her shoulder as he leaned close.

'That looks like real gold.'

'Gold leaf.'

'What does it say?' He'd gone too farsighted to read without specs, but her stone blue eyes were still sharp.

'It's an invitation to a wedding. On the ship! They were married on the ship!'

She gazed in wonder and delight, then turned it over.

'What's that?'

'Wee figures and squiggles. Greek to me.' She slipped the invitation reverently into the envelope and rewrapped the envelope in the oilskin.

'Don't you want it?' asked Mr Farquhar. 'It's pretty. I could make a frame for it.'

'Take it directly to Mr Thomas McGeady at the Cunard office. Tell him that I said to find this couple and send it to them.'

'You *know* Mr McGeady?'

'I own a pub, Mr Farquhar. I know everyone – Hurry! I'll hold your tea.'

'What's the rush?'

'Next month is their anniversary.'

San Francisco

On Nob Hill, in one of the very few mansions to survive the San Francisco earthquake and fire of 1906, Isaac Bell was telling Marion, 'It is possible that my eyesight is not as keen as it once was, so if I am to inspect this supposed wrinkle on your cheek you're going to have to come closer into the light, here on my lap,' when he was interrupted by a child who ran in with the morning mail, dumped it beside them on the sofa, and ran out.

After the supposed wrinkle had been thoroughly debunked, they went through the mail and discovered a large manila envelope from the Cunard Line.

'Captain Turner?' asked Marion, though it couldn't be. Over the years, Turner used to write on their anniversary. But he had retired from the line after the war and had become a recluse after being unfairly blamed for the torpedoing of the *Lusitania*.

Bell opened it with the knife from his boot.

Inside the manila envelope was a note from a Cunard executive: 'The company thought you might enjoy this. It was found by Mr Alec Farquhar of the Swan Works in Newcastle whilst refitting *Mauretania,* and sent along by Mrs Alison Skelton. The chairman joins me in offering the line's heartiest congratulations on your upcoming anniversary.'

Isaac and Marion recognized immediately the elaborate envelope that the ship's printer had run up for their wedding. Moisture had blurred the recipient's name. 'Whose was this?' Marion asked, leaning closer to study the faded letters. Wisps of her golden champagne hair brushed

Bell's cheek. 'Oh my gosh, this is *Clyde Lynds's* invitation. Oh, poor Clyde.'

Marion pulled out the invitation itself, only slightly less for wear. 'This is lovely. Oh, my dear, it's like being married again.'

Isaac Bell asked, 'What's this on the back?'

Five Years Later
The Strand Theatre on Broadway
in New York City

Isaac Bell was raising a glass of champagne to the resounding success of the premiere of Marion's new film, the screwball comedy *Listen Here, New York*, when he overheard a critic dictating his review from a coin telephone in the lobby:

'Marion Bell's *Listen Here, New York*, is a lulu about speakeasies, chorus girls, and gangsters. But while the first electrically recorded sound-on-film high-fidelity talking picture vastly improves *The Jazz Singer* with actual audible talk, a viewer still observes that the director ordered James Cagney and Edward G. Robinson to park themselves under a microphone before they delivered their snappy lines.'

Isaac Bell put down his glass.

Marion laid a restraining hand on his arm. 'Isaac, where are you going?'

'I'm going to punch that man in the nose.'

'Instead of punching a critic in the nose, which might influence reviews of my next movie, let's toast Clyde, whose plans made my picture possible – even though Talking Pictures was always more complicated than Clyde hoped it would be.'

Marion defused Bell with a smile and a moment later the critic redeemed himself, saying, 'Everyone agrees the talking pictures system will improve quickly, which in this critic's opinion cannot happen soon enough, at least when it comes to showing the bright, witty direction by Marion Bell. One hopes the studio will team her up again with Irene Vox, the Shanghai-based silent-film scenarist. Mrs Bell's direction made possible what this critic predicts will be the rarely successful leap from "silent" to "talkie".'

Bell was watching Vox across the lobby. The blond screenwriter was swathed in sable, dripping in jewels, and equipped with a dashing silver-haired escort. The rumors Bell had gathered so far claimed he was her cousin or her husband and either fabulously wealthy or a penniless refugee. To Bell's chief investigator's eye, he looked like a fellow who had spent time in jail. He said, 'I now know who that woman reminds me of.'

'Who?'

'She wasn't a blonde back then.'

'Who?' asked Marion. She had never met her writer until tonight, having communicated with the famously reticent scenarist by mail, cable, and telephone.

Bell said, 'I offered her a ride to their hotel. Take a good look at her in the car. Then you tell me.'

Vox and her escort were staying at the Plaza. Bell and Marion had come in their J-198 torpedo-body Duesenberg, which sat only two, so he telephoned the garage to send the J-140 town car instead. Bell drove, with the silver-haired gent seated in front beside him, and learned nothing, as the man spoke no English.

'Well?' he asked Marion as they pulled away from the Plaza. 'I saw you talking quite intimately in the mirror. What did she say?'

'We had a lot to discuss, having made an entire picture without ever meeting.'

'What did she say?'

Marion laid her hand on his as he shifted gears. 'She said that it's a custom in Shanghai for a woman writer to kiss a woman director's handsome husband firmly on the lips.'

'What did you say?'

'I said we were not in Shanghai.'

He just wanted a decent book to read ...

Not too much to ask, is it? It was in 1935 when Allen Lane, Managing Director of Bodley Head Publishers, stood on a platform at Exeter railway station looking for something good to read on his journey back to London. His choice was limited to popular magazines and poor-quality paperbacks – the same choice faced every day by the vast majority of readers, few of whom could afford hardbacks. Lane's disappointment and subsequent anger at the range of books generally available led him to found a company – and change the world.

'We believed in the existence in this country of a vast reading public for intelligent books at a low price, and staked everything on it'
Sir Allen Lane, 1902–1970, founder of Penguin Books

The quality paperback had arrived – and not just in bookshops. Lane was adamant that his Penguins should appear in chain stores and tobacconists, and should cost no more than a packet of cigarettes.

Reading habits (and cigarette prices) have changed since 1935, but Penguin still believes in publishing the best books for everybody to enjoy. We still believe that good design costs no more than bad design, and we still believe that quality books published passionately and responsibly make the world a better place.

So wherever you see the little bird – whether it's on a piece of prize-winning literary fiction or a celebrity autobiography, political tour de force or historical masterpiece, a serial-killer thriller, reference book, world classic or a piece of pure escapism – you can bet that it represents the very best that the genre has to offer.

Whatever you like to read – trust Penguin.

read more
www.penguin.co.uk